Charlotte's
Way

Also by Catherine Daly

All Shook Up

Charlotte's Way

CATHERINE DALY

POOLBEG

Published 2005
by Poolbeg Press Ltd
123 Grange Hill, Baldoyle
Dublin 13, Ireland
E-mail: poolbeg@poolbeg.com

© Catherine Daly 2005

The moral right of the author has been asserted.

Typesetting, layout, design © Poolbeg Press

13 5 7 9 10 8 6 4 2

A catalogue record for this book is available from the British Library.

ISBN 1-84223-191-X

Typeset by Magpie Designs in Goudy 10.5/14 pt
Printed by
Nørhaven Paperback A/S, Viborg,
Denmark

www.poolbeg.com

About the Author

Catherine Daly was born in Dublin and spent her childhood in Belgium and Ireland. After qualifying as a pharmacist from Trinity College, she worked in a hospital in Chichester in the south of England for five years. She returned to Ireland in 1996 and lives in Dublin with her husband and two children.

Her first novel, *All Shook Up*, was published by Poolbeg in 2004, the same year as she created www.writeon-irishgirls.com, a website and online community for readers and writers. For more information, or to contact Catherine, visit her official website at: www.catherinedaly.com

ACKNOWLEDGEMENTS

My first thanks are to all of you who bought *All Shook Up* and helped make it a success. And to those of you who sent me cards or e-mails telling me what you thought of the book – another Huge Big Thank-You! That kind of feedback really keeps a girl going!

On the home front, thanks to Denis, who keeps me sane(ish), and without whose love and support I'd have given up long ago. And to my two children, Lorcan and Cliodhna, who keep me grounded in the way only children can. ("Not another interview, Mum!" sigh!).

Thank you to my parents, Claire and Sean O'Donnell, to my parents-in-law, Jean and Michael Daly, and to Isobel, Keith and Christiane and Kieran.

My private sales-force-cum-PR-agency deserves a massive pat on the back – have you heard yet from someone, who knows someone, who knows a Daly, an O'Farrell or an O'Donnell? Don't worry, you will – their reach is global!

Thanks to my writing friends, especially Anne Marie Forrest, Sarah Webb, Pat Hickey, Marisa Mackle and Colette Caddle – always only an e-mail away. And to all the other 'Irish Girls'.

Thanks to everyone at Poolbeg for their friendship and professionalism; and to my agent, Ali Gunn, and everyone at Curtis Brown for their hard work and continuing support.

And finally thanks again to my editor, Gaye, for helping to make *Charlotte's Way* the best book it could be.

Thank you, all of you

xx *Catherine*

Dedication

To my godson,
Aidan O'Donnell

Prologue

1970

Sheila stepped into the middle of the convent parlour and looked around. The room was small and cold and even the smell of liberally applied furniture polish failed to banish the damp and musty unused odour. Instinctively, her eyes followed a beam of sunlight from a window high up in the wall to where it fell onto a wooden bench behind the door. Although she hadn't been aware she was holding her breath, she let it escape when she saw the two girls. They were her daughters. Hers as truly as if she had given birth to them. She turned to her husband, daring him to stand in her way. She issued her challenge in grim silence even as she tried to stop her face from breaking into a joyous grin.

But Robert seemed resigned now. He glanced briefly at the children, then turned to the nun waiting by the door.

"Mr Riordan?" the nun seemed uncertain what he wanted of her.

"The formalities," he muttered. "Best get them over and done with. We've a boat to catch." He took a well-used fountain-pen from his inside pocket and led the way out the door.

Sheila relaxed. She got to her knees in front of the girls, then sat back on her heels. It was a tiled floor and the cold seeped through her woollen tights, but as the only other place to sit was on another bench on the far side of the room, she stayed where she was. She smiled gently and resisted the urge to throw her arms about these two helpless mites, promising never to let them go. Because these two children already knew how easily promises could be broken. A moment of inattention, a busy main road, and all the certainty in their short lives swept away under the wheels of a London bus.

"You must be Charlotte," she said to the older of the two girls, a pretty red-headed child, no more than three or four years old who clasped her sister's hand protectively, and scowled at the world.

"And you must be Emily," Sheila said, turning to the toddler. A slight, blonde child, fighting sleep, whose free hand was clenched into a tight fist by her side. Her thumb was imprisoned within the tiny hand, as if freed it would fly of its own volition into her mouth and she had been warned once too often that this was not allowed.

Then she addressed them both:

"My name is Sheila. Would you like to come to Ireland and see where I live?"

1986

"I, Charlotte Riordan, take you …"

Even as she repeated the words Charlotte realised, in a moment of sheer panic, that she had no idea what to say next. That she had no idea what she was doing here. The heavy door at the end of the aisle yielded briefly to the wind; it creaked, then slammed shut again, sending a blast of icy air around the congregation gathered in the Trinity College chapel. The baby inside her wriggled, reminding her impatiently to get on with things, and Charlotte remembered. She was getting married. Soon she and her child would take on a new name and abandon the name Riordan. A name Charlotte had never felt comfortable with because she never felt she really owned it. Like a handed-down school uniform which had served its purpose but had never quite fit.

She smiled happily at the man standing beside her, and continued:

"… take you Donal Moran to be my lawfully wedded husband…" She clutched his hand tighter and he gave her a gentle, reassuring squeeze in return.

Emily sat on a small stool to the left of her sister, but none of the words registered. The ceremony was a distant background hum. She had only discovered that morning that Charlotte was pregnant, while she was helping her sister get ready.

As Charlotte had raised her hands over her head to

remove her loose sweatshirt, the slight swelling of her otherwise slender waist was unmistakable. Emily stared in amazement and wondered why she hadn't guessed sooner. Although Charlotte and Donal's whirlwind romance had surprised no one, Emily hadn't understood why steady, clear-headed Donal had been so adamant that they didn't want to wait before getting married, not even a few months for a spring wedding.

"You're not getting married just because…?" Emily blurted out before she had time to think. Nothing in her life had prepared her for this conversation.

"Of course not." Charlotte looked away.

"You don't have to get married just because you're pregnant," Emily babbled. "Not in this day and age." Immediately she wished she could unsay what she had just said – it was hard to imagine a worse thing to say on the morning of your sister's wedding.

Charlotte's sunny mood retreated.

"What's this day and age got to do with it?" Her green eyes glinted coldly. "Do you think it would be any easier for a child to grow up without its parents now, than it was in our day?"

Emily knew that Charlotte, being the older of the two of them, had always tried to shield her little sister from the reality of being 'parentless', adopted by a mismatched couple in a small Irish country town. But she had been unable to prevent Emily hearing whispers about "bad blood", and how Sheila and Robert Riordan had been "brave" to take in two fatherless girls. They both heard, in whispers that grew louder as they got older, that although one could understand how a girl (their mother) could fall once, you would have to be wary of a woman who made the same mistake twice. And, of course, while you couldn't blame the child for the sin of the parent... well, everyone had heard the saying "bad blood will out".

"You know that's not what I meant." Emily put her arms around Charlotte briefly to take the sting out of what she had said. "I wasn't suggesting you should go it alone, leave Donal out of the equation, but..."

Emily wasn't sure what she meant exactly. She had no doubt Donal would make a good father. Far better than Robert, their adopted father, ever had. Emily's misgivings were nothing to do with Donal; it was more the whole marriage thing. Marriage was so final, so terminal. A life sentence. Even before she knew what she had learnt today, Emily had been unsure about the marriage but she had not voiced her feelings because she wasn't sure she understood them. And she was afraid she might just be jealous. Up till now she had always been the most important person in Charlotte's life.

Now that she knew about the baby, however, Emily couldn't help feeling the marriage was a trap. A trap that Charlotte was walking into with her eyes wide open in some sort of self-sacrificial trance. But this was a hazy, wordless idea and Emily had no idea how to put her concern to Charlotte.

"It's just... that, well... you haven't been with Donal very long, and suddenly you're getting married, and..."

"You want to know, how can I be certain I love him?" Charlotte laughed that anyone could doubt she loved the man she was to marry. And to Emily's relief it was a warm, bubbly, genuine laugh; she couldn't help smiling herself in response to it. "I've loved Donal," Charlotte continued, hugging herself, "for a lot longer than any one realises. Longer than I realised myself!"

"But what about Marcus?" Emily felt she had to name Charlotte's first boyfriend out loud, although no one close to Charlotte had summoned up the courage to use the word 'rebound', even out of her hearing. "You loved Marcus, didn't you? And you told me only last Easter that you thought you had a chance of getting back with him."

"Well, I was wrong." Charlotte placed her hands on her sister's shoulders as she spoke, looked her straight in the face. "And Marcus was wrong for me," she continued slowly. "You all thought that. Learning that he had someone else was the best thing that could have happened to me. It left me free to realise that I loved Donal, and that I always had loved him without realising it. It was like coming home. So don't worry, Emily – everything's going to be all right."

Charlotte's face had an almost childlike joy to it. She hugged her sister, then catching sight of their reflection in the mirror, stopped and smoothed down the front of her dress with concern.

Now Emily wished she'd found the courage to have that conversation in the weeks leading up to the wedding, and not when it was too late for Charlotte to back out. Not that Emily suspected for one moment that she would have. She didn't doubt Charlotte's sincerity when she spoke about Donal and their future together, but that didn't mean she understood it. Personally, Emily didn't have much time for all this happy families crap. In four months' time Charlotte would be a mother. A few months before her twentieth birthday. Emily shuddered with distaste; she wouldn't fall into a trap like that. She would graduate at the top of her law class and then forge a brilliant career for herself.

She could see it now: Emily Riordan, barrister-at-Law. Champion of the underdog, expert on human rights. Feared by the major corporations and moral guardian of the state. It was a delicious fantasy.

She pulled her shawl tighter about her shoulders as yet another draught swirled around the altar and she noticed Charlotte's friend Anne-Marie doing the same. These filmy gold bridesmaids' dresses had not been designed with November in mind.

Anne-Marie, Charlotte's other bridesmaid, sat on her right side. The same place as she had taken throughout school, from the very first day that the new girl with the funny accent had joined her nursery class. She too shivered as the cold air swirled around her and she stole a glance at the bride in the hopes she wasn't feeling uncomfortable. But her friend looked radiant. The simple ivory dress and the fresh flowers she wore in her hair were perfect on her. Charlotte carried a bouquet made up of creamy white lilies wrapped in dark green leaves and tied with sprigs of miniature ivy. It was the perfect foil for her translucent skin, scattered lightly with freckles, and for the dark red hair tumbling freely over her shoulders. She looked, Anne-Marie thought, like a wood nymph from a child's book of fairytales. Charlotte wore flat shoes because she was only a couple of inches shorter than Donal who was nearly six foot tall. And Donal, with floppy light brown hair, a slightly crooked smile and piercing blue eyes, looked like every mother's favourite boy next door. They made a handsome couple. Although Donal wasn't, by any stretch of the imagination, stunning-looking, he was solid, reliable and he looked it. Just the kind of person Charlotte needed. And he adored her; anyone could see that.

Anne-Marie smiled and felt her eyes fill with tears when she saw Donal's expression as he began to recite his lines with a wobbly voice.

Suzy sat in the congregation and reached into her bag for a tissue. The pews in the old college chapel faced each other, so she lowered her head to prevent guests on the other side of the aisle witnessing her tears. She was a catering student who had lived in the bedsit below Charlotte's ever since her move to Dublin. The two girls became close friends.

So it was true, Suzy realised, as she watched her friend. Unlike the loose sweaters of the previous few weeks, Charlotte's dress did nothing to hide her pregnancy. Suzy had suspected, of course – there was very little Charlotte was able to keep from her. But she hadn't known for certain.

And now she wondered if it would have made a difference to have known about the baby sooner. If she could have acted on the knowledge.

But as Suzy listened while Donal was given permission to kiss his bride, she swallowed hard, blinking away unshed tears. No point thinking about it, Suze, she told herself sternly. It's too late to do anything. It's probably all for the best anyway.

Donal stood with his bride on the steps of the chapel as they posed for photographs, and he felt his heart would burst with happiness. Until a few minutes ago he hadn't really believed it was going to happen, but then Charlotte said "I do" and Donal pitied every other man on Earth. He grinned at his father who was pointing an oversized camera lens at them.

"Donal, Charlotte," the official photographer called out to them, "if I could just have you over there, under the campanile…"

Donal looked in the direction he was pointing, at the old stone monument, and nodded in agreement. But as he turned back to attract Charlotte's attention, a movement, spotted out of the corner of his eye, made him look across Front Square. His heart stopped as he saw someone disappear around the corner of the Long Library and he clenched a fist in anger by his side.

It couldn't be…

No, he told himself, and forced the calm smile back onto his face. There must be thousands of students with leather jackets like that. And that's all Donal had seen. A black leather jacket, dark hair and a way of walking that reminded him of… No, it could have been anyone.

Besides, even if Marcus had the nerve to turn up today, it was too late now; there was nothing he could do.

"Let's go," Donal said, linking his arms through his wife's. "Let's go and have those photos taken before you freeze."

Several hours later, Emily, Suzy and Anne-Marie sat in the residents' bar in the hotel where the reception had been held. Tara, a friend of Emily's who had joined the party for the 'afters' reception, was also with them. Most of the other guests had left by now and the girls instinctively huddled together to post-mortem the day. Although none of them said it, they were all thinking how strange it was that Charlotte was missing from their little group. And as far as Anne-Marie and Suzy were concerned, Tara, who brought their number back up to four now that the bride had left, was no replacement for Charlotte.

"I can't believe Charlotte didn't tell me she was pregnant," Emily said in a sulky tone.

"I can't believe it either," Suzy shook her head slowly. "I suspected, of course, but…" she fiddled with a beer mat, balancing it on the top of her glass of Coke. Then she placed it firmly to one side as she took a sip. "How did your mum take it?" she asked Emily. "Charlotte being pregnant, I mean."

"I don't really know. I haven't spoken to her about it. When I talked to Charlotte about it earlier, she said Mum had been great." Emily stared into her glass. "But then she's been so bloody great about everything to do with Charlotte lately, that I don't suppose that comes as much of a surprise."

"Tut, tut, Emily! Do I hear the little green-eyed monster talking? That's not like you." Anne-Marie was surprised. She had only brothers and often envied the easy relationship between the two sisters. She couldn't imagine jealousy featuring as part of it.

"Oh God, no! I don't mean that. No, she's been great with both of us but… maybe what I mean was that she was too understanding. If she'd put her foot down three years ago," Emily explained, "if she'd refused to let Charlotte leave school at sixteen and come to Dublin just because Marcus was here…" Emily ran out of steam.

"You knew Charlotte was never going to stay at home as long as Robert was alive," Anne-Marie reminded her gently. "And if Sheila had put up a fight, Charlotte would have left anyway and wouldn't have accepted any help. As it was, Sheila helped her get a job, persuaded her to enrol to do those three Leaving Cert subjects at night … and found her a flat as far as geographically possible from Marcus's!"

"I suppose so," Emily agreed begrudgingly. She knew Anne-Marie suspected her of being jealous of Charlotte's escape to the city, but she wasn't. Even if Robert hadn't died the winter after Charlotte left, Emily would still have stayed at home. Apart from her ambition to go to college keeping her at school, Emily had always managed to get along with her adopted father. Not in any positive way – it was just that she slipped beneath his radar, allowing them both to ignore each other. Whereas Robert seemed to expect Charlotte to thwart him at every turn; an expectation she spectacularly lived up to.

"I always thought Charlotte would have come home after Robert died," Emily continued. "Maybe that's when Mum should have put her foot down."

"Yeah, it might have saved Charlotte from getting into the mess she's in today," Tara snorted. The others turned on her with shocked faces and she realised what she'd just said. She went red and looked into the depths of her empty glass. She thought of how she'd give anything right now for a double vodka to help her dig herself out of this hole. "Oh God!" she blurted out. "I didn't mean … I mean …"

"Stop right there!" Suzy held up a restraining hand. "No matter how we might feel about today, I think we can draw the line at wishing that Charlotte and Donal had never got together! It's their wedding day, remember?"

The girls fell silent as they tried to banish the sour atmosphere brought on by Tara's comment. Suzy and Anne-Marie exchanged glances, confirming their shared opinion of the younger girl, while Emily tried to avoid looking at her friend altogether.

"So how *do* you feel about today?" Emily asked Suzy in a feeble attempt to change the subject. "Charlotte and Donal getting married, disappearing into the sunset … living happily ever after?"

No one had admitted out loud to believing that Charlotte and Donal were anything other than the most romantic tale since *Love Story* and Emily couldn't help wondering if Suzy had any misgivings about it.

"They're great together," Suzy answered, a fraction too quickly.

"Donal's perfect for Charlotte. Isn't he?" Anne-Marie asked Suzy firmly. She could see that Emily still wasn't convinced that the marriage was a good idea. "Charlotte needs someone solid. Suzy, you never met Sheila's late husband, but Robert was the most unfatherly figure you could ever come across. I don't know why he ever agreed to adoption."

"So do you think Charlotte was looking for a father figure?" Suzy asked after a pause.

"In Donal? Possibly," Anne-Marie said, shrugging. Suddenly she was uncomfortable discussing Charlotte's choice of husband. She knew it was only a matter of time before the subject of Marcus was raised … again.

"If she was looking for a father figure she couldn't have hit much further from the bull's-eye with her first choice!" Emily snorted, confirming Anne-Marie's prediction. "Marcus is hardly father material!"

Suzy opened her mouth to say something, but coughed to hide her change of mind. She didn't want to add anything to the discussion of Marcus either.

"Marcus was nothing but a childish prat!" Tara pronounced – delighted with the opportunity to redeem herself.

"Are you happy?" Charlotte asked.

She and Donal were lying in a four-poster bed in a

country hotel in Wicklow. The remains of a fire glowed in the grate and the occasional flame threw shadows onto the canopy over their heads. They had left their guests a couple of hours ago, to drive through the dark to start their short honeymoon. Charlotte admired the shiny gold band glinting on her finger. She had refused to let Donal buy an engagement ring because they needed all their money for the planned move to England in spring, after the baby was born. Donal had been offered a place in an insurance company's graduate training programme, and he planned to specialise in personnel management.

"Happy?" Donal answered. "The word doesn't exist to describe how I feel now."

He smiled, pulled her closer and kissed the top of her head.

"I felt a kick!" He sat up suddenly. His arm had been lying lazily across her stomach. "I really did, Charlotte! I felt a kick." Donal stretched his large hands over her. "There, again!" His eyes filled with tears.

Charlotte had been feeling movement for a few weeks – a light fluttering, bubbly feeling – but this was the first time it had been strong enough for Donal to feel.

"I think he wants to join in the celebrations! Could this day get any more perfect?" Donal was choked up.

"He?" Charlotte pretended to be indignant. "Who said it was a he?"

"He, she? I can't call it 'it'. Not now that …hey, I felt it again!" He leaned his head towards her small bump. "Hey, baby," he said in a deep voice into Charlotte's navel, "this is your daddy here. I know today's a special day, so I don't mind you staying up late. But from now on, no kicking and keeping your mummy awake after eleven o'clock. Do you hear me?"

"You're mad, do you know that?" Charlotte laughed.

"No, I'm not," Donal protested, laughing too, but with his eyes glistening. "You read the book. I've got to talk to him. It's so he'll recognise my voice after he's born."

"Well, if you're going to spend the night chatting to *her*, keep it down. I need to get some sleep." Charlotte yawned and closed her eyes; exhaustion taking hold of her as it seemed to do so often since she got pregnant. Within minutes, she was asleep.

Donal kissed her stomach and uttered a silent prayer for the child who had just made itself known. As he pulled its mother closer and she mumbled in her sleep before curling up under his arm, he thanked the baby for bringing them together for good.

Chapter 1

1993

Another town, another audit. Emily looked around her room with distaste. She could be in any town in Ireland, any hotel in the western world. The narrow twin beds with their pine lockers and pine-effect headboards looked as though they had come from a giant warehouse that kitted out hotels like this by the dozen. Even with her eyes closed, she could guess the layout of the room. The bathroom (five foot by eight, white tiles, chrome rails displaying over-washed but not threadbare towels) had been to her right as she walked in, so the wardrobe, in this case pine-effect to match the beds, was on the left. The low table on which she was supposed to balance her empty suitcase, but which she used to lay out six pairs of immaculately polished high-heeled shoes, was at the end of the bed nearest the window. There was a small desk or maybe dressing-table under the window, with a small cardboard sign on it saying that this was a non-smoking room and that Internet access was available at reception.

Emily took some files from her briefcase to read later. The audit, that she and the rest of the team from Barrett and Lyle Accountancy Ltd were carrying out tomorrow, was of a large meat processing plant and Emily knew from her initial study of the paperwork that it was going to be a tough, long-drawn-out job.

Only another few months of this, she promised herself. Then her contract would run out, and she would be free to start applying for other jobs. She had already been approached by a number of other accounting firms as a result of achieving one of the highest grades in the country in her final exams, but Emily had had enough of accountancy and audit for the moment. She wanted a job with some big company where she could work towards her final goal of financial director of some big corporation. Some mornings she woke up and wondered how she had ended up as an accountant instead of the barrister she had planned to be, but then she remembered that, on top of her years in college, training to be a barrister would have entailed several more lean years. Whereas Barrett and Lyle paid well for the privilege of recruiting the top few graduates in each year.

The phone on the bedside locker emitted a high-pitched bleeping, a signal Emily recognised as being a call from another room within the hotel. She came out of the steamed-up bathroom where she was hanging suits to shake out the creases formed despite her careful packing in tissue.

"Ready for dinner?" Richard Weston, Emily's manager,

asked her as she picked up the receiver. "The hotel din-ing-room is woeful, so I've booked a table at an Italian place about a mile away. Are you OK to walk? I need to stretch my legs after the trip down in the car."

"Give me half an hour, then I'll see you downstairs." Emily smiled as she hung up. He was eager. They'd only checked in twenty minutes ago.

She and Richard had arrived a day ahead of the rest of the audit team, as they occasionally did on a big job. It gave them two nights when they didn't have to worry too much about the prying eyes of the other accountants. She had been transferred to Richard's team a few months ago, which was convenient because they had been having an affair for nearly a year.

In the years since Charlotte's wedding, Emily had avoided any long-term attachment until Richard. And even Richard she regarded as a short-term boyfriend who she just hadn't tired of yet. As Charlotte and Donal's first child was soon joined by two others, Emily watched them juggle their lives around their offspring and she couldn't imagine ever wanting what they had. Or at least she couldn't imagine wanting it badly enough to give up her own ideal life. As soon as Emily had stepped inside the gates of Trinity to start her law degree, she had attracted hordes of admirers – and although she was too single-minded about her study to get seriously involved with any one individual, she soon discovered that if she chose her partners carefully, she could have a pleasant sex-life with no strings attached. Her one rule was that she would never sleep with any man who thought he was in love with her.

She had only nearly come to grief once when, just before her final exams, she slept with her best friend. Paul was older that the rest of the class, having returned to study four or five years after leaving school. He was on bad terms with his family, and although Emily got the impression that some bridges were mended in the few months before he came to college, family was a subject Paul was not willing to discuss. And this was what drew Paul and Emily together. While she never made a conscious decision not to discuss her family, only a handful of people, including Paul, knew anything about Emily's adoption, her adopted parents, or even her nephew and nieces in England. So, when after the two of them had been accepted to work for the same company after college, and a night of celebration had ended in Paul's bed, Paul assumed that they had moved to a new level of intimacy.

Emily still wasn't sure how she managed it, but she extricated herself from this attachment like every other and kept Paul as a friend. And now, although he seemed to have accepted that she had a different attitude to relationships than he had, she knew he believed her attitude to be flawed. He was always there for her, Emily suspected, so that he could rescue her whenever she inevitably needed rescuing. And while Emily loved Paul in her own way, she didn't know how to return his devotion. So in some ways she welcomed the distance between them, which her relationship with Richard

seemed to have brought about. It would make it harder
for her to inadvertently hurt him.

Emily pulled a black cashmere polo-neck over her head,
ran a comb through her hair and checked her reflection
in the mirror. Not bad, she decided. She looked younger
than twenty-five. She was letting her hair grow out of the
severe crop she had favoured when she started work.
Then she needed to look older, more authoritative. Now
the slight curl in her naturally blonde hair gave her a girlish appearance. Her Calvin Klein jeans completed the
teenage look. She had bought them for next to nothing
in a sale in Paris. There were advantages to struggling to
maintain her size six to eight waist. Her only disappointing feature, which caused her to frown for the briefest
moment, was her flat, almost boyish chest.

The phone began to bleep again and Emily grinned,
but didn't pick it up. She imagined Richard counting
down the seconds to thirty minutes so that he could ring
from reception to see if she was on her way. She picked
up her coat, took a last look around the room and locked
the door behind her.

Richard was slouching in an uncomfortable armchair
in the gloomy hotel lobby as she stepped out of the lift.
He shook his limbs free of the low chair and stood upright
like a puppet being raised by strings. He ambled towards
her, but didn't kiss or touch her; they both knew the
rules. He held the door open for her as they went out
onto the street and, as he guided her through it, his hand
rested gently on her back. It lingered for longer than

strictly necessary and she allowed herself a small smile.

In the restaurant, she studied him as he examined the menu. By the light of a candle perched in a straw-bound Chianti bottle, his hair looked as if it was strewn with sandy highlights instead of the grey he was so worried about when Emily met him. She had persuaded him to stop dyeing it and now his dark brown hair was alive and shiny rather than the dull and uniform bottled shade she remembered. His weathered face bore testimony to his level of fitness. He went running three or four times a week, sailed regularly although he no longer competed at the highest levels, and went skiing at least once a year.

They discussed the job ahead of them while they waited for their meal. Emily sipped a mineral water and Richard drank a glass of house wine from a tiny carafe. Since starting their relationship, he drank a lot less than he used to, and was delighted to see the waistline he had given up for lost beginning to return. He drank white wine rather than the red he preferred because Emily hated the smell of red wine off his breath.

"So how was your trip to England?" he asked as he tackled his deep-fried Brie.

"All right, I suppose." Emily frowned, remembering. She had spent the weekend with Charlotte and Donal and had flown back in time for this job. Then she made an effort to smile. "It was great seeing the kids again. Exhausting, but great. I don't know how Charlotte manages a full-time job and looking after three kids. The younger two use the crèche at Donal's work, and Gemma's school keeps her till half three ... but I don't think Charlotte and Donal get much time to themselves at all. I mean Charlotte's practically running that restaurant now. They have a couple of really good baby-sitters, but ..." Emily shrugged, "it wouldn't be my idea of fun."

"Just you wait," Richard smiled. "One day you'll get all broody, and you won't be able to resist."

"Never!" Emily shuddered. "Other people's kids are fine – you can hand them back. My nieces and nephew are particularly great because they're in another country."

She laughed as she gave her well-rehearsed reply. In fact she was mad about Charlotte's children and even the mention of them was enough to make her miss them like crazy. When she was with them she sometimes found herself wondering what it would be like to have kids of her own. But then she would remind herself that to have children she needed a man, and men like Donal were one in a million. Most men were more likely to turn out like her father Robert or like Charlotte's first boyfriend Marcus. Or they were like Richard. Who was sitting in a restaurant teasing his lover about children, safe in the knowledge that his own were tucked up at home with his wife.

"No sign of Donal and Charlotte moving back then yet?" Richard asked.

"Well, they're looking into it, but ..." Emily had experienced tension in England. She felt that it was something to do with the long-promised move back to Ireland, but any time Emily asked about it Donal or Charlotte changed the subject. It was nothing she could put into words and certainly nothing she wanted to share with Richard.

"Have you given any more thought to a weekend away?" Richard asked, after a long silence. He sensed that Emily was uncomfortable talking about her sister and didn't press her for fear of a brush-off. It was the same any time he tried to bring up the subject of her family; there was only so far that she would let him into her life. Sometimes he wished he could have more of her, but he knew he had to be happy with whatever crumbs she threw him.

Twice already he had asked her if she would come away for a weekend with him. Somewhere private. Somewhere they could spend two whole days together. And spend the whole night in the same bed.

"I don't know, Richard. It's a big step, and a big risk …" Emily stared at him with her big blue eyes. He stretched out his legs under the table to meet hers and in an automatic response she kicked off one shoe and rubbed her foot up and down his calf.

"Let me have a little longer to think about it, all right?" she said and wriggled her toes into the cleft behind his knee in a way she knew drove him wild. "I'll let you know when I decide," she promised when she was sure she had distracted him enough for him not to push her any further.

Richard knew that was a "No" to going away together, and that he shouldn't bring up the subject again. He smiled back, then reached down as if he were going to scratch his leg. But instead he caught her foot and ran a finger along the arch of it.

24

In the days after Emily's visit to England, Charlotte began to watch Donal carefully. She was worried about him. From the empty packets of antacids strewn around the house, she knew his indigestion was acting up again. Which meant, although he would never complain, that he was stressed out about something. While Emily was here, they'd had fun. A trip to the boat fair in Southampton, a couple of meals out and a day with the kids in Alton Park had forced him to relax for the long weekend. It made Charlotte realise that she missed his laugh and that his smile was less frequent and more strained than it used to be. As well as the smile lines that had always crinkled around his eyes, now an anxious frown line had developed between his eyebrows. Charlotte couldn't help feeling that Donal wasn't as happy as he should be and it worried her. She felt responsible for his happiness because if she hadn't become pregnant with Gemma there was no knowing where Donal would be now. When they were still just friends, when Charlotte was still with Marcus, Donal had talked about doing voluntary work overseas when he finished in college. He had talked about travelling. He had joked that after so many years intensive studying he needed to take some time out to explore his 'creative side' – although he needed to find it first.

Charlotte decided to tackle him about his indigestion first.

"You OK?" Charlotte asked after dinner one evening. "You're getting through too many of these." She held up a handful of empty Rennies boxes as evidence.

"I keep telling you, Charlotte," Donal answered, "I'm fine. It's just work. It's completely mad at the moment. I've a couple of people off sick, and two more will be leaving at the end of this month." He tried to grin, but as usual, whenever he talked about the work, his grin hardened into a grimace. "So are Amy and William coming to dinner on Monday?" he asked instead. "I haven't seen them in ages – we should have a good laugh."

Charlotte tried to ignore the way he'd changed the subject yet again, and confirmed that yes, William and Amy Costello, the husband and wife who owned the restaurant she worked in, were coming to dinner the following Monday. She'd become close friends with the couple – and not just because she was so grateful for a job that allowed her to work flexibly around the children's timetables. Amy and William were fun. A childless couple in their late forties, they had given up high-powered jobs in London to open a small bistro near where Charlotte and Donal lived. And after a few fraught years, during which William, the stockbroker, had to transform himself into William the chef, it was finally a success. It was their hobby as well as their job and William frequently sat drinking with regular customers long after the staff had gone home. Sociable and gregarious by nature, he loved the idea of work being an extension of his social life.

"Why did you keep avoiding the question when Emily asked if we were thinking about moving back to Ireland?" Charlotte asked. Two could play at the subject-changing game, she decided.

"I don't know." Donal leaned back in his chair, ran one

hand over his head, tangled his fingers through the hair at the back of his scalp and pulled on it. Then he swung forward again, freed his hand and looked as if he was about to stand up. Charlotte put her hand on his other arm and clamped it gently to the table.

"Don't know what, Donal? We always said we'd move home eventually. Do you think this would be a good time?"

"Do you want to move back?" Donal asked her.

"I asked first."

"I …" He held his breath for a few seconds, and then let it out in an explosive sigh. "I don't know what I want at the moment, love. Or if it's a good time to move. Gemma's settled in school. Tim can't wait to get started next term, you've got a good job…"

"There'll always be plenty of good reasons *not* to move," Charlotte said quietly. "Do you remember how, when we came over here first, we used to laugh at the Irish people who had come over ten, fifteen, twenty years ago? All saying they were only here for a few years? But any chance they got to move home, there was always a reason to stay: a new job, a kid starting school or doing exams. And then one day they realised that they were never going back, and that this was home. Well, that's fine. If we want to stay over here, let's make that decision and let's make this home. But whatever we do, I don't want to stay in England just because we never got around to moving back to Ireland."

"What do you want to do? Move back or stay?" Donal looked at Charlotte as he spoke, but it didn't stop him engaging in an intricate operation to remove the last trace of protruding nail from his left thumb. "And don't say you don't mind, like you always do," he added quickly. "I want to know what you really think."

The seriousness of his tone was relieved by a crooked, mischievous smile, as he pulled off the last bit of broken nail with his teeth. Charlotte toes curled up when she saw that the nails on his long fingers had been chewed right down to the bed.

"It's true, Donal. I really don't mind where we live. I don't have the same ties that you have to home. Mum comes to visit us here almost every month, and Emily… well, I'd love to see more of my sister, obviously, but moving back to Ireland wouldn't guarantee that. Her next job could take her anywhere in the world."

It was true – Charlotte didn't care where she was as long as it was with Donal and the children. Where did she call home? She was born in London and had lived there with her natural mother for the first few years of her life (although to her dismay, as she had children of her own, even the few memories she had of that time began to fade). While Robert, her adopted father, was alive, she had never felt that Castlemichael was home, and after his death she had moved to Dublin.

And Dublin she associated with her first boyfriend Marcus and the wild days she and Suzy had enjoyed as neighbours in Ranelagh. Now Suzy was a qualified chef working in London. And Marcus … Charlotte had no idea where Marcus was.

Home to Charlotte was not in any particular location,

not even in this comfortable house full of beautiful possessions that she had yearned for throughout her childhood. Home was in the man sitting opposite her and the three children asleep upstairs. With Donal, Gemma, Tim and Aisling, Charlotte knew she could make her home under a bush. And she would be happy wherever she was as long as she knew that Donal was happy. And that he still loved her.

Predictably, Donal changed the subject again after their exchange, but Charlotte was happy to let him, now that she knew she had set him thinking. She said no more about it for the rest of the week, but was pleased to see that whenever Donal was lost in thought he didn't wear the tense, ugly frown that meant he was worrying about work.

However, on Monday evening Donal came home from work in a foul mood. When he pulled up on the gravel outside the house, even the smell of cooking floating on the frosty autumn air barely lifted his mood.

He forced himself to smile and brought Tim and Aisling, whom he had collected from the crèche, into the kitchen with him. Gemma, sitting at the table pretending to do 'homework' but really colouring a Barbie comic, looked up in delight.

"Daddy's home!" The seven-year-old threw herself across the room at her father, while the two younger children clamoured to be lifted up by Charlotte. Donal's smile became more natural as the family was reunited in the warm, comfortable kitchen.

"You look shattered, love." Charlotte kissed him and cleared cookbooks off the armchair in an alcove in the corner of the room. "Bad day?"

They had bought the old chair in a junk shop in Brighton with the intention of reupholstering it and putting it by the fire in the sitting-room. It had found a temporary home in the kitchen, and was still there four years later. It looked as if it wanted to be there, Donal always thought. The kitchen used to have its own fireplace, where the cooker was now, and at night, in the dark, you could almost imagine the cottage's original resident, one of the local estate workers, sitting on the battered armchair by the dying embers of a wood fire. Charlotte's collection of copper cooking pots, hung on iron hooks on the brick chimneybreast, added to this illusion.

"Lousy day," Donal answered, letting out a long sigh.

"Do you want to go and sit down for a while?" Charlotte asked, recognising the signs. "Relax, have a drink or something? I can look after this lot." There was concern in her voice.

"What time are we expecting William and Amy?"

"Not till eight. Go and sit down in the front room. I've got everything under control here. I'm about to give the kids their tea, so if you want some peace and quiet, now's the time to get it." She moved expertly around the cramped room, neatly side-stepping the toys that Tim and Aisling had managed to spread liberally across the floor in the five minutes they'd been home.

Donal didn't move but watched her from the door. This was where Charlotte loved to be, he knew. She enjoyed her job in the restaurant but her heart was in her home where she had created the warm, love-filled family environment that she had never enjoyed as a child. Donal had never met Robert, who had died suddenly of a stroke just after Donal met Charlotte, but he knew Robert had at best a strained relationship with his adopted daughter. Which meant that after his death, Charlotte simply wrote him out of her life and refused to discuss him further. But Donal knew that Robert had shaped her in ways Charlotte would never admit. Her overwhelming need to love and be loved scared him sometimes, as if he was afraid of failing her.

"I'll just get a glass of wine and sit here with the rest of you," Donal said. "What are we eating?" he called out a minute later from under the stairs where they kept the wine.

"A pork casserole cooked with apples, sage and cider," Charlotte answered. "Only because I know you like a challenge!"

Donal groaned and emerged empty-handed. He came back into the kitchen and lifted the lid off the heavy cast-iron casserole, which was simmering over a low heat on the back ring of the cooker. He sniffed two or three times, then took a teaspoon and tasted, smacking his lips in appreciation.

"A challenge is right," he muttered, his bad mood forgotten. The only thing Donal enjoyed more than cooking an elaborate meal for friends was matching wine to a meal he hadn't had to cook himself. And he was surprisingly good at it for someone whose only training

31

was one term of evening classes.

"That white Rioja! The one we brought back from Spain last summer," he announced at last after a second taste of the casserole. "You're not going to add anything else to that between now and eight o'clock, are you?"

"Just a bit of cream!" Charlotte strained to keep a straight face. Donal took himself so seriously when choosing wine. "But we're having some pretty stinky Camembert for afters, so you might want a beefy red as well!" Her laugh escaped at last when Donal snorted and vanished into his "cellar" again.

"That was wonderful, as usual, Charlotte." William leaned back in his chair after the meal, and rested his hands on his considerable chef's paunch. "I think I might have to steal your recipe."

Donal listened as the three of them discussed the restaurant. It never worried him that his wife and her employers should discuss work when they all got together; he found the subject fascinating and he often joined in. For the first few years of married life, financial constraints and a lack of baby-sitters meant that Charlotte and Donal's social life had depended entirely on their learning to cook. Fast. And once Donal had mastered the basics, he discovered that he loved the ritual of food preparation. Entertaining satisfied his need for creativity and sociability and his instinctive organisational skills meant that he could knock up a meal for a dozen people at short notice and get nothing but a thrill from it.

"You were very quiet tonight, love," Charlotte said later as they were getting ready for bed. "Everything all right?"

"Yeah, I guess so. It's just work." He turned his back to her as he sat on the edge of the bed to pull off his socks. Then he swung his legs around, lay down and pulled the quilt up. To his dismay, Charlotte was sitting up in bed, looking very much awake.

"So what are you going to do about it?" she asked him.

"About work? What can I do? It's going to stay like this while we're short of staff, and we're going to stay short of staff as long as there's a recruitment freeze in place." Donal was grim again.

"No, I mean what are you going to do about you being so unhappy and frustrated at work?" She faced him squarely.

"I'm not..." He stopped and scratched his head. "It's probably just a phase..."

"A phase that's gone on for over a year now. You don't have to stay in a job that makes you that unhappy – there are other options. You know you could do anything you put your mind to." She crossed her arms across her chest.

"Anywhere else would be the same, Charlotte – believe me, I've been reading the professional papers." Donal closed his eyes, and reached for the bedside lamp to switch it off.

"So what could you do besides personnel?"

He froze, the light still on, and looked at her in amazement.

"But I've been working in personnel since ... well,

33

forever. What else do you want me to do?"

"Why are you a personnel officer, and why are you working where you are at the moment?"

Donal looked at her, not understanding the question.

"Why are you working in personnel?" Charlotte repeated. "Why aren't you a teacher like your sister, or a journalist like your cousin? Why are you not working in your father's building business? That's really picking up now. There's plenty of people who'd love to have a place in a family business they could fall back on."

"But I don't want to do any of those," Donal protested.

"You don't want be where you are at the moment either, by the sounds of it," Charlotte answered with a self-satisfied smile. Then she patted her pillows and lay back against them. But she didn't reach out yet to switch out the light. She obviously hadn't finished with him. Why did she always do her best thinking just as they were getting into bed, Donal wondered. "And," she continued, "you probably have another thirty years' work ahead of you,"

"What are you saying?" The hair began to stand up at the back of Donal's neck. Suddenly he was wide-awake.

She didn't answer; she waited for him to work it out.

"I don't have to stay in this job, or even in the personnel management field, if I don't want to, is that what you're saying?" Donal asked slowly.

Charlotte just shrugged.

"But what would we live on?" He shook his head

"Whatever you earn at another job," she suggested.

"What other job?"

"Well, if money was no object…" she began carefully.

"But it is!" he objected. "We've three kids, and a mortgage. Remember?"

"Forget that for a moment. Let's get into the realms of fantasy here."

"Did you buy a lottery ticket and forget to tell me?"

"Stop interrupting, Donal." She aimed a mock punch at his stomach. He curled up dramatically and mimed a zipping motion across his lips. "If money were no object, what would you most like to work at?"

He sat up in bed, and gave it serious thought. A small smile began to play across his mouth.

"That's easy. I'd love your job. Running a restaurant, I mean. Meeting people as they come in, making sure they have a great time, a good meal. Buying only the best ingredients so that my customers get the best. Talking to regulars about their food, discussing wine with them. Being more in control of my work, knowing that if I do a good job, we'll have a full house. And I know I'd do a good job." He stopped mid-fantasy, but his mind was in Costello's Bistro, showing a regular customer to his favourite table and telling William that Mr So and So was in, and would love to have the lamb dish he so enjoyed last month.

"So what's stopping you?" Charlotte asked gently.

Donal laughed bitterly.

"Generous though William and Amy are with your salary, I can't see us living the way we do, if both of us were on that kind of money. I know you love the job and, to be honest, I mean what else is there around here? But be realistic, honey, we couldn't afford for me to give up the salary I'm on."

He began to look depressed again and snuggled down into bed, punching his pillow into shape to put an end to the conversation.

"Amy and William make a good enough living," Charlotte whispered.

It took a few moments, but suddenly Donal was bolt upright again, looking at her with a mixture of awe and horror.

"You're not seriously suggesting we buy our own place, are you? Our own restaurant?"

"I'm not saying anything. Now it's after midnight, and we both have a full week's work ahead of us." Charlotte switched off the light and kissed him goodnight.

Donal saw a satisfied grin spreading across his wife's face as she dropped off to sleep. He, on the other hand, had a feeling that he was in for a sleepless night.

Chapter 2

"So when do I get to meet this man you're seeing?" Sheila asked Emily. The two women were sharing an early tea after one of Sheila's many trips to Dublin. Emily wasn't sure why she had finally admitted there was a man in her life – Sheila's interrogation on the subject had become routine and Emily had learnt to fend off the questions politely – but having spent so much time with Richard during the audit, Emily missed his continual presence so maybe talking about him had promised some relief. As she had walked along Grafton Street with Sheila, Emily had watched couples stroll carelessly along, arm in arm, and wondered what it would be like to spend an afternoon like that with Richard.

"So when do I get to meet him?" Sheila repeated when there was no sign of Emily having heard her question. "And what did you say his name was?"

"I didn't. And it's not that kind of relationship. The

meet-the-future-mother-in-law-type, I mean." Emily stirred the remains of her black coffee.

"Oh, I see." Sheila tried not to look hurt. "Well, I'll have to go by what others think then. What does Anne-Marie think of him?"

"She hasn't met him." Emily's spoon clattered around inside her mug.

"Oh. And Tara?"

Emily was silent.

"She hasn't met him either? Has anyone met him? I mean, he must call to your flat occasionally to pick you up."

Still nothing.

Sheila looked around Bewley's café. It was full of couples gazing into each other's eyes, groups of friends gossiping about their week's work and their plans for the weekend, mothers with daughters, laden down with shopping bags, or arguing about "that awful rag you wanted me to buy".

Sheila wished she were any of those other women rather than to have to ask the question which would confirm her suspicions.

"He's not married, is he, Em?"

She looked around fearfully, but no one seemed to have heard the awful accusation she had just thrown at her daughter. She wished she could take the words back and pretend the thought hadn't crossed her mind. That she hadn't wondered why her beautiful, clever daughter should be seeing a man she hadn't told her friends about.

"Is he, Emily?" Sheila was convinced that the noise

level in the café had dropped and that everyone was holding their breath as she was, waiting for Emily to answer.

"Would it matter so much if he was?" Emily challenged.

Sheila had her answer although her daughter seemed unable to say the words.

"I mean, as long as we keep it quiet and no one gets hurt. Does it matter so much? I mean, all I want from him is the occasional bit of company, conversation…"

"Sex?" The word slid out of Sheila's mouth with the force of a landslide.

And Emily blushed to the roots of her hair and couldn't look around in case the whole room was staring at her.

"Oh, don't look so shocked," Sheila continued. "I may be old, but I am human. And I read the occasional copy of *Cosmopolitan* in the doctor's waiting-room." She topped up her cup with lukewarm, tar-like tea. "So you're in this relationship for sex."

"No, not just …! I told you, we talk about books, have meals together, all sorts of things!"

"But you don't go out. He doesn't take you anywhere you might be seen together, I bet. He really has you exactly where he wants you, hasn't he, your married man?"

"I don't want more than that; it suits me. If he tried to get more involved with me I'd dump him so fast…"

The words were out before Emily realised what she was saying.

"Oh! So why don't you want to get involved with someone?" Sheila asked sadly.

Catherine Daly

"I don't have time. I've got my career to think of."
Emily got to her feet and started pulling on her coat.
"Come on, Mum. You're going to miss your train."

"Sit down," Sheila ordered. "I'll wait for the next train."

Emily sat. "Are you looking forward to your trip to England?"

"Stop trying to change the subject, Emily."

"I'm not. It's just that there's just nothing left to discuss. You asked me why I didn't want to get involved with anyone right now, and I told you."

"I don't believe it's as simple as that. Look at your sister and her husband. They're both working full time, and they still have time for each other and the children."

"Well, I'm sorry to be such a disappointment to you, Mum." Emily looked around the crowded café rather than look Sheila in the eye. "If I'd realised your idea of the perfect outcome was to be pregnant and married at nineteen, I'm sure I could have obliged."

"Don't be ridiculous. You know that's not what I meant."

"Then stop holding up Charlotte to me as the perfect role model," Emily snapped, a lot more viciously than she intended.

"I don't. Do I?" Sheila looked worried. "You know I only want for the two of you to be happy. And I can't help feeling you're not."

"Just because I don't fit into some model you have in your head of all the things a woman needs to be happy, doesn't mean I'm not fulfilled," Emily said, more gently

40

now. "Charlotte's got a great life, I'll grant you that, but I want more than that."

"More than three kids, a job she enjoys and a devoted husband?" Sheila raised an eyebrow sceptically.

"Sorry, that came out wrong." Emily waved her hands about as she tried to wave away her dismissal of her sister's life. "I don't mean I want more, but I want something different. I don't want my happiness to be tied up in someone else. I want to be in control of my own fate, not have to think about what the other person wants or expects from me all the time. Or needs from me."

Sheila pretended not to notice Emily shudder as she said the word 'needs'. She wondered was her daughter's determination to stay single born out of a desire to remain independent of others or out of a fear of failing them.

And she hoped that Emily's married lover could see past the façade and know that Emily wasn't as tough as she made out she was. She hoped he was fond enough of her to care.

Chapter 3

Summer 1995

"On Sunday I had the good fortune to revisit Moran's restaurant," Charlotte read aloud to the packed room. *"One of Dublin's best-kept secrets and one of my own personal favourites, I am almost reluctant to introduce it to the public via these pages, but in all conscience I can keep it to myself no longer. The Morans, Charlotte and Donal, have kept true to their original concept of providing good meals of consistent quality at prices which put many other establishments to shame. On Sunday, I enjoyed lunch in their newly opened first-floor dining-room with its spectacular views over Dublin Bay. Like the rooms on the ground floor, the clean lines of the Edwardian building have been sympathetically restored and the look is complemented with clutter-free modern furniture. The ambience is as warm as the Moran's welcome, and the staff are attentive and well trained. Chef Suzy Brady has put together an inspiring menu as well as offering at least two main course specials. On the day we visited, I chose..."*

"Wow!" Charlotte was choked up. This was their first review, despite having been open nearly two years now. They had built up a steady trade of locals but were beginning to wonder if locating out of the city centre condemned them to the critical netherworld. To receive such a glowing report in one of the bestselling Sunday papers, by a reviewer known to be difficult, meant a path would be beaten to their door.

Suzy grabbed the paper from Charlotte.

"Forget ambience and value, what does she say about the food?"

She nodded in appreciation at the description of the starters and main courses, but frowned when she read that the pastry in the chocolate mille-feuilles was a little disappointing.

"That review couldn't have come at a better time." Donal put his hand on Charlotte's shoulder, as he stood behind the chair at her desk. The entire restaurant staff were gathered in her office to read the review and Joe, the sous-chef, who'd been on duty the day of the reviewer's visit, was opening another bottle of champagne. He poured for those who hadn't received any the first time around and for those who had knocked back their first glass in one go. The atmosphere in the room was celebratory but cosy. Donal raised his glass in a toast, acknowledging the contribution made by everyone from the dishwashers to the chef, the cleaners to the head waitress. "We could do with the extra business the review will bring in, now that we've opened upstairs," he added finally.

They had debated for ages about whether they should go ahead with the first-floor dining-room, or buy a house. They were living in a small flat to the back of the restaurant and, although they were managing and it suited them to be close to the children so they needed less childcare, it was getting very cramped. In the end they had decided to go ahead with expanding the restaurant as they had been turning away too many diners and the bank manager had promised that they could have a home loan as well as the business expansion loan if they needed it.

"I think we should go back and have another look at that house," Donal said when the office emptied, leaving the two of them alone.

"Do you think so?" Charlotte was only half listening; she was re-reading the review. Picking out words, trying to read between the lines.

"I know so. Property prices are still shooting up, and if we don't buy soon there's no way we'll be able to afford a four-bedroom house within walking distance of this place. And I don't know about you, but I don't intend to spend half my week sitting in a car. And you do enough driving around as it is, seeing suppliers."

Donal and Charlotte had split the work of the restaurant between them; Donal handled the front of house, supervising the waiting staff, greeting the customers and discussing the menu with Suzy, while Charlotte dealt with the suppliers, any publicity requirements and all the paperwork.

"So, what do you think? The house?" Donal asked

again. They were in Charlotte's bright first-floor office rather than in his own cubby-hole under the stairs, conveniently located between the dining-room and the kitchen. "Do you want to go and see it again?"

"I suppose so, but that doesn't mean I'll necessarily agree to putting in an offer," Charlotte warned. "You still need to convince me we can afford it."

As ever she was the cautious one when it came to spending money. She could come up with the big plans and had the imagination and vision to bring them off, but as soon as Donal became enthusiastic, she would start to play devil's advocate. It was the same when they had decided to take the plunge and look into the possibility of starting their own restaurant. Once Donal was convinced that the plan was feasible, Charlotte had made him convince her of the wisdom of every step they took. They had looked at several properties before settling on this one and what swung it for Charlotte was the cramped but adequate flat attached to the rear of the old Edwardian house on the seafront. So with all their savings sunk into converting the building, they were able to live on site with no extra mortgage or rent to pay.

"I'll let Tom persuade you about the house – we're meeting him for lunch tomorrow," Donal grinned. Tom was their accountant, a friendly man in his early forties recommended by Emily's friend, Paul. He was normally extremely cautious and for the first few months he saved them from making some costly mistakes. But for the past six months he had been pressing them to buy a home. Like everyone in Dublin, he was obsessed with property and he worried that this young couple would get so tied up in their business that they'd still be living in the flat long after houses had risen above their price range.

"OK, we'll go and have another look at the house!" Charlotte laughed. "Now get out of here and let me get this work finished so we can take the kids to the zoo."

Their first year had been very tough – they seemed to be working all the time. They both loved it, but it was exhausting, and they worried that the kids were losing out. Although Suzy got the kitchen up and running with amazing efficiency, Donal and Charlotte had a lot to learn about running a restaurant. They lost two head-waiters before Suzy suggested her cousin Geri, and Charlotte felt that she was always reading CV's and doing interviews. So Donal had decided that keeping staff was cheaper than making economies by paying less, and he had gone to the bank, upped the wages, and everything was a lot easier since then. They found that customers appreciated seeing the same faces each time they visited, and the team they had assembled worked well together.

"Are you sure employing Suzy would be a good idea?" Donal had asked nervously when Charlotte first proposed it at the very beginning.

"What do you mean? You know she's dying to move back to Ireland, and she's one of our best friends. We couldn't not ask her."

"But, I don't know... working with friends and all that ... Would it not be easier to get someone we'd have a more professional relationship with?"

Charlotte had been surprised how uneasy Donal had seemed with the idea. It was as though there was something he wasn't telling her. Maybe he was nervous that Suzy was more Charlotte's friend than his and was worried that it might affect how she worked with him.

"Oh come on, Donal. You know Suzy's every inch the professional. It's taken her seven years and three jobs to get to where she is today. This restaurant would be perfect for her. She'd have exactly the same attitude to the venture as we have."

"Well, if you're sure. But you ring her, all right? It has to come from you," Donal had said at last, leaving Charlotte with the impression that he still had reservations he wasn't sharing with her.

Now, two years later, Charlotte longed to force Donal to admit he had been wrong. They had experienced none of the awkwardness he had expected with Suzy. Over the past two years they had established an easy working relationship which left room for friendship to survive. Outside her kitchen, Suzy acknowledged that the Morans were in charge, and although they had had a few run-ins on the subject of the menus, on the whole they worked well together. Suzy had assembled a good team around her and thanks to Donal's policy of paying slightly more than the opposition and Suzy's management style which involved a lot less swearing than many of her male idols, she had managed to keep most of them. But strangely, although they worked so well together, Donal was reluctant to discuss Suzy with Charlotte. If she hadn't known him better, Charlotte would have suspected Donal of protecting his own sphere of influence in the restaurant and not wanting the two women's long friendship to freeze him out.

And as running the restaurant became easier, Donal and Charlotte began to appreciate why they had moved home. Sheila was a regular visitor, and they saw plenty of Donal's parents too. Any coolness Charlotte had imagined from her mother-in-law when her engagement to Donal was announced vanished soon after Gemma was born. Hannah Moran was spending more and more time in the capital, visiting her grandchildren and socialising with the friends she had never lost touch with in all her years in Kildare. When she came to Dublin, she stayed in the basement flat of the house she had grown up in. When her mother died, instead of selling the house, Donal's father Paddy had suggested that they convert the huge house into upmarket flats for renting and keep the basement flat for their own use. He had always felt guilty for dragging his wife away from Dublin when they married.

"Now she has her own little pied-à-terre in the city, her bolthole for when the bog gets too dreary," he joked, as he had shown Hannah, Donal and Charlotte around the newly refurbished flat when it was complete.

Since Donal and Charlotte had moved home, Hannah seemed to spend more time in her little flat than she did in the big draughty house in Kildare. Sometimes, but not always, Paddy came with her on these jaunts, but his heart was in the fields he had bought as a retirement present for himself, and in the horses he was breeding in the fantasy of one day having a winner in the Curragh.

Charlotte sometimes wondered if she and Donal would lead such separate lives when they grew older and she hoped not. And occasionally too, she wondered what life with her first boyfriend Marcus would have been like; would the passion she had felt for him have survived the humdrum existence of everyday life? But when she looked around at her life and her family, she knew that she was better off without him. There was no denying she *had* loved Marcus. Her first love; her only love apart from Donal. But she'd never been sure whether he loved her back. Then he left her one Christmas, ostensibly to concentrate on his final exams, and Charlotte's world fell apart. She thought she could never love like that again, that part of her would always belong to Marcus, that the shivery passion she felt for him even when they were apart was in a hidden part of her that had died without him.

Then a few months later she met him in a pub. 'By chance.' It was where Marcus always drank on a Friday night and Charlotte wanted to see if she could behave normally around him. She sat at the bar on her own and kept looking at her watch as if she was waiting for someone. Finally he came up to her.

They talked and she managed to convince him that life had gone on as normal without him. He stayed with her when his friends moved on for something to eat. He bought her a drink (a Coke – she didn't trust herself around him with alcohol on board) and she finally conceded that she had been 'stood up' by her 'friend' so he offered to walk her home.

"Can I come in?" he asked as she fumbled with her key.

"I'm not sure that's a good idea, Marcus."

He looked at her without saying anything.

"Just for a coffee," she answered at last, meaning it at the time.

For another two months they met in secret. Charlotte knew only too well what Suzy, Emily and Anne-Marie would have said.

Marcus somehow managed to avoid admitting that they were together again. Although on that first night he told her how much he missed her, later he spoke vaguely of how the two of them had a "unique friendship". Charlotte, terrified of driving him away again, didn't try to press him to commit further.

And then she discovered why he had been so keen to keep the whole thing secret. Rather than leaving her to study for his finals, he had left her because he was already seeing someone else. A girl called Denise, the prettiest girl in his class. A student who would graduate with a degree in engineering like his own, and not an office-filing clerk without a Leaving Cert, like Charlotte.

"I thought you might like something to eat."

Suzy interrupted Charlotte's reveries, nudging the door open with her foot. On her tray she had a huge mountain of food, a glass of golden, bubbling liquid and a glass of freshly squeezed orange juice. She took off her chef's white jacket, revealing a white T-shirt beneath it. With it she wore her trademark black jeans. Charlotte sometimes wondered if Suzy owned clothes of any colour other than black and white.

Today her hair, permanently dyed black, was swept into a pony-tail, making her look younger than Charlotte, although she was the older by over a year. As usual, when Charlotte saw her friend bounce about comfortably in painfully tight jeans, she pulled in her own stomach and reminded herself that Suzy hadn't had her perfect figure stretched by three pregnancies.

"I'm going to join you for a girls' lunch, if you don't mind me disturbing your work." Suzy handed Charlotte the champagne, keeping the orange juice for herself.

"I wasn't working," Charlotte admitted, taking the champagne as she began to nibble at a piece of tortilla. "I was reading this review over and over." She grinned. "For the first time in two years, I can relax. I think we've finally got to wherever it was we set out to, at the start of this crazy plan."

"You never get to where you're going," Suzy said ruefully, "but it's a pretty good step in the right direction."

Suzy, who would never admit to being influenced by the opinion of a food writer, was enjoying her first review.. Up till now she'd always run in terror as some chef had ranted over a poor review, or basked in reflected glory when the establishment she worked in had received a favourable report. Now she was chef, and all the glasses were raised to her. She lifted her own orange juice, and tipped it against Charlotte's champagne glass.

"A long way from two grimy bedsits in Ranelagh!" Suzy said.

"They weren't that bad, surely," Charlotte protested; although she was never sure if her first little flat was as lovely as she remembered it, or if it was the sheer joy of having her own place and knowing that Marcus was only a few miles away. "And we had some great times."

"Yeah! We had fun. Who'd ever have guessed back then that I'd end up working for you and Donal!"

"If anything it should have been the other way around," Charlotte laughed. "You were always the sensible one. Working hard on your catering course. Minding me. Like the old mother hen you were."

"Someone had to," Suzy answered gruffly. "Mind you, I mean. Sweet innocent let loose in Dublin at seventeen, with Marcus the only person you knew in the city."

"While you, of course, were ancient. All of eighteen," Charlotte reminded her, steering her off the subject of Marcus. Her friend had never liked him and they'd never talked about him since. She also felt strangely uncomfortable talking about Marcus when she had been thinking about him only a few minutes previously. Suzy was so protective of Charlotte and Donal's relationship. Despite the length of time they had been happily married, Suzy was not above reminding Charlotte how lucky she was to have him.

They ate their way happily through the rest of the food before Suzy got up to leave.

"I'd better get back to work." She nodded at the review still open on Charlotte's desk: "We'd want to live up to that."

"And to plenty more good reviews, now that we

officially exist." Charlotte raised her glass towards her chef.

"To a great team!" Suzy grinned.

"To a great team!" Charlotte agreed, knowing that this was as close as Suzy would come to acknowledging that she and Donal deserved at least a share of the credit.

Emily joined the Morans for the trip to the zoo. Although she enjoyed spending time with her nieces and nephew, lately she was so busy that she had to make a real effort to save time for them. For Gemma in particular, who worshipped her aunt. She had turned into a real girlie girl and loved Emily's designer clothes and expensive cosmetics. Any time she came home after spending time with Emily, the girl sniffed in disgust at her mother's lack of interest in the important things in life and turned her nose up at Charlotte's supermarket-brand cosmetics and chain-store clothes.

"How's Richard?" Charlotte asked as she pushed soggy chips around her plate in the Zoo cafeteria. The six of them had spent an exhausting two hours battling through the crowds brought out by the first really hot day of the year, and although they had to queue for over half an hour in the cafeteria, the kids wouldn't hear of eating anywhere else.

"Richard's fine. He's in Dublin for the next few days, so I should be seeing a bit more of him," Emily smiled.

Shortly after Emily had left Barrett and Lyle for her current job in a big computer company, Richard had been offered a partnership as long as he was willing to move to

Cork. He kept a flat in Dublin as he still did business there, but his wife and family were safely ensconced down south. As a result of this, the relationship had continued longer than Emily had expected.

Immediately, Charlotte regretted raising the subject of Richard. She had said what she thought of the affair in the course of a big row with Emily, the worst of their adult life, just over a year ago. She had finally asked Emily why she was wasting her time on a relationship that she knew was going nowhere and her sister shouted back that not everyone wanted to waste the best years of their youth playing happy families.

It had taken two weeks and huge effort on behalf of Donal and Sheila to get them on speaking terms again and at least a month before the words were spoken with any warmth. Now Charlotte would ask after Richard occasionally, but it was hard to pretend to be interested in whatever opinion he had expressed about this film or that book.

"I see Barrett and Lyle got the contract for that big bank merger," Donal said out of politeness, sensing Charlotte's discomfort. "Is Richard involved in that?"

Charlotte looked at him gratefully. Although she knew Donal didn't think much of a man who would have an affair in Dublin while his wife gave up her own job to follow him to Cork, he was able to maintain a veneer of indifferent friendliness towards him.

"No," Emily answered, "the Dublin branch will handle the merger. But Richard has taken over some of their other big clients and that means he'll have to spend more

time in Dublin." She grinned, with a light in her eyes
that looked suspiciously like affection if not love. "So I'll
see a lot more of him over the next few months."

Charlotte's face tightened into a thin smile and Donal
jumped up and began to get the kids moving again before
she could express any opinion on this news.

Chapter 4

As she drove home from work about a week later Emily remembered that conversation in the zoo. She wondered if it was time to bring Richard out to meet Charlotte and Donal again. They had managed to discuss him without giving her one of their lectures. Or falling into disapproving stony silence at the mention of his name. In fact it was Charlotte who had brought up the subject. Yes, Emily decided – it was time to introduce Richard again. He was a part of her life and her sister would just have to accept that.

Even Emily was amazed that she was still seeing Richard. At the start of their affair, three years ago, she had expected it to last a few months at most, maybe a year. But soon, Richards' desire to see more and more of her, and even let some of their friends know about the affair had touched Emily. It made her fonder of him instead of making her run in the opposite direction.

There was no doubt that his move to Cork, or rather the removal of his wife to Cork, had also made things simpler.

Emily drove through the gates of the luxury development where she had finally bought an apartment a year before. When Tara, whom she had shared with ever since leaving home, had bought her own place, Emily had rented in this complex for a year. Then the flat upstairs went up for sale. She arranged to view it, telling herself that she was just curious, that she just wanted to see how her neighbour had the place decorated; but she fell in love as soon as she walked through the door. The apartment faced south and when Emily saw it the sun was warming up the balcony with its view over the Dublin Mountains. And although she had never intended buying until she was sure where she wanted to live, Emily put in an offer that evening. As her neighbour was in a hurry to sell, Emily moved in four weeks later.

She smiled as she looked up at her third-floor balcony with its two potted bay trees and small cast-iron table. She and Richard had sipped many a glass of wine on it, on their way out to some play or film.

Tonight Emily was meeting Richard at his flat, because they wouldn't be going out later and she preferred to end up in his bed rather than hers. Although Richard knew that she would never spend the night with him, there was always an awkward pause when he got up to leave her bed, as if he was waiting for her to ask him to stay. It was far easier for her to get up and leave him, smiling at his invitations to stay.

Recently, though, Emily had begun to ask herself if it

was time she got over her hang-up about spending the night with Richard. At the start of their affair she had stuck to a rule imposed on herself from the first time she ever slept with anyone: never spend the whole night with a man, and he can hardly claim that he thought you were in it for more than sex.

And she saw no reason to abandon this rule when she started sleeping with Richard. He was married, they enjoyed each other physically, and that was it. But as their fling developed into an affair and then into a long-term affair, she began to feel guilty at the hurt, hangdog look he gave her whenever she woke him up and pushed him gently towards the door. However, it had been going on for so long now that Emily was afraid that if she were to let him spend a night, he might read the wrong thing into it. He might think that she wanted more from their relationship. And because Emily was used to having Richard around and wasn't sure what she would do without him, she didn't want to scare him off by suddenly changing the rules. As long as Richard was chasing Emily for more than she was willing to give, he'd feel secure; he'd know exactly where he stood. If she were to give in to what he wanted, then he might wonder what he had to give in return.

Emily decided to wear a dress to celebrate the start of summer. She chose a pale blue cotton dress, which buttoned up the front. She chose her underwear carefully, imagining Richard's enjoyment as he slowly unbuttoned the dress to find the blue lacy confection beneath. She unclipped her hair out of the no-nonsense style she preferred for work and let the blonde curls fall about her shoulders, the way Richard liked it. Finally she chose a hand-knit chunky cream cardigan to keep off the night chill, and she was on her way.

Richard had the meal ready when she arrived, which was unusual, as they usually pottered around the kitchen together before eating. At home Marilyn hated it when he got under her feet while she cooked, so from early on, Emily had decided that one way to be completely different from Richard's wife was to cook with him. She wasn't much good at it, but she loved to watch him conjure up a sauce out of nowhere while she peeled vegetables and helped wherever she could.

Tonight Richard had made a special effort. There were candles on the table in the living-room and he had laid out the good cutlery and linen napkins robbed from his house in Cork because his wife hated the old-fashioned look of them. There were fresh flowers floating in a glass bowl between the two tall candles and the reflections of the flames danced between the petals. The music playing softly in the background was a compilation of opera preludes that Emily had given him for Valentine's Day.

"What's the special occasion?" Emily wondered out loud. Not only was the flat looking its best, but so was Richard. Freshly showered and with his hair still damp, he wore a pale blue denim shirt and a pair of faded black jeans. With a tan picked up on a family holiday in Spain, he looked a lot younger than forty-three. Emily felt warm affection seep through her as she observed him from the sofa where she was sipping a mineral water while he put the finishing touches to their starter. It was about time she began to trust him more, she decided.

"No special occasion," Richard replied, breaking into her thoughts, "just a special person." He smiled, but before their eyes could meet he looked away to attend to a pot bubbling on the cooker.

He's lying; Emily realised with a shock, and wondered what he was trying to hide. Richard had hinted lately that his relationship with his wife had deteriorated; although Emily didn't like him to talk about his other life.

Surely he wasn't about to leave Marilyn?

Emily's heart began to beat faster and she asked herself why she should jump to a conclusion like that. Did she want him to leave his wife? What impact would it have on her relationship with him? Would he want more of her?

About a year into their affair, Richard had offered to leave Marilyn for Emily. Totally unprepared for the question, Emily answered flippantly that if he wanted to leave his wife it was up to him, but she couldn't guarantee she'd still be there waiting for him when it was all over. Before she even had time to work out whether she had answered from the heart or out of reflex, Richard settled so comfortably into the routine of their affair that Emily couldn't help thinking that she'd given the right answer. So Richard stayed with his wife while Emily tried not to think too much about what might have happened if she'd taken up his offer.

But what if he left Marilyn now? Not because of any

pressure from Emily, but because his marriage was over? Emily told herself to stop being ridiculous; that she was jumping to conclusions. But she allowed herself a small smile at the thought that they wouldn't have to hide their relationship any more. If that's what he announces tonight, she decided, she wouldn't leave just after midnight as usual.

"Are you sure I can't help you with something?" Emily came up behind Richard and, standing on tiptoe, rested her head on his shoulder. She inhaled the delicious aroma of the lamb casserole he was stirring, mingled with the smell of an expensive after-shave. Emily tried to identify it but the cooking smells confused her. She nuzzled the back of his neck and felt him draw in his breath sharply.

"Just pour the wine and take a seat. If you distract me, we'll never get any dinner," Richard laughed, handing her a bottle of Bordeaux. Emily raised her eyes in appreciation when she read the label. He really was pushing the boat out tonight. She felt an unfamiliar flutter in her stomach.

They chatted over their starter of goat's cheese and tomato salad. He told her of a new shop near work, which sold the best olive oil and balsamic vinegar imaginable. She told him that before she met him she would never have imagined that you could put together such a delicious dish with such basic ingredients. He replied that before she met him, she wouldn't have touched anything that hadn't been defatted to within an inch of its life. And Emily let that pass without comment – well aware that her obsession with diet had bordered on compulsive.

Richard pushed the remains of his lamb around his plate. He usually had a huge appetite so Emily was surprised when he gave himself such a small portion and now seemed unable to finish even that.

"What's wrong?" she asked at last, pushing away her own plate and leaning towards him.

"I'm that obvious, am I?"

Emily said nothing but smiled encouragement, waiting for him to speak.

"Marilyn had an affair," Richard said, watching for a reaction from Emily.

She said nothing.

"It started shortly after we moved to Cork," he continued with a sigh. "She was bored and I spent so much time away. She met someone at one of her art classes. Ironic really, because I was the one who suggested she start back at art. I thought it would be a good way for her to make new friends." He shrugged his shoulders. "She's very good at painting and Mark seems to have inherited her talent. He won a prize in the Texaco art competition." He glowed with pride at the achievement of his nine-year-old, then remembered who he was talking to. "Sorry, I don't know why I'm telling you that." He knocked back the remains of his glass of wine.

He can't have tasted that, Emily thought with irritation. What a waste of a good St Emilion!

"Anyway, this affair – it lasted nearly two years. And I never found out about it – at least not until she told me."

Richard took the napkin off his lap and began to fold

it on the table in front of him. He frowned with concentration as he smoothed out the creases and rolled it up so that it looked as if it hadn't been used. He put it on his side plate and looked back up at Emily.

"Why are you telling me all this?" Emily asked in a voice that she barely recognised as her own. "When did you find out? I mean when did she tell you?"

"When we were on holidays. We got a baby-sitter one night, and went out for a meal in a local fish restaurant. She told me between the starter and the main course."

His face creased up in pain at the memory and Emily's desire to comfort him was tempered by the awareness of a hypocrisy she had never imagined him capable of.

"Marilyn wants to go into counselling," he continued. "She wants to rescue our marriage."

"Is that what you want?"

"I've got the kids to think of," he sighed, and looked at Emily with a silent appeal in his eyes. "But yes, I suppose it is what I want. Despite everything; I'm not ready yet to give up on this marriage."

"Will you tell her about us?" Emily stared intently at the flowers floating in the crystal bowl in front of her. She dipped her finger in and dripped water onto the open petal of a yellow rose. A perfect sphere formed on the velvety petal, shimmering in the candlelight. She poked the flower and the silvery drop ran off it.

"Will you tell her about us, Richard?" Emily repeated.

"I suppose I'll have to," he admitted. "Not in detail, of course. We don't need to go into names or anything. After all, I don't know the name of her ..." His face filled with confusion as if he were searching for the correct way of discussing his wife's lover with his mistress. He tried again: "I can't exactly sit there and let her spill her guts to some counsellor and act like the wronged husband. If we're to have a chance of getting this to work, I have to be honest."

Richard's face assumed a blank, neutral expression and he took a deep breath before continuing.

"You know what it means for us, don't you?"

"Why don't you tell me?" Emily spoke through clenched teeth.

"We'll have to end it. You do understand that, don't you? I wish it didn't have to be like this … but …"

After a long pause, he got up to make coffee.

"I'm going to put this place on the market," he told Emily. "In my heart it would always be our place…yours and mine." He walked through to the kitchen and continued to talk as he filled the kettle and spooned coffee into the cafetière. "I'm going to work things out at the office so that I don't have to spend so much time away. And if I do need to travel, I'll stay in a hotel. Maybe I'll be able to take Marilyn with me. Or maybe we'll just have to learn to trust each other…"

As she listened, Emily realised that she was already a part of his past. He explained the details of his new life, a life in which she would be no more than a memory. The subject of some challenging counselling sessions perhaps. The affair that meant Richard and Marilyn would face their future together on equal terms as the betrayal section of their matrimonial scoreboard read: *One-All*.

"I'll miss you, of course," Emily said, with a smile. "But we always knew this wasn't for keeps, didn't we? We'd have been foolish to think otherwise."

Richard looked at her with relief and sat down again. He reached for her hand across the table and enclosed it between both of his.

"Oh, thank God! I mean …I didn't want to hurt you. I was so afraid you'd feel that I was casting you aside or something … I'm sorry I misjudged you. I should have known you'd understand."

Emily looked at the man opposite her as though she was seeing him for the first time.

Of course, she understood.

Emily's hands shook as she tried to insert the key into her ignition. She kept missing, then she screamed silently with frustration as the keys slipped from her fingers and dropped to the mat between her feet.

As she retrieved her keys from the floor of the car and at last successfully got the engine started, she realised what had felt so wrong about their parting. For the first time ever, when she left Richard, he didn't beg her to stay. That small detail brought home the finality of their goodbye and as Emily pulled onto the main road the tears began to flow. She pulled a tissue from her bag and dabbed at her eyes to help her see ahead. She should pull in, she knew. It wasn't safe to drive like this. But she needed to reach the sanctuary of her flat. To stand on her balcony, look out over the city towards the dark shadows cast by the mountains against the night sky and to know she was home.

When finally she stood there, she pulled her cardigan tighter around her shoulders in a futile attempt to ward off the cool night air. The air she breathed in, in jagged gasps, was cold but comforting. The smell of the city, sulphurous, with a hint of rotting vegetation carried by a gentle breeze over the low tide, was as familiar to her as her favourite perfume. This is who you are, she told herself. Professional woman, owner of a large apartment in one of the most sought-after complexes in the city. You don't need Richard. Or any other man. Eventually you would have tossed him aside like all the others.

But she hadn't tossed him aside, she remembered with a sniff. He had discarded her.

"And that's the thing that gets to me, I suppose," she told Tara over dinner the next evening. All day, she had made an effort not to think about Richard, but now she decided that it was important to talk about him, to prove that she wasn't really upset at losing him. And Tara was a good person to talk to. Tara had a love 'em and leave 'em attitude to men. As undergraduates she and Emily had prowled together, picking up and dumping men, swapping notes afterwards.

They hadn't always been like that. In school Tara had been shy and gawky, stooping to conceal her height and blushing if a boy so much as looked at her, let alone tried to talk to her. Emily always had a string of hopefuls trailing after her, but as long as she was at home, and under Sheila's watchful gaze, she hadn't got involved with any of them.

"I've never been dumped before," Emily continued. "I've always done the dumping. I mean it's not really as if he was dumping me as such, if we could have carried on, we would have, but … I'm sure I'd have felt better if I'd realised what was happening, and ditched him before he could ditch me." Emily drained her glass.

Tara waved down the waiter and ordered another bottle of Chablis.

"So I take it you didn't really love this Richard guy then?" Tara had only met Richard a few times, at official functions to do with work. Usually it had been fairly late and she had a fairly hazy, alcohol-dimmed recollection of him. Although she had found it strange that she had seen so little of him, she thoroughly approved of the way Emily kept her boyfriend firmly in his box.

"Love him?" Emily laughed. It was a sound like crystal shattering. "Good God, no! Whatever gave you that idea? No, Richard and me was purely a convenience thing. His being married meant he would never try to tie me down."

"I didn't know he was married."

"Oh yes! Did I never mention it?" Emily knocked back her wine and gestured to Tara, who was nearer the ice bucket, to top her up. She noticed Tara's smile become stiff, and dredged up some vague rumours of Tara's father having had an affair, years ago. So Emily continued quickly. "Yes, married to the childhood sweetheart and all that. Two kids. Wife had an affair too, that's why he went back to her. Isn't that typical of a man?"

"So he's gone back to his wife," Tara said in strange, steely voice. "Don't you mind?"

"No, as I said, it had run its course. Onwards and upwards." Emily decided it was time to change the subject. "Did I tell you that there's a promotion coming up at work? I can't decide whether to go for it, or start looking for something outside the company. It's a relatively good move, but if I get it, I'm kind of tying myself in for at least another two years. What do you think?"

Tara, delighted to be off the subject of married Richard, and Emily's very much *not* broken heart, topped up the glasses and proceeded to give her friend the best career advice she could muster.

"I'm giving up drink for Lent," Emily moaned the next morning from under the duvet. Tara had switched on the light in her spare room and was standing at the end of the bed holding a monstrous mug of coffee. She was already dressed for work in a light wool trouser suit. Her make-up was immaculate and her blonde, shoulder-length hair was freshly blow-dried and straightened. Although tall, Tara always wore high heels and as she towered over her friend, Emily imagined what she herself must look like in her borrowed T-shirt, sleep-messed hair and hangover-ravaged face.

"Too late for Lent," Tara grinned. "Easter was a couple of weeks ago."

"Advent?"

"Months away… I think." Tara was no expert on the religious calendar.

"Forever then." Emily pulled a pillow over her head. "I'm giving up drink forever. Starting from now."

"Far too radical! I've a much better idea. I'll call in sick for you; you go back to bed till lunch-time, and we'll meet for a boozy lunch!"

Attractive though the prospect of a few more hours' sleep was to Emily, the mere mention of booze was enough to propel her at great speed into the bathroom. When she emerged a quarter of an hour later, after a hot shower, she felt alive enough to think about work.

"I can lend you a blouse and I've some brand new Marks and Spencer's knickers still in their wrappers if you'd like them." Tara offered. "You'd never get away with one of my suits, it'd be too big for you, but with a different shirt and if you iron the suit you were wearing yesterday, no one will figure out that you got too drunk last night to be left go home on your own."

She grinned wickedly, tucking in to her second bowl of Frosties.

Emily looked at Tara's breakfast, turned away and reached for the coffee pot.

"You need a carbohydrate breakfast, you do! None of that black coffee crap!" Tara held out the packet of cereal to Emily who turned green. "Are you sure you're fit to work, Ems? I'll call in for you if you like."

"For God's sake, Tara, grow up," Emily snapped. "We're not a pair of secretaries looking for an excuse to pull a sickie."

She knew she was being too aggressive, but she needed to vent her annoyance that while she had the worst hangover of her life, Tara had got away scot-free. And although Emily's memory of last night was delightfully vague, especially after they'd hit a club in Leeson Street, she could have sworn that Tara had drunk at least twice if not three times as much as she had.

"Sorry," Emily apologised at last as the caffeine began to hit home. "I didn't mean to lecture. I'm just jealous. I feel like death, and you look as fresh as a daisy. How do you do it?"

"Practice, I guess, and a strong liver." Tara stood up and tipped her breakfast things into the sink. "So, do you want to come and pick a shirt?"

Chapter 5

Later that evening Emily called Paul. She told herself that it was because she'd been neglecting her friends lately, tied up in work (and occasionally Richard), but in reality it was because she couldn't face sitting on her own all night. She invited Paul over to have something to eat, not intending to tell him about Richard, but he guessed that something was wrong as soon as he laid eyes on her.

"Are you sure you're OK?" he asked after kissing her on the cheek in greeting. He put a bottle of wine on the hall table and put his hands on her shoulders, holding her at arms' length. "No offence, but you don't look it."

Emily grimaced as she imagined what he was seeing. Pale face, dark circles and red-rimmed eyes she had convinced herself were the result of smoke and drink last night.

"I'm fine, honestly. But I went out with Tara last night, so still I'm suffering the after-effects!" Emily tried to make a joke out of it.

"You should have rung me," Paul reproached, still referring to her break-up with Richard.

"What on earth for? I told you I'm fine."

Emily wasn't about to admit that at about half one on Monday morning, after staring at the mountains for an hour, she'd picked up the phone to call Paul. She had needed to hear his voice more than anyone else's. More even than Richard's ringing to tell her that it was all a big mistake. But when she got through to Paul's number on the second ring and a woman's voice answered, Emily had dropped the phone as if it were red hot. She wanted to forget the stab of jealousy she had felt.

It was ridiculous to feel jealous; Paul was just a good friend.

"OK, you're fine." Paul clearly didn't believe her. "You know I didn't approve of the way he was stringing you along, but I have to admit Richard was good for you. So please don't go back to being the pre-Richard Emily."

"What do you mean?" Emily asked, amazed. She had expected Paul to say that the break-up was the best thing that could have happened to her, that she was better off without Richard, and that she'd been wasting her time with him. In fact she had been counting on that reaction. Hearing Paul be positive about Richard was threatening to make her break down.

"I thought you couldn't stand him," she whimpered.

"I didn't like the way he treated you … no, don't tell me, I know. You were the one to impose the rules." Paul held up his hand to stop Emily interrupting. "And no, I

don't like him. He took up three years of your life knowing that he was never going to offer you any more than …
any more than a few quick shags when his wife wasn't
looking. But on the other hand you changed while you
were with him, and not for the worst. He helped you grow
up in ways I would never have imagined possible."

"What do you mean?" Emily asked defensively, not
sure whether or not to feel insulted.

"I don't know…" Paul scratched his head helplessly. "I
mean you let yourself form an attachment to him… no,
don't interrupt; you know it's true. You'd never done that
with a guy before. I know the only reason you let your
guard down was because he wasn't available, but still …
come off it, Emily. This is me. You're not going to try to
tell me you didn't love him a bit?"

"I didn't love him," Emily answered, but even to her
own ears, the words were unconvincing.

"There's nothing wrong with having loved him, you
know," Paul went on as if he hadn't heard her. "Just so
long as you don't let it scare you off the whole idea of letting yourself fall in love again."

"I didn't love him!" Emily repeated, more vehemently
now. She got up to take a ready-made lasagne out of the
oven. "We used each other, that's all."

"I know you must be hurting like hell right now. But
that isn't the only thing that you get from loving someone."

Was Paul deaf or something, Emily raged. She'd just
told him she didn't love Richard.

"Think of all the good times you had with him too,"

Paul continued, oblivious to Emily's black looks. "And one day you'll find someone you love even more than Richard – someone you'll want to hang in there with. And if you're lucky, he'll love you too."

"I – didn't – love – Richard!" Emily slammed a plate in front of Paul and followed it with a wooden salad bowl. "Help yourself!"

"Yummy! Lasagne." Paul began to eat as if he hadn't eaten for a week.

Emily wondered if the woman he was with last night had cooked for him. Maybe they were too busy to think of food. Maybe he'd worked up this appetite last night.

Paul walked home through the darkened streets. It was pelting rain but he hardly noticed it. For as long as he'd known that Emily was seeing Richard, he'd longed for it to end, but tonight he was miserable. He hated seeing her like this and knowing that there was nothing he could say or do to comfort her. For God's sake, she wouldn't even admit there was anything wrong!

He was tempted to turn around now and walk the mile back to her apartment. But what would be the point? To prove himself right? To discover that she had broken down as soon as he had left, as he knew she would? At times like this he wished he didn't know her so well. He wished he didn't know that what she really wanted was to pretend everything was fine. If he didn't know that, he could have pushed her harder, made her admit to him that she was feeling crap and that she wouldn't mind a shoulder to cry on.

As always after Emily let her guard down with him, even the little she had today, Paul found his mind drift back to the day they had both been offered jobs. It was before they graduated, before they even sat their exams and it was impossible not to feel a sense of pride, even arrogance, that while so many other students would be forced to emigrate, they had already been offered jobs. They had celebrated, of course, had granted themselves a night free from study, and despite drinking very little (they still had to study the next day) the euphoria kept them going until the small hours of the morning.

"Come back to my place," Paul suggested after Emily had unsuccessfully tried to flag down several taxis. "I'm just down the road. It'll be easier to get a cab later."

They began to walk together towards his Baggot Street flat. They talked about case law as they walked and argued over whether one of their lecturers had given a real hint as to the content of the final exam. They diverted for food at Abrakebabra's and wiped sauce off each other's faces with scratchy napkins. They laughed together at a couple having a screaming row in the middle of the street ahead of them, and then laughed even louder, almost giddily, hysterically, when the woman pulled the man into a laneway and began to pull frantically at his shirt and the fastenings of his trousers.

They walked up the granite steps of the red-bricked building, arguing over nineteenth-century romantic literature. As Paul fumbled with the key to his flat they were comparing Mr Rochester to Heathcliff, but once he shut the door, and closed them both inside, they fell silent.

Paul's lips bruised Emily's – he couldn't kiss her hard enough to make up for how long he'd had to wait for this moment. He unfastened her blouse and fumbled with her bra. She wriggled free of her skirt and laughed with delight at the moan he let out when he realised she was wearing stockings and suspenders. They were both laughing as he lowered her gently to the floor.

Afterwards, he led her to his bedroom and they made love twice again before he fell asleep. When he woke up, she was gone.

He refused to believe it was a one-night stand.

Of course, Paul knew Emily had slept with other men in college. And he knew that she had vowed never to get involved. In fact she had even told him, 'jokingly', that the greatest compliment she could ever pay a man was to refuse to sleep with him because it meant she was interested in getting to know him properly. But Paul couldn't believe it applied to him.

"Emily, what was last night?" he asked her the next day when he finally tracked her down in the library and persuaded her to come for coffee. "Last night?" he repeated, when she showed no sign of having heard him the first time.

"Fun?" she tried weakly, then looking up she must have seen the flash of hurt cross his face no matter how he tried to hide it. "I have no idea, Paul, honestly," she continued lamely.

"It was more than just fun for me, Emily."

"I know, Paul. That's the problem." She couldn't meet his gaze.

"Problem? What exactly do you mean by problem, Emily?"

"You know what I mean. I can't give you more than this at the moment." She picked up one of the little plastic rods supplied for stirring, and dipped it in and out of her black coffee.

"So I'm to join the ranks of your male bimbos, am I?" Paul asked quietly. "The men you use and then dump before you can get involved. Before you can get hurt?"

"It's nothing to do with getting hurt." Emily's eyes flashed angrily. "I just don't want to get involved. It's too messy and I don't have time. I've finals coming up in three weeks' time. So do you."

"And after the final exams?" he challenged. "Will you have time then?"

"It's not that simple, Paul." Emily sighed. "You're my friend. I like you; I like you a lot. I love you even. And that's why this can't go on. I don't want to lose you."

"That's a load of crap, Emily, and you know it." Paul knew it was important to contain his anger, and he spoke slowly and calmly. To his ears, his speech sounded rehearsed, although he had absolutely no idea what he was going to say. "You've been repeating that kind of thing for years," he continued. "You don't really think I believe you, do you? Every time you dumped some poor bastard, just because he was getting too close, you told me that same story. This is me, Emily. Paul. I'm already as close as it gets and I'm not going to fall for that."

He studied her face and her shocked expression penetrated his anger.

79

"Oh Christ, Emily. You really believe it, don't you? All these years I thought you were just feeding us a line. The tough feminist who keeps sex and love parcelled up in completely separate compartments. You really believe you can pull it off, don't you?"

"And why not?" Emily bristled. "Men do, all the time."

"Not to the degree you do – you're pathological." Paul shook his head in confusion and ran his hand over his face, then up through his hair. "Tell me this, Emily. Do you expect to love someone one day, really love someone, fall in love?"

"Of course."

"When?"

"When I'm ready."

"When you're ready?" He laughed bitterly. "You think it's something you can plan? One day you'll be ready, and the next you'll meet him?"

"Don't talk to me like I'm a child, Paul." Emily got up to leave. She lowered her voice, aware that the cafeteria was filling up and people were looking at her. "I don't have to sit here and listen to this."

"Wait!" He put a hand on her arm. "Sorry. You're right."

She sat down, crossed her arms and waited for him to say whatever he was struggling to articulate.

"Look, I don't want to lose you either, Emily. You're my best friend too. And maybe I could live with whatever limits you want to impose on our friendship. But for the sake of my vanity, would you do me a favour and tell me what you thought about last night?"

"Amazing," Emily grinned.

"And do you not think there's even the remotest possibility," Paul had asked her finally, "that that might have been because for the first time ever you were making love rather than just having sex?"

Unable to wait for her answer, unwilling to put himself through her denial, Paul pushed back his chair and walked out.

Paul turned into his own street. He kicked at an empty drink can and it vanished into the gloom, coming to rest with a clatter against a wrought-iron gate at the end of the cul de sac. Even the sight of the small Victorian worker's cottage he'd bought a year ago and had been restoring ever since, failed to lift his spirits. He turned his key in the lock and pushed open the door. The hall was strewn with coats and bags. Only one more day of this, he reminded himself, gritting his teeth. Then he picked up the bags, flung them into the cupboard under the stairs and sat on the second step looking towards his front door. From here the house looked finished. He put one hand on the banister and stroked the mahogany lovingly. It wasn't in keeping with the house, but when he found it in the salvage yard he hadn't been able to resist it. The wood was alive with memories.

He was glad he'd found this house; if he hadn't he might have been tempted to chuck in his job with Barrett and Lyle and go back to carpentry. The love of wood was in his veins. The four years he'd spent working in his grandfather's business, before going back to college to study law, had been the happiest of his life. He'd still have been there if the old man hadn't forced him to face up to his responsibilities and finish his education, to return to the career he had planned to follow all the way through school.

"Carpentry will wait," his grandfather said, in a voice Paul knew it was futile to argue with. "Your father's offer to bury the hatchet and pay your college fees is only valid if you take up this place."

Martin Carey held out the flimsy computer-generated form offering Paul a place to study Law in Trinity College. Paul hadn't even known his grandfather had applied on his behalf. He imagined the hours Martin Carey must have spent practising his grandson's signature, when he himself had only learnt to write in his thirties. He pictured the scene as the old man begged his son-in-law, Paul's father, to reconsider, to give Paul a second chance.

It must have been such a blow to his pride, to have to beg like that, and there was no way Paul could throw the sacrifice back in his face. Paul's only regret was that his mother had attended his graduation alone. His grandfather had passed away three days after learning that Paul had achieved his honours degree.

Paul walked into the kitchen at the back of the house. He felt so restless that he longed to pick up a chisel and start hacking at the tiles. The kitchen was his current project. He couldn't leave it much longer. Every other room in the house had been renovated and redecorated, and this was all that remained. But every time he was about to start, something stopped him. Emily joked that he was allergic to kitchens, but that wasn't true. He hated cooking in here because he found it depressing to cook for one. But his reluctance to redecorate the kitchen went deeper than that. It was a room on which big decisions had to be made. Everywhere else, he had restored wood, plastered, painted, chosen colours. All things which could be changed easily. But a kitchen had to be planned, and he wanted to get it right. The kitchen was the centre of a home.

When he had bought this house he never imagined he would be so reluctant to tackle this last job. It never occurred to him that he wouldn't be able to sit down on his own and decide what to do with a space measuring no more than nine feet by twelve. But lately he had been forced to admit that his reluctance was about doing it on his own. He didn't want to design the centre of his home for use by himself alone.

He thought of Sharon and how things might have been, but quickly chased away that thought. It would have been disastrous; they had both realised that fairly soon. Even now, after a week in each other's company, they were able to remain civil only because they knew their time together limited.

He wondered why she had waited till now to ask him for a divorce. He had offered it to her as soon as they split up all those years ago and she went back to a former boyfriend. And now as Paul thought of her upstairs in his bedroom, where she was sharing his double bed with Scott, he felt an unexpected surge of jealousy. She had

Scott, and he had no one. But then who said life was fair?

Was it fair that he was in love with Emily who wouldn't admit that the emotion existed? Was it fair that Emily had fallen for a shit who'd dumped her as soon as he realised that maybe he couldn't have his cake and eat it?

Paul allowed himself to feel relief that it was finally over between Richard and Emily. She would get over him, he knew, but it would take time. He remembered how he had felt when he had first realised that Emily was dating Richard. It was only out of respect for her that he didn't act on his immediate, fury-driven desire for revenge, and report Richard to management. There were no official rules preventing married senior managers screwing trainee accountants who worked for them, but it would have given Paul some measure of satisfaction to see Richard bumped off the partnership track.

But soon he began to realise that far from damaging Emily, Richard seemed to be doing her some good, and Paul hated him even more for that. Somehow Richard was breaking down the walls Emily had erected to protect herself from the twin dangers of intimacy and love. The walls Paul had tried and failed to break down himself.

He looked around the kitchen again. The previous owner had put up hideous orange tiles, with brown flowers picking up every third one. No doubt bargain-basement seventies. When Emily had seen it, she had done her best to stop laughing, and couldn't understand why Paul wouldn't start straight into working on the kitchen. As far as she was concerned, you could live with the rest of the house, but those tiles…

The floorboards creaked overhead. Sharon or Scott got out of bed to go to the toilet. Listening, Paul deduced it was Scott.

Was this restless mood his ex-wife's fault, Paul wondered. He was only thirty-two – surely that was too young to be getting this horrible yearning to be settled, this fear of leaving it too late? Was it because Sharon had offered him the hope of a different life all those years ago when he was nineteen? Way too young to settle down, but they had been happy for a while, hadn't they? He couldn't remember. All he could remember were the fights and recriminations when the whole thing began to fall apart. He would never forgive her for lying to him. A huge lie, the biggest lie you could tell.

And yet here he was, desperate to try again with someone else. One particular someone else, for whom settling seemed as far from her mind as it had ever been.

Chapter 6

Suzy slammed the car door shut. She had broken as many speed limits as she could find driving up from Cork, but it made her feel no better. Two years ago, when she moved back to Ireland, she had promised that she wasn't going to let her father keep doing this to her. After all, she wasn't an only child. But when he phoned her at work two days ago, and begged her to come home, Suzy asked Donal for two days off and went to help him to sort things out.

She was furious that her father still hadn't told the girls.

Girls, Suzy thought. She was as bad for still referring to her sisters as "girls". May was twenty-eight and Tricia only a few months off twenty-seven. But even when she was living in England, it was always Suzy who got the anguished call in the small hours of the morning.

"Suzy, it's your mother. She's bad again."

And each time Suzy put her own life on hold for the few days it took to restore the house to some sort of normality so that her father could pretend nothing was wrong. Well, enough was enough. She had threatened to phone May yesterday and tell her to get herself home to help her father out, but he begged her not to.

"Next time, Suze, I promise. Next time we'll tell them. Maybe there won't be a next time, eh? Maybe this will be the last time, and then they'll never need to know."

I knew, she wanted to scream. I bloody knew. I had to, didn't I? From the age of ten I bloody knew. I had to hold this family together, and it nearly killed me.

But as usual Suzy said nothing. Next time, she promised. Next time they can help me cope with this and I won't have to go on pretending to be the strong one.

As Suzy stood beside the car, she looked along the seafront towards the restaurant. She still couldn't believe how lucky she'd been to find somewhere to rent this close to work. The carpark in front of Moran's was nearly full. Odd for a Tuesday afternoon. Then she realised that one of the cars was Emily's, another's was Charlotte's friend Anne-Marie's and she could have sworn a third was Tara's. Then there were a couple of little sporty numbers she vaguely recognised and the Morans' two cars.

"Oh shit, I haven't forgotten someone's birthday, have I?" She sneaked into her flat and checked her diary. No, she was in the clear: it must be some other celebration.

Suzy decided she had time for a quick shower before work. Joe, her deputy, was covering the kitchen for her while she was away and if she arrived back too soon it might look as if she was checking up on him.

She dressed casually, in black jeans and a long-sleeved black T-shirt, but took a bit more care than she usually would with her hair and make-up. Then she checked her reflection in the bedroom mirror. Not bad for an old bat just a few months off thirty-one, she decided. She tied up her hair and frowned at the brown roots. She had put off her regular appointment to get her hair dyed her trademark black, because the last time her hairdresser, spotting the beginnings of grey, suggested that she might want to reconsider.

Reconsider what, Suzy wasn't completely sure. She could no more go around grey than she could revert to her natural mousey brown. But he said she would have to use a different shade of black. A different shade of black! Tony was mortally offended when she laughed, and explained that the product he usually used on her wasn't recommended on older women.

Older women! Suzy felt quite justified in not leaving a tip. But now her roots were getting too long to ignore, and she would have to grovel to Tony and beg forgiveness.

Donal stopped Suzy as she came in the door of the restaurant.

"Welcome back – you're early! Don't even think of going near the kitchen, Joe's having a screaming afternoon, and he'll be terribly upset to be cut off in mid-rant. Besides, your presence is required upstairs, a bit of a girls' celebration."

"What's the big occasion? I haven't forgotten

something, have I?" Suzy asked, not particularly worried.

"My lips are sealed – I'll let Anne-Marie tell you herself. The whole gang's up there."

Suzy wondered when she had become part of the "gang". Charlotte had a habit of assembling her friends around her and creating occasions on which they all met together, even those who had nothing in common.

"Hey everyone, it's Suzy!" Tara shouted as she came upstairs. "Quick, Anne-Marie, show her the ring!"

So this was the reason for the gathering. Two of the restaurant tables had been pushed together, and there were about twelve women in the room, most of them already seated. Pink shiny helium balloons were tied to the backs of the chairs, and three crystal vases were crammed full of pink and white roses.

Anne-Marie shoved a huge sparkling solitaire in Suzy's face.

"Dave and I got engaged!" she announced somewhat unnecessarily, and hugged Suzy.

Yet another toast was proposed, and Suzy raised her glass with real feeling to congratulate the bride-to-be. When she had first met Anne-Marie, Suzy hadn't much time for the girl who had been Charlotte's best friend at home in Castlemichael. Only interested in clothes, make-up and boys, Anne-Marie couldn't ever get too worked up by anything in life. Even on the subject of Marcus, whom Suzy knew she had distrusted as much as Suzy herself did, Anne-Marie had had very little to say. She maintained that Charlotte would find out in her own time that he wasn't the right person for her, and she might as well enjoy the time she was having with him until then.

But Anne-Marie was impossible to dislike for long. She was just so enthusiastic about everything and everyone, and always had a kind word to say. After qualifying as a solicitor, she surprised everyone by taking the job with Paul Finlay's firm in Castlemichael that his own daughter, Tara, had refused. The slower pace of life in a provincial town suited Anne-Marie and Tara was delighted that she was off the hook.

"Dave got his consultant's appointment last month," Anne-Marie explained to Suzy, who had only met Anne-Marie's doctor boyfriend a handful of times because of his heavy schedule. "We had to keep it quiet until it was confirmed, but on the night my parents threw a party for him to celebrate, he proposed in front of everyone! It was just so romantic. The one-knee treatment and all!"

Anne-Marie omitted to mention that this was just the public proposal. The couple had become secretly engaged a few months before.

"So when's the big day?"

"Not for ages yet," Anne-Marie replied. "I told Dave there was no way I was getting married before I was thirty, and as I refuse to even *contemplate* a winter wedding, that means about this time two years."

Suzy looked around and wondered how long she needed to stay at this gathering. There were very few people here she would consider to be her real friends. Most were friends of Anne-Marie and Charlotte. Emily was sitting looking miserable at the end of the table, Charlotte was nowhere to be seen, and Suzy hadn't much time for Tara.

"Suze! You made it on time!" Charlotte returned bearing two more bottles of champagne, which she put down to give Suzy a hug. "And don't even think of doing a runner!" she hissed into her ear, putting a restraining hand on Suzy's shoulder. "Joe's got the kitchen under control, and if he even guesses you're in the building, he'll lose his self-confidence again."

Suzy sat down again with a bump, cursing the bad luck that had her seated next to Tara Finlay. She hoped the fact that it was only a Tuesday night and that most of the women here would have to work in the morning would restrain the evening somewhat. Although the number of empty bottles and the fact that it was only six o'clock dimmed that hope somewhat.

She took a sidelong glance at Tara. The woman scared her; she had a self-destructive streak Suzy recognised. Despite her brilliant job, a queue of men lining up to take her out and no shortage of money, Suzy guessed that deep inside Tara lacked self-confidence. And she tried to make up for it by pushing herself to the limit in every sphere in life. She had to have the most prestigious client in the firm, be working on the biggest merger, have the most men on the go at a time, and drive the best car. And it was a matter of pride to her that she could drink anyone under the table. She couldn't stay still for a moment. Every second of her time had to be filled; she worked and played harder than any one Suzy knew. Tara was like the driver of a powerful, fast car. While she was in control everyone admired her skill and daring, but Suzy didn't want to be around when she hit a curve she couldn't handle. When that happened, the crash would destroy her, and her tailspin would spread carnage amongst everyone around her.

Suzy did her best to chat to Tara but, after the meal, took advantage of the break before coffee, when all the smokers had been banished outside, to change seats. She slipped in beside Emily.

"Congratulations, bridesmaid," she whispered with a giggle. She couldn't resist it. She was sure she was the only one who had noticed Emily's momentary look of horror when Anne-Marie had asked her to do the honours. Of course, Emily had covered well, and oohed and aahed with the best of them until the attention was off her, but then she sank back into the gloom she had resided in all night. "Don't tell me this air of depression is because you're worried you'll never get hitched yourself?" Suzy teased. "I thought you never wanted to get married, and you had more or less the perfect relationship with Richard?"

"I never said I didn't ever want to get married," Emily said with a slight slur, "and I don't have the perfect relationship with Richard, not any more." She knocked back the remains of her glass of wine.

"Have you broken –"

"Sshhh!" Emily hissed, then whispered the bare details of the story. "I haven't told Charlotte yet," she explained, "and I didn't want to put a damper on the party."

That would hardly put as damper on proceedings, Suzy

thought, but said nothing. If anything Charlotte and Anne-Marie would celebrate all the more. She had never quite understood Charlotte's attitude to Emily's relationship. Charlotte was far less worried about the effects of the affair on Richard's wife and two children than she was about her little sister's heart getting broken. As far as Suzy could see, Emily had Richard exactly where she wanted him, and if she got burned – she was a big girl and knew the risks from the start. But Charlotte had always been over-protective of Emily, which Suzy thought ironic, because of the two sisters Charlotte was by far the more fragile with her constant craving for approval and love.

But she prepared to listen with sympathy, expecting Emily to expand on the story. To her surprise, however, rather than dwell on the ending of her relationship with Richard, Emily seemed keener to talk about Anne-Marie and Dave.

"They're a perfect match, aren't they?" Emily went on to extol Dave's virtues, and to say how lucky Anne-Marie was to have found him.

"So, are you on the look-out for Mr Right yourself?" Suzy asked, amused to see Emily wax so lyrical on the subject of love. Especially when that love ended up in marriage.

"Me? Never. No, if anything, Richard taught me that there's no point in tying your happiness up in a man. I mean, I'm sure that's what Richard's wife thought she was doing, and what did it get her?" Emily frowned angrily.

"An affair with another man, and she still gets her husband running home with his tail between his legs,"

Suzy replied wryly.

"I never thought of that." Emily sat up straighter. "What if she *did* know about us? Richard and me, I mean. Maybe she had an affair to get him back. Sly cow! I'd never stoop to that level."

"You might if you found a man you thought was worth the effort."

"No. No more men for me. Well, no more relationships anyway! I'm going to concentrate on my career from now on."

Emily raised her glass in a toast to the promotion she was hoping for.

"So you've applied for it?" Suzy had advised her that she'd be mad not to.

"Yeah, but I won't know till next week if I'm even going to be called for an interview," Emily answered modestly. In fact she was fairly confident that the job was hers. "Anyway, enough about me and my failed romances." Emily grimaced, unaware that as usual she had already ended the conversation about her love-life by starting a discussion on her career.

Suzy wondered if she did it deliberately, or if it was an instinctive urge to talk about the only thing that really mattered to her in her life.

"How are you getting along with that gorgeous Frenchman?" asked Emily.

Now it was Suzy's turn to grimace.

"Not good?"

"No, it's going great … but …" Suzy groaned as she thought of the grovelling she would have to do after dumping him at the weekend to go home. Her first Saturday night off in a month. She had more or less decided that she and Etienne would end up back in his breathtaking penthouse in Clontarf, and that she would stay the night for the first time. She was pretty sure that he had guessed her intention. "Yeah, it's going great, honestly. But I had to stand him up this weekend to go down to Dad, so I don't know how happy he's going to be about that."

"Well, is he the one?"

Suzy looked at Emily with amazement. Was this ice-maiden Emily asking her this? Love 'em and leave 'em Emily? "I haven't known him that long," she said finally, when she realised Emily was waiting for an answer, and hadn't asked just to fill in a silence.

"Have you ever been truly and madly in love with someone, Suze? Someone you'd want to spend the rest of your life with, I mean?" Emily reached for the wine bottle in front of her and drained the last few drops into her glass. She wasn't aware she'd asked the question loud enough for people on both sides of her to hear, and that they were all looking at Suzy now.

"Are you staying here tonight, or would you like to crash on my couch?" Suzy stood up, trying to ignore the fact that she was blushing right to the brown roots of her black hair. "Charlotte, do you have room for Emily, or will I take her with me?"

"I was going to get a taxi home. I've no clothes for the morning," Emily complained with a pout.

"If you get a taxi, your car'll be stuck here. Come on

with me. I'll be up early enough to throw you out so you can get home before the worst of the traffic." Suddenly Suzy wanted to get out of this stuffy room. She was uncomfortably aware that Emily's last question about falling in love was still hanging in the air, and she didn't want to answer it.

"Are you sure you don't mind?" Charlotte asked with relief. "I was going to drive Emily's car into town for her in the morning…"

"You've enough on your plate," Suzy said somewhat gruffly, thinking that it was about time Charlotte let her sister grow up and look after herself. Why should Donal have to put up with his wife running around and seeing to everyone else's needs? It wasn't as if they hadn't enough to do themselves with three kids and this place to keep running…

"I've an early start in the morning so I'm going now," Suzy explained to the other women, then turned to Emily: "Do you want to come with me, Emily, or will I leave the key out?"

"Take me home now! Before I do any more damage to my liver!" Emily groaned theatrically and staggered to her feet. "Sorry to leave so soon, everyone. Congratulations again, Anne-Marie! And give Dave a big kiss for me."

She hugged her friend and said goodbye to the rest of the room, then as they hit the cold air outside, she sobered up quickly.

"God! I couldn't wait to get out of there! Thanks, Suzy. They look as if they could be in for a long night."

Suzy realised that Emily wasn't half as drunk as she

appeared. They walked in silence the few hundred yards to a large seafront house which had been divided into flats. Suzy rented the first floor and had a view over the sea. It was dark out but, before she switched on the light, she could just about make out the black outline of Howth Head against the navy-blue sky. She closed the curtain and shut out the night. Turning back to the room, she noticed Emily looking around with interest. Guiltily she realised that although it was six months since she'd moved in, it was the first time Emily had been here. She wondered what Emily must think of it, Emily whose flat looked so distinctive, so Emily.

Suzy never tried to put her mark on the homes she rented. She lived with strangers' furniture and tolerated other people's taste without even noticing it. She never felt it worthwhile to put effort into flats she was only going to spend a limited amount of time in. To her, they were just temporary staging posts on the way to the real home she would one day own.

"What do you think of it?" she asked, waving her arm in a gesture that took in the whole living-room with its oatmeal carpet and brown corduroy sofa. She wished suddenly that she had at least a vase or two, a bowl on one of the low tables or a picture of her own on the wall. "Not exactly Terence Conran, is it?"

"No, it's nice. It's fine. Honestly. I mean you haven't been here that long, have you? You haven't really had time to do much with it."

"No, you're right. Coffee?" Suzy walked towards the kitchen.

A few minutes later Emily was stretched out on Suzy's sofa with a mug of her wonderful Java coffee.

"Don't think I didn't notice you avoiding my question earlier," she said

"Don't you want milk with that?" Suzy held out a jug.

"Not in this coffee, it's gorgeous. Where do you buy it?"

"Etienne gets it for me."

Suzy had met Etienne through the restaurant, and had been seeing him for a couple of months now. He was a wine supplier who imported a few unique wines from near his home town in the Languedoc region in the south of France. Donal loved them, appreciating the value they offered his customers. Etienne had also started importing other food lines, mainly to supply specialist food shops and restaurants, and Suzy had included some of his delicacies in her recipes.

They sipped their coffee, and nibbled Italian biscotti, another of Etienne's finds.

"You still didn't answer my question." Emily peered over her mug at Suzy.

"You're drunk," Suzy replied with a grin. "You're supposed to forget what you said more than two minutes ago."

"I didn't overdo the drunken bit, did I?" Emily giggled. "I had to get out of there. Too much rosy goodwill for me."

"I don't think anyone noticed. But what's wrong with rosy goodwill?"

"Nothing, as long as it's directed in another direction.

Imagine me as a bridesmaid! Yeuch! Anyway, by constantly avoiding my question about your one true love, you've now managed to convince me that you're trying to hide something."

"I haven't had a one true love. Plenty of applicants but no one who could stick the pace."

"Your job doesn't make it easy, does it?"

"No, the hours are a bitch. When most people are falling in love over a carefully prepared starter, I'm in the kitchen preparing their main course." Suzy frowned for a few seconds, then her face burst into the enthusiastic smile it always did when she talked about food and cooking. "But I wouldn't have it any other way."

With a start, Suzy realised that that was why Etienne was different. He really didn't mind her hours. He was happy to see her at odd hours, whenever she was free. Being his own boss helped, of course, and the fact that he was almost as obsessed with food as she was meant that he never got bored when she spoke about her passion. And he was more than happy to act as guinea-pig to test new dishes on. She resolved to make a special effort to make it up to him; she couldn't afford to lose him. She wasn't getting any younger and she would have to stop holding out for the impossible. Lost in her own resolutions, she was unaware that Emily was staring at her.

"What?"

"I asked if Etienne was the one. You know, the one you denied existed, the one you were so mad about you could see yourself settling down with."

"No, he wasn't. But he could be another one, I

suppose," Suzy replied before she realised what she'd said.

"Aha! I knew it. There was someone. Who? When?"

"A long time ago, and nothing happened. It was a case of right man, wrong time, wrong place."

"He was married?"

"No, not even going out with anyone when I met him, but it was obvious that he…" She stopped, remembering who she was talking to. "It was a long time ago. Now I don't know about you, but I'm going to bed. I'll wake you before I go out for my run in the morning, so you can have a shower. If you wait too long I'll come back and use up all the hot water."

"You run! I always wondered how you managed to maintain a figure that great when you're surrounded by food all day."

"I've no choice. I don't have the willpower not to eat."

But Suzy was absurdly pleased that Emily should think she had a good figure. Emily the Work-out Queen, who was a member of not one but two gyms, one near home and one near work. Emily thought she, Suzy, had a good figure!

Charlotte had waved off the last of the gang of girls over two hours before but she pottered about for so long that when she was finally ready for bed, Donal was already asleep. She crept in beside him, but within minutes knew she wasn't going to get to sleep. She tossed and turned for a while, then got up to make herself a cup of hot chocolate.

In the kitchen, the estate agent's leaflet for the house

they had looked at last week was on the table. Donal must have been looking at it; or else he had left it out deliberately so she'd see it when she came in. Charlotte picked it up and opened it.

Donal was right, the house was perfect for them. Five bedrooms, three large rooms downstairs besides the kitchen, and a gorgeous conservatory. It was the house of her dreams. And only three minutes' walk from this place. So why was she so reluctant to put in an offer on it?

Suddenly, she remembered Anne-Marie's comment from earlier: "I have no intention of getting married before I'm thirty."

Anne-Marie had made a life-plan in her late teens, and she had stuck to it. The college years, the job near home, the dependable man who would respect her need to have her own career, but be well off enough so that she wouldn't have to work too hard at it. And now she was enforcing a two-year engagement because she had sworn she wouldn't get married before she was thirty.

Charlotte tried to remember if she had ever mapped out her life like that. When she was younger, she had vague images in her mind of what her future would hold. She would be married, with loads of kids. A devoted husband, a comfortable house where her many friends would come and go as they pleased. Love and security had been the things she craved, although she might not have been able to put a name to them back then. She had fulfilled all her goals in a way she had barely dared dream possible. She had three terrific kids, Donal, the restaurant. So why did she keep getting the feeling that she had missed out on something along the way?

Maybe it was because she wasn't quite twenty-nine. Her oldest child was nine, she had a thriving business and they were in the position to buy a house far beyond what she would ever have dared aspire to. Was it all too soon? Suzy was still renting a small flat down the road. Anne-Marie was back living with her parents, and she and Dave hadn't even started looking at houses yet. Emily, although she had bought her own place, had no other commitments. Was that it? Did she feel crushed by her commitments? Her sister, her friends, most people Charlotte knew of her age, they could drop everything tomorrow and go to South America.

But Charlotte knew that she would never want to drop everything and go to South America, or Australia, or anywhere. She loved her life. She loved the people in it. She didn't feel tied down.

The milk boiled over on the stove, and Charlotte cursed as she wiped it up. There was just about enough left to make a small cup of chocolate. As she sat drinking, she looked at the brochure for Number 3 Elm Drive. The picture showed a solid twenties-built house, with leaded windows. The house was double-fronted and the bay windows to either side of the front door were framed by some kind of creeper. The photo had been taken earlier in the year when the creeper was bare, but when she and Donal had viewed the house, leaves were bursting out all over its tangled branches. To the side of the house, a garage had been converted into a study and beyond that again a new garage had been added in the seventies. The creeper had just about stretched to cover this concrete structure, which was at odds with the rest of the house.

The asymmetrical shape of the front of the house was not displeasing; it somehow made it stand out from the other houses on the road, which all looked the same. Something about its unbalanced appearance and gravelled drive reminded Charlotte of another house. A much bigger one. With a gasp she realised that the house her memory dragged up was Marcus's parents' home.

Charlotte remembered the only time she had visited the house, one night when his parents were away. The first time she and Marcus had made love. She blushed, and tried to drive the image from her mind. But it was no good: she felt a familiar heat spread through her, as her heart speeded up. Why should she suddenly start thinking of Marcus now? She was perfectly happy with Donal. Their lovemaking was a lot less frequent than it had been ten years ago, but they were grown up, they had children, and a time-consuming business. If she sometimes wished Donal could make her insides melt with desire the way Marcus had, just by looking at her, then she remembered how wretched her first lover had made her feel too. Donal was the man she really loved.

Charlotte picked up the estate agent's leaflet, and opened it to remind herself of the layout of the house. She smiled when she realised what was wrong with her. She needed a new challenge. The newspaper review had persuaded her that the restaurant was home and dry. A new house, to decorate and make her own, would keep her busy. After all, since their marriage, she and Donal had never stayed in one place for long, always moving to a new city, a new home.

She turned over the leaflet to where Donal had scribbled financial calculations of mortgages and interest rates to prove to her that they could afford the house. In a small space at the bottom, she began to write a list of all the things she would change about the house if their offer was accepted. First would be those awful green tiles in the kitchen. They would have to go.

A half an hour of planning left her eyes aching and when she dropped into bed, Charlotte fell asleep within minutes.

"What finally made you decide?" Donal was delighted. He hugged Charlotte as he told her their offer on the house had been accepted.

"I was just being over-cautious. You were right as usual – the house is perfect for us, and we really have to get out of here. It's all right for us, but it's not fair on the kids. They can't invite their friends around, and it's about time Gemma got a room of her own. Sharing with Aisling can't be much fun." The more she thought about it, the guiltier she felt for imposing such living arrangements on her children for so long. They were living on top of one another.

In an attempt to get some space, Gemma had taken to hanging out in the kitchens of the restaurant. The younger children were banned, so it was the only way she could escape them. At first Suzy had been amused at her goddaughter's fascination with her job, but soon she had begun to take for granted that the lanky nine-year-old would appear at her side after homework and hang around chatting. She had a calming effect on the other kitchen staff too. While Gemma wasn't the slightest bit fazed by the way tempers could flare with no warning in the steamy environment of the restaurant kitchen, Suzy found it amusing that the use of obscenities was drastically reduced when the boss's kid was about. And that suited Chef. If the testosterone-laden atmosphere of her kitchen was getting to her, she'd put on one of Gemma's Spice Girl CD's and the two of them would proclaim "Girl Power", and sing and dance around the kitchen as she worked.

"We can go up and see the house this afternoon if we want to – take the kids with us," Donal said. "It'll be six weeks or so until we can complete the sale and move in, so why don't you take the camcorder and video the house? That way you'll have a much better idea of what you want to do with it."

He'd seen Charlotte's scribbled lists and knew she was dying to get her hands on the place. This time they would do what they liked. This house was for keeps.

Five weeks later, Gemma sat in the middle of her new room, on the floor because the furniture wasn't due to arrive till the next day, planning the décor of her own little palace. Donal grimaced and Charlotte giggled as they looked over her shoulder at a picture of a four-poster bed draped with pink and purple curtains. The girl stuck her tongue out in concentration and looked around the room before choosing a yellow marker to colour the floor.

"I'm glad you're the one going shopping with her!" her father whispered, nudging Charlotte, and they both rushed out of the room so their daughter wouldn't hear them erupt into laughter.

They were all on a high. In the weeks since their offer on the house was accepted, Anne-Marie, acting as their solicitor, had pulled out all the stops to get the sale completed this fast. She had picked up the keys this morning and was, at this very moment, being shown the tree-house by a proud Tim.

"This is my real house," they could hear the little boy say through the window Charlotte had opened to blow out the musty smell. "But I'll have a room in Mum and Dad's house too, of course, for when it gets too cold out here."

They looked out at the garden, and watched Anne-Marie struggle her way up a rickety ladder to be shown around the little boy's pride and joy.

"I have to share it with the girls, of course," he explained, "but I know Gemma'll just say it's boring, and I can always push Aisling out if she gets on my nerves." At this point he looked up and saw the open window, and lowered his voice as he shared the rest of his secret plans with Anne-Marie.

"Happy?" Donal stood behind Charlotte as she strained to see the promised sea view from the master bedroom. He could just make out a small triangle of water between two houses and below a huge Scots Pine.

"Happy," Charlotte agreed, leaning back against him as he put his arms around her. "Do you think that tree will lose any of its greenery in winter to increase our view?"

"No, I reckon the property brochure boasting about the view must have been written fifty years ago, before the tree grew that tall and before the houses were built. Still, they block our view of the sea, but they also block the view of the restaurant. That can't be a bad thing, can it?" They held onto each other, staring out at the little patch of blue in the distance.

"Are you cold?" Donal asked in surprise a few minutes later. Despite the draught, the room was warm, as the sun streamed through the huge bay window. "I thought I felt you shiver."

"I'm fine. It's nothing." Charlotte's forced smile didn't drive away her worried look.

"Charlotte?" He turned her around to face him. "What is it?"

"Nothing, I'm being silly."

"Tell me."

"It's too much, Donal. I just suddenly got the feeling I don't deserve all this. As if it's all going to be taken away as soon as I believe it's really ours."

"Why can't you just believe in happiness, love? You once said we could achieve anything we wanted to as long as we stuck together. Don't you believe that any more?" There was sadness in his eyes.

"Of course, I still believe it! It's just that..." Charlotte pulled Donal's arms tighter around her. "Keep holding me and tell me what we're going to do with this room," she begged.

They discussed colour schemes, curtain fabrics and furniture, and almost managed to banish the ghost tiptoeing across Charlotte's grave.

"It's fabulous!" Emily gushed the next evening as she put the last of the cutlery into one of the drawers. "This kitchen must be at least five times the size of mine."

Charlotte smiled in agreement. Apart from the dark green tiles, which she had already hacked off leaving a mess for the plasterer and tiler to sort out, she was keeping everything else because the kitchen was almost brand new. It had been extended into a large conservatory with warm sand-coloured tiles running straight through from the hall. Whoever had designed the huge room had installed under-floor heating so the kitchen would be cosy even in winter. Pale pine units covered two walls, so there was more storage space than Charlotte had ever had before. The soft green paint on the walls was not the colour she would have chosen herself, but as she wasn't sure exactly what colour she wanted, and as the green worked, she was happy to leave it until she decided. But the natural light was the kitchen's best feature. The conservatory ran the whole length of the longest side of kitchen, and it faced west. Even the most watery of January sunlight would brighten the room.

"Come on. That's as much unpacking as I have the energy for tonight. Let's get a glass of wine and sit down." Charlotte rooted through the cupboards until she found glasses, and took a bottle of Sancerre from the fridge.

"Cheers!" Emily sipped the ice-cold white wine. It was actually too cold to taste properly because Charlotte had shoved it in the freezer to cool it down fast, and then forgot about it. She played with her glass, cupping it in her hands to warm it slightly.

The sisters sat in silence, enjoying the quiet of the summer evening. The two younger children had fallen into bed exhausted over an hour ago and Gemma, who couldn't get over the luxury of her own bedroom, was reading quietly.

"It's much quieter here," Emily said after a few minutes. "You can't hear the traffic from the main road at all." They both listened. Although the double doors were open onto the garden, the extra few hundred yards from the main road meant that they could hear only the occasional heavy truck .

"I wonder if I'll find the place too quiet," Charlotte said. "I mean, between the restaurant and the traffic, we haven't exactly led a quiet life for the past couple of years."

"And even the kids will seem quieter when they're spread over a bigger space," Emily laughed, remembering Tim and Aisling running through the house yelling, amazed that they were allowed to make so much noise. "Pity Donal couldn't get off tonight to enjoy your first night at home."

"Sneaky beggar!" Charlotte snorted. "As soon as he heard you and Anne-Marie would be helping me unpack, he suddenly decided work was *far* too busy for him to take a day off!"

She didn't mind really. It had been much easier to unpack and direct the movers without Donal thinking too hard about where everything should go. Charlotte just stood in the middle of the house issuing orders, and the job was done in half the time, with surprisingly few boxes ending up in the wrong place. There were still some anonymous-looking packages that they hadn't bothered opening since they got back from England, and Charlotte was looking forward to opening those in the weeks that followed. It would be like Christmas, rediscovering all their ornaments and bits and pieces that they hadn't had room for in the flat.

"It's a shame Anne-Marie wasn't able to stay longer. She was here for all the hard work, and not the enjoyable bit at the end." Emily held up her glass again for Charlotte to refill. The bottle was sitting on the tiles, and a puddle of condensed water had formed around it. Charlotte tried to catch the drips as she poured. When she had finished pouring, she put the bottle back in the fridge. The tiles, baked by the sun all day, had warmed up the wine so that it was no longer too cold.

"Well, it was a whole three days since she'd seen Dave, so she couldn't resist going to collect him at the airport." Charlotte grinned. "I'm really glad she's found someone that mad about her."

"Yeah, she's had a few disasters." Emily knew even more about them than Charlotte. She'd been the one picking up the pieces on the two occasions Anne-Marie had had her heart broken.

111

"And what about you?" Charlotte couldn't resist asking. She couldn't believe that Emily was as unaffected by Richard's desertion as she claimed.

"I'm fine. I keep telling you. I don't need Richard, or any other man for that matter. For God's sake, I'm only twenty-seven. I haven't started panicking yet about being left on the shelf." Emily grinned. "Besides I've got all my friends and family." She spoke in a tone that indicated she wanted to end the subject.

Chapter 7

Summer 1996

Charlotte sniffed the air and turned up the end of her nose suspiciously. All the windows had been wide open for the last few hours, but she still smelled paint. Faint, but present. It was no good trying to figure out if she was imagining it or not; she had lived with the oily fumes of new gloss work and the sweet, sickening scent of emulsion for so long now that it followed her around. In Superquinn last week, when she was doing her shopping, she had looked around trying to figure out who was renovating, before she realised that she was carrying around the odour in her hair.

She decided to have a shower, go for a walk on the seafront and let the wind blow her clean. Then she would come home and see if the house really did stink of paint, or if it was all in her head.

The frenzied spate of decorating was because Charlotte discovered Donal's plans for a 'surprise' party for her thirtieth birthday. Their guests were coming to the house for drinks, then walking as far as the restaurant for a late meal. When Charlotte heard this, she looked around the house in a panic.

She still hadn't worked her way through the redecorating planned last summer when they moved in. Lack of time was partly to blame, but Charlotte's leisurely pace as she stripped floors, painted and wallpapered was partly so she could put off the question: Is this it?

Her family, her home, her business. More than she had ever dreamed of, but there was something missing, and she couldn't figure out what. She loved Donal as much if not more than on the day they were married. Her kids, though a handful at the best of times and a fully qualified demolition team at the worst, filled her with pride when she was with them and an empty longing when she was parted from them.

And the restaurant? Their accountant was encouraging Donal and Charlotte to look into setting up a second restaurant in Temple Bar, so there was definitely nothing missing on the work front. Maybe, Charlotte thought to herself, it was an age thing. Maybe this restlessness was just because deep down she was depressed to be leaving her twenties behind.

Charlotte winced as shampoo flooded her eyes. She lowered the temperature of the shower and let the jet of water wash it out. Then she rinsed her hair and stepped out of the steamed-up cubicle. Her eyes were red and watering. To her surprise the tears wouldn't stop, so she sniffed then swallowed what felt suspiciously like a feeble sob. She looked in the mirror and frowned angrily at her reflection.

Get a grip, she muttered, as she stormed into her bedroom. The next-door neighbours' ginger cat lay curled up in the sun in the bay window. He lifted his head lazily, wondering who had come to disturb him. Charlotte flung the damp towel at him and he disappeared the way he had come in, slithering out through the open window. He really was getting to be a problem. They couldn't leave a window open anywhere in the house without 'Tommo' making himself at home.

"People who work all day shouldn't have pets!" Charlotte had raged one day when Donal had laughed at her animosity towards their feline intruder. "If they can't look after the bloody animal themselves, they can't expect their neighbours to!" But it was hard to stay angry with the animal for long. The kids loved him, and apart from his annoying habit of popping up when you least expected him, he was a friendly enough creature. Despite this, throwing the towel at him, and seeing him slither out the window in fear had the effect of cheering Charlotte up.

As she walked along the seafront a while later, Charlotte wondered if it would rain. Best to get all the rain out of the way before tomorrow, she thought. Donal was planning to serve drinks in the conservatory, hoping that their friends could spill out into the garden. Ominous-looking grey clouds gathered right across Dublin Bay, and Howth kept vanishing behind rain showers. Charlotte began to speed up. She wanted to call in to the restaurant before she collected Aisling from playschool.

The first drops of the threatened shower stung Charlotte's face. It was hail, not rain, a typical summer shower. Shielding her eyes, she looked up at the sky. It was going to be a quick shower, she hoped, and ran to a bus shelter until it passed. Hailstones the size of marbles hammered out a deafening rhythm against the side of the shelter. When the shower showed no sign of abating, Charlotte made a run for it and arrived at work just as the downpour stopped.

"Just a few messages for you, Charlotte. I've managed to deal with everything else," Geri, Suzy's cousin, told her as she towelled her hair in her office. She read from her list of phone messages. "O'Brien's are still querying last month's payment, but I wouldn't worry too much about that. They can wait."

Jack O'Brien, the Morans' meat supplier, couldn't keep records to save his life. Every month, as she sorted through his scribbled bills, Charlotte swore she would change suppliers, but then Suzy would cook her a steak and she would acknowledge that he supplied the best meat in the city.

"Anything else?" she asked wearily. Geri was right, Jack O'Brien could wait.

"Two phone messages. The first one's a wine rep. I told him he'd have to make an appointment, but he said he'd like to talk to you on the phone first."

"He can wait until next week. The other one?"

"A Denise O'Sullivan." Geri handed over the piece of paper, looking closely at her employer's face. Charlotte, who had her head down as she wrote herself a note about the other two messages, didn't notice her scrutiny. "She wouldn't say what she wanted to talk to you about. She left a number, but she said it's not urgent, and she'll ring you another time."

"Fine. Anything else?" Charlotte looked up, and was surprised to see Geri look away suddenly.

Geri updated her on restaurant business for another ten minutes, and went through the advance bookings for the next week. Charlotte was glad to see that they were as busy as ever, despite a new upmarket Chinese restaurant having opened only two hundred yards from them. Then Geri left her on her own to sign some cheques.

When she finished, Charlotte looked at the last message again. Denise O'Sullivan. The name rang a bell. Definitely not a supplier, or a rep she'd dealt with before. No, the name was lodged somewhere in the distant past. Someone from school? She couldn't say for certain but she didn't think so. She shrugged her shoulders and got up to leave, then scribbled *Ring Ms O'Sullivan* on her To Do list for Monday.

She froze.

Ms O'Sullivan or Mrs O'Sullivan? Denise.

The woman Marcus had left her for? Charlotte didn't even know if they'd got married, so that particular Denise might not be Mrs O'Sullivan at all. Her hand on the doorknob, she resolved not to think about it till she rang her on Monday.

Charlotte checked that her desk was tidy in case Geri needed to use it while she was off, and closed the door behind her. She went out through the kitchens to talk to Suzy. To her surprise, Suzy was reserved, keeping their chat to the purely professional. At first Charlotte was worried that she'd done something to offend her, then remembered her surprise party. Charlotte was supposed to pretend that she didn't know anything about it. No doubt Suzy was being careful not to give anything away. Smiling, Charlotte left the kitchen before her friend let something slip. As she walked across the carpark she stopped. It was no good. She would be thinking about Denise O'Sullivan all weekend.

"I left something upstairs," she told Geri who joked that she couldn't keep away from the place for more than a few minutes.

She closed the office door, then reached for Denise's number. Should she ring her from here, or from home?

From here, of course. For God's sake, she didn't even know who she was calling. What was she afraid of?

"Hello?" The phone was answered just as Charlotte was about to hang up.

"Hello, I'd like to speak to … ehm …" Charlotte hesitated, as if she were looking up the name. "Denise O'Sullivan, please."

"Speaking." The word was spoken in what sounded like a child's voice, or at most a teenager's. "Hello? Who is this?"

Charlotte realised that she had been silent for a few seconds.

"Sorry, sorry!" she blustered. "Sorry. My name is Charlotte Moran. Of Moran's Restaurant. I got a message that a Denise O' Sullivan had phoned me?"

Now it was the turn of the woman at the other end of the phone to be silent.

"Hello?" Charlotte felt the soft hairs at the back of her neck begin to stand on end. She ran her hand over them, smoothing them back into place. She continued to massage her neck as she often did when she had a headache.

"Mrs Moran," the voice said at last, "you don't know me. Or rather, we met, but it was years ago, so I doubt that you remember me."

Charlotte did. As soon as she realised that Marcus was leaving her for someone called Denise, she had dredged through her memory for the few college parties he had taken her to. And she'd remembered the diminutive blonde. Tiny, but able to captivate a whole room with her presence. Her little child's voice, which almost had a trace of a lisp to it, never had any trouble being heard in a room full of boisterous engineering students, because when she spoke they fell silent. The whole class was captivated by her, and Charlotte remembered the relief she had felt when Marcus told her that Denise had been going out with the same guy since she was seventeen and that they were probably going to get engaged after the finals.

"I used to be Denise O'Leary," the woman at the other end of the phone continued. "Until I married Marcus O'Sullivan, that is." She fell silent again.

"How can I help you?" Charlotte asked at last.

119

"I don't know. I just … well, I was wondering if I could meet you?"

"Why?"

"Don't worry. If it's too much trouble …"

"No, no, that's fine, if you want to meet …" Charlotte wasn't sure what else to say.

"Tomorrow, or over the weekend perhaps?"

"No, I'm tied up. How about next week?" Charlotte reached for the security of her organiser.

"When would suit you?"

"Any morning except Monday or Wednesday." Charlotte was amazed to hear herself sound so business-like as she arranged an appointment with her former boyfriend's wife. "And any time between ten and half eleven." That would allow her time to drop Aisling off and get back in time to pick her up. And no one need know she'd been gone at all.

"All right, let's say Tuesday then, at half ten?"

Both women were more comfortable now. Used to making appointments and scheduling meetings, they pencilled initials into their diaries, along with the time.

"I'll meet you at the restaurant then, will I?" Denise offered.

"No!" Charlotte gasped. "No, sorry, we can't meet at the restaurant." Why, she wondered; why couldn't they meet at the restaurant? "In town somewhere?" she suggested, unable to provide an excuse.

"Sorry, of course, I understand," Denise apologised. "How about in the National Gallery? In their coffee shop, I mean. Or would you prefer somewhere else? I haven't been back in Dublin for long and it's all changed so much since …"

"The National Gallery's fine. Perfect." Charlotte suddenly wanted to get off the phone. "See you then."

What on earth did Denise O'Sullivan want with her? And what did she mean about not being long back in Ireland? Had she moved back? Had Marcus? Charlotte had heard from Tara that Marcus had moved to Holland as soon as he graduated. Denise must have gone with him. When did they get married, she wondered. Had they lived in Holland ever since, or were they one of those cosmopolitan couples who only spent a couple of years in each city, moving to newer and better jobs to further their careers? And why was she suddenly so interested in how Marcus and Denise had spent the past ten years?

Charlotte suddenly felt swamped by the restlessness that had skulked in the background for the past couple of years. She tried to clear her mind. It was idle curiosity, no more. After all, she had spent nearly two years with Marcus, so it was only natural that she wonder how things had turned out for him – if he was as happy with Denise as she was with Donal…

Did she still feel anything for him? No, of course not. That was why she was going to meet Denise. If she saw his wife, and talked about him, then she could really put him into her past, couldn't she? She could enquire about him, ask whether he had any children, what he was working at now. Then he would become Marcus of the present rather than Marcus of ten years ago. She would know how he had turned out, rather than wonder what might have been.

"Bed! *Now!*" Donal growled at Tim, who appeared at the top of the stairs every time the door opened to admit another guest. He had been allowed to stay up for the start of the party, the family part, but then he had been banished upstairs and only Gemma was allowed to mingle with the adults. Tim thought this was grossly unfair. Ten wasn't that much older than seven and a half.

"I'll go, Donal," Fiona, the baby-sitter offered. "You should be enjoying your party."

"No, you relax and finish your drink," Donal insisted, smiling at her. "You'll be stuck here with the little monsters when the rest of us have gone down for dinner." He put his foot on the bottom step and Tim disappeared into his room. Until the next time.

A waiter was handing out drinks in the conservatory. The doors were open and the evening was warm. The garden smelled of warm, wet vegetation although the last stormy shower had blown itself out a couple of hours ago. Donal watched the party from the door of the kitchen. There was a gleeful excitement in the air, the result of the look of shock and surprise on Charlotte's face when Anne-Marie had brought her home an hour ago. Although Donal had let her in on the secret of the party, he hadn't told her that he had managed to get so many of their friends from England to come – most of whom she hadn't seen since they had moved back.

He was glad to see her so happy because he had worried about her lately. She was working too hard, and nothing he did or said would make her reduce her load. He had tried to persuade her to take on another baby-sitter to help out in the afternoons but she refused, saying it was a waste of money. So most of her afternoons were spent looking after the kids, doing any paperwork she had taken home with her and rushing around doing housework. And although Donal sent the restaurant cleaners up to the house twice a week, all that seemed to achieve was to send Charlotte around in a flurry of tidying before they came.

Donal did what he could around the house, but Charlotte's recent nervous energy ensured that there was rarely anything left for him to do. She couldn't stop moving if she thought there was so much as one pair of the kids' jeans left un-ironed or more than two garments in the laundry basket. And if by some miracle she did find herself with five minutes to spare, instead of relaxing, like he begged her to, she got out one of her damned lists and tackled the next task on it.

Charlotte's eyes still glistened with the tears she had almost shed when she saw William and Amy, the first people she spotted as she stepped into the hall. Donal had persuaded them to leave the bistro for a weekend to make the trip for Charlotte's birthday. Suddenly Donal realised that the guests in the house at the moment were all friends from more than three years ago. A varied collection of people from all over England, friends from Charlotte's Castlemichael childhood, and from the time she had spent in Dublin in her first flat. Charlotte, who collected friends like other people saved stamps, hadn't increased the size of her holding since they had returned to Ireland. There were some new faces, but they were mainly people they had met through work, or who Donal had met at the golf club.

"You've gone very quiet." Suzy appeared at Donal's elbow, making him jump. She was wearing a very stylish beige trouser suit which screamed money, but didn't quite work with her jet-black hair. She had come on her own to the party tonight as she was going through one of the 'off' phases of her on-off relationship with Etienne.

"Hi, Suze, enjoying the evening?" Donal asked her.

"It's a great party, Donal. Well done!" She put down her drink. "But I'm just going to pop down the road to check on tonight's meal."

"Oh no, you're not!" Donal laughed, grabbing her arm and forcing the glass of mineral water back into her hand. "Joe has everything under control and has threatened to resign if you dare to show your face in his kitchen tonight."

"His kitchen! Cheeky beggar! Who does he think he is?" Suzy clutched her drink in both hands and wandered off to talk to some of the people from the days she and Charlotte had been neighbours in Ranelagh. She joined the group who swooped on her with glee, then she manoeuvred the knot of people around so that she could listen to their conversation but watch the rest of the room at the same time. She saw that the Irish crowd seemed to have taken a step back from the birthday girl, allowing her to catch up on the friends who had travelled from England for her big day.

She noticed she wasn't the only one taking a step back and observing from a distance. Donal had resumed his watching brief from the door of the kitchen. Suzy wondered if he knew about Denise's phone-call. Geri had scribbled down the message on the reservations book before transferring it to the message pad, and Suzy had seen it when she was checking how busy they were going to be for the weekend. Geri didn't remember much about the call when quizzed on it, but came back to Suzy later and told her about Charlotte's strange behaviour after she had rushed back to the office to call Denise.

"You don't think there's anything going on, do you?" Geri asked, after Suzy had told her who Denise was, and had updated her on the history. "I mean, Donal and Charlotte look like the perfect couple."

"Of course, they are," Suzy said quickly. "Forget about it."

But she was unable to follow her own advice. She had noticed Charlotte's distant look these past few months and she saw how Donal seemed to be throwing himself further and further into his work. He claimed it was because he wanted to relieve Charlotte's load, but Charlotte was doing as much as ever. And now he had taken up golf as well. Surely they could hardly be spending any time together?

"Suzy!" Emily cried. "Where is that sister of mine so I can give her a great big birthday hug?"

Emily had just arrived, having flown in from the Far East from a tour of her company's manufacturing plants.

125

Paul had collected her from the airport, brought her home to change and was standing awkwardly at the door. Suzy felt sorry for him – he knew hardly anyone here. She went over to join him while Emily swooped on her sister and presented her with a small, perfectly wrapped gift.

"You made it!" Suzy said to Paul.

"Just about! Emily's Dublin flight was grounded in Schiphol because of fog. She was just about to try and get a train to Brussels when the fog lifted, but it still took ages to get the backlog of flights cleared. She doesn't look as if she's been travelling for over twenty hours, does she?" Paul looked fondly across the conservatory at Emily and accepted a drink off a tray that floated past him.

What is it about the Riordan sisters that they can totally captivate men and be totally unaware of it? Suzy asked herself for the thousandth time. She thought back to the year when Donal hung around Charlotte like a puppy, always waiting on the off-chance that she might leave Marcus. And Marcus too had been entranced by her, in his own way.

And now it looked like history repeating itself. Paul was smitten with Emily, and she accepted his friendship without being aware of what she was doing to him. Suzy guessed that, like Donal ten years ago, Paul was incapable of even looking at another woman. She watched with no small envy as a flock of men gathered around Emily and she began to wish that she had invited Etienne after all so she wouldn't feel so inadequate. But he had been getting too serious lately. He was trying to persuade her to move in with him, and she suspected that he wouldn't accept her excuse of needing to live near work for much longer. She couldn't understand why she was so reluctant to make a commitment to him. She loved him. He was perfect for her; they shared the same interests; they both dreamed of one day opening a restaurant of their own somewhere in the West of Ireland. But something held her back, and she wasn't willing to explore what it was.

"What do you think, Suzy?"

"Sorry, I was miles away." Suzy focussed her attention on Donal who had just joined them.

"Paul was saying that it looks as if it might rain again in the next half hour or so, so it might be as well to start making a move towards the restaurant now. I know it's only a short walk; but if we get caught in a shower like the ones we had all afternoon ..."

"I'll get everyone moving." Suzy was glad of something to do. She wasn't great at parties. Not being much of a talker, she preferred small gatherings where everyone talked at once and she could just listen, adding the odd comment or question now and again. At a big party, people broke down into small groups of two or three and she felt tongue-tied and awkward trying to make small talk with people she didn't know. Being the only non-drinker in most crowds didn't help either.

At dinner, Emily managed to seat herself between two of the few single men at the party. She had ignored Paul's attempts to keep her a place beside him, and for a few minutes she felt guilty. After all, he didn't know that many people here. But then she saw that he was beside

Anne-Marie and Dave and she relaxed. Paul liked Anne-Marie's fiancé, and Anne-Marie herself could make anyone feel comfortable.

So Emily concentrated on getting to know her dinner companions better. Craig, the slim, dark man to her left, she had met before. An Australian, of Greek extraction, he had lived in England since his late teens. Despite this, he looked and sounded foreign due to the strange mixture of Aussie, English and Greek accents and his Mediterranean colouring. He had lived next door to Charlotte and Donal when they first moved to England. To her right was Geoff. Pure English upper middle-class. Blond, rugged, tanned and broad-shouldered, he spoke with a plum in his mouth, an accent which had always made Emily's knees go weak. He had taken a week's holiday to come to the party and had sailed into Kinsale in his own boat on Thursday.

"Plenty there to blow away the cobwebs!" Tara leaned over and giggled into Emily's ear on her way to the toilet. Emily only just avoided spluttering her soup across the table. Apart from a fling on a winter sun holiday in the Canaries, Emily had endured a celibate year and Tara was convinced that she was growing cobwebs between her legs.

"Yes, it is a bit draughty in here, isn't it?" Craig looked at the open windows that Suzy had opened as soon as she realised how many of the party were smoking.

"Draughty?" Emily was confused.

"Cobwebs?" he offered.

"Oh, of course, yes," Emily answered quickly and felt

herself blush. She turned to her other side and Geoff, to hide her confusion.

"I wonder where your friend could possibly have seen cobwebs?" Geoff said with a knowing smile. "This room is perfectly dusted." His eyes dropped for a millisecond. Not quite as far as her legs.

Emily couldn't break away from his gaze, although now she knew that the slight pink on her cheeks was becoming a crimson stain from her cleavage all the way to the roots of her hair. Craig was forgotten as she began to enjoy Geoff's scrutiny. Never had a man undressed her so sexily with his eyes. He smiled at her, his lips parting just a fraction, and for a second she could have sworn that she saw the tip of his pink tongue dart out between his teeth.

Emily got up to go to the ladies' room. When she returned, Geoff had moved his chair a fraction closer to hers, so that when she sat down again, there was no way they could avoid their legs touching under the over-crowded table. He ignored her to talk to the woman on his right, and Emily began to flirt with Craig. All the time, she could feel Geoff's leg pressed against her own, sometimes pressing hard, sometimes barely touching her. She felt she would explode with longing. When she thought she couldn't get any more excited, he began to raise and lower his thigh by no more than a couple of millimetres, rubbing against her provocatively.

"Are you OK?" Craig asked her. "You look as if you're in pain!"

Emily was biting her lower lip in an effort not to cry out. But she would no more remove herself from the source of the problem than she would throw herself over a hundred-foot cliff.

"Cramp!" she muttered. "Leg cramp. I was sitting on a plane for most of the past twenty-four hours. I normally go straight to the gym after a flight, but I didn't have time."

"You need to stretch your legs." The suggestion came from her other side.

Emily nearly got whiplash she turned to Geoff so fast.

"I do?" she said weakly.

"Of course, you do. The best thing for cramp. I'll walk you down to the garden. I was going to go out for a smoke anyway." He held up a small black cigar. "I smoke these filthy things, and I wouldn't like to impose them on everyone else."

He helped Emily to her feet, and supported her out of the room. She found she didn't have to act – she really did need his help to walk.

"Which leg?" Geoff asked. They were standing in the back garden of the restaurant, on the gravel between Charlotte's raised herb and salad beds. He blew out smoke in long streams and Emily breathed in slowly, enjoying the mixture of smells: expensive cigar smoke and the lavender and rosemary she had brushed against on her way to this secluded part of the garden.

"Sorry?"

"Your cramp, which leg?"

She looked at him. Had he really believed the cramp story? She tried to remember which leg she had limped out of the room on.

"The right one, but it's better now. What are you doing?" Her question came out as a yelp, as Geoff squatted onto his hunkers and began to finger the back of her right calf.

"You need to rub out the lactic acid, or that cramp will come right back."

Emily was sure he was confusing his cramps, but the feeling of his rubbing the lower part of her leg was too enjoyable to ask him to stop. With each upward stroke, he ran his fingers slightly higher, and tickled the back of her knee. Now higher again. She gasped. Then he stopped, stood up and leaned towards her.

She could smell cigar smoke and feel his breath warm across her face. He whispered to her, his lips close enough to brush against the tender skin of her earlobe. "That was just an appetiser. Will you join me later?" He gave her the name of his hotel and room number. Not giving her a chance to answer, he led the way back inside.

"He's a bit of all right!" Tara nudged her as she walked through the toilet door. Nudging so hard that Emily was sure she felt ribs crack. "My guy's throwing a party back in his room later, if you want to join us!" She named the same hotel as Geoff's, where Donal had arranged a block booking.

"I don't think so, Tara. I've had a long flight and I'm hardly in party mood."

"Oh, you'd rather keep gorgeous Geoff all to yourself? Can't say I blame you. Happy shagging!" Tara tottered out unsteadily.

Emily was the only one left in the ladies' room. She

stared at the mirror and wasn't sure she recognised the woman looking back at her. The woman who would have had sex in the herb garden with Geoff if he'd offered it. And it wasn't as if she particularly liked him – he was just available, sexy and male!

Suddenly Emily thought of Paul. He had watched her leave the room with Geoff, and now he was probably wondering where she was. He worried about her, like the big brother she always wished she had. Apart from the fact that they'd had mind-blowing sex together, she remembered with a smile. Still that was all in the past.

"Don't leave without me," she whispered to Paul, pulling up a spare chair to sit beside him just as Donal tapped on the side of a glass to attract attention for a toast. "We can share a taxi home."

"Yeah, whatever," Paul mumbled, looking cross. Emily was about to ask him what was wrong, when he shushed and pointed to Donal.

Suddenly Emily was exhausted and didn't care less what Paul or anyone else thought. She had only slept for four or five of the previous forty-eight hours and the wine was hitting her harder than usual. She hoped Donal wasn't going to make too long a speech.

Chapter 8

The National Gallery was a lot more crowded than Charlotte expected for a Tuesday morning. Apart from the usual school groups and tourists, there was a scattering of damp shoppers sheltering from a sudden downpour. She was early so she wandered amongst the Flemish Masters without seeing a single painting. She wondered if Marcus and Denise had seen paintings like these in their home setting when they lived in Holland.

At last she made her way to the cafeteria. On her way through the gallery shop, she stopped to buy some cards to send thank-you notes for presents she had received at the weekend. Yesterday was officially her birthday and she had woken up feeling uncharacteristically depressed. She usually loved Mondays. A fresh week stretched out in front of her. A diary full of work appointments, all the kid's after-school activities, and the reassurance that there would be a hundred new problems for her to sort out at the restaurant. But this Monday was different. She was thirty. She didn't look any older than she did on Sunday, but she felt …well … thirty.

She stopped at the door of the cafeteria. A group of blue-rinse ladies got up to leave from a large table in the corner and the noise of their chairs scraping across the floor distracted her for a moment. Then she spotted a woman waving at her from a table near the food counter. Charlotte recognised her at once. Denise was petite, almost as slim as she had been as a student, and her elfin face looked even better now that her blonde hair was cut into a soft, layered bob. As a student she had worn it long, usually tied back in a ponytail, contributing to her waif-like look. She was wearing a pair of soft navy jeans, a white T-shirt and a loose black suede jacket. Charlotte felt overdressed in her jade-green summer dress, and overweight after all she had eaten all weekend.

Denise seemed unsure of how to greet the other woman when she finally reached her. "I …I …. thank you for coming. Can I get you coffee? A cake?"

Charlotte nodded in reply to both questions, and sat down. She watched Denise go to the counter, take a tray and queue up. What was she doing here? Why did this woman want to meet her?

"I wanted to meet you …" Denise began after taking her seat and handing Charlotte a coffee and one of the two slices of carrot cake she had brought. "I … well … oh God, this seemed really logical a few weeks ago when I came up with the idea." She concentrated on the cake in front of her, slicing it into four equal pieces. Then she rearranged the frosting so that each portion of cake had exactly the same amount of the orangey cream cheese. Finally she turned her attention to her coffee, adding two heaped teaspoons of sugar.

"How is Marcus anyway?" Charlotte asked at last, surprised at the sound of her own voice. It sounded so grown up. In her mind she had reverted to being the young girl who was in love with Marcus, and this woman in front of her was no more than another of his classmates.

"He's fine. I mean … I assume he's fine … We've split up. Marcus is still in New York and I haven't spoken to him in weeks."

Denise stirred her coffee, tasted it with tiny pursed lips, made a face and added yet another spoon of sugar. Then she stirred it again and repeated the tasting ritual. She didn't look entirely satisfied but took a proper mouthful none the less. She offered Charlotte the sugar.

"No, thanks." Charlotte pushed away the bowl, wondering how Denise stayed the size she was if she consumed that much sugar. "I'm sorry to hear you've split up."

"We only communicate through our attorneys now," Denise sniffed. "Sorry, I mean lawyers. The Americans call lawyers 'attorneys'."

"So why did you want to see me?" Charlotte interrupted before she was given a lesson in American English.

"It feels stupid now." Denise looked up and their eyes met for the first time. Charlotte was surprised at how sad and vulnerable she looked. She almost felt sorry for her.

"But I suppose I came back to Ireland to finish things for good, and I still couldn't get closure. That's an American term – it means –"

"I know what closure means!" Charlotte snapped. Then she regretted sounding so aggressive. "Television shows and that," she explained with a shrug.

"Well, my therapist in New York – he said that the only way I was really going to get closure was to meet you."

"Your therapist said you needed to meet me?" Charlotte couldn't decide who was the more crazy, the therapist in New York, the woman in front of her for believing in him, or herself for still being involved in the conversation.

"Yes, he said that you hung over my marriage like a shadow, and I needed to meet you so that I could establish once and for all that I wasn't to blame for our break-up."

"I hung like a shadow over your marriage …?" This was getting better. Or worse?

"Do you mind if I ask you a question?"

"Fire ahead!" Charlotte leaned back and nursed her coffee cup between her two hands. This was getting to be almost fun.

"When did you last see my husband? Marcus, I mean. When did you last see him?"

Charlotte looked at the other woman and saw accusation in her eyes.

"Do you think I had an affair with your husband?" Charlotte's hand shook as she put down her cup, splashing coffee over her uneaten cake. "I haven't seen him since before I got married. I only heard from friends that he was married. I didn't even know he was in New York." She stood up abruptly. "I don't know what kind of sick denial fantasy-land you've been living in, but I had nothing to do with the breakdown of your marriage." She turned to leave.

"No, wait! I'm sorry." Denise put out a restraining hand and touched Charlotte's arm. "I don't mean since then. I mean ... well, when he broke up with you, and started going out with me. Did you see him at all after that?

Charlotte hesitated, then sat down again, making an effort to calm herself. She took a long drink from her cup and considered her answer. She had never spoken to anyone about those months. Not to Donal, although he had occasionally tried to get her to talk about it when they were together first. Not to Anne-Marie. Not even to Suzy and they were practically living together at the time. All Emily knew was that Charlotte had run into Marcus in a pub and he had said he missed her; she had told Emily that she thought she might have a chance of winning him back. So why should she tell Denise anything? That part of her life was over. And she wanted it to stay that way. Buried.

When Charlotte didn't answer, Denise filled the silence by calling over a middle-aged woman in an apron who was dragging her feet around the café, a coffee pot hanging from her left hand. The waitress looked almost surprised when Denise suggested she top up their cups, and looked at the pot in her hand as if it had appeared there by magic. With their cups full, Denise began to speak.

"It was always Charlotte this, Charlotte that. I couldn't do anything without him comparing me to you." Denise's eyes filled with tears.

"I don't understand … He left me for you."

"I told Marcus he had to break up with you if he wanted to get serious with me," Denise continued as if Charlotte hadn't spoken. "And although he never said it, he implied that he'd given up too much to be with me …" She poured the last few drops of milk from the jug on their table into her coffee and stirred it. She tapped the spoon on the edge of the mug and watched a small group of bubbles swirling on the surface of the dark liquid. "Although he was going out with me, I always got the impression that he was still trying to choose between the two of us. I should have told him to go to hell, to go back to you, if he wasn't sure that he wanted to be with me, but by then it was too late. I was hooked, I was absolutely crazy about him, even if I didn't trust him completely." She looked up at Charlotte. "Was he still seeing you as well?"

Charlotte nodded.

"I always guessed, I suppose." Denise shrugged and continued to look at Charlotte, waiting for more.

Eventually the silence became too much for Charlotte and she began to explain.

"We used to … to see each other, after he started going out with you. Although I didn't know about you," she added hastily. "I thought I was getting back together with him. Then I heard that he'd started going out with someone … you." Charlotte winced, remembering the pain she had felt. "If I'd known earlier I'd …"

What would she have done? Fought harder for him? It didn't matter. She was with Donal now.

"I suppose I always guessed," Denise repeated. "But even though I suspected he was two-timing me, I put up with it, because I thought he needed time to make up his mind. And in the end he chose me. Or at least that's what I thought until recently." Denise was chewing her lip again, and Charlotte could see she was fighting back tears. There was a slightly hysterical tone to her voice when she continued. "I discovered later that he first proposed to me on your wedding day."

Charlotte couldn't decide if she was flattered or appalled by this. "How did you find out?"

"It was recently, after our last awful row. When I decided I had to come home and I was cleaning out the flat in New York. I found a newspaper clipping, his local paper from home. There was a picture of you and Donal in it, on your wedding day. I keep a diary and when I saw the date on the clipping I knew it looked familiar so I checked my diary from that year. And I was right. Marcus drove out to see me that night. He asked me to marry him and move over to Holland with him – we'd both been offered jobs there, in Eindhoven."

Denise stopped again and seemed to be lost in her own memories.

"So what did you do?" Charlotte prompted.

"I accepted the job, but I turned him down. I wasn't sure of him yet, you see." Denise smiled. "But he kept on and on at me. It was so romantic. Eventually he wore me down. He took me to Rome the following Valentine's Day and proposed, on one knee, in front of the Coliseum."

Charlotte remembered Donal proposing to her, in bed, after she told him she was pregnant.

"I accepted then and we got married a few months later in Amsterdam. We were happy. I really did love him. And I know he loved me. I think he still does if he'd only let himself. But we wanted different things from life."

"So what did you want?" Charlotte asked. She was surprised to discover that she had a morbid fascination with this woman. She was living the life that maybe she, Charlotte, might have lived if she'd stayed with Marcus.

"What does everyone want?" Denise asked. "A husband, a family, a home. Not at first, of course. I came from a crushingly 'normal' family. Mum stayed at home to look after us and Dad was out all hours working. He worked himself into an early grave as it happened … I swore I would be different, I was going to conquer the world, and Marcus said he loved that about me. We were an ideal couple really. I was into robotics and he was one of the best software guys in the business." Denise pushed her cake around the plate. "Then when I hit thirty, I got broody, I wanted kids. We were happily married. We had plenty of money. I didn't think it was too much to ask. But Marcus said I was changing the goalposts. He said I'd got him to marry me under false pretences." She took a deep breath and let it out slowly before she went on talking. She looked as if she was trying to control tears. "And to be fair to him, he had always said that he didn't want kids. And I didn't either. I mean what woman does in her mid-twenties, straight out of college? The difference was that Marcus had obviously thought about it and made a long-term decision. I just said what I felt at the time. You probably think I was mad to marry him at all, don't you?"

Charlotte shook her head helplessly. If Marcus had even mentioned the M word to her, she'd have had him down the aisle so fast ….

"And has it helped you to meet me?" She was aware that if she didn't leave soon she'd have to get Donal to pick Aisling up from playgroup.

"I don't know. It's silly really. I thought that the one thing I wanted to know was whether Marcus was seeing you during those months and whether he was trying to decide between us. While all along I already knew the answer." She laughed. "I thought that if I knew for certain, then I would be able to tell myself that he really had made a choice between us, and chosen me."

"But he did choose you. He married you."

"Did he choose me, or was I the consolation prize after you got married?"

"Look, Denise. You're doing yourself no favours here. He dumped me, so that he could go out with you. He stayed with you even when he started seeing me again. I was the hidden woman. We didn't tell any of our friends we were together. We ran around Dublin meeting in all sorts of weird places. He said it was because it would give us some space to decide what we really wanted, but really it was because he didn't want you to find out. So he cared about what you felt, not about what I felt." Charlotte was getting angry now. "So don't go feeling sorry for yourself. You won. You married him. If it went wrong, it went wrong later. It was nothing to do with him having chosen you too late. If he'd asked me to marry him, he wouldn't have had to ask twice. But he didn't. He asked you."

Charlotte glared at the woman sitting opposite her.

"Sorry."

"For what? I'm perfectly happy now," Charlotte snapped.

"No, I mean sorry if I sounded like I was whining, or trying to blame you in some way for my marriage failing."

They were silent for a few moments and Charlotte wondered how much longer she needed to stay.

"Do you have children?" Denise asked.

"Three," Charlotte answered.

"That's what I regret most about the past ten years. The time wasted. I'm thirty-four now, it's over with Marcus ... I might never ..." Denise forced herself to smile. "How old are they?"

"Gemma's ten, Tim's eight and Aisling's just turned five." Charlotte was beginning to feel uncomfortable.

"I bet they're a handful."

"You don't know the half of it." Automatically, as if a parental switch in her brain had been flipped, Charlotte began to tell some of the more hair-raising child-rearing stories from her repertoire. Soon the two women were laughing.

"It wasn't just me," Denise said suddenly. "I mean Marcus has to take some of the blame for our marriage breaking down. Maybe he should have married you, but you couldn't have made him any happier than I did."

"What do you mean?" Charlotte bristled.

"Well, you want the same things from life as I do, only you managed to find a man to give them to you. The children, the house …"

"Donal and I worked hard to get to where we are today. No one 'gave' anyone anything."

"That's not what I meant. Sorry." Denise began to turn her mug round and around on the table. A grain of sugar caught underneath made a grinding sound. "I don't really know what I meant. I suppose Marcus made me feel inferior for wanting precisely the things you have. He said that as a professional woman I should be more interested in advancing my career. He said that if he'd wanted a little wifey to stay at home and have kids –"

"But you stayed together till now," Charlotte interrupted, not wanting to hear the end of that particular sentence.

"It only really came to a head recently," Denise said, looking embarrassed. "Something happened … and then there was the money."

"Sorry?"

"I have lots of it. My father sold his engineering company a year before his death. My sister and I inherited a huge sum of cash each when we turned twenty-one.

Marcus and I were going to set up our own company, but then he went out on his own and people were falling over themselves to invest in him. He's loaded now, so the last thing that tied him to me is gone."

Charlotte was sure it wasn't as simple as Denise made it sound, but she couldn't stay any longer to question her further. She stood up and made her excuses to leave.

"We'll have to meet again some time. Now that we've got the history out of the way," Denise said as Charlotte was leaving. "You have my number. Call me sometime."

"Yes, of course." Charlotte didn't care if she never saw the woman again.

After leaving the museum, Charlotte walked around for a while to clear her head. She couldn't face going home just yet and was trying to figure out if she had got anything out of her meeting with Denise.

She knew what Marcus was up to now. And she knew why his marriage had broken up: he didn't want kids. Did that answer any of her own questions, or rather the one question which had ambushed her at regular intervals throughout the years: could she have made things work with Marcus if she tried? OK, so he told Denise he never wanted children but he never said that to her, did he?

Charlotte tried to laugh when she realised what she had been thinking about. Marcus was in the past, and she would make sure he stayed there. She called Donal.

"Any luck?" he asked.

"Luck?"

"Finding summer clothes."

"No, nothing yet," she answered guiltily. She had told Donal she was taking the morning off to go shopping. "Listen, hon, I lost track of time. Can you pick up Aisling for me? I'll never get back in time."

"No problem. Any excuse to get out of this joint for a while. Suzy and Geri are both acting premenstrual and Joe's in a strop because he can't take the August bank holiday weekend off."

"I'll be back as soon as I can," Charlotte promised.

"No, take your time. Aisling and I will have some quality time together, then we'll collect the other two from school. I've decided I'm going to stay out all day from work. I'm only encouraging trouble by being there – they're trying to play me off against each other. If I'm not there, they'll have to solve their own rows. So I'll cook dinner and you just enjoy your day."

"God, that sounds brilliant." Suddenly Charlotte was exhausted. "Maybe I won't come home till after the kids have gone to bed!" She laughed feebly.

"That's a good idea. Go to the health club on the way home, have a massage or something."

"I was only joking!"

"I'm not. You need some time to yourself. Dinner's at half eight – see you then!"

Sipping a latte half an hour later, suddenly the prospect of a day of freedom stretching in front of her wasn't as attractive as Charlotte expected. She didn't actually enjoy shopping that much, and when she rang the health club to book a massage, she felt so self-indulgent that she had only booked a half-hour one. She never felt completely comfortable in the luxury health and fitness club – the same club as Emily and Tara used, although they seemed to have no hesitation making full use of the facilities. Tara swore by a facial every Friday to put her in the mood for the weekend, and Emily didn't need to give her name to the beauticians because they recognised her voice on the phone. Charlotte decided to persuade Emily to come with her.

"You're where?" Emily asked when she picked up the phone. "On Grafton Street? Shopping? Right, I'll take a long lunch and we'll get you outfitted for the whole summer!" Emily was always trying to persuade Charlotte to come shopping with her. She was an expert at the art. "And yes, I will join you at the health club later for a massage, but only if we work out first. I haven't had a proper work-out since Hong-Kong and my joints feel as if they're going to rust permanently into place. And the waistband of my skirt was too tight for comfort this morning. Although I hope that's just fluid – I'm premenstrual. See you later."

Charlotte remembered what Donal had said about Suzy and Geri being premenstrual. He might be right; they were both in funny moods yesterday. She had spent a few hours at work in the morning, and neither had had much time for her. They hadn't even wished her Happy Birthday, although she knew she was being over-sensitive about that. After all, they had given up their Saturday for her party. But it was unlike Suzy not to mark the day with a card.

Stop feeling sorry for yourself, Charlotte told herself

severely. Do something constructive like thinking of an excuse for not working out, and think fast – Emily will be here soon.

"I don't have any sports gear with me!" were the first words out of her mouth after she greeted Emily. "So although I'd love to work out with you before our massage, I can't."

"You don't have any sports gear, full stop. This is the perfect excuse to buy some." Emily linked her arm firmly through her sister's and began to march her down Grafton Street.

"I'm not buying this!" Charlotte looked in the mirror in the sports shop. She looked great, but she wasn't going to shell out that kind of money for a few bits of Lycra and a pair of runners. She'd spent less than this on a whole outfit to go to a wedding last year.

"Yes, you are. It's perfect on you."

"It's too expensive, Emily! What's wrong with the stuff I normally wear?"

"I won't answer that. Besides, this is a bargain. Look, you get a free sports bag with it."

That nearly clinched it for Charlotte. She was a sucker for a bargain. She picked up the pink barrel bag with its designer logo on the side. She really would look the part with this. So much better than Tim's reject football bag, the one he'd decided he couldn't be seen dead with because no one in his class supported Leeds.

"This is leather, Emily, real leather, good leather!" Charlotte was horrified.

"And that's a problem? Have you suddenly gone

vegetarian or something?" Emily laughed.

"If they can afford to give out bags like this for free, they must be really overcharging for the clothes," Charlotte whispered.

"Of course, they are. The material in that top cost about fifty cent, the leggings thirty." Emily didn't add that that was probably more than the wages of the child in Thailand who sewed the seams; Charlotte might go all moral on her. "You're paying for that postage stamp sewn into the hem." She pointed to a designer label, discreet enough that you had to look for it, but visible enough to be seen by the person on the next exercise bike. Emily was getting impatient with Charlotte's lack of comprehension of the fashion industry. Her sister honestly didn't understand the difference between the clothes in Dunnes and designer gear. Apart from the fact that the Dunnes ones were probably better made. "You're not buying practicality or value. You're buying a look. A great look, I might add." Emily pointed to the mirror.

Charlotte hardly looked at the mirror. OK, she looked good in the outfit, better than she'd ever looked going to the gym before, but this bag … She fingered the leather lovingly, then tossed the bag over her shoulder. Wow, she really did look the part! And the bag was free …

She closed her eyes as she signed the credit-card receipt. It was her birthday present to herself!

She watched in admiration as over the next half hour, Emily charged the equivalent of a month's mortgage onto her own credit card, with nothing to show for it other than a minuscule handbag and a pair of strappy high-heeled sandals she wouldn't be able to walk the length of her flat in. Now that the tone for the shopping spree was set, Emily led the way, and Charlotte had to close her eyes a few more times as she notched up some purchases for herself. Donal would be thrilled, she thought. He laughed at the way Charlotte was willing to spend so much more on the kids than on herself. He claimed that Gemma must be the only girl in her school whose wardrobe contents cost more than her mother's.

"You didn't drop in on Sunday after the party," Charlotte remarked as they sat down for a well-deserved, if rather late, lunch in Fitzer's on Dawson Street. "I thought you might."

"Sunday ..." Emily scratched her head. "Sunday ... that was the day that should have fallen between Saturday night and Monday morning ... no, seriously. I think I slept through most of it."

"It was a good party though, wasn't it?" Charlotte remembered fondly. She had been almost dreading it, but once she saw how many people had turned up to wish her well, she'd relaxed into the evening and had even enjoyed herself. And when they got home, she and Donal had made love, slowly and beautifully, like when they were first married.

"The party, yeah, it was great. Although I'm afraid I don't remember much of it. I didn't realise how shattered I was."

"I forgot to ask you how your trip went. Did you have fun?" Charlotte tried not to sound jealous. It wasn't that she particularly envied Emily's lifestyle; she didn't. But it was hard to listen to Emily casually talking about KL and Hong Kong as if they were Cork and Limerick. Charlotte would have loved to believe that she would at least see Kuala Lumpur and China one day, even if she could never talk with such confidence about the best places to shop there.

"I'd hardly describe two and a half weeks in the Far East, on a whistle-stop tour of all our manufacturing plants, fun!" Emily answered, turning up her nose. "But I did manage to do some shopping in Bangkok!"

"A successful trip then?" Charlotte didn't try to hide her grin.

"And I found a way of saving twenty-three cents per chip in our Malaysian plant!" Emily proclaimed without conviction. The target had been eighteen cents, and the bean counters in head office were thrilled, but Emily didn't get the same kick out of it as she had when she started out. She had even caught herself thinking "It's only money!" during this morning's debrief, and then looked around fearfully as if the others could read her mind. How could an accountant even think such profanity? She hoped it wasn't because for the first time she had actually met some of the workers, seen the conditions they lived and worked in.

On the flight home she had even been tempted to reduce her saving to twenty-one cents and save thirty jobs, but then she realised that it wouldn't be long before the competition made the same saving and then there would be hundreds if not thousands of jobs at risk. So she had recommended a course of action which altered the lives of faceless workers thousands of miles away, and soon parents all over Europe and North America would be able to buy a computer for each of their children instead of forcing them to share with their siblings. Emily kicked her shopping bags under the table to where she wouldn't be able to see them.

"I have to go back to the office for an hour or two," Emily said quickly, knocking back the last few drops of her espresso. "Then I'll meet you at the club."

The sisters parted company, and Charlotte went to look for a present to bring back to each of the kids from her day in town. Getting back into her car near the National Gallery, she was proud to realise that she hadn't thought about Denise or Marcus all afternoon.

Chapter 9

Later that evening, Charlotte felt great as she pulled the bags from the boot of her car. Emily was right; she really should work out more often. And that massage afterwards ... it had left her in a pleasant state of total relaxation yet tingly all over. And she would have nothing to do for the rest of the evening except eat the meal Donal had prepared for her and then go to bed. That was a nice thought.

On Saturday night, just before they had both fallen into their sex-induced slumber, Donal had muttered something along the lines of "We really ought to do this more often ..."

At the time Charlotte had felt so guilty at the implication, that she had pretended she was already asleep, but now ... mmmm ...

Donal opened the door before she had even finished unpacking the car.

"What's wrong?" Charlotte asked.

153

The look on his face made her feel sick.

"Come inside, Charlotte, into the kitchen."

"What's wrong, Donal? Is it one of the kids? Has there been an accident – is one of them sick?" Half in and half out of the boot of the car, she was frozen, unable to move.

"The kids are fine. They're in bed. Come into the house." He picked up her bags and turned his back.

She had no choice but to follow him inside.

"Maura Slattery phoned about half an hour ago."

"Mum!" Charlotte put a hand to her mouth. Maura was her mother's best friend. She fell more than sat into the chair Donal pushed under her.

"Don't panic. Everything's fine. Well, not fine, but not serious either. Sheila had a fall earlier this afternoon. She's in hospital – she broke her wrist and twisted her knee."

"But how? You don't just have falls at sixty-five!" Charlotte protested. "She's not some old woman who can't see where she's going. They've got it wrong. And why is she still in hospital if it's only a wrist? I thought we were short of hospital beds in this country?"

"They think it was her heart."

"*What?* But she was fine …at the party … she drove home on Sunday …"

"They picked up an abnormal rhythm in her heart in casualty. If that happened earlier it could have been enough to make her faint. She was shopping at the time. Maura was with her and insisted on getting her checked out properly."

"Her heart?" Charlotte repeated and began to massage

her own chest with a balled-up fist.

"It's minor, Charlotte. Don't panic. She'll be on a monitor for twenty-four hours. Then, when they have a definite diagnosis, she'll probably be put on drugs."

"I have to go down."

"Maura says there's no point in going down till morning. The doctors would prefer her not to get overexcited while they're doing this trace."

"Overexcited? For God's sake, she can handle a visit from her daughter surely?"

"That's what I said, but Maura was adamant," Donal said quietly.

"And who's Maura to tell me when I can or can't visit?" Charlotte felt guilty that while she was spending money like water in Dublin, Maura was waiting with her mother in casualty. While she was working out in the health club, Maura was making sure that Sheila was getting the best possible care. While Charlotte was having her massage, Maura was watching Sheila being hooked up to a monitor. "Who the hell does Maura think she is, telling me that I can't visit Mum tonight?"

Maura was an easy target for Charlotte's guilt-induced anger.

"She's your mum's best friend, she's a nurse, and she's the one who has spoken to the doctors." Donal spoke gently but firmly. He pressed a drink into Charlotte's hand, which shook violently as she tried to push it away.

"Take it." He closed her fingers around the glass and watched while she drained half the gin and tonic in one go, then made a face.

"Not enough tonic!"

He went to get the bottle. He had deliberately made the drink strong. He didn't want Charlotte driving in this nervous state, and he knew she wouldn't drive if she'd had even one drink.

"I have to phone Emily. She's on her own –"

"I phoned Paul." Donal pressed Charlotte back onto her seat with very little resistance. "He's gone straight over – he'll let himself into the flat and tell her as soon as she gets in."

So even Paul knew about Sheila's illness before her daughters. The phone rang and Donal answered it.

"Emily." He held out the phone.

As Charlotte spoke to her sister, she broke down in tears. Donal put his arms around her and tried to comfort her as best he could. Soon she was nodding, wiping away her tears and sniffling. When she put the phone down, she looked stronger.

"We're going to go down tonight." She held up her hand to silence Donal's protest. "Paul's driving Emily's car down and he'll get the early train back tomorrow. They're on their way over to pick me up now. We'll talk to Maura when we get there and, if she still doesn't want us to go to the hospital, we'll wait till morning."

Donal nodded. He was happier that Paul would be doing the driving, and that he'd be in the house with them tonight, although he wished he could take Paul's place. But he knew he had to stay with the kids.

Charlotte felt strange leaving her bag in her old bedroom. She hadn't slept a night here since she was married.

Maura had made up the beds for them, and a bed for Paul in the living-room. She had been in the house when they arrived and was waiting downstairs to talk to them. She said that what she had to say was important, so Paul had gone for a walk to let them talk alone.

"Sheila got a fright this morning. It made her realise that she's as mortal as the rest of us." Maura hesitated before she went on. "She got quite agitated – that's why I asked you not to go in. But she was terrified that she might have died without telling you what she knows about your natural parents."

She looked from one girl to the other for a reaction. They were unable to look her in the eye. Unable even to look at each other.

"She shouldn't be worrying about things like that." Charlotte was the first to break the silence. "She should be concentrating on getting better."

Emily walked across the room to the window. She pulled back the curtain and, despite the light in the room, she could see that the sky was filled with stars. You could never see stars like this in Dublin, she thought. It was never dark enough.

"I don't want to know anything," she said slowly, without turning around.

Charlotte and Maura exchanged a look.

"Why not, Emmy?" Charlotte was unaware she had reverted to using her sister's childhood pet-name. "When we were growing up you always said you wanted to know all you could ..."

"I was a child then. Full of stories of princesses, kidnapped and brought up by wicked sorcerers and who find their real mother, the queen, at the end of the story. Well, life's not like that. Our mother was a single mother, who died, leaving us alone. We were given to strangers because our father wasn't interested in us." Emily didn't turn to face the other two. She was trying to find the star Charlotte had told her was their mother looking down on them. She hadn't thought about that star, or looked for it, since she was nine or ten years old.

"What are you afraid of, Emms?" Charlotte was surprised by the vehemence of her sister's response "Are you afraid you'll be disappointed?"

"I'll never be disappointed by our mother, because as far as I'm concerned, she's lying in a hospital bed less than ten miles from here. I don't know how you can deny she's our real mother, not at a time like this!"

Emily stormed past them in tears. Maura held Charlotte back, shaking her head as they heard the door of her room slam. The years melted away, and Charlotte felt she was back in the eighties, and she and Emily had had a row over something.

"Sheila's quite determined to tell you."

Charlotte jumped; she brushed a few unshed tears from her eyes before turning to Maura. "Why now, after all these years?"

"Like I said, she got a fright. Maybe she's afraid that if she died without telling you, she'd be failing in her duty to –"

"You said it wasn't serious!"

"Calm down, Charlotte. I said 'if' she died. Not now – whenever. This thing with her heart just made her realise that she was going to die sometime. But you can understand why I didn't want you to go straight to the hospital. I wanted you to be forewarned. I don't know whether or not you're going to like what you hear, but it'll be tougher on Sheila than anyone. For all her bluster, she's sick and she needs rest before launching herself back into your childhoods."

Maura left before Charlotte realised that she knew more than she was admitting to. She had winced when Emily said they'd been adopted by strangers, and she'd said she wasn't sure if they'd like what they heard.

Paul returned, and locked the house up for the night. It was strange to see him do it. Robert had always made such a performance about checking all the doors and windows, but after his death the ritual was dropped. Emily came back downstairs sheepishly.

"Is she gone?"

"Yes, but we need to talk." Charlotte pushed her towards the front room.

"Oh God, Char … I can't bear it…" Emily burst into tears. Paul had his arms around her on the couch before Charlotte could register a stab of jealousy that he had replaced her as her little sister's protector.

"Sheila wants to tell us about our real parents," Emily told him in a toneless voice.

Paul looked over her head at Charlotte, who shrugged. She had no idea what to say.

"What's wrong with that?" he asked at last.

"Because Sheila's our mother, that's why!" Emily spat, sitting upright. In pulling away from him she knocked her head against his chin, and he rubbed it absent-mindedly. He ran his tongue over the teeth that had crashed together.

"But surely this won't change anything, Emily? Your mother, your natural mother will still be dead, and Sheila will still be here."

"Then surely it doesn't matter about her. Our natural mother, I mean. Why do we need to know anything about her, or the man who walked away from us?" Emily looked at Charlotte and Paul triumphantly.

"Don't you want to know about her?" Paul asked gently. "The woman who gave birth to you, whose blood runs in your veins? And the man she must at least have had some feelings for?"

Charlotte watched them, clenching her hands, digging her nails into her palms. This conversation scared her. She was afraid of saying something wrong.

"What's blood got to do with anything?" Emily asked Paul. "And what the hell would you know about it anyway? Are you adopted? Did your mother die? Did your father abandon you?"

"No, but don't tell me family doesn't matter, blood doesn't matter."

"Read it somewhere, did you?" Emily sneered, although she longed to give up the fierce independent act and accept comfort.

"My wife let me love a boy I believed to be my son,"

Paul said slowly. "She didn't tell me he wasn't mine until after we split up and she applied for full custody. So I think I am in a position to be able to comment on the importance of family ties. You're not the only one to –"

"Your wife!" Emily gasped. "You're not married!"

Charlotte watched them nervously. Why was he telling them this? She wanted to tell him to stop, that she didn't want to hear any more. How could the conversation suddenly have turned to this? She didn't want to hear about Paul's marriage or about the boy he had believed was his natural child. But, like a driver slowing down at a fatal accident, Charlotte was unable to fight her fascination.

"I *was* married," Paul went on. "The years between school and college, the years I never really talk about? I was married for two of them."

Emily shook her head in confusion. "You told us you were working for your grandfather, you had a row with your father …"

"Sharon got pregnant the summer we left school. I wanted to marry her – my father freaked out. He said he'd have nothing to do with me if I went ahead. He said she was only after me for my money or rather his money, and that the baby might not be mine anyway. The fact that he was right on both counts just made me hate him all the more when it all fell apart two years later."

Emily couldn't cope with the pain on Paul's face. She walked to the window and looked out at the night again.

"I don't see what all this has to do with me."

"I loved Scott. He was a gorgeous kid and I'll never

161

forget the day he was born ... But something inside me changed when Sharon showed me the blood-test results. He couldn't have been mine. I tried to fight it, I felt ashamed, but there was nothing I could do about it. I just couldn't feel the same about him. Later I often wondered: if I'd known from the beginning that he wasn't my son, would it have been different? Was it that I'd been duped, or the fact that he was some other man's child? Because I still loved Scott. And yet when Sharon made it clear that she didn't want me to be a part of their lives any more, all I could feel was relief that I didn't have to make the decision myself. I hated myself for it, but I couldn't change how I felt. But for you, Emily, it's different. You've always known what your relationship to Sheila was. How can that change now?"

Emily felt numb. Paul had bared his soul to her to help her and she felt guilty that she couldn't do more to acknowledge his trust.

"I'm not afraid of what it'll do to my relationship with Sheila. Nothing could change that. I'm afraid ..." The words dried up again.

"Of what, Emily? Say it." Paul stood behind her; she leaned back against him and he put his arms around her. Neither of them saw Charlotte slip out of the room.

"Afraid of losing the dream about our real mother. I don't remember anything about her – I can only go on what I was told. That she was raising two small girls on her own in London, that she died and that she left instructions for us to be kept together. What if that's all a lie? What if she's not this tragic, sad, figure? What if she's still alive somewhere and she abandoned us after all? What if she was … I don't know … mad, or a criminal or something, and we were taken away from her? I don't want to know anything like that. I'd rather keep my dream."

"Do you often think like that, Emily?" Paul asked carefully.

"Like what?"

"That there was something wrong with your mother, that she wouldn't live up to your dreams?"

"Sometimes." Emily shrugged. "At night. When I'm not sure where my life is going. When I don't feel in control, and I wonder if everything's already mapped out for me in some genetic time-bomb. I get scared that maybe I'm wasting my time trying to build the perfect life for myself, because I'm going to go mad some day and lose it all. Does that sound crazy?"

"No, but soon there'll be nothing left to worry about."

"What do you mean?"

"This time tomorrow you'll know the truth." He kissed the top of her head.

They stood like that for a while, then Emily turned to face him. His eyes were full of sadness. She knew he was thinking of his wife and the child he had thought was his. She wanted to comfort him, wanted to know more, but she couldn't cope with any more emotion, any more revelations tonight. She needed comfort herself. She stood on tiptoe and kissed him gently on the lips. He pulled her into his arms and returned her kiss. She felt so safe with him then; she could stay like this forever. He continued to kiss her mouth. Then her jaw, then her neck. Emily pressed herself harder against him, loving the heat from his body. This was so right. Why had she fought it for so long? He looked into her eyes and she begged him silently to read words there that she couldn't say out loud. But he pulled back.

"Not now, Emily. I can't cope with this right now. I'm sorry."

Paul walked away from her, out of the room, without looking back.

Upstairs, Charlotte heard doors open and close, heard Paul go upstairs to use the bathroom, and then retreat into the back living-room. She listened for Emily to come upstairs.

Although Charlotte had waited all her life for what Sheila was about to tell them, she felt now as if things were getting out of control. This wasn't how she had imagined it would be. Finding out about her past was supposed to be a quest. She should be feeling a sense of achievement on the eve of having everything revealed.

Shortly after moving to England she had tried to find some trace of a woman called Caroline Wilder, the young unmarried mother named on the sisters' birth certificates. A woman who had lived and died somewhere near Kingston upon Thames where Charlotte and Emily were born. But there was nothing to find, apart from a final, impersonal entry in the register of deaths. Nor had the investigator she hired found anything. The man was sympathetic but warned Charlotte that she could spend a lot more money and still get no results, so Charlotte had abandoned the hunt. The only way to pursue it further was by asking Sheila for more information, and she was unwilling to take the risk of hurting her at a time when she was going through so much change herself. Robert was only a few years dead, Charlotte had moved to England after making Sheila into a grandmother, and Emily was away studying in Dublin. And Donal, although he had supported Charlotte throughout her search, seemed relieved when it brought up nothing new. It made Charlotte wonder had she rushed headlong into it without thinking how it would affect everyone around her.

But despite that, Charlotte had always imagined that one day she would pick up the few remaining threads of her mother's life and try to follow them further. She had imagined a paper trail, letters and phone-calls, and at each stage a decision about where to go next and whether she wanted to go there. She had imagined being in control. When Robert died, Sheila gave the girls their original birth certificates, and although she never said it, she implied that she had no more to tell them. But now, with hardly any warning, she was going to blow open their past.

Charlotte kept listening but Emily didn't move up from downstairs. She knew Paul had settled in for the night, she could even hear gentle snoring through the floor, so Charlotte wondered what had happened between them that kept Emily awake downstairs on her own. She wondered if she should go down and see what was wrong with her, but before she could make a decision either way, she fell into a troubled sleep.

The next morning the house was empty when Emily made her way downstairs. She began to root around the kitchen to make breakfast, amazed that Sheila still stored her teabags, teapot, plates and cups exactly where she remembered. It soothed her to wander around laying the table, boiling the kettle. It was like turning back the clock, as if she had never left. Even the bread bin was the same: a bottle-green-painted metal box with a hinged lid that didn't fit properly. Charlotte and Emily had bought it for Sheila for Christmas, when Emily was six.

"Paul wanted to get the earliest train possible," Charlotte explained when she returned from the station. "He insisted I didn't wake you, that you needed your sleep."

"How come you were up so early?" Emily tried to hide her disappointment that Paul was gone and had left no message for her.

"I heard him moving about and I couldn't get back to sleep. Years of conditioning as a mother, I suppose." Charlotte grinned. "I rang the hospital. Mum's doing fine, and we can go in and see her whenever we like. Are you not going to eat anything?"

Emily was standing against the counter with a mug of tea in her hand, but the plates she had laid were clean.

"No, I'm not hungry." Emily shook her head although she was surprised at the question. She never ate breakfast.

Charlotte looked at her sister. Emily knew her eyes

were red-rimmed, and her face puffy. She knew that
Charlotte would guess that this was more than the few
tears she had shed last night in the front room.

"What's wrong, Emms? You look like you didn't sleep
all night. Were you worrying about what Sheila might
tell us today?"

"No, it's not that …"

"What then? Paul?"

Emily winced as she remembered how he had walked
away from her when they were kissing. But she didn't
want to talk about that. She wasn't even sure what there
was to say.

"No, it's not Paul."

"So you didn't have a row or anything last night?"
Charlotte asked. "I'm not saying he was in a hurry to
leave this morning, but I was surprised he didn't want to
say goodbye to you."

"No, no row, honestly. He probably just had an early
meeting or something."

Charlotte poured herself a cup of tea from the pot
Emily had left on the cooker. She stirred it slowly before
asking: "Did he say anything more about …" she watched
her sister closely, "well, you know, his son, Scott, or
rather the child who wasn't his son? Did he talk about
him at all? Is he still in touch with him? Does he have any
feelings for him now? Did he say how it might have been
different if he'd known the truth all along?"

"No, he didn't say anything else," Emily answered.
"Well, that is, I didn't really ask him. I suppose he might
have if I'd pushed."

"So you weren't interested in how he felt now about the boy? You weren't curious enough to pursue it further? Find out how he felt to discover ..." Charlotte raised her arms in a helpless question. "It must have been a huge thing for him, to find out his child wasn't really his own. Doesn't that interest you at all?"

"Why are you so interested in how Paul feels, all of a sudden?" Emily asked. Goose bumps made the hair on her arms stand up on end. She suddenly got the same feeling as when she woke from a dream, feeling that in her sleep she had remembered something important. And the harder she tried to recall it, the further it sank back into her subconscious.

"No reason." Charlotte turned away quickly. "It's just that he's a friend of yours. I thought you'd try to get an insight into how he felt about it." She put her coat back on. "Let's go in and see Sheila. By the way, did I tell you Donal rang while you were still asleep? He's coming down this evening to see her."

"Did you tell him about –?"

"No, I didn't," Charlotte interrupted. She hadn't wanted him rushing down sooner to 'support her', when what she might need was some time to herself to think things through. "This is just between us."

"My God, Charlotte, am I that sick?" Sheila laughed as she hugged Charlotte. "Look at that pile of magazines." She pointed to the bundle Charlotte was unpacking onto her locker. "And that bag of fruit, Emily. Honestly, how long do you expect me to stay in for? I was told I could go home tomorrow."

"They're only letting you home tomorrow because they want some peace and quiet here. " Emily gave her a hug.

They had spoken to the doctor who said there was nothing to worry about. Sheila had a slight arrhythmia, not uncommon at her age, and it would be easy to control it with drugs.

"How are the kids and Donal?" Sheila asked. "I hope I haven't given everyone a fright. I kept telling Maura she was overreacting, and I wouldn't let her phone you until I had got the all clear. I wish you hadn't come rushing down here, putting everyone out like that." But she was clearly glad to have them with her.

"Maura was very good," Charlotte said. "She met us at the house last night. We were quite late down, but she waited for us."

"Oh." Sheila's face fell. "What did she say to you?"

"She said you wanted to talk to us."

"I see."

"You don't have to." Charlotte wished she hadn't said anything. In the light of day, Sheila might have changed her mind "You just concentrate on getting better. I'm sure it's nothing that can't wait."

"So she told you what it was about . . . Don't worry …" Sheila held up her hand, "she was right. You've had some time to prepare." She reached for the half-empty glass of water beside her bed but Emily got to it first and refilled it before giving it to her.

" I'm only sorry I didn't tell you sooner. I should have

169

… but …" Sheila stuttered.

"Mum, leave it! You don't have to tell us anything." Emily was getting agitated

"Yes, I do."

Chapter 10

"The easiest way to do this is to get it all out in one go," Sheila began. She took a deep breath: "You know who your mother is, or rather was, from your birth certificates. What you don't know is that…" Sheila paused; her eyes darted between her two daughters, studying their faces. It was obvious from her nervous, almost scared expression that what she was about to say would shake them. "What I never told you … I mean what Robert forbade me to tell you … is that he was your uncle. It was his brother, your Uncle Martin, who was your … your *biological* father." With barely a pause, she rushed on. "So as well as being your mother, your adopted mother that is, I am also your aunt – well, aunt by marriage. Do you remember your Uncle Martin?"

Neither girl answered. In order to put off processing this information, Charlotte tried to remember Uncle Martin. She didn't think she had ever met him; he was a distant figure in their childhood. He used to send a five or ten-pound note at Christmas and their birthdays. Strange, foreign-looking notes, English money. He died when Charlotte was thirteen years old and the only thing she remembered feeling at the time was cheated, because Emily had just received her envelope while Charlotte's birthday was still a few months away

Then the implication of what Sheila said hit her like a blow to the chest: Her father had died in England, and all Charlotte could feel was cheated out of her ten-pound note. She had felt guilty at her callousness at the time and lit an extra candle for him at Mass; but now she was having trouble breathing.

Emily's reaction was different. First her face paled as she clenched her teeth and her hands formed tight fists by her side. Then an ugly red stain spread blotchily across her face. "So we were related to him. To Robert," she said slowly. "We had as much right to the name Riordan as he had."

Sheila looked anxiously at her, waiting for the explosion of anger.

"Every day of our childhood, he tried to make us feel grateful for having been given a gift of the precious Riordan name, when really it was ours by right." Emily's hysterical laugh made her sound like she was choking. "Don't wear your skirt that short. Don't run in the street. Don't look around in Church. Don't make a laughing-stock of the family. We were made to feel like outsiders in this town. Suspicious little blow-ins! Charity cases!" Sheila winced as Emily's words hit her like blows. "And all the time our roots were as firmly entrenched as any-one else's, in the sodden, mucky, *shitty* soil of this area! Our father grew up here. He probably went to the same bloody school as we did." She was gasping for breath now. "Bloody Hell, he grew up in the same house. One of us," Emily turned to Charlotte, pleading with her to join with her in this feeling of outrage, "one of us even slept in the same bedroom our father would have slept in as a boy. Do you realise that? How the hell could Robert have done that to us? Let us go on feeling excluded like that?"

There were tears streaming down Emily's face. As fast as her anger had exploded, it died away. She shook her head and shrugged her shoulders helplessly. Too late she realised that although she blamed Robert, Sheila had, by her silence, been his accomplice. Now she wanted to understand rather than accuse. She turned to her sister in the hope she could be gentler.

"We were family, Mum," Charlotte said quietly, sur-prised by the sheer force of Emily's reaction. After all it was Charlotte who had borne the brunt of Robert's dis-approval when they were children. "How could he have wasted that? Why would he have wanted to? I don't understand. And why did…" She found she couldn't say the word 'uncle'. "Why did Martin not want us?"

"I'm not sure if anything I say will excuse Robert…" Sheila hesitated, "or, I suppose, even myself for going along with him…" She looked from one daughter to the other, but neither was able to meet her eyes. Not just yet. She sighed and went on: "Martin was Robert's elder brother. He was the older by quite a few years so they

were never close. He went to England to work and did
well for himself, much better than Robert, who stayed at
home with his parents and eventually, when they died,
took over the shop. He married late – a few years after
Robert and I got married – and I know Robert was dreading the announcement that Martin was expecting a
child. By then it was obvious that Robert and I were not
going to be blessed and if Martin had children it would be
one more thing he had succeeded at where Robert had
failed. When Martin did no better after a few years, you
could see that Robert, while maybe not being pleased,
was at least relieved. His older brother had always
excelled at everything, always been better at everything,
and at least here they were equal."

Sheila stopped and reached for her water glass. She
emptied it and Charlotte took the jug and refilled the
glass. When Sheila took the glass back, her hand shook
as she raised it to her lips and she spilt some down her
nightdress. Emily picked up a tissue to wipe it off but
Sheila waved her away impatiently.

"I wanted children so desperately, but Robert wouldn't
agree to apply for adoption. To do so maybe would have
been to admit he had failed, I don't know. I suspect that
was why Martin wrote to me, not Robert."

Martin had written to her that he knew of two girls,
whose mother had just been killed in a road accident, and
that he would have some influence over placing them
into an adoptive family. He said he had thought immediately of Robert and Sheila. The two sisters were to be
kept together; it was what their mother would have

wanted. Sheila persuaded Robert that they should at least go and see the girls and that was when they learned that they were in fact Martin's own children by an affair.

"The possibility of his adopting you wasn't even discussed the day we met him," Sheila said. "He had obviously already made his decision about that. He said that if we didn't take you, he would use an adoption agency. And you would go to strangers, maybe even be separated. So Robert felt trapped. Not only had Martin outdone him again in managing to father children, but also to Robert duty was everything. There was no way he would walk away from his own flesh and blood. I realised of course, but Robert didn't, that that was exactly what Martin had intended. He knew that his little brother would be unable to resist taking the high moral stand. I knew that I was storing up trouble for the future, and that maybe I should have walked away, but I couldn't, and Martin had counted on that too. When I saw you, you were so young, so helpless, so beautiful. And I wanted you so badly."

Sheila stopped and looked at her daughters, and her face was sad.

"Robert couldn't love you because of who you were. Maybe he tried too hard. Or perhaps loving you would have meant accepting a gift from Martin. A gift he could never possibly repay. Whereas by raising you because it was his duty … well, that allowed him to feel superior to his brother."

"So Uncle Martin … our father … never tried to have anything to do with us after that?" Emily asked in disbelief.

"Not exactly. He wanted to help out – you know, contribute to your upkeep or whatever, but Robert forbade it. He said if we were going to adopt you it was going to be done cleanly and legally. All ties should be cut. I think he thought he was punishing Martin but, to be honest, Martin was probably relieved. You see, the woman he had married was the only daughter of a huge building magnate in London and Martin's own business relied on him. He owned a plumbing company and he got the contracts for fitting out all this man's new developments. If she found out about the affair and divorced him, he stood to lose all that."

"I can't believe he could have just walked away from us like that," Charlotte said, thinking of her own children and how she would kill anyone who tried to take them from her.

Sheila's face tightened into a frown. "I'm afraid Martin wasn't a very nice person. Not half the man Robert was, for all his success in life. I'm sorry to have to tell you that, but there's no other way of explaining it to you. Martin was ambitious. Money and status were more important to him than people. I felt sorry for his wife – she was no more than a girl when they married and he married her to further his own business ambitions, not because he loved her. If you consider that he was only five years married when your mother died, and Charlotte, you were over three… Well, you can do the maths and work out that the affair was either already under way, or started very soon after he stood in that church in Islington and took his wedding vows."

"But when Martin died," Charlotte said, "it meant nothing to us. And it should have. Why couldn't you have told us then?"

"Do you think it would have made anything easier for you?" Sheila asked, shaking her head slowly. "Martin left this town at the age of seventeen. He never returned, even to visit his parents. He never sent money home to them, just the odd letter boasting of how well he was doing. Before he went to England he was disliked because he was arrogant, but to neglect your parents, especially when you're doing well, is the ultimate sin in the eyes of small-town Ireland. Believe me, to have it generally known that you were Martin's illegitimate children would have done you no favours. Remember that if Robert wanted to look good he could have let it slip at any point who you were. It would have made him look like such a Christian, caring man compared to the brother who abandoned first his parents and then his children. But Robert wouldn't do something like that, and it was for your own sakes."

"I suppose you're right," Charlotte admitted reluctantly. "Unknown 'bad blood' was bad enough, without them being able to trace every bit of misbehaviour, every undesirable trait back to Uncle Martin."

"And there was Martin's wife to think of too," Sheila reminded them. "In my innocence, I suggested to Robert that we go as a family to the funeral. To pay our respects. I thought that one day, when you knew where you came from, you would at least have the comfort of remembering your real father's funeral. God, how could I have

177

been so stupid?"

"Do we look like him?" Emily asked.

"At thirteen, Charlotte looked enough like him to have raised eyebrows at his funeral."

"And what about our mother? What can you tell us about her?" Emily asked, after they had all been silent for a couple of minutes. Emily needed to know whether she took after her mother. She was surprised at the jealousy she felt when Sheila said that Charlotte looked like their father but hadn't mentioned Emily.

"Your mother," Sheila smiled, relieved to have finished explaining about her and Robert's motives in keeping the girls' past from them. "Obviously I never met her. But I did speak to one of her friends, who used to come and visit you at the home before the adoption came through. Your mother's name was Carrie, Caroline Wilder, but you knew that from your birth certificates." Sheila turned to Emily as if she guessed what was going through her mind. "Apparently even as a toddler you were the image of your mother, Emily. She was petite like you are. And blonde. She was a waitress at a restaurant near where Martin lived. Before he got married he used to eat there after work. Her friend said Carrie was besotted with him and even when she learned he was married, when she was pregnant with you, Charlotte, she couldn't give him up. She couldn't walk away from him although all her friends begged her to."

"And family? What did her family have to say to that state of affairs?" Charlotte whispered.

"It seems that when Martin chose his subject for an

extended extra-marital affair, he chose her well," Sheila continued with what could only be described as a sneer. "He obviously didn't want an enraged brother or father knocking on his door. Caroline was the only child of elderly parents. Her father died when she was in her teens and her mother remarried a few years later to a man Caroline didn't like much. She moved to London from Liverpool and didn't have much to do with them after that. In fact, her friend said …" Sheila's face lit up as she remembered. "Fiona, that was the friend's name. Caroline's friend. Anyway, Fiona got the impression that Caroline hardly exchanged a word with her mother's new husband from the day she left home till the day of her mother's funeral."

"So, she's dead too then. Our grandmother," Charlotte said, unaware that her eyes were glistening.

"I'm sorry, Charlotte." Sheila put her hand over her mouth in shock as if she had only just realised the implications of what she had said. "Had you hoped to find her?"

Charlotte shrugged her shoulders, unwilling to admit that that was specifically what she had set her investigator to find. A mother for Caroline Wilder might have led to a father, brothers, sisters. An extended family for Charlotte and her children.

She looked at Emily to see how she was taking the news. After her earlier outburst, her sister looked calm, relaxed. Almost, Charlotte thought, relieved. She supposed it made sense. Emily with her mania for control and neatness, need never now fear that there was anyone out there to upset her tidy world.

And although she understood Emily, Charlotte couldn't help but feel a stab of irritation at her. She wanted Emily to be more shaken up. She wanted her to realise that apart from Charlotte's kids, and a sister of Sheila's who was a missionary nun in Africa, her whole family was here, in this room. She wanted Emily to share her sense of loss for the other family that could have been out there somewhere.

For a while longer, they spoke about the past, Sheila digging through her memory for anything she could remember Fiona telling her about their mother, Charlotte and Emily doing their best to reassure her that she couldn't have behaved any differently than she had towards them, and that no matter what they had learnt, she was still their real mother. None of them mentioned Robert, and Charlotte knew she would have to re-examine her memories of her adopted father, rewrite the past. She would need to find a way of judging him less harshly, and certainly forgive Sheila for having loved him despite the way he had failed to love his daughters.

"What do you want to tell the kids?" Donal asked as they drove back to Dublin the following evening. Emily had taken a few days off to be with Sheila when she got back from hospital so, once Charlotte saw she was settled in, there was nothing further to keep her away.

"Sorry, what did you say?" Charlotte opened her eyes and woke up with a start. She had slept very little the night before.

"How much do you want to tell the kids?" Donal repeated.

Charlotte thought about it for a while.

"Nothing yet. I have to get my own head around it first." She smiled across the car at him. "Do we need to tell them anything?"

"Well, they might like to know that Sheila's your aunt," Donal suggested gently. "I know that to them she's their granny, but they know about you being adopted, so in time I'm sure they'll start asking questions. It might be easier to get the whole thing out in the open now. We'll never know if any of them are thinking about it. Letting it stew inside. Especially as you can't seem to open the newspapers or turn on the television lately without another story of adopted children searching for their parents."

"Do you think so? Do you think they might worry about it?"

"Probably not at the moment," Donal said. "But … well … I suppose everyone must want to know where they came from. It was important to you. Why should it be so different for them just because it's a generation down the line?"

"And do you think the truth is so important?" Charlotte asked carefully. "I mean, does it make such a huge difference who you're connected to biologically?"

"I don't know," Donal replied after a short silence. "You'd know more about that than I would."

They drove in silence for a while. Then Donal cleared his throat.

"There's something else we need to talk about, Charlotte." Donal pulled into the carpark of a pub near their home.

There was a strange expression on his face and Charlotte felt a hard little ball of dread form in her stomach. What was wrong? She thought about the last few months, and how she had worried about a distance she imagined growing up between them. She had told herself that it was just because they were so busy with the business, and with the children now that they were growing up and were more demanding. She kept telling herself that it wasn't distance that was growing between them, but familiarity. But the look on Donal's face worried her. Surely he wouldn't pick a time like this to talk about their marriage? She followed him wordlessly into the lounge and found a table in the corner.

"What did Denise O'Sullivan want?" Donal asked, after he brought drinks over.

"Denise O'Sullivan? What …? I mean, how …?" Charlotte shook her head in confusion, wondering why Donal should raise the subject now. Then she realised that although it seemed like another age it was only two days since she met Denise.

"I saw her name and phone number in the reservations book," Donal answered quickly before she could ask. Donal didn't want to have to tell Charlotte he had only seen the name after Suzy drew his attention to it.

He remembered the feeling of being punched in the stomach.

"Denise O'Sullivan?" Suzy had asked aloud as she

looked at the message on the reception desk. "I wonder if that's Marcus's wife? What could *she* want with Charlotte?"

It wasn't Denise's name, or even Marcus's that sent Donal reeling that morning, but the look on Suzy's face. The knowing look. She looked right into his eyes, trying to read his mind. There was only one possible reason that Suzy was asking Donal rather than Charlotte about Denise's call – she wanted to make sure he knew about it.

For the first time in ages, Donal wondered had they done the right thing in offering Suzy the job.

"I met Denise on Monday, for coffee." Charlotte's answer brought Donal back to the present. "What's this about, Donal?"

"Why did you meet her?"

"She wanted to meet me. That's what she rang about. And I didn't really know how to refuse." Even as she said it, Charlotte knew it sounded foolish. She was an adult, a wife and mother as well as a respected businesswoman, but just as she had been unable to refuse Marcus anything when they were together, now it sounded as though she had transferred that obedience to his wife.

"What was it about?" Donal asked.

"I'm not sure, to be honest. She said she wanted to meet me, that she had this therapist in New York who said she had to meet me to get closure." Charlotte forced a silly little laugh to show how ridiculous the whole thing was. "She said I hung like a shadow over her marriage. Donal, what's wrong?"

She realised his face was like a mask. Not a happy or a

sad mask. Or even an angry or a suspicious mask. More like a death mask, as if Donal was making a conscious effort to wipe all emotion from his features.

"Why didn't you say anything to me?" he asked carefully.

"I didn't know I needed to. If you like, I'll print you off a copy of my schedule every Monday." Her flippancy hid a real fear.

"Stop messing about, Charlotte. You were meeting Marcus's wife. It's not the same as meeting an old friend from school, or the wine merchant."

"Why not, Donal?" Charlotte got angry. "Marcus is in the past. I haven't seen him for ten years …"

"Is he, Charlotte? I want to believe that. Is Marcus really only in the past?" Donal looked carefully at Charlotte. "You never talked about him … I could never be sure you were completely over him …"

"I married you, Donal. I love you. Marcus is in the past." Charlotte wished she could feel the certainty she expressed. "He's in New York. He and Denise have split up. She wanted to meet me. There's nothing else to know."

They glared at each other. Donal broke away first, taking a long drink from his pint. He wiped foam from his upper lip, leaving a tiny bit, just below his nose. Charlotte almost had to sit on her hands to stop herself wiping it off for him.

"I'm sorry to hear that – that they've split up, I mean." Donal heard Charlotte draw in her breath in a hiss of annoyance. "Only because it's sad to hear of people splitting up. Do they have any kids?"

"No, Marcus didn't want kids." Charlotte was surprised to see Donal relax. "Denise said that's what they split up over." This conversation was becoming more surreal than the one she had held with Denise herself. "Denise asked about our kids, and realised that I couldn't have made it work with Marcus any better than she could, because my need for a family would have split us up in the same way. Donal, what is all this about?"

They stared at each other in silence for a while. Then Donal reached over and took one of her hands between his two huge ones.

"I was afraid, Charlotte. Afraid he was going to come back into our lives and change things. But that's not going to happen, is it?" he pleaded. "He's in New York. You're here. That's the way it's going to stay, isn't it? He's not going to wreck things for us, is he?"

Charlotte shook her head, unable to speak, unable to answer Donal's question because she wasn't sure exactly what he was asking, what he was afraid of. They had never discussed Marcus, so she had no idea what was really going on in his head.

In Castlemichael Emily put down the phone. Sheila had gone to bed soon after Charlotte and Donal left, so the house was quiet. She had been phoning Paul all day but kept getting his machine. It was unlike him not to check his messages, so she decided he must be avoiding her.

What did he regret about Monday night? Telling her about his ex-wife, Sharon, and the child, Scott? Kissing her? Emily touched her mouth; it tingled from the memory of his kiss. But stronger than the memory of his kiss was the memory of watching his back as he had walked away from her into the other room.

But the kiss was real; she knew that. For years Emily had fought the feelings she felt for Paul, but now she knew she wanted him and she was afraid she had left it too late. The way Paul had said 'Not now, Emily. I can't handle it', convinced her she had. That there was probably someone else.

That was it then. She had left it too late. She shrugged and fought against the pain she felt; after all, she had no one to blame but herself. For a brief moment she thought about fighting for him, but gave up on the idea immediately.

Paul was her best friend; she would do what she could to rescue the situation and not lose him as a friend. If he'd found someone else, she had no right to screw it up for him. Why should one kiss make any difference, she argued. She had been under stress at the time He was back with that other woman now, and he was probably feeling guilty that he had kissed Emily in a moment of weakness. But they had got over something like this before; they would again. It was probably all for the best.

"Emily!"

Paul was glad she had picked up on the third ring – it was late to be calling her. He had avoided her calls all day because he had no idea how to talk to her. He almost wished that he had taken advantage of the opportunity which presented itself the previous night, but as soon as the thought formed, the words 'taken advantage' stood out in bold italics.

"I didn't wake you, did I?" he asked.

"No, you know me, a right night owl. Sheila's gone to bed though."

"How is she?"

"Fine. The doctors are pleased with her."

"I'm sorry I didn't call you back before ..."

"No, that's fine. You don't need to explain ..."

"How did yesterday go? Did Sheila tell you about ..." Paul wished he were there with her. Again he thought that maybe it had been a mistake to walk away when they were kissing, but he didn't want to give Emily any more excuses. He had been waiting for that kiss for years, ever since the night when they were still in college. He wasn't going to let her pretend it was just because she was upset and needed comfort. The next time they kissed, it would be the start of something real.

"I'll talk to you when I get home," Emily said briskly and Paul shivered. "I'm staying down here until Sunday night."

"Oh ... all right." He hid his disappointment. "Will I see you then?"

"It'll probably be late. Maybe for a drink during the week sometime?"

Paul wasn't about to let himself be brushed off like this again.

"Emily, about Monday night. I'm sorry if I –"

"It's all right Paul. I understand," Emily interrupted. "It

was an emotional situation." She paused, then rushed on before he could interrupt. "We let ourselves … look, let's pretend it never happened. I wouldn't want it to stand in the way of our friendship. To be honest, I'd prefer to pretend it hadn't happened at all. Listen, I've got to go. I think I can hear Sheila moving about upstairs. I'll call you next week sometime."

Paul stood listening to the beep-beep of the hung-up phone. She'd done it to him again! He picked up a little porcelain figure on the hall table. Sharon had given it to him as a thank-you present.

It had been an exaggeration to say that he'd lost all feeling for Scott when he discovered that he wasn't his own child. When he saw how the boy had turned out, spoilt and truculent, he felt a surge of anger at the two people who had the right to call themselves his parents. Scott had been a sunny and laughing baby – what had they done to turn him into this? Unless she was criticising him or they were arguing, Sharon hardly acknowledged the boy's presence, and it was clear that her latest partner had little time for the child.

Above all, Paul resented the guilt he felt every time he met Scott. The child wasn't his, and at twenty-one he could hardly have been expected to put up that strong a fight to take on the responsibility for another man's child. But Paul knew that no matter how awful his relationship with Sharon, he could have been a better father to Scott than the man who contributed half his genes. Scott didn't remember the years with Paul as his 'daddy', but whenever they spent time together now, Paul felt that they could have at least have been friends. And he hated himself for not making the effort to be some sort of constant presence in the boy's life. So when Sharon, unsure of where else to turn, had phoned Paul in a panic, saying that Scott was in trouble, that he'd been mixing with a bad crowd and had been cautioned by the police for vandalism, Paul stepped in. He had 'loaned' Sharon the money to send Scott to the school he went to, then paid the boy's fare so that he could spend the summer with cousins in the States.

Paul tossed Sharon's gift up and down absent-mindedly. It landed in his palm and he looked at it as it nestled, small and fragile-looking, in his hand. The little porcelain shepherdess was hideous. Did Sharon really know him so badly that she could have thought he'd like it? There was no way Emily would ever buy something like that. He felt no guilt when the figure shattered to a million pieces against the wall. But the destruction did nothing to relieve his pain.

Chapter 11

Spring1997

Donal pushed open the door of Charlotte's office and stuck his head around it. When he saw she was alone, he came in with two mugs of coffee and she took out a file on their new restaurant in town, which was due to open in two weeks' time. Suzy was going to take over the new kitchen and Charlotte was relieved that they would see less of her. Somehow since the summer, her friendship with Suzy had become strained, although the other woman wouldn't admit that anything was wrong.

"First cup of the day," Donal grinned, handing her the steaming coffee. They had taken to drinking tea with breakfast because, since Gemma had started drinking the strong coffee they brewed at home, Charlotte was worried that it might be contributing to her recent bolshy behaviour. Anyway, she was too young to be drinking strong coffee.

"Hi. How are things your end?" Charlotte smiled at her husband. She had come to love these morning cups of coffee at work. They would sit and chat about the restaurant, keep up to date with each other's areas and sort out any problems before they blew up out of proportion. Sometimes it seemed to Charlotte that it was the only time they really spent together throughout their busy weeks.

"Don't ask!" Donal groaned, and proceeded to tell her anyway. "The kitchen's like a war zone. Joe's flexing his muscles to prepare for when he takes over, and Suzy contradicts every order he gives. 'It's still my kitchen!'" He mimicked the Cork accent she hadn't lost, despite not having lived at home since she was eighteen.

Charlotte looked with concern at the look of sheer frustration that crossed her husband's face every time he said Suzy's name. He had the opposite problem with Suzy. While Charlotte made every effort, only to be rebuffed, Donal went out of his way to avoid her only to have her seek him out at every opportunity to ask his opinion or simply chat.

The two of them had never really discussed Suzy properly. Charlotte wondered was it because Donal was loath to say "I told you so", having been the one who was reluctant to employ such a close friend in the first place. She had been about to raise the subject, but when she saw Donal's expression, she put it off again. Instead she went through the lists of staff who were moving to the new restaurant and the final plans for the party. They exchanged bitchy comments about some of guests for the official opening and laughed over some shared jokes.

Donal left the office still laughing, and Charlotte looked after him. He was still enjoying it, she reassured herself. She had worried when they married first that she had trapped him into a life of working to pay bills and support his family. He was the first in his class to get married, and by far the youngest to start a family. She was always afraid that he would hold it against her one day. In that awful period in England, when he had begun to hate his job, she had lain awake at night, trying to read blame into some small comment he might have made during the day. She felt so responsible for his happiness.

And Charlotte had to believe he was happy in his work, because she wasn't sure how happy they were at home. Not that there was anything particularly wrong. Not that you could put your finger on. They hardly ever argued, they enjoyed family occasions and they still made love, though not perhaps as often as Charlotte would have felt comfortable with (it wasn't so much that she wanted more sex, but she felt that Donal probably did).

She tried to put it out of her mind and phoned Emily to confirm that they were meeting up that evening in the health club. Then she got down to paying bills before collecting Aisling from school.

The three women pedalled furiously on the exercise bikes. Charlotte was glad she was beside Anne-Marie, so she wouldn't feel inadequate alongside Emily who had already worked up enough miles to take her to Belfast and back. Anne-Marie was in Dublin for the day to choose wedding invitations. She had narrowed it down to two, but the stationer she had really wanted to check out had been closed.

"Look on the bright side," Emily laughed as she swigged from her water bottle. "Now you have to do even more shopping."

Charlotte and Anne-Marie exchanged a look. That laugh was the final straw. Emily wasn't even breathless! They got down off their bikes in disgust and sank to the carpet until their legs recovered. They regained just about enough breath for Anne-Marie to be able to whisper to Charlotte, with Emily unable to hear over the mechanical whirring of the bike.

"Sexually frustrated!" She looked knowingly at Emily's glistening legs pumping furiously. "What she needs is a good –"

"What are you two whispering about?" Emily jumped off the bike and began to do a series of stretches. "You should join me, you know. You're going to be horribly stiff tomorrow otherwise."

"I'll risk it," Charlotte groaned. Emily's contortions looked too much like hard work. "Let's go and join Tara in the Jacuzzi."

She and Anne-Marie trooped off leaving Emily to chat to one of the fitness instructors. They eased themselves into the swirling bubbles.

"I'm going to regret this tomorrow." Anne-Marie leaned her head back against the side and closed her eyes.

Tara was on the other side of the circular bath. It would just about fit the four of them when Emily joined them; it was a good thing the club was quiet. Charlotte studied Tara who had her eyes open and was staring at the ceiling. When they had arrived, Charlotte wondered how Tara could look so fit and slim without joining them in the gym. All she ever seemed to use the health club for these days was the Jacuzzi, steam rooms and beauty salon. Now that Charlotte saw her in her swimsuit, with no make-up on, she realised that Tara didn't look as great as at first glance.

She had lost too much weight, and where she used to have well-toned muscles now her limbs looked weak and spindly. There were dark circles under her eyes, and the hay fever, which had struck for the first time the previous spring, still seemed to be bothering her. Her eyes were red-rimmed and she had a constant sniffle.

"You look well, Tara," Charlotte lied. She'd learnt there was no point in bringing up the subject of Tara's hay fever; Tara was fed up with well-meaning friends suggesting allergy experts and alternative remedies. And it didn't seem to have slowed her down one bit. Charlotte got exhausted just listening to descriptions of the social life she led. And that on top of a demanding job in which she seemed to be excelling.

"How's the love life?" She asked.

"Non-existent," Tara muttered with a sniff without looking up. "But if you want to hear about my sex-life …" She sat up, eyes gleaming.

Charlotte wished she hadn't asked, but nodded and oohed and aahed in all the right places as Tara gossiped about the intimate details of the famous men she had

slept with lately. She was going through an enter-
tainment phase at the moment. Singers, actors and television personalities. Charlotte shuddered when she
remembered how Tara and Emily used to go out on the
prowl together, years ago in college. She was glad that
Emily was over that phase. Tara seemed to be coping, but
she wasn't sure that her little sister would have stood the
pace.

Emily dropped thankfully into the Jacuzzi beside them
and just about avoided throwing her eyes up to heaven
when she realised what Tara was talking about.
Sometimes she was amazed at the way they had remained
such good friends when their lives had gone in such different directions. Emily was no angel, but she was glad
she'd left her wild days behind. She remembered how,
when she first went to college in Dublin, she'd been
determined to make new friends and leave Castlemichael
in her past. But after three years, Tara and Anne-Marie
were still the best friends she had. College hadn't been
the life-enhancing experience she'd expected. For one
thing she had to work too damn hard to keep up at the
top of the class. And the way she picked up and dropped
men in those early days had made her few female friends.
The only real friend she had kept in touch with since her
law-student days was Paul.

She sighed when she thought of Paul. She felt guilty
because she saw so little of him these days. Since last
summer the atmosphere between them had been decid-
edly awkward – she'd been wrong to think they could put
that kiss behind them that easily. When Emily met up

with him to tell him all about Sheila's revelations about her mother, he'd talked it through with her just like a good friend would. But she knew his heart wasn't in it. She tried to draw him out again on the subject of his own marriage, and the boy he had thought was his son, but he always changed the subject.

They still went out for the odd drink together, and they went to films or to the theatre, but when they talked they stuck to safe subjects. It had become so hard to spend time with him that Emily left longer and longer gaps between their meetings, and wasn't surprised when he didn't try to make up for it by calling her. She hoped she hadn't lost him for good, but she knew it would take something big to shake them out of the rut they were in at the moment. She hoped it didn't happen too late.

She had heard nothing more of the girlfriend she had speculated about, the woman he had supposedly rushed back to from her mother's house the previous June; but she hadn't pressed him about it. It mustn't have worked out for him. Occasionally she was tempted to try and recapture whatever they had during that one kiss but she was terrified of driving him even further away. If he had wanted to take things further, he'd have done something about it by now, so the safest bet was to leave things as they were and hope for the best.

Emily's snort, and her eyes cast up to heaven had not been lost on Anne-Marie. Like her, she had tuned out of Tara's kiss-and-tell monologue. Maybe she was being a prude, but she kept waiting for Tara to grow out of her

197

sex-mad phase as Emily had. She looked over at Emily, who had closed her eyes now and was letting the warm water soothe what must be tingling muscles. Anne-Marie knew her friend well enough to know that when she was this fit, she wasn't happy. She'd seen her exercise regularly to the point of exhaustion, just so that she could sleep at night. And Anne-Marie knew that she was dieting as well. Not just calorie-counting to keep trim, but fanatic over every morsel which passed her lips. Organic, biotic, dairy-free, yeast-free. Cleansing, purifying, detoxifying, antioxidant. To be edible, it had to have a 'label'. She was an advertiser's dream. Anne-Marie wondered what aspect of her life Emily had lost control over that she was imposing such discipline on her body. She had been like this in her early twenties, before she had started going out with Richard. Maybe she needed another Richard to shake her out of it again.

No, not another Richard, Anne-Marie decided on second thoughts. She just wished to God Emily would get it together with Paul. He worshipped the ground she walked on and he'd be perfect for her. Anne-Marie suspected that if she'd only let him, Paul could teach Emily what it was like to really be loved. And he had a great body!

Anne-Marie felt herself blush at that thought. She was getting married soon, so why was she admiring other men's bodies? Dave was all she needed. Though she'd never admit it to Emily or Tara, he was the first and only man she'd ever slept with. It was strange how they'd all been so different about sex, wasn't it? Charlotte sleeping with her first-ever boyfriend, Marcus, and falling for him in a big way. She was the typical can't-separate-sex-from-love type. Then Emily who had had great fun in her early twenties without getting involved with anyone, and now seemed to have sworn off the opposite sex completely. Tara … well, Anne-Marie had never really understood Tara's attitude to men. It was like some kind of scary dependency.

And then herself. One of the first in her class to kiss a guy, plenty of boyfriends throughout school and college, but she'd never felt the need or even the desire to share herself completely with someone. Until Dave. She was so lucky to have found him. Anne-Marie had never believed in fate, but she was sure that everything in her life had been leading up to the moment she met Dave. They were soul mates.

She had accepted the job with Tara's father because she hated working in Dublin, hated the rat race, the competitiveness, the anonymous bustle of a city practice. Life as a small-town solicitor suited her. Finlay's was known for miles around as the best place for wills. Paul Finlay senior, Tara's grandfather, had a way with people and any will he was involved with was fair and water-tight. His son, Tara's father, just didn't have the same gift with people and was glad to leave that side of the business to Anne-Marie. With old Mr Finlay's help she gained the trust of their clients and soon she had taken over his mantle as the will expert for the county. So it was to her that Dave had come, distraught, on reading his father's will. Everything had been left to him on his father's death. The house, his father's money, shares, everything. A paltry allowance, and the widow's entitlement of two pensions had been all Mr McMorrow had seen fit to leave his wife. Dave wanted to sign everything back to his mother without her finding out that her husband had trusted her so little with money.

As he sat in Anne-Marie's office, signing away the best part of a six-figure sum, the look of sheer relief and joy on Dave's face had convinced Anne-Marie that she wanted to see more of this gentle giant. So when he invited her out for a drink afterwards to celebrate, she accepted. And when that drink extended to a late dinner, she was doubly sure this was a man she wanted to get to know better. She could have listened to his soft, gravelly voice all night, and she was disconcerted to feel the need to fold her hands tightly, to stop her running her fingers through his wiry, rust-coloured hair.

She had always had a thing for doctors. And Dave was a good doctor, or so the sister in charge of the geriatric unit confided to Anne-Marie. It had taken a while for the fierce Sister Morley to accept Anne-Marie. She had seen women come and go, all attracted by Dr McMorrow's rugged good looks and obvious consultant potential; and they had all ended up hurting her precious doctor. But she soon realised that Anne-Marie was different. Anne-Marie came onto the ward and chatted to the nurses or the patients while she waited, rather than sulked that Dave was late for yet another engagement.

Anne-Marie remembered the afternoon she had come to collect him to drive to Wexford for the opera festival.

She had managed to get a pair of tickets, worth their weight in gold, and they had been looking forward to this trip for weeks. She couldn't wait to see him dressed up in a tuxedo instead of the crooked tie and loose chinos he wore under his white coat. When Anne-Marie arrived on the ward, an hour after Dave was due to have finished, he was with a dying patient in a side room. The woman was in her late nineties, had suffered from dementia for the last decade of her life, and had outlived all her relatives and friends. In her three weeks in hospital, she had recognised in Dave some man from her past called Jonathan. A son, a brother, an old boyfriend, no one really knew, but the only time the woman stopped moaning piteously was when "Jonathan" was in her room, chatting to her, checking up on her. This evening he was sitting with her, holding her hand. He looked up when Anne-Marie poked her head in the door, apology written all over his face. She handed him a cup of coffee without saying anything, knowing the woman would shriek in terror if she heard a stranger's voice. As she listened to him babble soothingly to his patient, she knew this was the man she wanted to spend the rest of her life with.

It was dark by the time Dave was finally able to leave the woman, having closed her eyes for the last time, and far too late to travel to Wexford. Instead of being upset that they had missed the opera, Anne-Marie was relieved that the woman hadn't died alone and afraid, while they were away. The love she felt for Dave that night was so great, so consuming, that when they finally got home to his dingy rented flat, a stone's throw away from the hospital, she fell gratefully into bed with him, and they made love for the first time. The next morning, he asked her to marry him.

"*Yearrgh!*" Anne-Marie spluttered. Tara had just swooshed a huge wave of chlorinated water in her face. She shook herself off and looked at the other three women, doubled up in mirth.

"What?" she asked, feeling herself go red. "What?"

"Who were you dreaming of?" Emily asked. "I only hope it was Dave. I've already booked the time off for your wedding, and I'd hate to have to cancel it because you've run off with someone else."

"I wasn't dreaming of anyone," Anne-Marie protested, slipping further under the water in a vain attempt to hide at least some of her blushing.

"Come on. Let's get out of here. I'm turning into a prune," Charlotte said, seeing that Anne-Marie was getting more and more embarrassed. "Dinner's booked for nine."

Emily had insisted that, as Anne-Marie was spending the day in Dublin doing weddingy things, they all had to go out for dinner to plan a hen party. When they finally sat down to eat, they were all in such fits of giggles that it felt like a rehearsal.

A few weeks later, as Charlotte drove across Dublin towards Emily's apartment, she opened the sun-roof and turned up the stereo. It was the May Bank Holiday, and she was on her way to Anne-Marie's hen weekend. Three whole days away! She felt like shouting for joy. Three days of not worrying about the staffing crisis in two restaurants. Three days without school runs or after-school activities. Two nights of not being woken by childish footfalls on the landing. (Two nights of not wondering if she should reach out to Donal in the middle of the night.) Three whole days of having all your meals prepared for you by someone else. Two nights of getting plastered with your closest friends. (Three days of wishing Anne-Marie hadn't invited Suzy. Three days of wondering what had happened to that particular friendship.) Three days and two nights in Killarney on Anne-Marie's last fling as a single woman. Three days of sunshine according to Met Éireann.

Charlotte ran up the small flight of steps to Emily's apartment block and rang her buzzer. Soon the sisters were heading towards the Kerry road.

Tara and Emily had tried to persuade Anne-Marie to hold her hen-party somewhere like Barcelona, Paris or Milan, but Anne-Marie had insisted on Killarney. She had rebuilt her network of school friends, and very few of them could afford a trip abroad. Anne-Marie had booked out a whole guesthouse for the long weekend, and planned long walks, golf and relaxation to break up the three days' drinking. With only two weeks to the wedding, Anne-Marie had declared that what she needed most was a chance to de-stress. Her mother had insisted on a white wedding with all the trimmings and already Anne-Marie had rung Charlotte three times in despair, begging her to talk her out of eloping to Bermuda.

"Who else is coming this weekend?" Emily asked her sister as they eased onto the Naas dual carriageway.

"You, me, Tara. Anne-Marie, obviously. Her sister-in-law Antonia." They both made a face. "Two of Anne-Marie's Kerry cousins, the twins – you remember Phil and Terry? Then there's a few of Anne-Marie's class from school, a couple from college and two' of the girls she worked with when she did her solicitor's training."

"Articles," Emily corrected automatically.

"What?"

"Her solicitor's training, it's called … oh, never mind. Chewing gum?" Emily reached into the bag at her feet.

"No, thanks. I need something more fattening than that. Would you ever reach for that bag on the back seat and grab me some chocolate?"

Emily twisted around in her seat and picked up the dingy purple beach bag with distaste. No doubt this was another of Gemma's cast-offs.

"What kind of rubbish have you got in this bag?" Emily lifted out bag after bag of treat-size chocolate. "How many people are you planning on feeding, Charlotte?" She was glad she wasn't sharing a room with her sister. She could feel the pounds pile on just by looking at Charlotte's bag of chocolate. She wasn't even staying in the same guesthouse. They were one room short so Tara had nobly volunteered herself and Emily to stay in the Park Hotel instead. If they couldn't go to Barcelona, then they could at least get some serious pampering in the height of luxury.

"Anne-Marie needs fattening up. At her last fitting,

her dress was hanging off her," Charlotte explained.

"So how are Donal and the kids?" Emily asked, changing the subject. She was uncomfortable talking about Anne-Marie's dress fittings. As chief bridesmaid, she should have gone to those with her, but she was in Malaysia on business for the first one, and she couldn't get out of a meeting for the most recent one.

"Everyone's fine." Charlotte was equally anxious to get off the subject of Donal. "How's work?"

"Driving me mad. I have to get out of there soon or I'll lose it completely," Emily moaned.

"Oh," was all Charlotte could answer. Emily's work was usually such a safe topic.

"So, you're thinking of changing jobs?" Charlotte asked at last when it was clear that Emily wasn't going to elaborate any further.

"No, not really. To change jobs I'd have to have some idea of what I wanted to do."

"I thought you loved your job?"

"I did." Emily sighed. "Look, let's not talk about this now. We're supposed to be enjoying ourselves." She reached into Charlotte's bag of goodies and took out a small finger of Twix. She nibbled all the chocolate off one side, then the other and pulled the caramel off the top. Then she crunched her way slowly through the biscuit.

"I could have eaten a three-course meal in the time it took you to eat that," Charlotte muttered.

Emily just snorted in reply, reached for a jumper to roll up as a pillow and promptly fell asleep. Charlotte watched her sister fondly out of the corner of her eye. She drove the rest of the way carefully so as not to wake her – if Emily was able to sleep in that contorted a position, she needed the rest.

"Here already?" Emily woke up when the car stopped, and straightened out her neck. It began to tense up.

Charlotte watched with amusement while she began to gyrate her head and shoulders as she stood in the gravel carpark of the guest house.

"I'll just go and check if anyone else is here yet," she laughed.

Anne-Marie sat watching her friends. She was in the corner of the hotel balcony, and they were gathered around her on stools and aluminium chairs. Most of them wore skirts or shorts and they were angled to catch as many of the sun's tanning rays as possible. They had gathered in the hotel to wait for the rest of hen party to join them. Every new arrival made some joke about this being Anne-Marie's last weekend of freedom, and she obligingly raised her glass and pretended to be a lot drunker than she was.

She had been sorry when Suzy rang last night to say she couldn't make it after all, but the relief on Charlotte's face this evening had worried Anne-Marie.

"What happened between the two of you?" she asked.

"I honestly don't know. Over the last year or so we've just drifted further and further apart. I thought that maybe she was finding it uncomfortable working for me, and that things would get better when she switched into the new place, but if anything it's got worse." Charlotte sighed. "Maybe the friendship's just run its course."

"What does Donal think?"

"We don't really talk about it – if I raise it, he mutters in a noncommittal way for a minute or so, then changes the subject. He had reservations about taking her on in the first place, remember? Mixing work and friendship or whatever. Maybe he was right and doesn't want to say 'I told you so'. The ironic thing is that she seems to go out of her way to be friendly to him."

Anne-Marie sighed now, as she looked at her friend giggling with Emily and Tara. It hadn't escaped her notice either that, as soon as she mentioned Donal earlier on, Charlotte had changed the subject. Anne-Marie ignored the nasty little voice in her head asking if it could have anything to do with the fact that Marcus had moved back to Ireland a couple of weeks ago. He had dropped into Anne-Marie's office to ask about an Irish family lawyer to help sort out his separation from Denise. Anne-Marie knew that it wasn't just client confidentiality that stopped her from telling Charlotte he was home.

She shook her head resolutely; she wasn't going to worry about the state of other people's marriages this weekend. This was her hen party.

The weekend flew past and Charlotte couldn't remember feeling this relaxed for years. Any time she rang home, the kids were in great form, with Donal spending extra time with them and Granny Hannah spoiling them rotten when he had to go in to work. She refused to worry about what crisis could have suddenly stopped Suzy from joining the party for the weekend; maybe she had just chickened out. The only time Charlotte had managed to get Donal himself to the phone, he had seemed distant, almost distracted; but that was probably because of all the extra hassle he was facing looking after the kids on his own for a change. And she *wasn't* going to let herself feel guilty about that.

Charlotte got up early on Monday morning, the last day of their stay, and she had the breakfast room to herself. She knew it would be hours before the others emerged and she didn't want to waste the morning. She chatted to Mrs Lynch, the landlady, a friendly woman who enjoyed having a group of giggling women fill her guesthouse for the weekend. She decided, on Mrs Lynch's recommendation, to visit Muckross House for a walk before she drove back to Dublin. They hadn't done nearly as much walking as planned over the weekend, and Charlotte could feel the waistband of her jeans tighter as a result of all they had eaten and drunk.

The sun was out again, after a disappointing Sunday, and Charlotte marvelled at the stillness of the water and the reflections in the lake. She couldn't remember when she'd last had this much time to herself. She decided not to bother with visiting Muckross House but to walk through its extensive parkland and think. In the calm, she came to the realisation that she wasn't completely happy with her life at the moment. Everything she did was about someone else. The house, the kids, Donal. Even the restaurant, although she was proud of what they'd achieved, had always been more Donal's dream than hers. But what was her dream? She couldn't remember.

If I found a magic lamp and the genie offered me three wishes, what would I wish for, she asked herself. Good health for my family, obviously. Security? Yes, that too. Her walking slowed down, and she began to hit at the seed-heads of grasses with a dried stick.

Her mother-in-law had tried to persuade her to join an evening class with her and they had gone along to the open day together. Hannah signed up for Cordon Bleu cookery and an Italian class but Charlotte hadn't found anything to interest her though she accepted a bundle of leaflets on the way out the door. Now, as she sat on a grassy slope, looking back over Muckross House, she took one of them out of the pocket of her jeans.

It was a timetable for Leaving Certificate subjects for next year. As she stared at the creased leaflet, Charlotte worked out again how she could find time to take Geography, History and French. It was possible; she knew it was. She had spoken to a tutor in the centre, who was convinced that Charlotte could manage the three subjects. Her French had always been good in school and she'd kept it up since then with the odd evening class or video because it was useful for work. History had always been her favourite subject and the only reason she hadn't chosen it ten years ago was that it didn't fit in with her plan to work and study at the same time. Geography she could take or leave, so why was she so anxious to give it a go? She folded up the timetable again and walked on.

"Admit it, Charlotte," she said out loud. "Geography

brings you to three subjects, and with the three you took ten years ago, that makes six." The magic number of subjects she needed to submit on a university application form.

She speeded up. The thought of going to college hadn't entered her mind until the tutor in the education centre had mentioned it, but now... She stopped suddenly, looking up at the mountain whose reflection she had admired in the lake.

Because it's there. Isn't that what climbers replied when asked why they risked their lives to reach a peak? Charlotte knew she wanted to have another go at education because now she knew she could.

When she got back to the car, she searched through her handbag, then her glove compartment for a pen. Emily would have been able to find a pen in ten seconds flat, she thought, as she scribbled on the back of a checkout receipt to get the ink flowing, then smoothed out the crumpled leaflet. On the back page was an application form. She filled it in and, with her heart pounding, wrote out a cheque for the deposit. She stopped at a newsagent's and bought an envelope, which she addressed and sealed. Then she picked some fluff off a stamp she found lurking in her purse. Charlotte held the envelope with trembling fingers before letting it fall into the green mouth of the letter-box. When she heard it land, with a whisper, on the rest of the mail, she checked the time of the next delivery and took a deep breath.

She couldn't wipe the excited smile off her face. For the first time in far too long she was doing something for

herself. For her, Charlotte. It wasn't going to benefit the
kids, Donal, the house or the business. It might not be of
any great benefit even to herself. She was doing this just
because she wanted to and Charlotte was surprised at
how unfamiliar that felt. And at how good it felt.

Emily sighed with annoyance at the form lying comatose
on the bed beside her own. At the time it had seemed a
good idea to come and stay in the hotel with Tara, but she
had missed out on the giggling companionship the others
must have shared in the guesthouse. Last night Tara had
vanished after they all stumbled out of the night-club.
She had been chatting up a couple of American advertis-
ing executives all night, and must have hit it off with one
of them. She'd fallen into the room she was supposed to
be sharing with Emily at about half five, and was lying,
still dressed, on top of the covers. Emily cursed the fact
that Anne-Marie had arranged for Charlotte to drive two
of the others back to Castlemichael because it meant that
Emily had to go with Tara. It would be hours before they
could leave judging by the alcohol fumes which assaulted
her nostrils.

After showering, she decided to let Tara sleep it off.
She scribbled a note and went to get a quick cup of coffee before going for a walk around Killarney. When she
got back, she was surprised to see Tara bright-eyed in the
lobby, waving off the two Americans. For the hundredth
time, Emily wondered how she did it. She should be lying
in bed with the mother of all hangovers, but here she was,
looking tired, but certainly not acting it.

"Which one did you get lucky with?" Emily asked, only because she knew she was expected to. They were having breakfast in the bright airy dining-room, not because Emily was particularly hungry – even after her walk – but because she wanted to delay their departure without telling her friend that she didn't trust her to drive until at least some of last night's booze had cleared her system.

"Oh, was I supposed to pick only one?" Tara replied with a look of mock-horror, then burst into a high-pitched giggle. "The blond, of course. I know you prefer dark men, so I thought I ought to leave him, just in case… No, seriously, Brad was a bit of an animal, if you know what I mean. He really knows how to party… I haven't enjoyed myself that much since…"

Emily got up to go to the buffet so as to avoid a blow by blow account (literally), of exactly what Tara meant by "animal". As she piled fruit onto her plate, she told herself to stop being such a prude; after all it wasn't that long since she'd been Tara's partner in crime.

"Hay fever bothering you?" she asked as she sat down again. Tara was blowing noisily into tissue.

"Mmmh? Yeah!" Tara mumbled. "Country air's a killer." She continued to sniffle, then took out a cigarette and lit up.

"I thought you'd given up again?" Emily said in despair. Over four hours to Dublin in a smoky car?

"What's the point? We're all going to die sometime." Tara exhaled a stream of blue-grey smoke. "Are you about ready to hit the road?"

"Shouldn't we go and say goodbye to the others?"

Emily tried to calculate how many hours it was since Tara had had her last drink. She looked fine, if a little bleary-eyed, but that could be the hay fever. Maybe Emily could offer to split the driving, take the first leg. They could stop for lunch for about an hour, and by then Tara would surely be OK to drive.

"We're going to see them all in two weeks at the wedding," Tara insisted. "No, let's hit the road. I have to be back in Dublin this evening. I'm meeting someone."

"A man?" Emily was surprised. Tara didn't normally worry about keeping men waiting.

"Yes, as it happens it is a man, but not what you think. Come on, let's check out." Tara hammered the bell on the reception desk despite the fact that there were already several uniformed receptionists dealing with other guests. Emily slunk off in embarrassment.

Charlotte was glad she'd arrived back in time to have dinner with Donal. They picked through the remains of their take-away Indian meal.

"Honestly, Charlotte. I think it's a great idea." Donal had gone very quiet after she told him about her plans to start studying again. "I'm just worried that you might be taking on too much."

"I did it before." Charlotte tried to forget how hard she had found it to work and study at the same time.

"You didn't have three kids then …" Donal tried to point out, almost mirroring Charlotte's own thoughts. Maybe she was crazy. Maybe it was too much to take on.

"I want to give it a go, Donal," she interrupted before

he could convince her. "If it's too much, I promise I'll drop one of the subjects.

"But I want to start with three, and I've worked out how to fit them round the kids' school. The French is at night, and Fiona's dying to get some more baby-sitting money. I know your mother would be delighted to help out – she was very disappointed when I didn't sign up for something straight away last week." Charlotte looked at him carefully. "It won't impact too much on you, if that's what you're worried about. Geri practically runs Moran's here, and you spend most of your time in the Temple Bar restaurant, so you don't need me there. It's only twelve hours a week, Donal."

"I know, I'm sorry. You're right. I just worry about you, that's all." He smiled. "Seriously, I am pleased for you." He moved up to her end of the couch, and put his arms around her. "And I'll help you with anything I can."

Charlotte suddenly realised that the subjects she'd chosen were ones he'd never studied. He'd hated French in school, choosing Spanish and German instead, and the rest of his Leaving Cert subjects were science and maths based. Had she picked her subjects like that deliberately, so that he couldn't get involved? So that this would be something she could achieve totally on her own? No, that was ridiculous. She snuggled closer to him.

"Happy?" he asked, kissing the top of her head.

"Happy," she confirmed.

"Sure?" He pulled away and looked for something hidden in her eyes.

"What?"

"Well, you've been, I don't know – miles away for the past few months. There's nothing wrong, is there? Nothing you want to talk about?" His face was too serious.

"What could be wrong?" Charlotte stood up, shivering and reached for the cardigan hanging on the back of a chair. She was suddenly cold, although the room had been warm up to then, almost uncomfortably so. "I just need to do this, Donal." She picked up the leaflet she'd shown him earlier, and sat down beside him again. "You do understand that, don't you?"

"Of course, love." He put his arms around her, and kissed the top of her head again, but now he was the one who was miles away. "If there was anything, you would tell me, wouldn't you, love?"

She didn't answer. She didn't know what he was asking.

A cold wave swept through her and she got the feeling that something, somewhere, was terribly wrong.

Chapter 12

Charlotte stood in the intensive-care unit and stared at the battered body in the bed closest to the nurses' station. She put her hand to her mouth to stop the bile from rising in her throat. It's just the smell, she told herself, the smell of disinfectant. The smell and the fact that it was four in the morning and that she'd been ripped from sleep by a doorbell only three hours ago.

It wasn't the sight of her sister that was making her feel sick. No matter what Emily looked like, she was Charlotte's baby sister and Charlotte was going to look after her.

Although she still wasn't convinced it was Emily. She'd spoken to Emily only this morning in Killarney, and she'd been fine then.

Charlotte tried to ignore the tubes, some draining blood, some attached to pumps which forced liquids into the veins of the crash victim on the bed. She tried to see past the dressings and around the ventilator tubes. She needed to study the woman in the bed to spot some feature which would confirm that it was all a terrible mistake. That the woman lying there wasn't Emily. That it wasn't her bright, vibrant, beautiful sister who could run a mile in less than five minutes.

The poor unfortunate creature lying there was lucky, the doctor said. She had a good chance of pulling through. Despite a host of internal injuries, colossal blood loss and too many broken bones to count yet, they had patched her up and now it was up to her.

And suddenly Charlotte felt a surge of hope. Of course, it wasn't Emily. There was no way Emily would have let them cut her up like that. Emily, who exercised and dieted to keep her body looking perfect, the way she wanted it, would never have tolerated a surgeon taking a scalpel to her perfect skin. Would not have sat back passively as they shaved half her head or cut a hole in her chest to insert that awful tube. Charlotte almost laughed out loud at the notion. It was ridiculous. She could just see her now, scolding them. She remembered Emily, at ten, coldly informing a young doctor in Castlemichael infirmary that if he left a scar on her knee from the stitches he was putting in, she would sue.

So Charlotte knew she had to find Donal, to stop him from making all those phone-calls. No need to panic people unnecessarily. Then she saw him coming through the door of the ward. He looked drawn and pale and his hair was tossed. The neon lights gave his skin an almost grey hue. The rugby shirt he wore was crumpled; like

Charlotte he had grabbed the first clothes to hand. His rubber soles squeaked on the vinyl floor. Those shoes normally irritated Charlotte, the way they squeaked like that, but tonight she loved them. It was a human sound amidst all the humming, clicking and purring of machines. It was a sound she associated with Donal walking on the wooden floors at home, or on the tiles of the restaurant kitchen.

He tried to smile at Charlotte when he saw her and put Emily's small purple address book back in his pocket – the book the policeman had taken from her pocket at the scene of the accident.

Charlotte looked back at the bed and knew she had to face the truth.

"She's back from the operating theatre, then? How is she?" Donal propelled Charlotte towards an orange plastic chair and lowered her gently on to it just before her legs crumpled beneath her.

Charlotte shrugged, unable to talk. The words she needed were lost in the muddy swamp that was her brain. She tried not to think that this might be what Emily's brain was like now. When Emily was brought back from theatre a doctor had spoken to her, but the only phrases Charlotte could remember were "stable", "head injury" and "next few days". It was like a script from *ER*, and Charlotte wanted to get off set. She had an urge to shout "*Cut!*"

"Who did you call?" Charlotte forced herself to speak, to regain some control over what was happening.

"Just your mum, Tara's parents and Paul."

When the nurse suggested tactfully that Emily's family should be called and might want to come to her bedside, Donal knew Paul would want to be here.

"And how is … *she?*" Charlotte couldn't say the name Tara. Tara who had been driving. Who had failed to stop at a red light. Who had hit a truck and almost taken the side off her car. The passenger side.

"Tara's fine, considering." Donal said slowly. "Badly bruised, a couple of broken ribs, but the air-bag took the worst of it."

"Did you ask her what happened?"

"No, I couldn't go in to her. She's asleep … sedated." He added the last word quickly when he saw the look of shock on Charlotte's face. Donal too had found it hard to believe. In fact the sight of six women asleep, when his sister-in-law was fighting for her life on the operating table, had sickened him. He wanted to shake the whispering nurse, make her understand that this wasn't just another nightshift. Emily might be dying, might already be dead.

Donal left Charlotte and went into the glass-enclosed nurses' station. When he came back, a nurse followed him. Donal kneeled at Charlotte's feet, and rubbed her icy hands between his own. He spoke slowly, enunciating each syllable carefully.

"Emily's going to pull through, love. She's strong." He stopped to clear the huge lump in his throat. "She's heavily sedated at the moment and that's why she looks so awful. Her body needs to rest and her brain's swollen. The tube to help her breathe is there because of the anaesthetic; they'll leave it in for a few days so that they can keep her doped up. All the other tubes are providing her with the fluid she needs, and the drugs."

The nurse took over then and explained every tube and machine to the couple, breaking down Emily's life support into manageable bits. She knew how afraid they were. The first time she had walked onto an intensive care ward, as a student nurse, it had terrified her. The unnatural quiet disturbed only by the click and purr of pumps and respirators. She had uttered a prayer that day that she would never walk onto one as a relative. And tonight, as always when confronted by a family like this, she thought of her own children asleep at home, and of her husband, and repeated her prayer.

"Your sister's alive, Charlotte," she repeated gently. "And being kept alive until she can take over for herself. Now all we can do is wait."

Donal held his wife as she finally broke down and sobbed.

Paul laid his fingers on Emily's forearm, the only bit of unmarked skin he could find. He wanted to hold her hand, but one of her fingers was clamped in a clip, connected by wire to a machine displaying glowing green numbers. The numbers fluctuated around the high nineties. He stared. Ninety-nine. Ninety-seven. Ninety-eight. Ninety-nine.

Hit one hundred, you bastard! he screamed silently at it. If he wanted it enough, if he really willed it with all his strength, Paul knew the machine would hit one hundred, and Emily would wake up. But it danced away to its own rhythm, teasing, with several ninety-nines in a row. He had come to hate that machine. This was the third time he had sat with Emily and it was the first time he was on his own.

It was less than thirty-six hours since the accident. Too soon to tell anything yet. The most recent brain scan showed some improvement but, although they had lightened the sedation, Emily was no nearer regaining consciousness.

"Can she hear anything?" Paul asked a nurse who was writing on Emily's chart.

"It's unlikely at this stage – she's still sedated, but there's no way of knowing for sure. Talk to her. It might help." The nurse didn't add that the person it would help most was the unshaven, red-eyed man beside the bed.

"Emily …" Paul leaned towards her. "Emily, I don't know if you can hear me. Please wake up, Emms. I miss you." The tears began to flow down his face. Now that he was on his own with her he could cry. He had felt guilty at his urge to break down when Charlotte was there. She was doing her best to hold up for Sheila's sake, and they had so much more claim on Emily than he did.

"Emms," he sobbed, "try to wake up! Try to listen to me. I'm going to keep saying this until you do wake up, so if you want to yell at me for being stupid, you'd better hurry. I love you, Emily. Not in the way we've pretended to love each other for years, as best friends, or brother and sister, but in the way I've always loved you. I want to spend every minute with you, every minute of the day and night. So wake up and push me away like you always do. You have to wake up to do that, Emms. And until you do, I'm going to sit here and bleat in your ear how much I love you. Just wake up, damn you!"

Paul leaned over, putting his ear closer to her mouth in case some word was trying to make its way past that infernal tube. But all he could hear was the *hiss-thump-hiss* of the machine forcing air into her chest, making it rise and fall with clockwork regularity.

He jumped when he felt a hand on his shoulder. He swiped his sleeve across his face, ashamed that Sheila should see him crying. She'd held up better than all of them so far. She put a hand out to stop him, shaking her head, reaching into her pocket for a tissue.

"Charlotte will be a while yet," she said, meaning that he could cry all he wanted. She sat on the chair beside Paul's and took his free hand in hers. They sat in silence until Donal and Charlotte returned.

Then Paul, wanting to leave them alone with Emily, but not ready to leave the hospital, found himself in Tara's ward.

"She discharged herself against medical advice about two hours ago," a nurse told him.

Paul felt his body deflate as the air hissed out of it in a big sigh. He had no idea why he had come to see Tara. She was the last person on earth he wanted to see. But he had to have an answer to his question. Not that it would change anything.

"Had she been drinking?" he'd asked Donal when he heard that Tara was driving. Donal shrugged his shoulders; it hardly mattered now, did it? But it did, to Paul it did. He'd always known Tara was trouble, but he'd never warned Emily and it was all his fault.

"Where did she go?" Paul asked the nurse, shaking his head. He couldn't believe Tara had just been able to get up and walk out.

"Home, I presume – she called a taxi. She'd have been discharged tomorrow anyway, but she wouldn't wait." The nurse looked at the stricken look on the face of the handsome man in front of her. "Are you a friend of hers? A relative?"

"Ehmm, a friend."

The small blonde debated for a moment or two.

"You should warn her," she said finally. "The Guards were in, enquiring about the results of her blood tests. She took off soon afterwards. But they came back about an hour later and they were none too impressed that she wasn't around to answer their questions."

"How long ago did you say she had left?"

"About two hours ago. Why?" The nurse shook her head, puzzled at the speed Paul took off down the ward.

"Tara, pick up! Answer the phone – I know you're there!" Paul yelled into his mobile phone. "Don't do this, you bitch. You've done enough damage!"

He bellowed in frustration as the answering machine cut him off again. He looked at the scribbled address on the car seat beside him and checked the names of the apartment blocks. Why the hell couldn't they have numbers?

"Tara!" He hammered on her door when he finally reached it. He'd pressed every buzzer in the block until someone let him in. "Tara, open the goddamned door!"

A neighbour poked her head out the door in alarm.

"Is she in there?" he yelled at her.

"I'm going to call the police if you don't leave," the old woman threatened.

"Tell me, did you see her come home? Is she in there?"

The woman retreated inside her door.

"Call an ambulance while you're at it!" Paul screamed after her, then stepped back and threw his weight against the door. It shuddered but didn't yield.

The neighbour, alarmed by talk of ambulances, abandoned all thought of the police and came outside again. She stepped forward hesitantly. "Tara leaves me a key. Do you think there's something wrong?" She held out the key, then snatched her arm back when the terrifying young man grabbed it from her outstretched hand.

"Tara! Tara! Where are you? Check the other bedroom!" he shouted to the elderly woman hovering at the door. "No, don't bother, I've found her! Call an ambulance! Tell them it looks like an overdose."

He dropped to his knees in the en-suite bathroom, and picked up Tara's lifeless body.

"Wake up!" he screamed. "You have no bloody right to do this to them. They've been through enough. Wake up, you self-indulgent bitch!" He shook her and slapped her face.

Her eyes fluttered open for a moment, then closed again.

He lifted her to the edge of the bath, draped her body over the edge and turned the cold shower on her head. She spluttered and opened her eyes again.

"What did you take?" Paul pulled her up by the hair so that she could see him. He told himself that he was just trying to wake her up but he knew that he was being rougher than he needed to be. That he wanted to hurt her. "What did you take?" he repeated, clenching his hand into a fist and seeing her wince with pain as his fingers pulled at the roots of her hair.

"Ebberysing," she slurred. "But not nuff." She began to sob but her eyes fluttered closed again.

"Stay awake, damn you!" He shook her.

"Paul!" Tara opened her eyes and a vacant, lopsided smile deformed her face. "Whah choo doing here?"

"What did you take?" he cajoled. He spoke with a deadly calm now. He was afraid she'd lose consciousness again and he wanted to be able to give some information to the ambulance staff. He looked around the bathroom for bottles, but saw only one packet of headache tablets, almost untouched. *"What – did – you – take?"* He tried to contain his anger.

"Ebberrrryssing....." She closed her eyes again.

"What?" He shook her.

"Coke, lotsh of coke … and pillsh, all my pillsh, all my lovely pillsh …"

"Where are the bottles?" He wanted to read the labels.

"Oh, Paul," she giggled hysterically, "my special pharmash … my special sharmaph … my special chemist doesn't shupply in little bottles …" She giggled

226

again at the notion.

Shit! Paul thought to himself, a cocktail of illegal drugs.

"Do you know what you took?"

"Oh Paul, you're no fun ..." She reached up to touch his face, then fell asleep again.

He lifted her up and contemplated sticking his fingers down her throat to make her vomit, but was afraid of choking her. He lay her on her side on the living-room floor, a rug covering her, while he searched for some clue as to what she might have taken.

But she had told the truth when she said she had taken everything. The only trace he found was the remains of a suspicious-looking white powder in her make-up bag. He gave it to the paramedics when they arrived.

"Do you want to come with us?" one of them asked him as they loaded her onto a stretcher.

"No!" The thought repulsed him. "Where are you taking her?"

The ambulance driver named the hospital Paul had just left.

"Shit!" he said, wiping his hands on his trouser legs as they carried the stretcher out the door.

Somehow he had imagined they would take her somewhere else. Although if they transferred her to the other side of the country, it still wouldn't be far enough from Emily.

"Ahem!"

Paul jumped. He was still standing in Tara's flat with the door open. He had no idea how long had he been standing there. He had a vague recollection of Tara's neighbour saying he looked like he needed a cup of tea, but she hadn't come back with it yet. Instead two uniformed gardai stood at the door.

"This is where the young lady from the ambulance was found?" one of them asked.

Paul nodded.

"Can we come in?"

"Of course. I mean, I don't know." His law degree snapped into action in his mind. "It's not actually my place, so you need the owner's consent if you want to search it, unless you have a search warrant."

They looked at him strangely.

"You found her?"

"Yes."

"How did you get in?"

"A neighbour gave me the key – I tried to break down the door, but I couldn't."

"How did you know …?"

"Any idiot could have worked it out! I can't believe she was allowed to just walk out of the hospital …" Suddenly he realised that they had no idea what he was talking about. "Do you mind?" He pointed to the sofa and collapsed into it. He put his head between his hands and tried to frame his thoughts. "She was involved in an accident a couple of days ago. She was …" Paul's legal training kicked in again. Convinced though he was that Tara had been drunk, even under the influence of something else at the time, he didn't know it for sure, and he had no right to say it to the young officer scribbling in his notebook. "She was the driver. Her passenger was injured. Your lot came looking for her blood-test results from the hospital, and she just took off. It didn't take a genius to work it out."

"You know her well enough to guess this was the kind of thing she might do?"

Paul nodded, realising he probably did.

"Are you her – boyfriend?"

"No!"

"Do you know where she got the drugs for this?"

Shit! Paul was pretty sure he hadn't mentioned illegal drugs to them. To the ambulance men, yes, but the guards hadn't arrived till later. The paramedics must have passed on the information when they reported the overdose. "I don't know what –"

"Look, we just need to know what you were doing here, that's all." The older man wore a neutral expression.

Paul realised they suspected him of something. Maybe even of supplying the drugs.

"Emily – I mean, the other woman, the passenger in the car – she's ... she's ... my best friend." God, that sounded pathetic. "She's very special to me. She nearly died. She still hasn't woken up. They don't know if she will. I went to see how Tara was. And when I heard how she'd taken off, I just didn't think Emily's family needed ..." he gestured helplessly towards the bathroom. "Not on top of everything else."

"Sorry," the older man said gruffly. He handed Paul a peach-coloured tissue from a box on Tara's bookcase. Paul hadn't even realised he was crying. "Do you want a lift to the hospital?"

"No, my car's downstairs."

"Can we leave you here to lock up?"

"I'd rather not." Paul walked to the door before they could object. "Her neighbour has the key."

Chapter 13

Charlotte felt tears flowing down her cheeks as she watched Dave lift the veil and kiss his new wife and she swiped at her eyes with a tissue in frustration. She was crying too much lately. She'd cried this morning in Anne-Marie's house when Emily had phoned from her hospital bed to wish her friend well on her wedding day. She had cried for hours when her sister finally woke up a week ago after five days in a coma. She cried when she heard about the list of operations Emily would still have to endure, although she'd tuned out of the details. (She felt faint when the doctors talked about repairing Emily's bowel, inserting a feeding tube into her neck, pinning and plating her mangled bones.)

She'd cried when she heard Paul tell Emily over and over how much he loved her, and she cried even harder when she realised that he'd stopped saying it now that she was awake again. She'd cried when the first words

Emily spoke, after being told what happened, were to ask after Tara. And she cried when she had to tell Emily that Tara had been charged with causing the accident, and that she had signed herself into psychiatric care after her overdose.

And she'd done enough crying, she now decided. Today was Anne-Marie's big day and she owed it to her friend to do her best to share it with at least some enjoyment. She forced a huge smile onto her face as Anne-Marie turned to walk down the aisle of Castlemichael church, but felt a lump in her throat as she saw her own two daughters lead the way, scattering rose-petals on the red carpet.

"OK?" Donal squeezed her hand.

"OK." She smiled back at him. She had so much to be thankful for, hadn't she?

Marcus sat in his car outside the Parkview Hotel. What the hell was he doing here, he asked himself for the hundredth time. OK, so he had rung both of Charlotte's restaurants several times in the past two weeks, and had been given the run-around, but this was tantamount to stalking, wasn't it? If he was still in the States he could be arrested for this. He wondered why Charlotte wouldn't take his calls. He couldn't believe she hadn't been at work at least one of the times he'd phoned. And what about the messages – surely they would have been passed on?

Marcus just wanted to see Charlotte. He couldn't really understand why. Since returning to Ireland he hadn't been able to put her out of his mind. It was as if, adrift now that he had to start again here, he had been thrown back in time to the months after he heard she was engaged to Donal Moran. Marcus hadn't really believed she'd go through with it, but he was still eaten up with jealousy. He'd hung around the Long Library in Trinity, almost expecting to see her running out of the chapel at the last minute, and instead he'd had to endure watching her being congratulated by friends and family on her wedding day. Her wedding to someone else.

And here he was lurking outside another wedding. He'd been in the lobby of the hotel, hoping to catch a glimpse of Charlotte, maybe even say a few words to her. But as he waited, and some of the guests arrived ahead of the main wedding party, he saw Suzy. Suddenly Marcus realised he had no right to be here. Being here might even cause trouble for Charlotte, and anyway, her best friend's wedding was hardly the day to confront her.

So he retreated to the car, convinced that no one had recognised him, and here he was, hoping to get a glimpse of her. How pathetic was that? He put the key in the ignition and drove off.

Charlotte got through the day with only one more burst of tears. Anne-Marie made a speech after the meal, and asked everyone to remember Emily who should have been here today as bridesmaid. The other missing guest, Tara, wasn't mentioned.

Suzy was sitting at the Moran's table where Charlotte had asked Anne-Marie to put her in Tara's place so that there wouldn't be an empty seat. Besides, Suzy'd been great for the past two weeks. She couldn't do enough to help Donal and Charlotte. She'd even let Gemma spend all day Saturday under her feet in the much smaller kitchen of the second restaurant. Now she was chatting animatedly with Donal, a strange brightness in her eyes. If she didn't know that Suzy never drank, Charlotte would have sworn that she'd been hitting the champagne too hard. She was surprised how relieved she felt that their period of estrangement seemed to be over. Sometimes it took a tragedy to bring people together.

Charlotte smiled and turned to Etienne who was sitting beside her. She felt slightly sorry for him. Suzy was concentrating so much effort on making up for lost time with herself and Donal, that she was neglecting her boyfriend a bit. The Frenchman was uncharacteristically quiet. Charlotte had never known him not to have anything to say for himself, but then she usually saw him in the restaurant where he was waxing lyrical about some new wine he was trying to sell, or extolling the virtues of a new truffle supplier he'd unearthed.

"It's a good day, isn't it?" Charlotte was surprised to realise that she didn't know what to talk to Etienne about, other than work. "So when are you and Suzy going to give us a day out?"

"Sorry?" Etienne's English didn't stretch to that particular idiom.

"A day out – an excuse to buy a new outfit!" Charlotte laughed. "When will you be inviting us to a day like this?"

"Hmmph," the Frenchman snorted, looking over at

Suzy who had her hand on Donal's arm as they shared a story. Then he turned back to Charlotte and gave her one of his enigmatic smiles. "You know Suzy."

Charlotte smiled, though lately, she wasn't sure how well she did. And she could never figure out her friend's relationship with Etienne. He'd asked Suzy to move in with him several times, but each time she'd come up with another excuse. Charlotte hoped Suzy wasn't stringing him along. Maybe she was holding out for more than living together. She was certainly holding out for something.

Charlotte watched Suzy as she turned to Gemma who was sitting on her other side. For a moment she looked annoyed at having been interrupted, then her face lit up with a smile and she chatted easily to her goddaughter, and even Tim who was on his best behaviour for once. Donal smiled as he watched Tim and Gemma compete for Suzy's attention, then turned his attention to Sheila who was sitting on his other side. Yes, thought Charlotte, although Emily may be lying seriously ill in hospital, I have a lot to be grateful for.

Paul spent the day with Emily because he knew she was upset not to be at Anne-Marie's wedding. He was supposed to be at it with her. He had longed to hold her as she fought back tears after phoning Anne-Marie.

"I let her down, Paul. I was supposed to be her bridesmaid. I never went to any of her fittings, she as good as organised her own hen party, and now I'm not even there on the day."

He was ashamed at his relief not to be watching yet another of their friends getting hitched, while he sat again with the only woman he could ever imagine himself making that kind of commitment to. In the week since she had woken up, he had spent most of his free time with her, only leaving when he got the impression her family were beginning to get irritated by his hovering presence. But today, at Emily's insistence, they had all gone to the wedding, and Charlotte had been relieved when he said he'd stay with her.

Emily was no longer in the intensive care unit, but in a private room. It was bright and airy, with huge windows, but Emily wanted the blinds closed.

Paul kept telling himself that she'd been through a lot, and that it was only a week since she'd woken up, but he was worried about her. Her moods swung from elation at surviving to morose refusal to discuss her condition. She closed her eyes any time the nursing staff came into the room to check her feeding tube and dressings, or to administer drugs, and she submitted silently to their ministrations. Paul had tried, despite his own squeamishness, to bring up the subject of the operations she had already gone through and those she had yet to face, but he gave up when he saw her eyes glaze over.

Instead he brought her videos and books and gossip. They had such similar taste in reading that he knew she would enjoy anything he liked himself. It also meant they had something to talk about.

He had never had any trouble sharing silence with her before, but it was never silent in this room. Any gap in conversation made his flesh creep as the whirring of the pump, feeding milky liquid through a tube into her veins, got louder and louder. He noticed that Emily never tolerated quiet either. The television, radio or video were always blaring when she was alone, and at night she fell asleep with earphones feeding sound from the portable CD player on her locker.

Paul cursed the fact that he hadn't been there when she woke up. If he had, he might have had the courage to tell her what he'd repeated hour after hour as she lay unconscious. But when he walked into the unit, and saw her surrounded by Charlotte, Sheila and Anne-Marie, he'd stopped dead. There was an air of false jollity. With her eyes open, most of the bandages off her face, and the tubes removed from her mouth and nose, she looked like Emily again. And she looked bloody awful. Although her head had miraculously avoided any major injury, her face was bruised, cut and swollen. She looked weak and broken and it broke his heart. The sheer joy he felt when Charlotte phoned him to tell him that Emily was awake evaporated when he looked at her and realised how much further she had to go. One step at a time, he tried to tell himself, but it was no good. The woman he loved was going to go through hell on earth for the next few months and there was nothing he could do to help her. A declaration of love at a time like this seemed selfish and self-indulgent. She needed to focus all her energy inwards, to get better.

Emily opened her eyes and reached for the remote

control as soon as she was sure Paul was gone. She hit the button for Sky News and closed her eyes again. She fought the tears, which had been threatening to spill from her eyes as they had discussed the latest novel he had brought her. She had only skimmed through it, unable to concentrate, but she had to get some idea of what it was about if she was going to be able to nod in agreement whenever he came in and rabbited on about it for hours. She wished she had the guts to say biting and caustic things to him, to drive him away, but she needed him. Even though he was so obviously repulsed by her in the state she was in.

She couldn't blame him; she hated herself for the tenacious hold she seemed to have on this broken wreck of a body. Everyone said, wasn't she great, a real fighter? But she wasn't. She was a coward. She was afraid of dying. Even poor old messed-up Tara had more courage than she had.

While she was still in the intensive care unit, Emily had felt lucky. She was alive. Against all the odds, she was still here. But now, if someone ignored her angry order to "Shut the door!", she could see other patients walking past in their nightclothes or even ordinary clothes while she was still in a hospital gown. No couturier had ever designed a garment to fit over the contraptions attached to her. Frames to immobilise her hips and legs. Bandages across her chest. One arm up in the air at an odd angle, plastered to repair her collarbone.

This was lucky?

And the tubes. They were the worst. She'd been awake

for nearly a day before it occurred to her that she hadn't had to face the indignity of asking for a bedpan. The nurse explained that she wouldn't need one. There were as many tubes coming out as there were going in, it seemed, but Emily didn't want the details. She felt that she was reduced to a bundle of cells being managed from the outside. They forced a series of healing and feeding liquids into her through one set of tubes, and they collected and measured her filth through the rest.

And Emily was devastated that Paul couldn't cope with her like this. Her family loved her because she was family. But so far he was the only non-family member to visit her and he didn't seem to love her any more. She kept waiting for him to say that he still loved her; that none of this mattered, but he didn't. Paul who had told her he loved her at the most inopportune moments, who had kissed her with a longing he couldn't hide, couldn't tell her she was lovable now that she needed it most.

He was here because he pitied her, and although she hated his pity, she couldn't help wanting him near her.

The morning after Anne-Marie's wedding, Charlotte dropped a few items she didn't really need into her trolley in the supermarket in Castlemichael. She'd handed in some photos to a one-hour developing booth, and she needed to kill some time. Donal had drunk a bit too much last night and was still in bed in the hotel, so Charlotte wanted to let him sleep it off. She couldn't begrudge him the rest. He really deserved it. He'd done so much the past couple of weeks, keeping everything together, when Charlotte could have let their whole world fall about her ears and not notice.

"Put those back, Tim!" Her son had picked up three multi-packs of crisps and snacks and was about to throw them into the trolley on top of Aisling, who had beaten her brother in the race to climb into the trolley while their mother wasn't looking.

"We'll need something to eat on the journey back, Mum!" He protested.

"It only takes an hour to get home. Don't be ridiculous." Charlotte looked at Tim's truculent face and then relented. He'd been so good yesterday. "Oh, all right then. One bag. And not Monster Munch, Aisling hates them."

"Cool, Mum!"

"Still sensible, I see, Charlotte," someone said behind her.

Charlotte's heart stopped as she recognised the voice. She turned around slowly, hoping she was imagining things.

She wasn't.

She examined Marcus. He hadn't changed much. His hair was slightly shorter, but it was still thick and wavy and dark, stopping just short of his collar. He looked heavier, but there was no fat on his face, and she could see the outline of muscles under his T-shirt. He'd obviously been working out. In the gloomy supermarket, his dark eyes looked blacker than ever. Even without their history, Charlotte suspected that he'd have rendered her breathless by his sheer good looks alone.

"Are these your children?"

Tim stood defending the trolley, and Aisling looked up suspiciously at him from where she was sitting amongst the groceries. Charlotte realised they were all waiting for her to say something.

"This is… Marcus," she managed at last. "A friend of Mummy's from when she was … when I was younger. This is Tim, and this is Aisling."

"Tim's not your eldest, is he?"

"No, Gemma's with her grandmother." Charlotte muttered a silent prayer of thanks.

"Are you all visiting?"

"What?"

"Are you all visiting Granny?" Marcus smiled. "You live in Dublin now, don't you?"

"I … we … yes, we live in Dublin. We're down for Anne-Marie's wedding. You remember Anne-Marie, don't you? She got married yesterday. To a guy called Dave McMorrow – he's a doctor, a consultant actually, in geriatric medicine, or whatever it is they call it. That's her fiancé, well, her husband now I suppose seeing as they got married yesterday. They're going to Florence on honeymoon." Charlotte stopped, aware that Marcus was smiling at her babbling. "I didn't know … I mean … when did you get back to Ireland?"

"Only a few weeks ago. I tried to call you …"

"Why?"

"Just to say hi. I tried both your restaurants, but you haven't been in much …"

"Hectic few weeks." She didn't want to explain. It

would take too long. She wanted to get out of this shop and back to the hotel, to Donal and safety. Marcus was having a disturbing effect on her and it scared her.

"... and I didn't have a home phone number for you ...?" He paused, hopefully.

"No, I suppose you didn't. Look, I'm sorry but Donal's waiting for me back at the hotel. We have to go back to Dublin. They're expecting us at work." She had no intention of going anywhere near work for the rest of the weekend. "Saturday lunch-time is always busy."

"I'd like to meet up with you sometime, Charlotte."

"I don't know ..."

"Just as friends. I've lost touch with most of my friends in Ireland ... and I'm separated from Denise ..."

"I know."

"Oh." Marcus looked pleasantly surprised.

"I really have to go." Charlotte piled her shopping onto the counter, ignoring the disapproving look the cashier gave her when she saw such a big child sitting in the trolley. She paid, picked up her two bags of groceries, then realised Aisling was still in the trolley and was unwilling to get out on her own.

"Here, allow me." Marcus swung the six-year-old out with a big jump and pushed the trolley over to the others.

"Thanks," Charlotte mumbled resentfully.

"Anytime. You have two very beautiful kids. Aisling's the image of you, Tim I can see a bit of Donal in, but he has your eyes. And your hair obviously." He ruffled Tim's carrot hair with his hand. "Who does your eldest –

Gemma, wasn't it? Who does she take after?"

"Donal," Charlotte said firmly, pushing Tim and Aisling in front of her to the door. "Although she has blonde hair, a bit like Emily's."

"It was nice seeing you again, Charlotte," he said to her retreating back. "Say hello to Donal for me."

Why now? Charlotte threw her bags of groceries into the boot while the kids fastened their seatbelts. Have I not enough on my plate at the moment? She drove to Sheila's to collect Gemma and then back to the hotel.

"Hi, gorgeous!" Donal stood up from where he had been sitting in the lobby and kissed Charlotte full on the lips. He lingered, obviously still in the afterglow from last night's lovemaking. He smelled of soap and shampoo and he tasted of toothpaste and coffee. His hair was still damp from the shower. Charlotte leaned against him in giddy relief.

"I've paid the bill, but the bags are still in the room," Donal said, breaking free from her. "Will we hit the road?"

"Yes, let's go." She was glad to keep moving; she'd wait until they were in the car before she mentioned meeting Marcus.

That evening Charlotte turned her key in the front door and leaned against it as it opened. She was exhausted. She'd taken a taxi back from the hospital where Donal had dropped her on the way back from Castlemichael. She'd called in to show Emily the photos of the wedding but it had been a difficult afternoon, with Emily in a weepy mood. Although she tried not to cry in front of people, the atmosphere was strained when she was holding back tears. Charlotte wished to God she'd just let go, and bawl her eyes out. She had asked the nurses if her sister was behaving normally, refusing to cry, but they just said it was early days and every one had to cope in their own way. But if Emily burst into tears then Charlotte could put her arms around her, comfort her. She'd feel like she was doing something useful. She realised with shame that she had half hoped the wedding photos would break the dam and let the tears out.

The house was quiet. Donal had taken Gemma into work with him and the other two children were with Hannah. They'd slept more nights in her flat than they had at home for the past two weeks and Charlotte couldn't imagine how they'd have coped without her.

But life would have to struggle its way back to normal now, she thought as she ran a bath. The children were at school for another couple of weeks before the summer holidays, the restaurant needed Charlotte's input and she would have to stop relying on other people to keep the house habitable. The nurse in charge of her sister's care had pulled her aside as she left this evening. He explained gently that Emily had months of recovery ahead of her. She needed the support of her family and friends, but Charlotte had to make time for her own family too. It was time Emily let other people visit her, he said. The ward had received streams of phone calls from friends and colleagues asking after her, but she kept saying she was too tired or too weak to see anyone.

"Emily can't go out at the moment, so she's got to let the world come to her," he pointed out. "She has to see that there are loads of people who want her to get better, who care about her. She can't keep pretending that life's on hold until she's ready to join it again. It'll be hard for her, seeing her friends visit then leave again while she's trapped there, but …" He shrugged.

Charlotte knew he was right. Emily was surrounded by trained experts dealing with every aspect of her physical recovery, so her family and friends had to work on her mind.

She sank into the bubbles, feeling the hot water suck some of the tension from her muscles, and closed her eyes. What a day!

She still hadn't told Donal about Marcus. She'd waited for one of the kids to mention meeting someone in the supermarket, and then she'd say something along the lines of "Oh wow, I forgot. You'll never guess who I met?" But as they drove into Dublin, and Donal pulled onto the road to the hospital, she realised that she was always meeting people she knew in Castlemichael, so the kids hadn't thought it the slightest bit remarkable. Before she could think of another opening, she was on her way in to visit Emily.

Then she thought that maybe she'd practise talking about Marcus to her sister. Try out a few lines, maybe even take Emily's mind off her own troubles, but she hadn't found a way to start the conversation with her either. "You'll never guess who I saw down the supermarket?" sounded too much like the opening line of a comedy act and Emily was in no mood for laughing.

In the end Charlotte decided to say nothing about meeting Marcus. She remembered how Donal had reacted to learning she'd met Marcus's wife for coffee and, after all, it was pure chance that she had run into him. If he rang the restaurant again, then she'd talk to Donal about it. There was no point causing trouble if Marcus decided, after the way she'd treated him today, that he didn't want to have anything more to do with her.

Chapter 14

A few months later, in the steaming heat of her kitchen, Suzy Brady was having a bad day.

"Those scallops are overdone!" she screamed, poking the offending shellfish. "Pure rubber!" She bounced one off the floor to demonstrate, then flung the whole plate on the counter in front of the chef responsible. "Do another lot."

She was being a total bitch today, but she couldn't help it. If she hadn't been screaming at Tony about the duck salad, he wouldn't have overcooked the scallops, she realised. She'd apologise to him tomorrow. When she'd decided what to do about Etienne.

His ultimatum had come out of the blue, just when Suzy thought they were settling into a comfortable pattern. It was so long since he'd asked her to move in with him that she assumed he accepted that she wanted to keep things as they were. She valued her independence, her privacy. Not that she didn't want to settle down one day... But she wasn't one hundred per cent sure that

Etienne was the right guy. In fact she couldn't be eighty, seventy, even sixty per cent sure.

"Idiot!" She screamed as much at herself as at the waitress who'd brought the wrong starter to table two.

There was nothing wrong with Etienne. She loved him; he loved her; she was happy with him. One day they were going to open a restaurant together. One day they were going to settle down together and fill a little stone cottage with children. So why did the fool have to ruin it all by asking her to marry him? Now of all times? He hadn't said it was all off if she refused, but she knew. When she didn't say yes straight away, he said he'd give her time to think about it. He was going back to France for an uncle's funeral. He would extend his stay, see some suppliers, renew some contacts and come back to Ireland in about a month's time. They agreed not to talk about his proposal on the phone, but to wait till he got back.

Oh, Etienne was so reasonable that sometimes Suzy wanted to scream at him. But most of the time she wanted to say 'Yes! Yes! Yes! I will marry you. I love you, take me back to France with you and we'll open up our restaurant there. Away from the mad insanity of my life in Ireland'. But she knew she couldn't. She could no more break the string that tied her to the Morans than she could turn her back on her father, when he rang in the small hours of the morning to say her mother was bad again.

Tara took a deep breath as she pushed open her front door for the first time in four months. Her counsellor would probably go ape-shit if he thought she was trying to face this on her own. But then Marty was a bit of a wet. He thought that fifteen years' alcoholism and gambling qualified him to understand the depths that she, Tara, had sunk to.

No, this was one thing she had to face alone. This was going to be so much more difficult than the others. She'd faced her father with his pity; her mother with her hurt questioning; she'd faced her sister; she'd faced Charlotte. She'd even faced Emily. And always Marty, or some other professional was there, silently in the background, to help her as much as to prevent her chickening out. But this, she had to face herself. She had to come to terms with the fact that she'd tried to run away from them all.

There wasn't a speck of dust anywhere. The cream throws on the overstuffed sofa had been dry-cleaned. There was a smell of cleaning fluid and bleach lingering in the air. She'd rung her cleaner, Dolores, and said she'd be back sometime in the next two weeks and the poor woman must have dropped everything and come over straight away.

Tara smiled as she checked the drinks cabinet in her living-room and then the cupboard beside the fridge and then the fridge itself. She wondered who'd cleared them out. She'd told Dolores to take anything she found, but she had a feeling her father would have got there first. Hiding behind his jovial pity was shame. Shame at the way his daughter had fallen, let him down. He'd do his damnedest to make sure she didn't relapse …

She was in the main bedroom now. Her bedroom. Stark and minimalist, like the rest of the apartment, it was almost devoid of colour. The ragged pink teddy bear lying across her pillow was the only sign that this was a room that belonged to someone, that it wasn't a hotel room. An angular black ash bed-head with two lockers contrasted with the soft white counterpane, the white walls and the floor of the palest wood she had been able to find. Hopelessly unfashionable now, but she loved the look, and the feeling it gave her to come home to. This was her space, her safe place. She never brought anyone in here but she wondered would it ever feel safe again.

The bathroom door was ajar, revealing a few black mosaic tiles on the floor and the pedestal of the small sink.

"Breathe," Tara reminded herself out loud.

She took a step closer to the door and reached out until she could almost touch it. Then she leaned forward and pushed it open. The bathroom looked no different.

Why did Tara feel almost disappointed? What trace, what signs had she expected to find? Proof of the drama that had played itself out here four months ago?

Tara sat on the edge of the bath and tried to remember. She still hadn't answered the question. It haunted her. She'd searched her soul, her memory, her conscience but she didn't know the answer. Every psychiatrist, therapist, counsellor had asked it in some form or other.

She'd wept, screamed, meditated even, but she still didn't know if she had really intended to kill herself.

When she stumbled out of hospital after the accident, she was desperate for a fix. Desperate to lose the pain and to escape from what had happened to Emily. But rather than numbing her, the drugs had heightened her senses, made her aware of what she'd done, terrified of what she'd done. And terrified of the consequences – already the guards wanted to ask about the accident. And that was why she couldn't really answer the question. Had she really wanted to die when she took more and more. Had she really wanted to smash her life into oblivion? Or had she just wanted to escape the consequences of her actions? Had she been glad when Paul found her; glad that now they would all know how disgusted she was with herself, without her having to make the whole sacrifice? She couldn't remember. She could remember nothing from the moment she'd lined up the coke, and laid out all her pills in a little row.

The room began to close in on her. Suddenly Tara knew she'd been mad to come here alone. She tried to stand up. She pulled herself up on the sink but her legs were like jelly. She made it as far as the bed, then sank onto the edge of it in panic.

"I need a drink."

The words shattered the silence. Tara realised they'd come from her own mouth, and she was terrified. She knew that if there was a single drink in the place, she'd be back on her downward spiral.

She punched numbers on the phone in her living-room.

Engaged. "Shit!" She tried again. "Marty!" she moaned. "Hang up; I need you." The engaged tone mocked her again.

She began to cry. How could she get out of here? She remembered all the pubs and off-licences between here and the sanctuary of her father's flat. She'd been a fool to go out alone. One step at a time, they'd said before she left the treatment centre. Two days out and Tara's confidence was shattered. She was going to fail, she knew it. How did she think she could do this on her own?

"You're not alone," a voice inside her said.

She went into the kitchen and picked her bag off the counter. She began to work her way through the numbers in her mobile phone. The first answer she got was Moran's Restaurant.

"Chef …" The receptionist quaked with terror at the door of the kitchen; she'd already borne the brunt of Suzy's temper today. "Sorry to disturb you, Chef, but there's someone on the phone. She was looking for Charlotte or Donal. She sounds pretty desperate. She says her name's Tara Finlay."

"Better?" Suzy was waiting outside the parish hall.

"No, but I think I can survive the next few hours without a drink." Tara grinned feebly. "Thanks, Suzy. I'm sorry to take you out of work like that…"

"It doesn't matter," Suzy waved away her apology. "The staff probably cracked open a bottle of champagne when I left. I've been a total bitch all day."

Tara had hoped to reach Charlotte, or even Donal when the phone was answered in Moran's in town. When she was told that they were away for the weekend, she had cried into the phone. It was the sixth number she had tried and no one was in at this time on a Friday. She was surprised when Suzy came to the phone, spoke to her calmly and took her address. Meekly she let Suzy into the flat when she arrived, allowed her to push her arms back into her coat sleeves, then followed her to this old church hall. She didn't resist when the other woman pushed her through the door and found her a seat at the back of the already crowded room. It was the first meeting she'd attended on the outside and she was terrified. She didn't know any of these people. They all looked so normal. Imagine what they would think of her if they knew why she was here? After a while, she began to relax. They were just like her. Some of them had been through worse, and they were still here. Still dry.

"Thanks, Suzy. I don't know what I'd have done …"

"Night, Suze!" One of the men who had been in the hall greeted her on his way past.

Tara was suddenly aware that quite a few people had nodded or smiled at Suzy as they filed past into the evening air.

"How did you think I knew there was a meeting on?" Suzy smiled, answering Tara's question before she asked it.

"But you don't drink!" Tara protested. "I've never seen you drink."

"One day at a time. Come on, let's get out of here. I'm freezing."

"My mother was an alcoholic. *Is* an alcoholic," Suzy corrected. They were sitting in her flat, the remains of pizza and garlic bread hardening in a flat cardboard box on the coffee table, while they shared a tub of chocolate ice cream. "No one will admit there's anything wrong

253

with her. She functions normally for weeks on end, then goes on a binge, which could last a week." Suzy pulled her legs up under her and gripped her coffee cup. "When I was young, I could come home from school and find her passed out with a bottle beside her, or crying at the kitchen table. Once she was crying because the bottle was empty. I'd have to tidy her up and get her to bed before my younger sisters came home. It scared me. I didn't understand why she could suddenly change like that. It was always when my father was away – he was a travelling salesman. When I tried to tell him what was happening, he wouldn't believe me. Told me not to talk about my mother like that. One day I'd had enough. There was some vodka left in the bottle on the table. When I put Mum to bed, I came back down and drank it. I wanted to see what the attraction was.

And as soon as the liquid hit my stomach, I understood. I stopped caring that my mother was upstairs passed out. I wasn't worried that I'd have to make a meal for the others. It didn't matter that Dad was away and wouldn't be back until Friday. I had been stupid to think my problems were so huge. A few mouthfuls of vodka had put it all back into proportion for me. I was twelve.

"For the next five years, I think I probably had something to drink every day. It was painfully easy. I'd raid the drinks cabinet as soon as I came home from school, I knew where Mum kept her stashes, I hung around with older kids who drank cider from brown plastic bottles in the field behind the school." Suzy shuddered as she remembered the things she'd had to do to keep in with that older, mainly male crowd. "I think Mum guessed I was drinking. When she was drunk herself, she didn't mind. It meant I couldn't judge her. When she was sober, she felt too guilty to admit it, and it never occurred to Dad that there was anything wrong. Until I was seventeen. Then the school called him in. It had taken them that long to realise I was coming into school drunk or hung-over. I was bundled off to an aunt in Dublin, I went into treatment, and I've never lived at home since."

"And your mother?" Tara broke the silence.

"She still drinks. Not as often, but when she does … You see, we never admitted that there was anything wrong with Mum. Dad won't accept that the woman he married's a drunk. If he did, then maybe he might have to take responsibility for all the time he was away from home when I was young. No one at home knows why I left. The story was that I wanted to go to college in Dublin, and my aunt, who has no kids of her own, offered to let me live with her so that I could do my leaving in the Institute. I had missed so much school through 'glandular fever' that they said I needed a grind college. Even my sisters don't know the truth to this day. About me or Mum."

"Suzy …" Tara was almost afraid to ask, "did you ever drink … I mean after …"

"You're not supposed to ask that," Suzy grinned.

"I'm just so scared …" Suddenly the memory of earlier that evening was too much for Tara and her eyes filled with tears. "What if you hadn't been there? What about the next time? If I take another drink again … drugs … I can't go through all that again."

"Once." Suzy began to clear debris from the coffee table. While she was speaking, they'd consumed the tub of ice cream between them. "I came very close to drinking plenty of times, but only once I actually did."

She dumped the rubbish in the kitchen and came back with the coffee-pot to top up their mugs.

"A friend of mine, someone I loved, was about to make a huge mistake with his life. The person he trusted and loved was betraying him. I tried to tell him, but I couldn't. It would have meant destroying too many lives, and I wasn't sure of my motives – it could have been jealousy... And I suppose I couldn't be one hundred per cent certain ..." She sighed. "And she was a friend too. When it was too late, I hated myself for not saying something. So I hid from myself the only way I knew how."

Suzy remembered leaving after the reception, almost at a run. She tried to get a taxi, but ended up walking back to the flat her sisters shared in Harold's Cross. They were away for the weekend. She wanted a drink so badly. She'd watched the man she loved marry ... She opened the fridge. Her sister Tricia's six-pack of Budweiser stared out at her. She drank her way through it but it wasn't enough. Half a bottle of vodka was hidden in the bottom of May's wardrobe. She finished off the vodka, then ransacked the flat looking for more. She ended up downing a bottle of mouthwash before getting on the phone to someone from one of her meetings.

"And afterwards?" Tara had to know.

"I stopped again. I skipped lectures for about a week, so

that I didn't have to avoid going to the pub afterwards. I went to every meeting I could. And that was the last time. I've been tempted though. I think back to that time and I say, I got over it then, I can do it again … But the bottom line is that I don't know for certain if I can."

"Did you ever take … anything else?"

"Drugs? No, I never got into the scene really. I suppose I would have if they were available – towards the end no amount of vodka was doing it for me. But I wouldn't have known where to look. I was seventeen, living in a small rural town. The only option was glue …" She shuddered. "And that wasn't an option."

Suzy got ready for bed. She and Tara had talked well past midnight, then Suzy called a taxi to take her home to her father's place. Tara told Suzy about how her mother had been depressed throughout her childhood, a condition Tara suspected had been brought about by her father's many affairs. Tara was painfully shy – which wasn't helped by the fact that her mother wouldn't let her bring friends home. She discovered at an early age that a few drinks loosened her up, made her funny and attractive to guys.

A few drinks at the weekend developed into the inability to go and meet anyone without having a drink first. Then, when she was working and able to afford it, she discovered cocaine, which helped her drink more because she could cope with the hangover. Then she added one drug after another to deal with the downside of the last. She never realised she had a real problem until the accident.

257

Suzy realised that she was lucky to get away from drink before she could get into drugs. Tara's recovery was going to be a lot more difficult than her own had been. Suzy's whole life had changed when she got off drink. She was living away from the source of the problem; she was at a different school; none of the triggers for her drinking were there. Whereas Tara had relied all her adult life on drink and drugs. She had never functioned without them. She had to go back to the same life, the same job, without the crutches she'd relied on up to now. She had good reason to be terrified.

Suddenly Suzy realised life was too short for compromises. Tara's story could have been her own. Or she could have been in the seat of a car that had careered into a truck.

It was time she took life by the neck and shook it until she got what she wanted instead of waiting for fate to deliver it to her on a plate. She'd have to wait till Monday to do anything about it, but she rehearsed in front of the mirror.

"Donal, I hate to be the one to have to tell you this … but I can't bear to see you made a fool of all over again …."

She tried a few more openings. No matter how she said it, it sounded wrong. As though she was telling tales. Betraying Charlotte. But Donal was her friend too and Suzy believed she'd been silent for long enough. If Charlotte didn't know how lucky she was to have Donal, she didn't deserve him. And after what Suzy had seen this afternoon, maybe she didn't.

Chapter 15

Charlotte came out of the bathroom wearing nothing. He was standing by the window looking out but he turned and smiled at her when he heard the door open. He wore a suit and tie and she was suddenly embarrassed by her nakedness.

"Come here, Charlotte."

She walked towards him and stopped when she was close enough to feel the heat of his body. She waited for him to reach out and touch her, to feel his body against hers, to remember him.

"Look," he said.

She looked out the window at the river. The sun reflected off the water and people scurried along, hopping on and off the pavement as they moved past crowds towards the bridge.

If any of them look up they'll see me naked, she thought. But she couldn't move.

Marcus still hadn't touched her. He came closer and stood behind her.

At last he kissed her shoulder and lifted her hair so he could reach the back of her neck. He remembered where she loved to be kissed. He turned her around to face him and began to kiss her on the mouth. Over his shoulder she watched them both in a full-length mirror. She was surprised that she felt nothing. He continued to kiss her, tracing patterns on her back with his fingers. Still she didn't move. Still she felt nothing. He pulled her closer, still kissing her. His eyes were closed, but she watched the whole scene in the mirror behind him.

The door opened. A man came in, towing a laughing woman behind him. She couldn't see who the woman was. The man stopped when he saw Charlotte and Marcus, and laughed.

"Sorry, we'll find another room."

"Donal!" Charlotte screamed.

"Charlotte, Charlotte! Wake up, love! You were having a nightmare."

"Oh God, not again!"

"Do you remember it this time?"

"No," she lied. "Hold me."

It was always the same dream, and she'd been having it, sometimes two or three times a night, since the day she'd seen Marcus in the supermarket. It started with her coming out of the bathroom, and ended with the door opening. Sometimes it was Marcus in the room and Donal at the door, sometimes the other way around. Each time she woke up sweating, and each time she cursed the fact that she hadn't looked to see who the woman at the door was. She knew that she could almost see her, if only she could remember to turn her head sooner ...

"Maybe you should see someone?" Donal cradled her head on his chest. "It feels like you've been having these dreams for months."

Four months. Donal thought it was since Emily's accident, Charlotte knew it was since she had seen Marcus.

"I'm sure they'll pass. Besides, what could anyone do? I can't even remember the dream. What woke you? Did I say something?"

She was terrified that one night he'd hear her scream "Marcus!"

"I don't know, but you were crying and moaning when I woke up. It sounds as if you're really upset about something, Charlotte."

"I'm fine now. Go back to sleep. I don't want to waste our weekend away."

She snuggled up beside him and soon Donal's breathing become regular again, but Charlotte couldn't go back to sleep. As she lay beside him, she wondered again what the significance of the dream was and why Marcus and Donal's role in it kept reversing.

She still hadn't called Marcus, despite a number of messages he had left for her at work. He had taken to calling only their first restaurant, as he'd found out that that's where she spent most of her time. A week ago she had decided that she would have to talk to him, if only to beg him to stop calling. Maybe it would put an end to the nightmare. She still hadn't told Donal about their chance meeting four months ago, and if he ever saw messages stuck to her desk with Marcus's name and number on them, he didn't comment.

But Charlotte knew that even if she wanted to talk to Donal about Marcus she wouldn't be able to. Lately, when they were together, they stuck to a list of safe topics including the kids, work and Emily's progress. When they exhausted these, they busied themselves to avoid talking at all. At times she and Donal reminded her of a bull and his matador, circling each other in a series of choreographed moves designed to delay either of them from delivering the final, fatal blow.

And now tonight, as she lay with Donal on their first romantic weekend away in years, Charlotte looked up at the canopy of the four-poster bed and felt her heart beat with the remembered shock of seeing a familiar figure getting out of a car outside the restaurant only that afternoon, as she had left to go home and get ready for this weekend away with her husband.

She turned left as soon as she recognised Marcus, pretending she hadn't seen him. Then she made a big show of putting up her umbrella and hiding under it.

"Charlotte!"

A car sped past between them, and she walked faster as if she hadn't heard him.

"Wait, Charlotte!" Marcus crossed the road towards her.

Charlotte saw one of her neighbours out walking the dogs despite the downpour. The woman looked around on hearing Marcus call, and seeing Charlotte on the other side of the road, raised her hand in greeting.

It would look too weird if I continued to ignore him, Charlotte realised; it would look as if I were hiding from something.

So she stopped and waited while he crossed the road towards her.

"Marcus, what are you doing here?" she asked, not caring that she sounded annoyed rather than surprised to see him

"Looking for you," he answered. "I can't get you on the phone and you never return my calls."

"I've had a lot on," she answered and watched him stand in the rain, the water beginning to plaster the hair to his head.

He lifted a strand of it off his forehead and shook his head just as a drop of rain fell into his eye. "I'm getting soaked here. Can we shelter somewhere?"

Charlotte's head turned in confusion towards the restaurant and then to the corner of the road that led home.

"How about my car?" Marcus nodded towards a navy blue BMW on the other side of the road.

"OK, but I haven't long. I have to collect Aisling from school."

She was surprised to see him put his key in the ignition and start the car when she sat into it.

"What are you doing?" she asked, resisting the urge to reach for the door handle.

"We're parked on a double yellow line. I was just

watching for you to come out – there's a carpark a hundred yards up the road."

"What do you want?" she asked when he stopped the engine again.

He didn't say anything for what seemed like ages. Charlotte watched the rain stream down the windscreen. Through it she could just make out the grey sea, whipped into white tufts by the sudden September squall.

"Can we not just be friends, Charlotte?" he asked at last, without looking at her.

"I don't know, Marcus. Not at the moment. There's too much going on." Despite herself she told him about Emily, about how she was worried that Gemma was going off the rails with increasingly difficult behaviour, and about how she was returning to studying again.

"All right, but I want you to know I'm here," Marcus told her. His hands gripped the steering wheel and he stared straight ahead, out the front window of the car, out to sea. "I was a shit to you all those years ago, and I'd like a chance to prove that I really regret it, and that I'm not really like that, not any more."

"Maybe when all this has settled down …"

"You'll call me?"

"I have your number."

"Can I call you if you forget?"

"I'd prefer you didn't, but I won't forget, I promise." Charlotte realised she was telling the truth.

"I'm sorry, Charlotte."

"For what?"

"For hurting you. Back when…"

"It's a long time ago. Look, I really have to go."

"I'll drop you off." Marcus offered, starting the car. "You'll get soaked."

"No, it's easing off." She opened the car door quickly. "I will call you, Marcus. I promise."

Charlotte moved closer to Donal and, in his sleep, he put his arm around her and pulled her closer. She remembered the last time they had slept in this room, the first night of their honeymoon, the first time Donal had felt Gemma kick.

Charlotte knew she had to find some way of breaking the invisible bond between her and Marcus, the tie that stopped her from cutting him out of her life completely.

Emily switched on the light and looked around the room that had been her home for the past four months. She had longed to get out of this prison, but now she was terrified. It was confirmed – she could go home this week. And Sheila had already moved into the second bedroom of her flat to be on hand if she needed anything.

But Emily was terrified of leaving the sanctuary of the hospital. Here she had perfected her survival mechanism. Everything that happened to her here, she had delegated to a third person, casting herself as interested observer. It was how she tolerated the pain of daily physiotherapy sessions during which she forced her wasted muscles to retake control of her pinned and plated skeleton. It was how, in the first few weeks, she had been able to bear the indignity of having no control of her bodily functions;

265

the bags and tubes were attached to Emily Riordan, patient (female), room 104. It was how she was able to discuss calmly, and with a smile, the operations to restore her gut and removed the loathsome bag.

But now she was going home. In her beloved flat, surrounded by the things which she had collected throughout the years and which helped to identify her, Emily knew she would no longer be able to pretend that this was happening to someone else. She would have to face up to the fact that she had changed. The body she had worked so hard on, to make it into something she could be proud of, had changed. The Emily who returned on Wednesday would be a different woman than the Emily who had closed the door behind her the weekend of Anne-Marie's hen-party.

On Sunday afternoon, Sheila was watching her grand-children in the garden. Tim and Aisling were kicking a ball around and Gemma was lying face down on a rug, pretending to read, but kicking her legs in time to the music in her headphones. Sheila was baby-sitting for the weekend. Although she'd been delighted when Donal told her he wanted to take Charlotte away for a couple of days, Sheila would be glad to escape this evening when they came home. She had thought Charlotte must have been exaggerating when she complained about Gemma's recent behaviour, but now she could fully sympathise. Nothing was right as far as Gemma was concerned. She was like a parody of a teenager. Nobody understood her and everyone was a moron.

"Stop it!" Gemma hissed, without even turning round.

"Stop what, Gemma?" Her grandmother was puzzled. She hadn't moved for the past ten minutes.

"Staring at me."

"Staring at you?" How had the girl known she was thinking about her, let alone looking at her? She hadn't looked up from her own book for the past hour.

"Yeah, staring at me. S-t-a-r-i-n-g. You're always doing it. I'm fed up of it. You and Mum and Dad, you're always at it. Staring at me. Watching me like you expect me to grow a third head or something."

"A third head?"

"Yeah, well, I assume I must already have two. And you all keep looking at me in a kind of worried way to see will I sprout a third one."

"I didn't know I was staring at you and I'm sorry if I upset you," Sheila apologised to the back of her granddaughter's head. The girl rolled over, unplugged her stereo and sat up.

"It's all right. You don't do it that often. Staring, I mean. I shouldn't have shouted at you. It's Mum and Dad who really get on my nerves."

Sheila wondered if the row had been engineered so that Gemma could talk to her about it.

"Do you want to come in and have a pot of tea with me?" she nodded her head in the direction of the kitchen.

"Don't mind," the girl shrugged.

"To be honest, I'd like some company. Those two," Sheila looked Gemma's younger siblings, "can get to be a bit wearing."

They sat at the large pine table and Gemma looked longingly at the packet of chocolate hobnobs. That was the trouble with Gran, she always bought the yummiest biscuits; it made Gemma want to eat a whole packet, and then she'd just look like a greedy kid.

"Maybe your mum and dad are just worried about you, Gemma."

"Funny way of showing it. Staring at me whenever they think I'm not looking."

"What do you mean, staring at you?"

"Just that. Staring. I get this funny feeling at the back of my neck, I look up and one of them's staring at me. I don't even have to look at them any more – I know what I'll see."

"Have you tried asking them about it?" Sheila regretted it as soon as she said it; she kept forgetting this was an eleven-year-old she was talking to.

"What'd be the point? The way Mum and Dad are lately…"

"What do you mean?"

"Oh, you know … staring into space, talking about work the whole time, I don't know, weird."

"Weird?"

"Yeah, especially when we're around, they like… talk to each other through us."

Sheila knew what Gemma meant but didn't know how to discuss the fears she had for Charlotte and Donal's marriage with their daughter.

"Maybe it's just all the extra stress with Auntie Emily's accident," she suggested lamely.

"Nah, it's been going on much longer than that. The staring anyway. They never do it to Tim and Aisling."

"Maybe they do, but you don't notice."

"They don't." Gemma took a biscuit from the packet in front of her and nibbled her way around the edges in silence. Sheila, sensing that she still had more to say, topped up the cups, although Gemma had hardly touched hers.

"Gran …" Gemma mumbled through a mouthful of crumbs. She had stopped nibbling and bitten off over half the biscuit. "Gran … they'd tell me if I was adopted, wouldn't they?"

"You're not, but what on earth gave you that idea?"

Gemma shrugged, and reached for another biscuit. She began the nibbling ritual again. Sheila had to bite her tongue to prevent hersef from interrupting the youngster's train of thought.

"Remember, last year, when you were sick?" Gemma asked at last.

"Yes."

"And remember how you told Mum that you were her aunt, and then she told us? About her being adopted, and you being her aunt, but it not making any difference about how she felt about you, 'cos you were still her mum?"

"Yes."

"Well, it was since then."

"What was?"

"That they started watching me. It was as if they were waiting to see what I thought of it. I'm not adopted, am I?"

"You're not, love, I promise." Sheila came around the table and put her arms around her granddaughter. She wiped a few tears off her cheek, then she sat down and pulled Gemma onto her lap. The girl didn't object to being treated like one of the younger kids. "I remember the day you were born. You kept us all waiting, miss, I'll tell you that. Three times your mum went into hospital thinking you were about to grace us with your presence, and three times she was sent home again. Then the night she did go in, we didn't know whether to believe it or not. It wore on and on, and she didn't seem to be making any progress. In the end everything happened really fast and they had to deliver you by …" Sheila hesitated.

"I know what a caesarean is, Gran. I've seen the scar."

"OK … and at last, there you were. Your mum was still asleep when I saw you, all red and angry. You had a pair of lungs on you that nearly knocked the window out of the recovery room! It was just getting bright, so after your mum saw you and she fell asleep again, your dad took you to see your first sunrise. You screamed at that too!"

Gemma digested all this information. She'd heard most of it before, but hearing that her mother had lived with half-truth all her childhood, she had begun to wonder.

"Neither of the others were born by caesarean, Gemma." Sheila broke into the girl's reverie.

"What?"

"Tim and Aisling were born in England and they were both delivered naturally."

"So?"

"So, that caesarean scar, it's your own personal little entrance to the world. And I promise you, you're not adopted."

"OK." Gemma jumped off her grandmother's lap, suddenly embarrassed. "Can I go over to Lisa's house now?"

"Welcome Home!"

Tim and Aisling had painted a banner to stretch along the hallway and Emily's neighbours were outside the lift to wish her well. She was glad that she had insisted on leaving the wheelchair in the car. She was tired and in pain, and she knew she would be glad to sink into it later, but she had wanted to walk out of the hospital and into her home unaided. If you could call it unaided, hobbling with a crutch, her sister to one side of her, and Paul on the other in case she stumbled and fell.

She had known there would be no way of avoiding the inevitable hullabaloo when she was finally released, so she hadn't even attempted to ask to return home alone, but Emily was glad now that there were so many people around as she put the key in the door. Charlotte must have guessed how she felt though, because there was no one inside, and as Emily limped into her hallway, they all waited at the door. She pushed open the door to the living-room and walked over to her balcony. Sheila had taken good care of her plants and nothing else seemed to have changed. She sank into the sofa with relief, and didn't try to hide the tears which flowed down her face even when the others joined her. She had been wrong to worry about coming home. This was her place – she

271

could face anything here.

A party materialised and over the next couple of hours, friends drifted in and out to wish her well.

"Thanks!" Emily murmured to Charlotte the first time she managed to get her alone.

"How does it feel to be home?"

"Great!"

Charlotte felt tears begin to sting her eyes as she saw Emily's smile. She had forgotten what her sister's real smile looked like. She had got used to the cosmetic confection Emily pasted in place whenever she felt that a smile was the most appropriate response. Today her smile lit up her whole face and gave life back to features that had become uniform in pallor and sharpened by tension since the accident. Just an hour today, in the evening sun on the balcony, had restored some colour to her cheeks. In hospital, the bleaching of Emily's skin by being trapped indoors had gone unnoticed, but on her return she looked deathly pale compared to her guests.

"You need a few sunbed sessions!" someone from work had joked. But Charlotte knew it would be a long time before Emily plucked up the courage to undress in the health club and expose her scars.

"Where's Donal gone?" Emily had noticed her brother-in-law leave shortly after the party began.

"Crisis in town. Suzy sends her regrets too. Something to do with Tony, Suzy's deputy, having had a major row with Maria the pastry chef, and both of them threatening to quit over it." Charlotte had been annoyed that it had cropped up this week of all weeks, and was relieved that

Donal seemed happy to deal with it himself. It must be serious though; she'd hardly seen him since Monday and he looked preoccupied and angry whenever he was home. "Your boss is a nice guy." Charlotte wanted to change the subject off Donal. Crisis or no crisis, she was annoyed that he'd rushed off without saying a word to her.

"Yeah, Malcolm's been great. The company's health insurance has picked up anything my own insurance didn't cover, and I'm still officially on sick leave. I'll have to think of when I'm going to go back though," she grimaced.

"No point in rushing things," Paul joined in the conversation. He had his jacket on. "Take your time; be sure you're ready before you go back full time. Now, I'll have to love you and leave you, I'm afraid. Some bastard at work arranged an evening meeting of all the managers and partners." He kissed Emily on the cheek and squeezed her hand. "Take care, Champ! I'll call you tomorrow."

He walked away, stopping to say good-bye to a few more people on the way out. At the door he turned to wave one last time and Charlotte saw Emily force herself to smile back at him.

"How are things going between the two of you?" Charlotte asked.

"Paul? Oh, fine – he's a real friend," Emily answered quickly. Too quickly, as if she had rehearsed the reply. "He'd do anything for me," she added.

Despite the smile, Charlotte saw some of the light go out of her sister's eyes. It was none of her business, she reminded herself, as she had a hundred times since Emily woke up from her coma. She wondered if her sister had any memory of the hours Paul had spent beside her bed telling her he loved her. Or had he declared his love and been pushed away again?

The party wound up soon and Charlotte ushered the last of the guests out the door so that Emily could get some rest. When she got home she rang the restaurant to let Donal know she was home, then settled the kids in bed. At last she was able to pull out her bag and get started on some history homework.

"Hey, you're home early. I thought you'd be hours yet," Charlotte called out and looked up reluctantly from her history book when she heard Donal's key in the front door. Although the term had only just started, she'd found very little time to study so far and she had assumed that tonight, with a problem at work, it would be after eleven before he came home.

"I didn't make any dinner – did you eat in town?" she asked when he joined her.

"I'm fine."

Donal sat at the dining-room table opposite her and ran a hand through his hair. He looked tense and tired. Charlotte tried not to sigh as she put her books back in her bag. He obviously wanted to talk about whatever was wrong in the restaurant.

"Did you sort everything out?" she asked at last when Donal said nothing.

"What?" he asked, looking confused.

"The row at work. Tony, Maria? Threatening to quit?"

"Oh, that. Don't worry about it." Donal waved his hand dismissing her question. "Storm in a teacup."

Charlotte bit her lip and tried to hide her annoyance. Storm that kept you out of here the last three days, and turned you into an Antichrist when you were here, she thought.

"In that case …" She reached back into her bag for her history book.

"Charlotte, we need to talk."

She smiled and pushed her bag out of reach. At last! All weekend she had looked for opportunities to say just that.

"About what, Donal?" She would let him go first.

"About Marcus."

"Oh," was all she could manage when she got her breath back.

"You've seen him." Donal's tone was hostile.

"I ran into him, shopping, the day after Emily's wedding."

A cosy domestic scene, shopping together, with Marcus giving Aisling a hug and lifting her up, was how Suzy had described it to him before he could tell her to stop.

"And on Friday?"

"God, Donal, are you having me watched?"

As she arrived at the restaurant, Suzy had seen Charlotte get into Marcus's car and drive off with him.

"On Friday, Charlotte, a few hours before we went for our romantic weekend away, you met Marcus. Ring any bells?"

"I didn't plan it. He was waiting for me outside the restaurant when I came out."

"Why was he waiting for you?"

"Because he's been phoning me for months, and I haven't taken or returned any of his calls," Charlotte snapped.

"Oh."

Now it was Donal's turn to be at a loss for words. A look of hope flickered in his eyes, trying to displace the pain and anger there.

"It was pelting rain," she explained, "so I got into his car, which was parked illegally. He drove a hundred yards down the road to a seafront carpark." Charlotte waited for some reaction from Donal. "He just wants to meet me, he says. He wants to apologise for the past, show me that he's not really the shit I must think he is."

"And will you? Meet him, I mean."

"I don't know. Yes. Probably. But that's all it will be, to talk."

"What's so difficult about leaving the past in the past, Char? It's over between you and him, isn't it?"

A silence grew between them, and Charlotte began to realise what had been going on for the past year. Ever since she had met Denise, Donal had been watching her for some sign that Marcus was going to come back into her life. And now he had that sign. They had been seen together. Although she knew it was ridiculous, although there was no way Charlotte would ever let anything come between herself and her family, she felt like her marriage was on trial. She swallowed hard before continuing.

"Of course, it's over, but ..."

"Is this about Gemma?" Donal interrupted, the words exploding from his mouth as though they had been trapped inside under pressure. "It's to do with Gemma, isn't it? Otherwise you'd just be able to tell Marcus to go to hell after the way he treated you, wouldn't you?"

Charlotte forced herself to take slow breaths. She tried to see her husband's face, but it was obscured from view by a swirling mass of red dots. There was a pain in her chest. She tried to still the *whump whump whump* of her heart, by pressing against it with her fist and lowering her chin to meet it. Was this what a heart attack felt like? Was she going to die?

Donal reached across, took her hand, uncurled it and enfolded in his own. With his other hand he touched her chin, lifting her face to force her to look at him. As her vision cleared, Charlotte almost wished she had died rather than see the fear in his face.

"There's a chance Gemma's his, isn't there, Char?"

Donal didn't need an answer: it was written on his wife's face. He had spoken gently, as if to a frightened child, but now a huge sob broke from him: "Oh God no, I always hoped ..."

The world closed in on them. The cars on the main road went silent, no light shone from their neighbours' houses, the night sky was starless. Even the furniture in the room around them vanished; all they could see was each other's faces, each other's eyes.

Charlotte broke the silence first. "How ... I mean, when ... how long have you known?"

"Always. From the beginning I suppose," Donal answered. "I mean, I didn't know for sure, but…"

"I didn't know, Donal. I swear, that wasn't why…" Charlotte remembered the first night they spent together. She couldn't bear that the memory should now be sullied by any suspicion. "What we had was between us, it was nothing to do with Marcus, or me thinking I was pregnant. I swear it."

"I believe you. I think…" Donal hesitated and looked down at the table before asking: "So you slept with Marcus…"

"About a week before us," she interrupted.

Donal tried to control an anger which he felt was irrational and yet couldn't escape feeling he was entitled to.

"A week before we made love for the first time," he enunciated slowly and carefully, "you and Marcus slept together for the last time." He repeated facts as if he needed to confirm them. Like a barrister badgering a witness. "At least I assume it was the last time. Was it?"

Charlotte's appalled expression when he asked her this made him close his eyes in shame. He pressed fingers into the corners of his eyes, then pulled them downwards along the bridge of his nose. "You're right … I shouldn't have said that. I'm sorry." But despite himself, he felt he had scored a point in some undeclared competition.

"You have no right to be so angry, Donal," Charlotte said slowly. Although for years she had imagined this moment, any logical arguments she had rehearsed crumbled under the weight of Donal's emotion. "I never betrayed you. You knew how obsessed I was with Marcus.

You came to me to console me when I realised he was…"
She didn't want to say cheating on her, because that
would imply that she and Marcus had made some sort of
commitment to each other. "The only person betrayed
in this whole mess was me. By Marcus. I thought I was
getting back together with him. I didn't know about
Denise …"

"And then when you found out, you come running to
me. The consolation prize."

"It wasn't like that, Donal. It was…" Charlotte tried to
put it into words. "You were always there, and I really did
love you – I just couldn't see it until Marcus was gone.
Properly out of the picture. And now we have Gemma,
Donal. *Our* daughter. I don't care who happened to be
there at the moment she was conceived. She's *our* daughter Donal."

"But it does matter, Charlotte, doesn't it?" Donal asked
sadly. "You're the proof of that. From the day I met you I
don't think I ever heard you mention Robert more than
once or twice. The man who raised you as his daughter.
But since you discovered he was your uncle, you can't
stop telling the kids stories about your childhood. Stories
that include Robert."

"That's not fair, Donal. My attitude to Robert didn't
change because he was my uncle, but because… Well,
because I understood more about his position. Why he
behaved the way he had. It was nothing to do with dis-
covering I was related to him." But Charlotte wondered
how true that was. She had never really questioned her
change of heart. Could Donal be right? Could she be

forming this retrospective attachment just because they were related?

"I need a drink," Donal said. But what he really needed was a few seconds on his own. "Do you want one?" He got up and walked out to the kitchen without waiting for her to answer.

Charlotte heard him rummage through bottles in the kitchen; then she heard the rhythmic creak of metal being screwed into cork followed by a squeak and pop as Donal uncorked the bottle. He came back into the dining-room with the bottle and two glasses.

I need to buy some more wineglasses; those ones have dulled in the dishwasher, Charlotte thought as he laid them on the table. Donal poured. She watched as he swirled the wine in the bottom of his large glass, then sniffed. She wondered had he noticed any of the aromas and flavours or was he merely seeking comfort in ritual. She herself took a large mouthful and tasted nothing, but was grateful for the hot sting of alcohol at the back of her throat.

They drank in silence for a while, each of them following the other's smallest gesture with their eyes so that they wouldn't to have look straight at each other.

"Promise you won't do anything foolish without discussing it with me first," Donal said.

"Sorry?" Charlotte had an insane vision of coming to Donal to ask his permission to have an affair with her former lover.

Affair. That was the first time the word had ever entered her consciousness. It had only done so, she knew, because she suspected that it might be hovering in Donal's mind too.

"I mean, don't tell Marcus he's a father without discussing it with me first."

"Donal, we don't know that he is the – father. It could just as easily be you."

"I know." Donal poured another glass of wine and remembered the hours he had spent with an obstetric calendar and a medical textbook. "I know from the scans, the due date they gave us. They put her conception … well, around our first night, but …"

"Do you want to get a blood test?"

"*No!*" Donal was surprised by his own ferocity. "No," he repeated with a weary tone. "I'd prefer to live with uncertainty than know that she wasn't…" He couldn't say the words. "Have you ever thought about it? Getting a blood test, a DNA test or whatever?"

"Not really," she lied. Of course, like Donal, she had thought about it and like him she had rejected the idea. Like him, she was afraid of the result.

Donal asked himself if Charlotte realised what he had been going through ever since Gemma was born – when they moved to England first and Charlotte had tried to find some trace of family for her birth mother – when Sheila had revealed what she knew about Charlotte's past. Every time Charlotte had talked about her own origins, surely she must have been questioning Gemma's? All those times Donal had longed to force her to talk about it, but he'd been afraid. Afraid of somehow forcing her hand.

"I should have told you sooner, Charlotte, I'm sorry. About my knowing, I mean. It wasn't fair to you to have to keep it a secret for so long."

"How did you know?" Her voice was a lot calmer than she felt. He was being too damned reasonable. She wanted to scream at him that this was important, that they should be throwing things round the room by now. This civilised politeness scared the shit out of her.

"I knew you were still seeing Marcus, when you wanted us all to believe it was over. It was something he said after a teachers versus past pupils rugby match, something about having his cake and eating it. He laughed about not worrying that Denise wasn't 'coming up with the goods', as he put it, because he had an ex on the side. He was drunk, Charlotte," Donal added quickly when he saw the distress on her face. "I don't think he even realised I had heard him. Not that he'd have worried, the little shit – all he cared about was looking like the big man in front of his mates. He was using you, Charlotte. How could you have let him do that to you?

"I didn't know about Denise," she snapped back at him. "Unlike you, I wasn't privy to locker-room gossip. And although I didn't see Marcus that often, he told me it was because he was studying for his finals. If anything, the time we spent together between Easter and the summer, was far better than the previous two years. We had fun. We never fought over anything." Charlotte didn't understand why she wanted to emphasise how happy she was. She knew that every word must be digging the knife deeper into Donal but she couldn't stop. "I can see now that it was just sex," she continued , "but at the time ... I thought Marcus loved me."

Charlotte's tears caused Donal a jolt of such pure jealousy that he gasped with pain. He had planned, before he confronted her, to finish up by holding her, telling her it was all right, that they would go on as before. That sharing this secret would only make them stronger. But now he wasn't so sure. He was afraid that he might have just released Charlotte from having to pretend any more. And that all these years perhaps it wasn't love that had kept Charlotte with him, but fear of discovery.

"When I realised you were pregnant ... remember, I guessed before you told me?" He forced himself to go on. "I tried to figure out when it could have been. I was hoping to God that you'd tell me your last period was the day before we ... but it wasn't, so I knew there had to be a doubt."

"Why didn't you say something?"

Donal looked ashamed. "I was afraid you wouldn't marry me."

"Oh Donal..."

"Well, would you have? If I hadn't managed to persuade you that Gemma could have been conceived that first time we made love, or even in the week after that. If I had confronted you with the knowledge that I thought the baby might not be mine, would you have married me?"

Charlotte was silent. She wasn't sure what she would have done. Would she have told Marcus about the child that might be his? Would she have raised Gemma on her own, like her own mother had tried to do?

And could she have married Donal knowing that he knew?

"I suppose you did the right thing, Donal," she admitted at last.

"She might be mine. She was born very late to have been his," Donal said.

They both remembered the agonising wait, and the several false alarms, neither of them realising at the time that they weren't alone in wishing Gemma would delay her arrival as long as possible.

"And then when she was born, I thought it didn't matter. She was my daughter, no matter whose chromosomes she was carrying. When I looked into those eyes, and I watched you sleeping, she was all the more special to me, because she'd given me what I wanted more than anything in the world. You, Charlotte, as my wife. Even then, I couldn't fool myself into thinking that we'd be married by then if it wasn't for Gemma. So I couldn't love her any more, even if there was no doubt."

"Oh, Donal!"

"Marcus doesn't deserve her, Charlotte," he pleaded.

"I hadn't planned to tell him," she said.

Donal believed her. Charlotte probably felt no sense of duty to Marcus. But what about to Gemma? In ten or twenty years' time, when their daughter was getting married, leaving them to start a family of her own – how would Charlotte feel then?

"But you can't forget about it either, can you?" he asked.

"Can you?" she challenged. She knew they had both watched Gemma with worried faces in the year since Charlotte had met Denise.

"Yes, I can forget it, Charlotte. Gemma's my daughter, you're my wife and I don't want to lose either of you."

Although Donal was crying, and Charlotte longed to put her arms around him, reassure him that he wasn't losing anyone, she couldn't. They were being honest with each other and she wouldn't make promises she wasn't certain she could keep.

Across the city, Paul stared with undisguised hostility at the man facing him. The partners' meeting had broken up just few minutes earlier and Richard had followed him when he left the boardroom. Now they were in Paul's office.

"I think Emily could do without the kind of friendship you'd have to offer," Paul hissed.

"I wasn't asking your permission, Paul. But I know how you feel …" Richard held his hands out in front of him in a warning expression. "I know you're her best friend, so I was telling you out of courtesy. Shit, I don't know why I was telling you. But Emily needs all the friends she can get at the moment, so you're not going to stop me from going to see her."

"Wife left you again, has she?" Paul sneered.

"My marriage is fine, thank you for asking." Richard sat down and crossed his legs.

Paul sat down as well, visibly deflating.

"Why can't you just leave her alone, Richard? She

doesn't need this right now."

"Need what, Paul? All I want to do is see her. I wrote to her when she was in hospital and she phoned me a few times." He noticed the other man's surprise. "You didn't know that, did you? Well, now, I just want to see how she is."

"Why didn't you go and see her in hospital if you were so worried?" Paul challenged.

"I wanted to, but she asked me not to."

"Has she asked to see you now?"

Paul would be surprised if she had. Although Emily's scars weren't as bad as she had a right to expect from the severity of her accident, she seemed to think she was hideously deformed and didn't like to meet any more people than she absolutely had to. He had noticed that the party earlier this afternoon had been an ordeal for her. As she met friends for the first time since it happened, Emily had scanned each face for signs of revulsion. And although she saw nothing but relief that she was all right, he knew it was of no comfort to her. As ever Emily was her own harshest judge.

"No, she didn't ask to see me. And if she doesn't want to, I won't turn up on her doorstep unannounced, if that's what you're worried about."

"I'll kill you if you hurt her again, Richard."

"I won't."

Paul didn't want to believe him. He didn't want Richard anywhere near Emily, especially at the moment. In the months since the accident, she had become withdrawn, had built up a shell around herself and Paul wanted to be the one to chip away at it, be the one she turned to. He was terrified that Richard, with his detached bonhomie, might be the one to make Emily smile again. He stared angrily at the other man, wanting to find the words to make him stay the hell away from Emily. But he knew that even if he found them he wouldn't use them.

To his relief the phone rang.

"Excuse me." Paul reached for the receiver on his desk. "Close the door behind you," he ordered without looking up. "Barrett and Lyle, Paul Hamilton speaking," he said in his professional voice.

"Paul, it's Tara here. I need to talk to you."

"Oh God. What now?"

"Can I get you a drink?" Tara called over a waitress as Paul sank into a comfortable chair in a secluded part of the Shelbourne lobby.

"I'll have a pint of Guinness," he told the girl who came over to them. Then he saw Tara's coffee. "Sorry, just make that a coffee, would you?" He went red.

"He'll have the pint. And I'll have another coffee." Tara waited until the waitress left. "The whole world doesn't have to stop drinking just because I have, Paul."

"Sorry. How are you?"

He hadn't seen her since bundling her off in an ambulance. She'd regained some of the weight she'd lost and her hair shone like it had when he first knew her. As ever, her make-up was immaculate but now it enhanced her natural beauty rather than covering up the ravages of her former life. For the first time Paul recognised that Tara was a very attractive woman. Not his type, but attractive none the less.

"I'm not doing too badly, considering."

Tara smiled for the first time since he'd come in and Paul got the impression that he was seeing her smile for the first time ever. But surely that couldn't be true? He'd been at countless parties with her in college and later, and she always seemed to be having such a good time.

"I never thanked you for saving my life," she said in a small voice.

Paul was saved from answering by the arrival of his drink. He stared at the creamy foam, and took a deep drink before saying anything.

"I didn't really do it for you," he admitted.

"I guessed as much, but it doesn't matter. You were there, and I'm here today. Thanks."

Paul felt awkward. He picked up his pint, took another small sip and put it down again. He didn't know what to do with his hands. His drink had been served on a small round, plastic-backed paper coaster. He would give anything right now for a stout cardboard drip mat that he could spend the next ten minutes shredding.

"What did you want to see me about?" he asked at last.

Tara's calm was unnerving him. He had never seen her like this, almost serene. The old Tara tapped her fingers, swung her foot, fiddled with her hair, unable to stop moving for a second. Now she sat still except when she leaned forwards to take a small sip from her cup. It made Paul's nerves scream with tension. He picked up his glass again.

"I saw Emily again," Tara said.

"She told me." Paul didn't want to be here. He had expected to feel anger, hatred for the woman sitting opposite him, but he felt nothing.

"I wish she could get more angry with me." An anguished look flashed across Tara's face. Anger, frustration, anxiety? Then she resumed her feline calm. Suddenly Paul realised it was all an act. Tara was terrified of being here with him. Knowing how he must feel about her. He was intrigued as to why she was subjecting herself to it.

"*Emily* doesn't blame you." As soon as he said it, Paul realised he had emphasised the word 'Emily', implying that everyone else did.

"I blame me," she replied.

Paul shrugged. What was there to say? They sat in silence for a while.

"She's got a long way to go still," Tara said.

"She'll get there, she's strong."

"She'll need all the help she can get."

"What do you mean?" Paul was suddenly reminded of Richard.

A tall slim man came out of the bar in the Shelbourne and spotted Tara. His face broke into a grin and he made his way towards their table. Paul wondered what there was about his own expression which had put the man off, because at the last moment he veered away, waved at Tara, and mouthed "See you around" at her. Tara smiled warmly in reply before turning her attention back to Paul.

"Emily won't sue me."

Paul shrugged again.

"She's got to." Now Tara became animated. "You've studied law too. Will you try to talk sense to her? Tell her I know it's nothing personal but, if she doesn't sue me, my insurance company will screw her."

"She was afraid you had enough on your plate."

"Nothing I don't deserve."

"I already told her all this."

Suddenly Paul was ashamed of the way he'd badgered Emily into suing her friend. She was going to be off work for a long time and although her boss had indicated that he would make sure there was still a job for her when she got back, Paul wanted to make sure that she had a decent financial cushion to fall back on. This accident had taken a lot out of her; she was entitled to any compensation she could get.

"I reckoned you would have, that's why I came to you. Charlotte just agrees with anything Emily says," Tara said, breaking into his thoughts.

"I don't know what I can say to change her mind." He had tried just about every argument he could think of.

"Would you just come with me to talk to her?" Tara pleaded. "She might listen to us both together."

"All right. We'll give it a try."

Charlotte tried to go back to her books in a futile attempt to take her mind off the scene with Donal. She was trying to pretend that her whole world hadn't just fallen apart. That all that had happened was that the air had been cleared, that she and Donal would just need to sit down and talk this out properly and then they'd be able to get on with their lives. He'd gone out, saying he was going for a walk, but that was two hours ago. Charlotte wondered if she should ring the restaurant; maybe he'd gone there.

She stared at her history book, but all she could see was Donal's hurt face staring at her. Stop thinking about it, she ordered.

Suddenly, although she tried to fight it, the memory of her last night with Marcus came to her. It was a few days before her nineteenth birthday. A letter arrived for Charlotte at work, marked personal and hand-delivered. Although she didn't recognise it straight away, the writing looked familiar. Inside was a plain white card with the words: *Burger King, O'Connell St. 6PM Wednesday.* Now she knew who it was; it was Marcus, writing in block capitals. What was he up to now? Although they didn't meet often, he always had to make it as exciting as he could. It was as if, now that they were seeing each other again and Charlotte hadn't told anyone, they had all the excitement of a secret affair.

"Is this seat taken?"

Charlotte looked up from her table in Burger King, to see Marcus in a suit and tie he must have been wearing for a job interview. She thought she'd never seen him look so sexy.

"John Smith, pleased to meet you." He held out his hand to her as he sat down.

She giggled. If Marcus was planning a stranger-seduction fantasy, surely he could have come up with a better name?

"And you are …" He raised an eyebrow.

"Why don't you guess?" Charlotte decided she may as well play along.

"Mmmh, let me see …"

She giggled again.

"Sophie, Alicia? How about Tanya?"

"That's it, Tanya." She held out her hand. "Pleased to meet you … John." She managed to suppress the giggle this time.

They walked along the quays at his suggestion that they find somewhere a little less crowded, then he took her arm and steered her into the lobby of a hotel.

"Let's have a drink."

They sat in a rather seedy lounge and ordered sandwiches to go with their drinks. She told him she was a model while he claimed to be the owner of a multinational computer company. Apart from the first handshake, they had hardly touched since meeting and Charlotte felt sick with longing.

When Marcus/John Smith had suggested they order a bottle of wine and he would show her the view of the river from his room, she got up with as much dignity as she could muster, while he asked for the key to his room.

"You had this planned!" she squeaked with indignation in the lift.

"What do you mean, Tanya?" Marcus frowned slightly; it was the first time she'd stepped out of her role as glamorous stranger.

"Nothing, sorry." She didn't want to spoil the mood.

As she remembered, Charlotte was sure he had been laughing at her all those years ago. She had thought they were sharing some delicious fantasy: a businessman, maybe married, maybe not, picks up a woman for a night of uncomplicated sex. And all the time Charlotte really was his bit on the side, the woman who kept him ticking over while he waited for the woman he wanted to marry.

They'd gone into the bedroom. The room from Charlotte's nightmare. He showed her the river from his window, and started to undress her, kissing her all the time. After they made love, they lay in each other's arms, with the window open, and the evening sunlight streaming through.

"I love you too much for this, Charlotte," Marcus mumbled just before falling asleep.

Charlotte didn't dare speak, spoil the moment. He'd never said he loved her before.

She left the next morning before he woke up because she had to get home and change for work. She left a note, thanking him for a great time and signing it *Tanya*.

It was the last time she saw him until the day after Anne-Marie's wedding.

Chapter 16

In the months after Donal and Charlotte's discussion about Gemma, Charlotte did her best to repair their life. But everything she said or did seemed to go wrong. When she pleaded with Donal to just let things go back to how they were before, he looked at her sadly and asked how that would change things. And of course he was right. In fact, given the power to go back to any moment she chose in their relationship – which one would she return to? The time when they were both pretending nothing was wrong, and yet studying Gemma for any sign of Marcus's chin or eyes? Or back to before they were married, when she was pregnant and couldn't be sure who by? Or maybe if she hadn't found out about Marcus and Denise, or if Donal hadn't come to her when she did, she would never have slept with him – and then what?

So Charlotte tried to start again. She did her best to

arrange little romantic interludes to bring them closer. One Friday night she planned a late supper after the kids had gone to bed, but in the middle of the afternoon, Gemma's teacher rang to say that she had been causing problems in school. Charlotte decided to deal with it quickly by grounding her for a week rather than ruin their evening, but then Gemma phoned her dad to complain about her punishment. Although he supported Charlotte when he was speaking to Gemma, later Donal wanted to know why Charlotte hadn't discussed it with him. Without saying it, he implied she had deliberately excluded him from a decision about Gemma. Needless to say, their romantic supper went cold.

Another day Gemma was cheeking Donal, and Charlotte told her to apologise to her father at once. The way she said "Sorry, *Daddy*, I won't ever say anything like that again, *Daddy*" in a sarcastic tone of voice, made both her parents wince and avoid each other for the rest of the day.

So Donal decided he should move out. He wasn't going far: just down the road and around the corner to the flat behind the restaurant, where they'd lived before buying their home. He promised he'd be in and out of the house almost as often as if he was living here, so the kids would hardly notice he was gone.

"We need some time apart, Charlotte," he had said, two nights after a disastrous Christmas.

"You might. I don't," she said panicking, terrified that if she let him walk out, she might lose him forever.

"I'm not saying it's over, love." It was as if he had read her mind. "But we're getting nowhere. We may live in the same house, but we're miles apart. Trying to pretend everything's fine just puts more pressure on us and I can't go on living like this."

"What do you want me to do?" Charlotte pleaded. "I want you to stay so we can work this out."

"It's as if we let an evil genie out of the bottle after I told you I knew about Gemma," Donal shook his head sadly, "and we can't just put it back in."

"But you said it didn't matter who Gemma's father was."

"Not to my relationship with Gemma ..."

"But you can't love me any more. Is that what you're saying?"

"I do love you, Charlotte. But it changes things between us. You have to admit that?"

"No," she replied stubbornly. "It shouldn't."

But she knew he was right. She had married him for Gemma's sake. She knew that now. And when he said he'd do his best to ensure the children didn't suffer, was it fair to keep him tied to her, when she couldn't be certain it's where he wanted to be?

"What will you do?"

"Nothing, I'll just wait." He got up and paced the room.

"For what?"

"To see if living apart can make things any clearer for us. Help us see what we want to do with our futures. I don't want to rush into anything."

Rush into anything? she wanted to scream. You're the one moving out.

Charlotte closed the suitcase she was packing with a violent thud and the clasp slid shut with a sharp click. She would bring the case over to the flat later, before Donal came home, so he couldn't protest in front of the kids that she'd done his packing for him. It was stupid really, but Charlotte had always packed for the whole family, and packing Donal's cases now was a silent reproach; she was making the point that as far as she was concerned, nothing had changed.

Donal had taken the kids to Cork for the weekend. He needed to look at premises for a third branch of Moran's and he had decided to take advantage of the trip to visit Fota Wildlife Park.

He had decided not to leave until after the kids had gone back to school, not wanting to ruin the Christmas holidays for everyone. But since he had made the decision to go, Charlotte was in some crazy way glad that the day had finally arrived. For the past couple of weeks they had danced around each other in a series of rehearsed moves. They were polite, humorous even, when they talked, but emotion was banned. Charlotte even felt awkward kissing or hugging the kids if Donal were around. Afraid that he would notice the difference between the hugs and kisses she lavished on Gemma, Tim and Aisling and the quick pecks on the cheek they gave each other.

She prayed that he was right about space being what they needed to help them see clearly again. But she wasn't convinced. Her instinct was to plaster over the cracks in their marriage, strengthen what they had, build on what had worked so far.

A few miles away, safe in the confines of her apartment, Emily looked in the mirror in her hallway as she picked up the phone. She found that if she practised smiling at the mirror when she spoke, her caller was less likely to pick up on her black mood. She could hear their almost audible relief that Emily was all right and that they didn't have to offer to 'pop over for a chat'. She wished they'd all just leave her alone. But instead she had to deal with at least three or four kind, solicitous phone-calls a day. This time it was Malcolm, her boss, checking how she was getting on and wondering when she was coming back to work.

Why couldn't they understand how hard it was for her? It wasn't just a case of negotiating the office, with the stick that she could manage without but didn't yet dare leave behind. Or even the terror she felt every time she got into a car. It wasn't that she was afraid of facing her colleagues, knowing that they pitied her or were vaguely curious as to what scars were hidden under her business suit. It was simpler than that. She wasn't sure if she could do the job any more. Although her concentration had improved and she no longer fled in terror from a sheet of figures, she just didn't care enough to be bothered to do her job properly.

"No, really, Malcolm," she said, grinning into the phone as she spoke in her rehearsed 'cheerful' voice.

"Really, it's not necessary to call over… Oh, you'd like to? When? This evening?" Emily tried in vain to think of some prior engagement to stop her boss dropping in on his way home. "Oh, all right then, about eight, so."

Oh God, she thought miserably. That means I have to get dressed up properly. I have to wash my hair, get changed and put on some make-up. It was all just too much effort.

Unable to galvanise herself into motion, Emily went on staring at her reflection. Her once blonde, curly hair hung limp and dank on her shoulders. She hadn't been out for so long that the blonde highlights she got naturally from the sun had faded into the greasy mess. Her face was pale, and without make-up she could see the scars clearly. She traced the bigger of the two visible scars, along her lower jaw and down the side of her neck. As she pushed against it, she could feel a pulse. She looked at the second hand of her watch and counted the beats. After thirty seconds Emily groaned. On top of everything else she was horribly unfit. She felt like crying.

But after her shower, she felt slightly better, almost glad that she had been forced to make the effort. She dressed quickly in the bathroom, back into the sweat-pants and top she had been wearing before Malcolm's call, and then she slouched into the bedroom to examine her wardrobe.

She was pleasantly surprised when she finally re-examined herself in the mirror. Her jeans seemed to fit better than they had a few weeks ago and her hair, although she had dried it without much enthusiasm, had regained some of its old bounce. Emily attacked it with a soft brush and left it framing her face in a fluffy halo. It needed a trim, but it had nearly grown long enough to cover the scar on her neck. With foundation, her face looked healthy again, and she even went so far as to draw on some green eyeliner to bring out the blue in her eyes.

In the bathroom, Emily had heard the answering machine click on, and Paul's voice as he left a message saying he would call by with a video and some takeaway. Her annoyance at the way people just assumed she'd be in, whenever they announced they were dropping by, was set aside this time by relief. Paul would probably arrive while Malcolm was here and they could talk to each other. Little did she know they had been chatting before either of them spoke to her.

"I was just asking Emily when she was thinking of coming back to us." Malcolm got up to shake Paul's hand when he came in.

"Well, you know what I think, Emms. I think you're more than ready to go back. The sooner the better." Paul ignored her killer look and kissed her chastely on the cheek before sitting down.

"I'm not ready…"

"What's stopping you?"

"Weelll …" She hesitated. "To be honest … I'm not sure I want to go back at all. I've so much on my plate, what with the law case. I'm still doing physio twice a week …"

Emily fizzled to a stop. She hadn't expected to get this

far. She'd been sure they'd both explode as soon as she said she was quitting. Or at least Paul would; Malcolm might just be relieved.

"Your compensation case could go on for years, Emily. And I'm sure Malcolm won't mind you taking time off for your physio …" Paul said carefully.

"Absolutely," her boss beamed.

Emily seethed; they were ganging up against her. She turned to Paul again but he just smiled and turned towards the kitchen to put the foil takeaway containers into the oven.

"But seriously, Malcolm," Emily stumbled over the words, "I really was planning to hand in my notice. I just hadn't got around to writing my letter of resignation yet…"

"Well, don't bother," Malcolm said, still smiling but with a grim determination in his eyes.

"What?"

"Because I won't accept it."

"But –"

"And I would like to remind you that you have to serve out at least three months' notice with us." Malcolm looked at her sternly. She hated the way he suddenly made her feel like one of the clerical staff who'd misfiled an important report. "And given that you've been off on sick leave for so long, I reckon you owe the company some loyalty. Should we say six months?"

To her horror, Emily saw Paul, who was standing at the kitchen door, nodding in agreement.

"You couldn't hold me to that …" She choked in

terror. "It would never stand up …"

"Probably not, Emily." Malcolm couldn't look her in the eye any more. As if he was ashamed of what he had to say. "But I'd try, I promise, and publicly. And I know you wouldn't want the whole of Dublin to think you were chickening out."

"I'm not chickening out. How dare you talk to me like that?" Emily was on her feet in rage. "I'm the best accountant the company's ever employed in Ireland and you know it! It just so happens that maybe I want a change."

"That's better. That sounds more like the woman I promoted," Malcolm replied with relief. "So, I'll see you on Monday then."

"Oh." Emily collapsed back onto the sofa as Malcolm got up to leave.

"I'll offer you a deal, Emily," her boss said from the door. "You come back, and if you still want to leave after a month, I'll accept your notice. On one condition."

"What's that?"

"That you know what you want to do instead."

"He's right, you know." Paul put the reheated containers of Chinese food on the table between them.

"I suppose." All the fight had gone out of Emily. "But the thing is, Paul, I was thinking of leaving even before the accident. Now I dread going back."

"I know. But believe me, it'll be much easier to go back to somewhere you're known than having to start from scratch. You've no confidence at the moment. Use the company for a few months, let it build you back up again and then leave if you still want to." Paul tucked into his spare ribs.

Emily realised he wasn't going to be sympathetic, and listen to her fears all night. Maybe he was right. But it didn't stop her feeling angry with him. He was Paul; he was supposed to be there when she needed a shoulder to cry on.

"Richard's in Dublin this weekend." Emily had the satisfaction of seeing Paul wince. "He wants to take me out to dinner. He's been asking me for months, but I couldn't face it. Maybe I'll go. As you said I need to get out in the real world again. A night out with Richard would be good for my self-confidence."

"Sounds like a good idea," Paul said, refusing to rise to her bait. "Will I put the video on?"

She felt like throwing it across the room.

"No, I've changed my mind. I think I'll get an early night. Do you mind?"

Paul just shrugged. He was disappointed, but took care not to show it.

Later, as he put on his coat, he asked, "How's Charlotte?"

"Managing, I suppose." Emily shrugged. "I haven't spoken to her since Sunday."

Paul gave her a funny look as he closed the door. Her sister's marriage was crumbling and she didn't seem to care. Donal was moving out this weekend; the old Emily would have camped on Charlotte's lawn rather than leave her to face it on her own.

Paul hoped to God he'd done the right thing in calling Malcolm. He'd tried everything else to shake Emily out of this depression. He'd even dragged her to a psychologist but, after the one visit, Emily refused to go back. There was nothing wrong with her, she said.

Well, if there's nothing wrong with her, Paul thought savagely, she can bloody well get out there and prove it.

Late on Sunday night, Donal stood in the kitchen of Moran's Restaurant. The light he'd just switched on flickered to life over his head, throwing eerie shadows across the stainless-steel worktops. He couldn't sleep and, as he hadn't had time to shop for food yet, he'd come to forage in the restaurant fridges. He wondered had he done the right thing in moving out. Tim and Aisling were understandably upset, although they'd come round a bit when he said he'd be living in the flat, only two minutes down the road.

Gemma had been remarkably sanguine.

"You're not getting divorced?" Her young face creased into a frown of concentration.

"No."

"You're not getting separated even? Not officially?"

"No."

"So you just need some space." The girl's eyes flicked between her two parents. "Well, I can understand that. You can't even bear to be in the same room as each other lately."

Donal's heart ached when he thought how she must have worried.

"I suppose as you're not really splitting up, just seeing how you get along apart, it's not so bad. You might even get back together again."

"We can't make any promises, love."

"I know. But you'll still be friends, won't you?"

"Yes." By now Donal was finding it hard to speak. He was glad they'd chosen to talk to Gemma first, on her own. He looked across at Charlotte who was chewing her bottom lip, trying not to cry.

"Well, that's a lot better than Lucy's parents." Gemma was referring to a friend whose parents had recently split up. "They were screaming and shouting at each other, in front of everyone. It was so embarrassing. Maybe if they'd taken some time apart, they might have got back together again."

Donal and Charlotte hugged their eldest daughter, both wondering how they had produced someone so wise for her age.

But whatever about the kids, Donal knew he had to get out. Charlotte's admission, or at least her refusal to deny that she had married him for Gemma's sake, had hit him harder than expected. After all, he'd always known it, hadn't he? And it wasn't as if she wanted to end their marriage; she was hurt that he couldn't try to put it behind them and make the best of it. But Donal couldn't stay on those terms. The months between finding out for definite and leaving had been hell. Not knowing if she was staying with him out of pity, duty, loyalty, or love. He might have been able to persuade himself that it would all work out if it hadn't been for the sex. It had become so cold and mechanical. It had got so that he could guess when Charlotte would make her next dutiful advance towards him, get it over with as soon as possible, then turn over in relief and pretend to go asleep. The passion was gone. He was afraid to touch her, to try and hold her in case he was putting pressure on her. He was terrified she would shrug him off.

He wondered what his life would have been like if, all those years ago, he hadn't waited until Charlotte was free. He'd been tempted to ask Suzy out. The only thing stopping him was that he knew she was crazy about him, and he wasn't sure he could return that devotion. If things had gone sour between them, Charlotte would have hated him for hurting her best friend.

Her best friend. That was a good one.

He groaned when he thought about telling Suzy that he'd moved out of home. She had split up with Etienne again, and Donal wouldn't allow himself to suspect that it was because he'd told her how things were between him and Charlotte. He was sure she must be over what had basically been a girlish crush on him a long time ago.

He couldn't remember quite how it had started, but he and Suzy had formed a habit of having coffee and a chat together in his office, any time he was in the restaurant in town. She had been genuinely upset telling him about Charlotte meeting Marcus, and now she seemed to see it as her duty to be there whenever he wanted to let off steam. And she was so easy to talk to. She never judged or offered advice; she just listened. If it wasn't for the fact that she'd been the one to tell him in the first place, he'd probably think of her as his best friend at the moment.

"I just couldn't bear to see you made a fool of again," she'd said with tears in her eyes. "If you face up to this now, you have a chance to sort it out properly this time."

So she must know, or at least have guessed about Gemma. What the hell was he going to do about her?

Donal had suggested that Suzy might like to take over the Cork restaurant when it opened. He'd even offered her a partnership, thinking that she'd like to be closer to home, and knowing that Etienne had always loved Cork. That was when she told him she'd split up with Etienne and that her life and all the people she cared about were in Dublin.

Charlotte still didn't know that it was Suzy who had forced him to confront her about Marcus. He didn't want to cause trouble between them, and Suzy seemed quite happy to maintain her friendship with Charlotte now that, as she put it, "I don't have to feel guilty about hiding anything".

He was a coward not to tell his wife; he knew that. But Suzy got on so well with the kids, and for Gemma to lose her beloved godmother now would break her heart. But he hated himself for keeping the secret; it was as if he shared something with Suzy that excluded the rest of the world, and he wasn't sure he liked the feeling of intimacy it implied.

Chapter 17

Spring and summer 1998

On a sunny afternoon about four months later, Marcus parked his car in the Stephen's Green Centre, then wandered through the shops to kill some time. Charlotte had finally agreed to meet him. Since hearing about her separation from Donal, he'd spoken to her on the phone a few times, but this was the first time she hadn't made some excuse as soon as he suggested they meet.

He walked out of the shopping centre and crossed the road to St Stephen's Green. After a long winter, summer was surprising everyone by skipping spring altogether. It was the hottest day of the year so far, and although Marcus was too lazy to take off his jacket, he had to laugh at the park full of summer clothes. There were even a few pairs of shorts. You'd never have seen shorts in April when he was a student, he thought to himself; no one would have dared reveal blue knobbly knees so early in the year. But most of the legs on display nowadays were tanned, although some did have tell-tale streaks of orange at the back of the ankles.

He walked around the lake and stopped to watch a family feed the ducks. He felt the familiar pang. He was talking to Denise again, not through lawyers, but face to face. He'd been unfair to her. All it took was for him to make that one admission and they were able to talk like friends again.

He wondered did Charlotte and Donal still talk like friends. Whenever he spoke to Charlotte on the phone, their conversations lasted only five or ten minutes, not the ideal forum for him to bring up the subject of her separation. And she never referred to Donal at all.

The waiter was just pulling some tables outside onto the pavement on Chatham Row when Charlotte arrived. The sun had put her in a good mood, so she sat outside and asked for two menus. Because she was early, she ordered a glass of wine and sat back to watch the street. She'd eaten at Mao, a sort of Eastern Fusion restaurant, before, but never outside. Some of the windows in the College of Music across the road were open and piano scales drifted out to compete with traffic noise. A car pulled up by the kerb near where she was sitting.

Only six weeks to her exams – of course, the weather was improving, she thought, as she pushed her sunglasses onto the top of her head and closed her eyes. She was surprised at how well her study had gone. It helped to take her mind off her problems with Donal, as she dived into her books any time she was tempted to think. Her teachers were pleased with her and she'd done well in her mock exams in March. She was well on her way to getting a place in college as a mature student.

She looked up when the waiter brought her wine, thanked him and poured half the little bottle into the glass. Then she saw Marcus. He was walking from Grafton Street, on her left, and he hadn't spotted her yet so she had time to study him. He was wearing a black leather jacket, jeans and a white T-shirt. It was a timeless outfit, but it dated him, aged him somewhat. Charlotte couldn't help thinking of the way Donal always looked well-dressed and effortlessly fashionable. Then she thought she was being unfair. Marcus only looked dated because that's what she remembered him always wearing, but the jeans were designer now, and the jacket had the lustrous sheen of expensive leather.

"Charlotte, hi." Marcus took off his sunglasses and put them in the inside pocket of his jacket. Then realising they were going to be sitting outside, he put them back on again. Still standing, he seemed unsure what to do with his hands. For one awful moment, Charlotte thought he was going to extend one of them for her to shake.

"Marcus!" She jumped up, scraping the metal legs of her chair on the pavement as she did so. She stepped forward, glad of the table between them, touched his arm and leaned towards him, just far enough to kiss him quickly on the cheek. Before he could respond, she was sitting down again.

"What are you drinking?" She caught the waiter's eye

and called him over.

"The same," Marcus said pointing at her glass. "Will you have another?"

"No, I'm fine." Charlotte addressed the waiter: "Could we have a jug of water too, please?"

They studied their menus and made their selections. They ordered when the waiter returned with Marcus's drink and a large jug of water. Charlotte poured two glasses of water and sat back in her chair. She refused to feel awkward. He was the one who'd suggested they meet; let him get the conversation going.

"Amazing weather for April really," she said at last when the silence had stretched to fifty, maybe sixty seconds.

"Yeah, I'd forgotten what a bitch an Irish winter could be."

They both grinned, then laughed shyly.

"Hey, we're Irish, what else would we talk about?" Marcus shrugged his shoulders and took a sip of his wine. Then he swapped glasses and took a long drink of water.

Now that he was here, he had no idea what he wanted to talk to her about. Or rather he knew he wanted to ask her about her marriage. But that wasn't exactly what you talked about on a first date was it?

God, is that what this was, a date? He hadn't really thought of it like that.

Charlotte wondered how long he would go on staring at her like that. She was glad she was wearing sunglasses so he wouldn't see what direction her eyes were turned. To help her feel less awkward, she looked at the next table to theirs. There was a woman sitting alone and, although she had arrived after Charlotte, she had ordered immediately and was now eating a crispy duck salad. Charlotte watched with interest as she tried to eat lettuce with chopsticks. Not crunchy sliced-up lettuce, but a huge, dark green leaf of floppy butterhead lettuce. She admired the way the woman used her chopsticks to fold the leaf carefully, over and over, wedging it against the side of the plate to hold it still. Then she swirled the little parcel around her plate to coat it with shiny dressing and popped it into her mouth. A masterful performance; Charlotte felt like applauding.

"How are the kids?" Marcus dragged her attention back.

"Fine. Looking forward to the summer holidays." Charlotte could only meet his eyes for a fraction of a second as she wondered why he asked about kids first.

"How are they coping since …?" Marcus knew he had to be careful; Charlotte's smile had straightened and thinned. "Well …since you and Donal separated." There really was no other way of putting it.

"We're not separated." Charlotte cursed silently; she should have known he'd have heard – this city was too bloody small. "We just need a bit of space, that's all."

"Sorry, I didn't –"

"And the kids are coping fine. I mean, they actually see a lot more of him now. So do I for that matter. See Donal, I mean. He's in and out of the house the whole time. Things are better between us now than they were six months ago."

As she spoke, Charlotte realised she was telling the truth. Since Donal had moved out, the atmosphere in the house had lightened and after the first few awkward weeks, a pattern of sorts had emerged. They could talk and laugh about things together without trying to read meaning into every word. Because they both knew that Donal was going home to his own bed, neither of them had to worry about sending out the wrong signals. It was only after he left that Charlotte ached for him and wished she had reached out to touch him, or brushed against him as they passed in the kitchen so her skin would have a recent memory of him to carry her through the long nights.

Because in the months between their discussion about Gemma and the day Donal announced he was moving out, they had made love only a handful of times. Each time it was Charlotte who had initiated it – mainly because it felt like too long to have gone since the last time. And afterwards she always felt that Donal had gone along with it only to humour her. She was afraid to be too passionate, in case he rejected her, and afraid of asking him what was wrong when he rolled over afterwards and turned his back to her.

"I'm sorry. I shouldn't have asked about you and Donal – it's none of my business." Marcus could see she was miles away and tried to bring her back.

"You're right," Charlotte agreed, feeling no pity for his embarrassment. "It's not."

The waiter brought their meals, breaking the tension between them. They admired each other's dishes, and busied themselves with the food.

After they had eaten in silence for a while, Marcus put down his knife and fork. Charlotte stopped eating, a large prawn suspended in mid-air, clutched firmly between her chopsticks.

"Can we start again?" he pleaded.

Charlotte put the prawn in her mouth, chewed slowly and swallowed without tasting it.

"What do you mean?"

"This – conversation, lunch – whatever." He'd been about to say 'date'.

"Oh." Relief flooded through her. She smiled. "All right."

"I just wanted for us to be friends, if that's possible after the way I treated you."

"It's a long time ago."

"Not forgotten though, is it, Char?" Marcus nearly said 'babes', the endearment she had pretended to hate.

She put down her chopsticks and abandoned any pretence of interest in the food.

"Can you just answer one question, Marcus? To help make sense of those two years."

"Shoot."

"Did you love me?"

"What?"

"Did you love me at all, or was it all a big game to you?"

Marcus took off his sunglasses and put them back in his pocket. He stared into her face. Charlotte lowered her glasses as well, and looked at him properly for the first time, although with the sun in her eyes she had to squint.

315

"Wow! What a question!"

Charlotte shrugged but said nothing.

Marcus knew that if he was ever wanted to see her again he had to be honest.

"I … well, that is … yes."

"You never told me, you know, not in two years." Charlotte refused to think about their last time together, the time that maybe Gemma had been conceived.

"At first … you're right; it was a bit of a game. You … I don't know if you have any idea what kind of effect you had on me, Charlotte. You were beautiful, you seemed so old, and yet so young, and I wanted you so badly. More than I ever wanted anyone or anything before. But you're right, I didn't love you then, not really. That was later, much later …" He'd been about to say 'when it was too late'.

"OK." Charlotte began to regret asking the question. His answer was making her uncomfortable. She picked up her chopsticks and forced herself to eat some more.

Marcus began to eat again too.

"Do you want coffee?" he asked after they had finished their meal in silence.

"Not really." Charlotte looked at her watch.

"Sorry, do you have to get back to the kids?"

"No, Donal's picking them up. He'll mind them till I get back."

"Fine." Marcus didn't know why her answer unsettled him. He wanted to ask if Donal knew she was meeting him. "How about a walk, and then maybe we could get a coffee later?"

"Yeah, that's a good idea. I need to stretch my legs, I was sitting in a classroom all morning."

They wandered down Grafton Street.

"So you've gone back to studying again?"

"Yes, another three Leaving Cert subjects. It may have taken me thirteen years, but I'll have a full Leaving Cert to my name at last," Charlotte grinned.

"Well done."

"I'm hoping to go to college next year, as a mature student," she admitted as they walked through the front gates of Trinity College.

"Here?" Marcus waved a hand around, in a gesture that took in the whole of Front Square.

"Maybe." Charlotte was suddenly embarrassed. "I've applied here and UCD. But I may not get in anywhere."

"How will you manage? With the kids and work, I mean."

"Donal's been great, and his mother's living almost full time in Dublin now. She's really keen for me to do it. And we've two really good baby-sitters. And as for work, a few hours a day runs both places. I've a really good assistant too – Suzy's cousin Geri. Remember Suzy?"

"How could I forget Suzy?" Marcus grinned. "She never approved of me, did she? Remember sneaking up to your flat when it was supposed to be over between us?"

Charlotte didn't answer; she didn't want to remember that time in their relationship.

"I suppose she was right," Marcus said, after they had walked the length of the college cricket pitch without talking.

"Who?"

"Suzy. She was right. I was no good for you. You deserved better. You got a lot better in the end, didn't you?"

They turned around the end of the cricket pitch, and sat on a bench. There was no one playing, but the sloped edges around the field were dotted with students sunbathing. Two runners were doing laps of the running track.

"I could never have given you what Donal gave you," Marcus went on, ignoring her silence. "You wanted a family, stability, all that. I'm really glad you got what you wanted with Donal."

"I don't want to talk about Donal, all right?" Charlotte's voice was weary rather than hostile.

"Sorry." Marcus shifted uncomfortably on the wooden bench. He'd sat down first, and she'd sat as far from him as she could without being rude. The space between them felt embarrassingly wide. On the next bench to theirs, two couples sat holding hands. "Do you want to go and get a coffee now?"

They had a quick cup of coffee in the Kilkenny Design Centre, and talked about safe subjects such as Charlotte's study and gossip about Castlemichael. Then he walked her back to the carpark.

"Can we do this again sometime?" he asked without much hope.

"Yes, I'd like that."

"OK, when?" They were standing in the pay area of the carpark. Charlotte had paid for her ticket, and a queue was forming to get to the machines. Someone jostled against her and Marcus caught her as she stumbled.

"Sorry." He let go of her arm as if it had burnt him. "When would suit you?"

"I'll call you. I'll have to sort something out, and I've a lot of study to do."

"I seem to remember that excuse came up quite regularly last time round." He tried to grin, but his senses were electrified by the brief contact between them, and all he managed was a grimace.

"And as far as I can remember, you were the one who made the most use of it," Charlotte replied.

"Yeah, I guess so. Sorry." This time his grin worked. "I'd better let you get back to your books then. Bye." He turned towards the door to the street, then swung round again. "Charlotte ..." He hesitated. "I really enjoyed this afternoon."

"So did I." Her face was a mixture of surprise and amusement.

"Till next time then."

She smiled through the closing lift door.

Marcus walked quickly along Stephen Street, past Break For The Border and towards his car. He was whistling. Just before he reached the door of the shopping centre, he turned and walked back down Grafton Street. He stopped at the first flower stall and selected a mixture of tulips, which he asked the stall-holder to tie into a big bunch. He was driving to Castlemichael, for dinner with his parents. Slowly, he was beginning to bridge the gap that had separated them since he was a teenager.

As he placed the bunch carefully in the boot of his car, he tried to remember the last time he'd bought flowers for his mother. Then he realised he'd never bought flowers for his mother. As he drove out of the carpark he was reminded of all the lousy decisions he'd made in his life. He thought of Charlotte. She had agreed to meet him again, but she hadn't given up on her marriage. He uttered a silent prayer to a God he didn't believe in, that he'd do the right thing by Charlotte this time, that he wouldn't screw things up for her.

Anne-Marie stopped at an amber light, nearly causing the car behind to rear-end her. Since Emily's accident, she was a much more cautious driver and, normally, the behaviour of the man behind her, flashing his lights and waving his fist at her, would have her fuming with self-righteous indignation. But today she felt like getting out of the car, going back to his open window and telling him that it was all right. Life was great. It was thirty-four days since her last period!

"I'll buy a pregnancy-test kit in town. I'll put it back in the car, and then we'll do it together, tonight." She imagined Dave's face.

They'd been trying for a baby since a couple of months before they got married. Month after month, Anne-Marie had cried as she realised they hadn't managed it yet, and month after month Dave told her not to worry, they hadn't really been trying that long. And now they were coming up to the one-year mark. The line in the sand, the time when they had to decide to do something about it. But now they wouldn't need to! Anne-Marie felt like singing for joy.

She bounced into the restaurant where she was meeting Emily, and kissed her friend on both cheeks, before hugging her and taking a seat opposite her.

"You look great, Emms!" she said honestly. "Have you gone back to the gym?"

"No, I've just been walking, trying to run, but I can't manage that for very long."

"Would it not be easier in the gym, or the swimming pool? Less impact on your joints and all that?"

"Maybe, I don't know. How's Dave?" Emily didn't want to admit that her real reason for running was that she could change in the privacy of her own bedroom.

"Dave's great. You'll have to give this marriage thing a go, Emily. I never thought I could be any happier than I was with him before –"

"It certainly suits you." Emily cut her off. She didn't want to hear Anne-Marie extolling the virtues of marriage.

"Oh, no!" Anne-Marie mistook the reason for her friend's sour expression. "I keep forgetting about Charlotte. How's she doing?"

"Not too bad, considering." This was another subject Emily wished they didn't have to discuss. She felt guilty whenever she thought about her sister's separation, and how unsupportive she'd been when Charlotte needed her most.

"How's work?" Anne-Marie continued cheerily. It really was so hard to talk to Emily these days.

"I've got to get out!" Emily said with real feeling.

"I seemed to remember you saying that over a year ago, before …"

"Well, now I mean it. I've been scanning the job pages and the Internet, but nothing catches my eye. I don't really know what I want to do."

"Why not take some time off altogether?"

"And do what?" Emily shuddered as she thought of the months before she had gone back to work; she never wanted to go through a period of inactivity like that again. She'd finally agreed to go back to the psychiatrist a few weeks after starting work, and he reluctantly agreed that she needed to keep busy to keep the depression at bay. And work helped, especially since he'd cut her dose of Prozac.

"How about travel?"

"I thought about that, but I was never much good at it. Travelling without a goal, I mean, just to see things, soaking up atmosphere and all that. Besides, I'm no good at being on my own. And I can't think of anyone who'd drop everything to bum around the world with me."

"How's Paul?" Anne-Marie had thought of him as soon as Emily mentioned being no good at being on her own.

"Fine," Emily grunted.

"And …" Anne-Marie took a deep breath and forced a smile, "Richard?"

"He's well. He's just been made senior partner. He's not able to get to Dublin as often as he used to." Why did everyone always ask about bloody Paul first? It was no secret that Emily had been seeing Richard on and off for the past couple of months. Couldn't they just accept that he was what she needed right now? "Tara was asking for you." Emily swirled the crisp Chablis around her glass and watched Anne-Marie's face for a reaction.

"How is she doing?" Anne-Marie folded and unfolded her napkin. She hadn't spoken to Tara since the accident.

"Not too bad. She's back at work. She's been banned from driving, of course, but she says it doesn't bother her too much. I think the police would have liked to charge her with possession – they found some coke in her flat. But I gather Paul got a barrister friend of his to point out gently that they didn't have a search warrant, so it went away. I think it was too small an amount for them to get their knickers in a twist about, and as she was doing well in treatment …"

"Why did Paul do that? Help her out, I mean. The day after your accident he'd have happily strangled her with his own two hands."

"He said it was because he felt guilty for letting them into her flat in the first place, but I don't know. He's a big softie at heart."

"Or he was doing what he thought you'd have wanted him to do?" Anne-Marie watched Emily closely but she just shrugged and refused to look up. Sod it, she thought. Life's too short to pussy-foot around. And Emily more than most should know that you can't afford to let opportunities go by, because you might not be there tomorrow. "I can't see why you'd be the slightest bit interested in Richard with a man like Paul around," she said.

Emily looked up, startled, and felt the blood rush to her cheeks.

"It's like Charlotte and Donal all over again," Anne-Marie went on. "You Riordan sisters really know how to pick them, don't you? You let the bastards sweep you off your feet and leave the men who really love you waiting on the sidelines. At least Charlotte saw sense in time and got together with Donal. How long are you going to keep Paul waiting? I know you feel something for him. I know you too well."

"Richard's not a bastard, and he hasn't swept me off my feet. We're just friends this time round."

"And Paul?"

"I don't want to talk about this, Anne-Marie, all right?" Emily begged her friend, then she dropped her eyes to her plate again. "Anyway I think I left it too late for anything else to develop between me and Paul. We'll only ever be good friends now."

"If you want more you should go for it – you've nothing to lose."

"Yes, I have." Emily was amazed at Anne-Marie's flippancy. If she understood that Emily had feelings for Paul, then she must also understand that she was terrified of losing him altogether. "Can we talk about something else? I seem to remember we were discussing Tara before you changed the subject."

"I thought we'd finished talking about her. What else is there to say?"

"She's moved on, Anne-Marie. She's changed. Can't you give her another chance?" Emily pleaded. "For my sake?"

"What for? We were never particularly close anyway."

"She feels awful about … you know, screwing up your wedding and all that."

"My wedding?" Anne-Marie slammed down her knife and fork and the red wine sauce from her steak splashed the white tablecloth. It looked like stale blood. "What the hell has my wedding got to do with anything?"

"You know…" Emily answered carefully, baffled by Anne-Marie's reaction. "Tara landed me in hospital so I couldn't be your bridesmaid. And it must have cast a bit of a shadow over the day."

"And you think that's why I can't bear the thought of seeing her again?" Anne-Marie's eyes sparked with anger. "What kind of self-centred bitch do you think I am?"

"I never –"

"Tara nearly killed you, Emily. I was in that hospital watching one of my best friends fight for her life, and the other torn apart by the fear that she was going to lose her sister. Tara may have been driving, but if I hadn't insisted on dragging you all down to Kerry that weekend – if I hadn't asked Charlotte to give Antonia a lift back to Castlemichael – you'd never have been in that car."

"Oh my God, Anne-Marie!" Emily looked at her in horror. Her eyes filled with tears. "You feel responsible …"

"It was Tara's fault." Anne-Marie clenched and unclenched her hands as she spoke. "She got behind the wheel of a car, drunk and high, and she nearly killed you. That's why I hate her, Emily. It was her fault but I feel guilty."

"Well, stop it! I'd been in Tara's car a million times. I'd

got into the seat beside her dozens of times knowing she was over the limit – after some party or some late-night reception, when I just couldn't be bothered to go looking for a taxi. I feel guilty too, you know."

"You do?" Anne-Marie looked at her in disbelief.

"Yes. I was supposed to be her friend. She was falling to pieces in front of my eyes, and I didn't do anything to help her. None of us did. Tara, the life and soul of the party. Tara who could drink us all under the table and still get up the next day and go to work. How the hell did I think she could do that? I never asked, I didn't care. And then when she started to snort white powder up her nose, and take God knows what other tablets, when she started hanging around with dangerous people, when her nose and eyes were permanently streaming, and she lost weight, I didn't want to know. It was none of my business. How do you think that makes me feel? If it hadn't been for the accident, would I have sat back and watched, while Tara buried herself in a chemical grave, or ended up a vegetable from some overdose? It happened, Anne-Marie, and we have to get on with our lives. I was put together again with steel pins and catgut whereas Tara has to hold herself together. And she's not doing too bad a job of it. But I know she feels bad about you. Could you not even pretend not to hate her for a few hours, and say you forgive her?" Emily was aware that she was talking louder and louder. The man from the next table was looking at her. He turned away when she caught his eye. She returned her attention to Anne-Marie. "Well?"

"I'll try. I won't promise anything, but I'll try." She

326

paused. "Why don't you sign me in as a guest at the health club?"

"I haven't been back …"

"Well, maybe this would be a good opportunity." Anne-Marie finally looked up, the unspoken challenge in her eyes.

"OK. The health club," Emily agreed at last. She could change in a cubicle, she decided, and she didn't have to get into the Jacuzzi.

"So how did it go?" Richard asked a few days later as he arranged flowers in a vase while Emily tossed a salad.

"Not too bad. Do you want to eat on the balcony? This weather might not last – we may as well make the most of it." Emily opened the sliding doors. It was a beautiful early summer evening, and there was some warmth left in the air. She reckoned that they could eat the meal out here and retreat indoors for coffee. "It was a bit awkward at first," she went on, in reply to Richard's question about the visit she, Tara and Anne-Marie had made to the health club, "but soon we were all chatting away. Strained, but at least talking. No one mentioned the war."

"Do you think Anne-Marie still blames herself?"

"I don't know. I haven't spoken to her since the day in the gym."

"And how did that go?" Richard asked, watching her closely. "Going back to the gym, I mean. How did that go for you?"

"No big deal." She turned her back on him. "I was

stupid to leave it so long. Imagine paying my subscription for a year and never using the place."

But Emily would never forget the panic she felt as she walked into the large communal changing room, one wall covered in tall wooden lockers, another two with sparkling mirrors. An aerobics class was about to start in one of the studios and the wiry fitness instructor was chivvying along the stragglers. Some of the women changed quickly, pulling baggy T-shirts over flabby torsos while others lingered, standing in their bras and knickers, casting surreptitious glances at their own reflections. In the corner, emerging from the shower, two women recognised Emily, greeted her, then continued their own conversation, gossiping about work, talking to each other but watching their reflections as they smoothed body lotion onto tanned, muscular bodies.

I can't do this, Emily thought suddenly.

Then Tara, seeing her discomfort, chose to get changed in one of the curtained cubicles and Emily fled into another.

No big deal, she repeated to herself now. Loads of people prefer to change in a cubicle.

Emily poured a supermarket cheese sauce over the pasta she had just drained, and mixed through some grated Parmesan. She piled it onto two plates and sprinkled some fresh herbs on top.

"Will you grab the wine, and two glasses?" she called over her shoulder to Richard, and stepped out onto the balcony.

He touched his glass against hers as they began to eat.

"Cheers!"

"Richard," Emily said after they had been eating in silence for a few minutes, "Richard, I want you to stay the night."

He put down his fork. "Are you sure? I mean …" He took her hand and waited for her to raise her eyes so he could read her expression. Even at the height of their affair he had never spent the night with her and, although they were seeing each other again since the accident, they hadn't even kissed properly, let alone slept together.

"Don't you want to?"

"You know I do." His eyes were hungry. "But you know I can't promise …"

"I know. Same rules as before."

"Marilyn and I –"

"Ssh! I'm not asking for any more than you can give me."

"I'm not sure it's a good idea …"

"I am. Finish your pasta." Emily pointed to his meal and wagged her finger sternly. "No dessert until you clear your plate."

Emily switched off the video halfway through.

"You were right. It is a crap film."

"You can't say I didn't warn you." Richard smiled at her from his end of the sofa and went on rubbing her stockinged feet.

"Go on through," she nodded towards the bedroom. "I'll follow you."

"Are you sure about this Emily?"

Her heart skipped when she saw doubt on his face, then she relaxed as it was replaced by pleading lust.

"Just go," she ordered, swinging her legs off his lap.

He was already under the covers when she came into the bedroom. She stopped in the doorway and looked at him. He had pulled up the quilt as far as his waist. Some of the hairs on his chest were grey now. She wondered how grey his head was now that he'd started dyeing it again. She remembered the feel of his chest under her fingers. She knew all the things he loved. It was going to be all right.

She switched off the bedroom light and went into the bathroom to undress. Turning off that light too as she went back into the bedroom, she slipped quickly under the covers beside him. He gasped at her nakedness as she wrapped herself around him. To her relief she felt his erection press against her stomach. She flipped onto her back and dragged him with her.

"Now, Richard!" she hissed, pulling him to her.

"Wait, darling." He began to run his hands over her body, touching her, stroking her. She felt his fingers run over the knobbly, taut skin of the scar on her abdomen and she stiffened. "It's all right, Emily," he whispered. He kept his hands clear of it. When his searching fingers found the scars on her hip and then her thigh, they moved on quickly, noting their positions, never to return there again. He raised himself on his arms and began to kiss her breasts; he tugged on her nipple and she felt his teeth as he sucked it into his mouth. To her surprise she began to feel the stirrings of her own, forgotten passion. It spread through her body like a shiver. Now when she moved with him, she was no longer acting.

"Oh Richard!" she called out.

"Sshh! Darling," he whispered into her hair after collapsing on top of her. "It's all right now. It's all right."

He stroked her hair as she cried against his chest, sobbing with gratitude.

Chapter 18

In the months that followed their first meeting, Charlotte and Marcus met a handful of times. Always during the day and always for a meal or a coffee in town. Apart from a quick kiss on the cheek to say hello or good-bye, they never touched. They talked about safe subjects. He asked how her study was going; they discussed television or work. Each time she met Marcus, she asked Donal to mind the kids. She never said where she was going, or who she was meeting on these occasions, but she always left a long silence in their conversation, just at the point where she would usually have explained. It was a code she knew Donal understood.

That was how Charlotte wanted it. She didn't want to sneak around behind his back, but she knew he didn't want the details. Each evening, when she arrived home from one of these meetings, he would ask politely if she had enjoyed her afternoon and search her face for some

333

clue that things had changed between her and Marcus. She would tell Donal where she had been, what she had eaten and drunk, without mentioning Marcus's name.

But this evening was different. She felt that she was cheating on her husband as she got ready to go out. Marcus wanted to take her to a new restaurant in Dun Laoghaire to celebrate the end of her exams and Charlotte had asked Fiona to baby-sit. It was only because she was going out for the evening, she told herself. Donal might be needed at work, Friday being the most hectic night of the week.

Marcus met her at the DART station in Dun Laoghaire. He had offered to collect her from home – he said he didn't want her driving because she had to be able to have a few drinks to celebrate. When she had refused a lift, he had suggested the train and she agreed readily. The DART didn't run all night; she would be home by midnight at the latest.

"The table's booked for half eight," Marcus said as he kissed her cheek at the top of the steps up from the platform. "Would you like to get a drink or go for a walk?"

Charlotte looked up at the clock on the town hall. It was approaching half seven.

"Let's go for a walk. I love the seafront in this weather."

They walked away from the station and, before they'd gone a hundred yards, Charlotte had to take off her jacket. The evening's warmth was too much even for lightweight linen and although Charlotte hadn't intended exposing her shoulders in her spaghetti-strapped dress, it was that or roast.

"I like your dress." Marcus smiled as he put out his hand to take her jacket. "The colour goes well with your hair."

Which particular colour, Charlotte wondered. Her dress was light and silky white covered in thousands of flecks of different turquoises, blues and greens. Self-consciously, she smoothed the light fabric down over her stomach and hips and noted with annoyance that it had creased while she was sitting down in the train. She had lost weight since Christmas. With Donal not in the house, she tended to feed the kids early and often didn't bother with dinner herself. She loved this dress, the first size twelve she'd bought since the kids were born – and bought to congratulate herself on doing what she hoped was really well in History and reasonably well in Geography and French.

Marcus swung her jacket over his shoulder. They must make a handsome couple, she realised. He was wearing, as usual, jeans and a white T-shirt. Why did he always wear the same, she wondered. Had Denise never taken him shopping? Charlotte would love to see him in … she stopped midway through her train of thought. She'd been about to contemplate buying him clothes.

"Where are we going?" she asked.

They had turned off the seafront and were walking up a street of gleaming, almost all newly painted, Victorian houses. Then they stopped in front of one, which bore a large brass plaque on the iron railing: M O'*Sullivan Systems Ltd*.

"Original name!" She traced out his name, carved

into the cold metal. "What do you do?"

"At the moment, mainly software for mobile phones. But I've also got some people working on a new Internet security system."

"How many people do you have working for you?" Charlotte stepped away from the gate when he put his hand on it.

"Twenty-two." He grinned when he saw her raised eyebrow. "Quite the entrepreneur, aren't I? Of course they're not all here. Some of them work from home, just pop in now and again. I've even got three guys still in New York." He opened the gate. "Would you like a tour?"

"Of the office? OK." She walked up the granite steps ahead of him.

"Hi, boss!" A tousled blonde head appeared from behind a computer screen as they walked into the first office. Charlotte thought he looked like a teenager. "I've nearly got it cracked. Take a look."

Charlotte watched as Marcus and the boy he introduced as Ozzy peered at his screen. She wandered over to the window and tuned out of their excited discussion.

"Sorry." Marcus came up behind her making her jump. She could feel his breath on her cheek. He pulled back before she had a chance to react. "Got a little carried away there. Ozzy's a genius programmer. Aren't you, Oz?"

"Pay me more then!" The youth didn't reappear from behind his screen.

"Would you like a drink while you're here?" Marcus

asked a few minutes later, after they'd seen all there was to be seen. They were standing at the bottom of a wide staircase with a locked door at the top.

"Why not?" Charlotte took a deep breath and followed him upstairs.

"The building was divided up into four flats when I bought it," Marcus explained as he took a bottle out of the fridge. They were in a small kitchen at the very top of the house. "White wine OK?" He searched for a corkscrew when she nodded her assent. "This top flat was the biggest, so I didn't have to do too much to it. Most of the work was downstairs, converting the office space."

He opened the bottle, poured wine into two glasses that didn't match and handed her the more elegant of the two.

"Come on. We'll take these down to the living-room."

There were two doors on the landing below.

"That's my room," he said pointing to the closed door. "There's a bathroom and another bedroom down there." He nodded towards the back of the house and the flight of stairs they had just come up. "This is the living-room." He led the way.

"It's gorgeous!" Charlotte looked around at the large, high-ceilinged room with two bay windows. It had a dark gold carpet, rich cream walls and ornate plasterwork which gleamed with white radiance from the ceiling. Sunlight flooded through one of bay windows, but it was into the other that Marcus walked.

"Look at this."

Charlotte followed his gaze. She looked down the

street they had walked up and beyond that to the sea. Hundreds of tiny white sailing boats broke up the deep evening-blue water.

"I love water!" He gave a deep sigh of satisfaction. "I don't know how I lived for so long in New York. In Holland we were near the sea ..." He stopped as if remembering that in Holland and New York he was with Denise. "I can't imagine ever living away from the sea again. Funny really, when you think I grew up so far from it in Kildare."

Charlotte sipped her wine and stared at the sea. Marcus stood a couple of feet behind her and to her right. The silence between them was comfortable for the first time. She breathed deeply, luxuriating in the comfort of that silence, like a warm bath. When he took a few steps forwards, so that he was standing right behind her, she could hear him breathing. Slow and measured breaths. He sounded as relaxed as she was.

She turned to face him. He was slightly taller than Donal, so even though she was wearing heels, she had to tilt her head upwards to see into his eyes. He looked happy and she knew it was because she was here with him. It made her feel powerful. She didn't move when he gently took her glass and balanced it on the sash of the huge window, then he leaned forward from the hips and touched his lips to hers. At first that's all it was, the softest of touches, but when she didn't pull away, he began to kiss her gently. He put one hand on the back of her head and rubbed the back of her neck with his fingers.

Stop! she tried to tell herself. But her body, longing to

be touched, tried to shut down her mind. I shouldn't be doing this, her brain screamed inside her head. But she let him go on, pulling gently on one of her lips then the other, and darting his tongue in and out between her parted teeth. He tasted of white wine and toothpaste. Then he pulled back a bit, their lips still touching, to see what she would do. After a fraction of a second's hesitation, she began to kiss him back.

This has gone far enough, her mind told her. But she sucked his tongue hungrily into her mouth. He placed his other hand on the base of her spine and applied the gentlest pressure. She responded by moving forwards, pressing her hips into him. Her body began to remind her of the last time they had made love. The hundreds of little kisses he had rained all over her body making her feel like a rosebush with a swarm of butterflies alighting on it. Her skin tingled with the memory. He had told her he loved her that night.

Surely something which felt this good couldn't be wrong? It was so long since she had been made love to. If she closed her eyes she could pretend he was Donal.

"No!" she cried out and broke away from him.

Marcus stood alone in the window. The flotilla of little boats seemed to have lined up, almost motionless. A gun sounded and they surged forwards together, like hundreds of parts of the one organism.

It felt like they had been kissing for hours, though it was probably less than a minute.

Charlotte was sitting in a brown leather bucket armchair, her elbows on her knees, her head in her hands. He walked over and stood in front of her. She gave no sign that she even knew he was there. He got down on his hunkers and touched her chin gently. Still she didn't move. At least she didn't pull away from him.

"Charlotte, look at me."

She tilted her head up to meet his eyes.

"I'm sorry," she whispered.

"Charlotte, I have to know. Am I even in with a chance here? Because if I'm not, I'd rather know now."

Was he? She honestly didn't know. She wanted Donal back. How much she wanted him she had only just realised. But suppose it was too late for them? Turn Marcus away now and she might regret it for the rest of her life. But was it fair …?

"I don't think I can answer that question, Marcus."

"I understand."

"I hope you don't," she said so quietly that he barely heard her. She was ashamed of the way that she was keeping him in cold storage, just in case …

"I'll wait, Charlotte …"

"No …"

"Sshh. I'll wait until you tell me to stop waiting, all right?"

She shrugged her shoulders and he handed her back her half-finished wine. They sat and sipped in silence. A clock over the fireplace chimed, making them both jump. It chimed eight times. Only half an hour had passed since she left the station. As she looked at the clock, Charlotte decided that it was a very ornate piece for a man to choose. Black marble inlaid with gilt curlicues, a white enamel face and strong black Roman numerals. Maybe it was a family piece, or maybe it was left over when he and Denise had divided up their belongings.

Their divorce wasn't through yet, she remembered. She was kissing a married man. And she was a married woman, with three children.

"Shall we say this never happened?" Marcus suggested. He must have been reading her mind. "Can we go back to the way things were before?"

She nodded gratefully, unsure if they could or not.

"Should we go to dinner?" she asked, draining her glass.

"I'll get your jacket."

Fiona yawned, stretched, and switched off the television as Charlotte came in.

"Donal called in for a while when you were out. He asked could you give him a call sometime tomorrow. He and Gemma had a great chat about something." The teenager grinned. "I think it might have had something to do with your birthday."

Birthdays were big occasions in the Moran Family. Donal's own birthday in February, coming so soon after he had moved out, had been so awkward that Charlotte dreaded her own. Donal must dread it too, she guessed, because there were only a few days to go and he hadn't tried to contact her about it. She had been tempted to let it slide, except that Gemma would want to know why. It was one of the things the children had been promised. The whole family would still celebrate birthdays together.

She tried to ring the flat after Fiona had gone, but hung up when the answering machine picked up. Then she tried calling the first restaurant. Geri was surprised she hadn't reached Donal in the flat.

"He must have gone into town after all. He said he might. He's left on every light in the flat though," Geri snorted with disgust. She was quite the environmentalist.

Charlotte rang the Temple Bar restaurant. He wasn't there either. Eleven o'clock. Where the hell was he? She rang the flat again and waited for the beep of the answering machine.

"Donal, I got your message. You can call me if you get back within the next hour. It's eleven now. Bye."

Donal stared at the phone. The caller ID display showed she was at home. He had nearly picked up the first time she called, but this time he waited to see what message she would leave. She was letting him know what time she'd got home. Perhaps she had a guilty conscience. Earlier Donal had wondered what had changed that Charlotte had asked Fiona to baby-sit this time. She always made a point of getting him to take the kids when she met Marcus, rubbing his nose in it. And when Donal had heard from Fiona that Charlotte had caught the DART, he was sure it was out to Dun Laoghaire. God! Did the man not even have the courtesy to pick her up?

The first time Donal realised she was meeting Marcus was in April. Charlotte had arrived home from one of her French classes and asked Donal if he wanted to share a late evening snack with her. When he refused and pulled on his jacket to leave, she'd clenched her teeth defiantly and asked him if he could collect the kids from school on Friday. She didn't say where she was going. The message was clear. If he wasn't going to come back, then she would meet Marcus.

She didn't understand that he couldn't come back until he was sure Marcus was out of her system.

That first time he had examined her when she came home, looking for some clue that she had suddenly realised what Marcus was really like. She was grown up now; surely she couldn't fall for the crap he had fed her as a teenager? It wasn't until she'd been out with him three or four times that a horrifying thought occurred to Donal. What if Marcus had changed too? What if all these years later he still had the power to make her love him, not as the spoilt boy he was then, but the man he was now?

Donal was tempted then to abandon his high-risk strategy and ask her if they could try again. But he knew she would take him back, and he would never know if she wanted Marcus, or the father of her children. Well, most of her children …

Don't think like that, he told himself, slamming his hand on the table hard enough to hurt himself. Gemma's yours. Charlotte believes it too. If she really believed Marcus was Gemma's father, she'd have told him by now. She's too honourable to hide it from him.

Donal stared at the answering machine blinking accusingly at him, knowing that he should ring Charlotte back. He got up and wiped the message to stop the red light flashing and decided he needed some fresh air.

He walked around the side of the building, to avoid going through the restaurant, and began to walk almost at jogging pace along the seafront. It was warm and muggy, but there was an ozoney smell to the air which warned him that rain was on its way. He walked on anyway, relishing the prospect of a drenching. On his way back, it was still dry, but the sky was dark and clouds obscured the stars. He diverted to walk past the house. It was almost midnight but there were still lights on downstairs. Charlotte had no more study to do, and she never watched television this late at night, so she must have stayed up in the hope he would call. Donal stopped at the gate, tempted to go in.

And say what? He walked on, slower now, despite the first few drops of warm rain.

Chapter 19

"This job would entail a huge drop in salary for you – why do you want it so badly?" The chairwoman of the children's charity looked at the young woman in front of her. She was by far the most qualified of all the candidates, overqualified for the job advertised, so overqualified that had it been up to Marcy, she mightn't have given her that first interview. But Emily had impressed everyone with her enthusiasm and grasp of world economics. She would be perfect for the job, if she was taking it for the right reasons.

"This may sound stupid, but money isn't that important for me right now," Emily explained. "I've earned a good salary as long as I've been working, I've made some lucky investments, and my compensation case from a car accident is coming up soon. I'm more than comfortable."

"So what is? Important, I mean," Marcy asked.

"Making money work, I suppose. I've spent my whole

career chasing pennies to add pounds onto the portfolios of rich people. And I was good at it. They said I could spot a wasted cent halfway across the world. But chasing money for money's sake isn't fun any more. You, however, your charity, spend money and you spend it where it's needed most. But if you don't mind my saying so, you also waste a lot of it." Emily was warming to her theme. "I really admire the kind of person who can go and live in some godforsaken village in the back end of nowhere and care for the people there. I know I could never do something like that. But those volunteers deserve to know that the money raised in their name is being well spent."

The interviewer nodded in appreciation. All the other applicants had bleated on about helping the under-privileged children of the world. But what Marcy needed was someone who could sort out the finances of the foundation. Someone who understood how money worked and who could work with foreign governments and other aid agencies to make sure that the money went where it was needed. And at the salary the foundation could afford to pay, she knew she had no right to hope for someone like Emily.

"What about travel?" Marcy asked. "Although you would be based in Ireland, the foundation has offices in New York and Nairobi. And you would need to visit the countries whose projects we support in Africa, Asia and Eastern Europe. Would that be a problem?"

Emily knew she had the job when Marcy asked her about travel. The advertised job had been to work on the accounts of the Dublin branch only, but Emily knew she wouldn't have stayed there for long. She was glad Marcy realised it too. They talked on for a few more minutes, and then Emily went to wait in the next room while Marcy came to her decision. She still couldn't believe she was here. It was her second interview and, as far as she knew, she was the only one called back. Marcy had flown in from New York to meet her, and the two women had hit it off immediately. Marcy had a much better grasp of the finances of the organisation than anyone Emily had met in their Irish office, and Emily had spent almost as long quizzing her up as she had answering questions. The more she heard, the more she knew she could really make a difference.

She was excited; this was something worth getting out of bed in the morning for! Emily remembered the thrill she used to get from reading law books in first year, the way she used to daydream about becoming the voice of the oppressed. She had long ago suppressed that dream, but for the first time in her life she was willing to admit that she needed a dream. For the first time since leaving college Emily felt a real purpose to her life and she could almost persuade herself that one day she might be really happy. That she was entitled to be happy. And that happiness might be something more concrete than a job you like, a decent salary to give you security and a reflection in the mirror you could be proud of. Because since the accident, Emily had started to hate her job, she loathed looking in mirrors and despite having more money in her bank account than ever before, her sense of security was shot to hell. And yet, to her surprise, she wasn't

347

miserable. In fact she didn't feel much different to how she had felt before she lost all the things she thought were important. For the first time she began to wonder had she ever been really happy.

Emily looked up as Marcy called her back into the room. Fergal, the Irish volunteer co-ordinator and the man who chaired the first interview panel, had joined them. He grinned as he stood to shake Emily's hand.

"Welcome on board, Emily. Marcy agreed with me when I said we should grab this opportunity with both hands. Although I suspect," Fergal continued, winking at his boss, "that we won't have you to ourselves for long. Marcy will have you jetting all over the world."

Emily's eyes met the older woman's while Fergal busied himself with a bottle of wine and paper cups to celebrate her appointment. They would work well together. The thrill of the challenge facing her made Emily's pulse race.

"I got it!" Emily laughed into the phone as soon as Anne-Marie answered. "I got it. And I've got you to thank for pointing me in the right direction in the first place."

A couple of months before, when Emily was moaning, yet again, about her job, Anne-Marie had suggested she do some voluntary work for a medical charity Dave was involved with. Emily sorted out their books in the course of a few evenings and the woman she worked with joked that Emily was just the type of person her boyfriend Fergal needed. That was how Emily met Fergal, and he talked her into applying for this job.

"Are you going to take it?" Anne-Marie was surprised at the rate things had moved.

"I've already accepted it. I have to work out my notice, but I'm going to start with them as soon as I can. And I'll get to work on their Dublin books straight away, in the evenings and at weekends." Her enthusiasm was infectious.

"Let's meet in town for a drink to celebrate," Anne-Marie suggested. "Although it'll just be a soft drink for me." Her baby was due in a few months. "Will Charlotte join us?"

"If I can get hold of her. Now that she's a student, I never know where to reach her. And she keeps forgetting to switch her phone back on after lectures."

They met in Neary's Pub, which, typically for a Friday, was heaving with people although it was only six. Charlotte would join them later for a meal, but she had her first history essay to hand in, so she was in the library doing some research.

"How's Charlotte finding college?" Anne-Marie asked.

"She seems to love it, although she never has a minute to herself. Donal wants her to get an au-pair to help out, but she's not keen on the idea."

"They're getting on so well together, lately," Anne-Marie said with a groan. "I feel like locking them in a room together and not letting them out until they sort things out. I thought he'd have moved home months ago. What the hell's wrong with them anyway?"

"You know she's seeing Marcus occasionally?" Emily asked carefully.

349

"Yeah. I met them in town last week." Anne-Marie frowned. "But I'm sure there's nothing between them. I saw them before they saw me, and well … they're not a couple. They just don't look right together."

"Actually they look stunning together, but I know what you mean. Charlotte and Donal look like a couple … they *are* a couple, I really don't understand what's going on."

"Have you tried to talk to her?" Anne-Marie had, and failed.

"She says they're just friends. Her and Marcus, I mean. That they have too much of a shared past for her to be able to shut him out of her life altogether."

"What's that supposed to mean?"

"Search me. There's very few of my ex-boyfriends I'd ever want to see again." Emily stared into her drink. "Enough about my sister. How's the bump?"

"Fine." Anne-Marie smiled fondly, and laid her hands on her stomach. "Lively, especially at night."

"Everything going OK?" Emily was almost afraid to ask. There had been a few scares at the start of the pregnancy, including a threatened miscarriage. Then a month ago Dave had insisted Anne-Marie give up work when her blood pressure went up.

"Yes, my blood pressure's fine again. But, of course, Dave's still checking it whenever he gets near me with the cuff, and at least twice a week he shoves a little plastic pot at me and orders me to pee in it." Anne-Marie wrinkled her nose in disgust.

"Hey, he's just being careful, looking after the two most

350

important people in his world." For some strange reason, Emily felt her eyes sting as she said this. She jumped up to hide her confusion. "Another drink?"

"You must be joking. Since we've been here I've already been to the loo twice. Anyway, isn't it about time we went to meet Charlotte?"

The next morning, Emily was padding round her flat in bare feet. Anne-Marie had stayed the night rather than drive home, so Emily stripped the sheets from the spare room. She opened the window and stuck her head out to breathe in the morning air, which was just beginning to warm up. As usual when she was in the small spare room, she wondered at the sanity of the architect who gave this poky boxroom the best view. Her own spacious bedroom looked out over the carpark and beyond that the street. She bundled up the sheets and went back into the kitchen. She slammed the door of the washing machine, and watched the drum fill with suds.

"Damn you, Richard," she growled at the phone, remembering the conversation she'd had with him just after Anne-Marie left. Then she picked up the phone and dialled Paul's number. She was surprised when he answered almost straight away.

"Hi, I thought I'd be talking to your machine. No football today?" Paul had started helping out at a local sports club where he was the coach for the under-elevens.

"I'm just back. How are things?"

"Great. I've got some news. Do you want to get a drink later?"

"How about lunch? We could try that new Italian place that's just opened down the road from me," Paul suggested.

"Brilliant! Oh no, wait!" Emily remembered the dinner she had planned for Richard. It was a bit heavy for lunch – but if she did a salad with it … "Why not come here? I'll cook. I reckon I owe you one." That was true. Any time they met, they either went out or Paul cooked. And he wasn't to know he was getting the steaks Richard had cancelled on.

"I can hardly refuse an offer like that! I'll have a shower and tidy this place up a bit. About an hour's time suit you?"

"Fine, see you then."

Paul's hand felt clammy as he put down the receiver. She had news for him. Shit! It had to be something to do with Richard. What was he planning? Paul knew that the other man's marriage had finally ended a few months previously. Two weeks ago, the final property settlement had come through and Paul had handled the paperwork in which Marilyn gave up any claim to Richard's interest in the firm. He didn't want to move back to Dublin to be with Emily, did he?

He still couldn't believe they'd got back together. What did Richard have to offer her? At first, before they resumed their affair, Paul had to admit that Richard had worked some of his magic on Emily again. At least she'd started going outside her flat occasionally. And when she was at home, she took an interest in her appearance, unlike those awful few months after she came home from hospital. But when they'd started sleeping together, Paul found he could hardly bear to be in Emily's flat any more. Any time she invited him over, he found some excuse to meet elsewhere. He couldn't have used cups, glasses, the bathroom, wondering if Richard had been the last person before him. He only accepted her invitation this morning because she'd caught him off guard.

"Shit, shit, shit. Fuck, fuck, fuck," he told his naked reflection in the bathroom mirror.

Tara and Suzy were enjoying an early lunch in the Avoca Handweaver's restaurant outside Dublin. They'd been for a walk up the Sugar Loaf Mountain and were tucking into large quantities of fattening things to compensate.

"I need to go on a diet," Tara moaned, finishing her quiche and reaching for her meringue. "I've put on over a stone since giving up – well, everything."

Eating, especially high-sugar, high-fat foods, sometimes helped take the edge off the ever-present craving. And maintaining some social contact usually involved eating now that drink was off the menu.

"How's it going?" Suzy asked. She was amazed at the inner strength the other woman seemed to have been able to call on.

Tara shrugged. "As long as I keep moving." The nervous energy which she had always displayed seemed to have got even more intense. She was like a shark in deep water: move or sink. "Sometimes it gets so bad …" she hesitated. "Can I ask you something?"

"Fire away. There's very little we don't know about each other at this stage."

Tara thought about it. Suzy was right; the two women had shared a lot since the day of the AA meeting.

"Did you ever keep something to remind you…? You know, to take out when you felt close to the edge?"

"I don't think so." Suzy shook her head. "But I'm not sure I know what you mean."

"Well … look, just tell me if you think this is really sick." Tara reached into the bag beside her chair and took out her purse. She removed a folded up piece of newspaper and handed it to Suzy. "If I get really bad. If I feel that the only thing in the world I could possibly do is take a drink, or go and find some drugs, I look at that."

"Can I open it?" Suzy held the tattered piece of paper away from her, as if it was hot.

"Go ahead. I haven't even told Marty about it." Tara was afraid her counsellor would call it some kind of a crutch and that she should be reaching inside herself to find the resources she needed to fight her addictions.

Suzy found what she expected, but seeing it made her gasp. She couldn't see how anyone could have been extracted alive from the car in the grainy picture. The photo showed Tara's mangled vehicle being hoisted onto the back of a tow-truck.

"Not that I need reminding," Tara said at last. "But that makes it real somehow. Maybe because it's in the newspaper. Do you think I'm sick to carry it around?"

"No, if it helps, I suppose …"

"Emily's case comes up next month."

"Are you dreading it?"

"I keep telling myself that I'm just a witness. And Emm's been great. She says I'm just being brought along to tell them all about the actions of some madwoman called Tara. A woman who doesn't exist any more. I've never denied anything, and I've even been charged with causing the accident, so Paul reckons my insurance company will settle at the last minute. I hope to God he's right."

They sat in silence for a few minutes.

"Hey, I never told you the best news of all!" Tara sat up suddenly with a grin. "As of next week, men are back on the menu."

"What do you mean?" Suzy laughed, relieved at the lightening of the atmosphere. She pushed the newspaper clipping back across the table to Tara who folded it and returned it to her purse without looking at it.

"I was off men for a year. Marty's orders. Apparently my predatory nature was part of my addictive behaviour. But now I'm free to prowl again." Tara frowned for a second "Well, not exactly. That's a bit of a problem."

"What is?"

"Marty says I should only have sex as part of a meaningful relationship." She made an ugly face. "Yeuch!"

"You're joking! That's a bit pervy, isn't it?" Suzy laughed.

"What is?"

"Marty dictating your sex life. Are you supposed to report back to him?"

"God, I never thought about that. Maybe I am. That's

355

put me right off the idea." Tara frowned at Suzy. "Trust you to spoil the one thing I've been looking forward to for months!"

"You could always go down the meaningful relationship route." Suzy grinned and raised one eyebrow sceptically. She'd never known Tara to be involved in a meaningful relationship.

"You're a one to talk. You haven't been near anyone since giving Etienne the brush-off." Tara noticed a sudden change of expression on Suzy's face. Her amusement was replaced by lip-chewing anxiety. "There is someone, isn't there? Come on, tell me. This gut-spilling goes both ways, you know."

"There's no one."

"But you wish …"

"It's not going to happen. I know that now."

"Then there's no reason why you shouldn't tell Auntie Tara. Hang on, I'll get two more coffees."

She returned from the counter bearing two mugs piled high with whipped cream. "Shoot!"

"Forget it, I said." Suzy looked uncomfortable and she was beginning to turn red.

"I'm not giving up. Tell me. You'd never know; I might have some useful insight."

Suzy spooned cream off the top of her coffee, and licked her spoon. She stared at the mug. The truth was, she really did want to talk about it. She'd lived with it for so long now…

"Promise that if I tell you anything, it's between us?" she pleaded.

"Of course." Tara was looking forward to this. She had a feeling that it was something mega. "Who is it?"

"Donal."

Tara's jaw dropped.

"Charlotte's Donal?" She had to be sure.

Suzy nodded wordlessly.

"Nothing happened though, did it? That wasn't why …"

"No. Nothing happened between me and Donal. At least …"

"At least what, Suzy?" Tara tried not to sound hostile – after all, Suzy had listened to hours of her confessions without judging her. But this was different. Charlotte was a friend.

"Marcus was contacting Charlotte before she and Donal split up," Suzy said in a small, almost whiny voice. "She met him. Twice."

"You didn't tell Donal?"

Tara saw from the way Suzy couldn't meet her eyes that she had, and she wanted to shake her. Although she and Suzy had become friends recently, she owed more to Charlotte and Emily. It was Emily's forgiveness and Charlotte's acceptance of it that had made Tara believe that there might be something of herself worth saving. It was as much to live up to their trust that she had stayed clean as it was to forge a new life for herself.

"Why, Suzy? Why would you try to break up his marriage? Charlotte's marriage. I thought she was your best friend?"

Tara wanted desperately to understand and she felt

357

herself trembling with unfamiliar emotion. Since giving up drink and drugs she had learnt to care deeply for the people closest to her. And it was a hard lesson to learn, because she knew she was leaving herself open to the risk of being hurt by them. Now, for the first time she was being faced with the evidence of how these people could betray each other. And she was terrified she would have to choose between them.

Suzy didn't answer.

"You know something," Tara said with false cheeriness, as she tried to retreat into her old, cynical, persona, "you've just made me feel a whole lot better about myself. I may have nearly killed *my* best friend while I was out of my skull on drink and drugs but, in the final judgement, when it comes to handing out medals for shitty behaviour, you'll be way ahead of me in the queue."

"You don't understand. It's not that simple."

"Try me," Tara snapped.

Suzy took a deep breath.

"Do you remember, years ago, the night of Charlotte's birthday party? When you let slip about Marcus having a new girlfriend?"

"Ye-es …" How could Tara forget? Charlotte had almost collapsed on the floor with shock and everyone at the party blamed Tara for upsetting her on the day of her birthday although afterwards they all admitted that it was the best thing that could have happened to her.

"Well, the reason Charlotte was so upset … the reason she was so upset was that she was still seeing Marcus and I think she thought they were back together. No one knew. Well, except for me – I saw him coming to the flat a couple of times."

"That was what, ten or eleven years ago? What the hell has it got to do with anything?"

"Thirteen years ago. Charlotte was still sleeping with Marcus. I'm almost sure of it."

"So …?" Tara didn't like what she thought was coming next.

"I think there's a chance Gemma might be his – Marcus's, I mean."

"Fuck!"

Tara stared at the woman opposite her, exhausted by her revelations. All her instincts screamed at her to get out now, make some wisecrack and end the conversation. Being grown up and responsible was too much effort. In her old life she could have taken refuge in drunkenness, safe in the knowledge that no one was going to ask her advice because it was well known that she didn't give a shit anyway.

"Does Donal know?" she asked, because she knew that the new Tara couldn't escape. She had to go to wherever this conversation was taking her. And she wouldn't be able to pretend in the morning that she couldn't remember any of it.

Suzy shrugged.

"Did you tell him?"

"I wanted to. Before they got married. But I couldn't be one hundred per cent certain. I mean, she hadn't even admitted she was pregnant. She only told Emily on the morning of the wedding. And even if I felt there was a chance that the baby was Marcus's … I wasn't sure of my reasons for saying anything. I was afraid I was just jealous. But it was more than that. I mean Donal was crazy about Charlotte. He always was, even all the time she was going out with Marcus. If I had been the one to destroy all that …"

"He'd never have been able to look at you again. So instead you waited until you got a chance later. And then you tried to destroy their marriage." Tara pushed away the remains of her meringue. Suddenly she'd lost her appetite.

"I wasn't the one meeting my ex-boyfriend without telling my husband!" Suzy snapped. She couldn't understand why she was trying to justify herself to Tara. Who the hell was she to throw stones?

"Did you ever ask her about it? See if there was a perfectly reasonable explanation for it?"

Suzy shook her head.

"And Donal? How did he react?"

"I think he already knew. About Gemma, I mean."

"*You* didn't say anything?" Tara looked at her in disbelief.

"No, of course not! But when I told him about Charlotte meeting Marcus … he… well, he looked at me strangely and got me out of his office as fast as he could. As if he was afraid I was about to say something else. And if I put it into words, it would make it real – he'd have to do something about it."

"He did, though, didn't he?"

There was a long silence.

"What should I do?" Suzy tried to attract Tara's attention again.

"You haven't done enough?" Tara asked wearily.

"I mean, I've been thinking of telling Charlotte … you know, that it was me who told Donal…"

"And that would make you feel better, would it?"

"I dunno, I suppose." Suzy played with her spoon. She had spilled the contents of the salt cellar onto the table and was drawing ornate patterns in it with the spoon handle.

"Well, then, by all means go ahead!" Tara said, her mouth twitching with sarcasm. "Go ahead and tell Charlotte she's been betrayed by her best friend. Tell her the secret that she and Donal lived with for all these years isn't such a secret after all. Let her spend the rest of her life worrying that you might have told someone else. Do all that if it makes you feel better. I mean – that's all that matters, isn't it?"

"I have to do something. I caused this mess. I have to sort it out."

And looking at her, Tara knew that Suzy really believed that. Suddenly she realised that while she had thought Suzy to be strong and reliable, in fact her fear manifested itself in a need to control everything around her.

Tara knew that the next few hours would be that hardest she had ever faced without a drink, but she knew she'd get through them. She had a debt to pay.

"No, Suzy. Please, leave them alone," she began. "If you've any decency in you at all, you have to stay out of it and leave them to sort this out themselves. Come on," she stood up. "Let's go home."

Paul pushed open the door of Emily's flat and took a deep breath. He breathed in a mixture of shampoo, shower gel and expensive moisturiser.

"Hi, there!" She gave him a hug and kissed his cheek. She was wearing a pair of loose navy trousers and a pale yellow, round-necked, long-sleeved top. Although she hadn't had time to finish drying her hair, or even put on shoes, her make-up was immaculate. It made Paul long for the care-free Saturday mornings when they had shared brunch and she would tan herself on the balcony in shorts and a skimpy T-shirt or bikini top. Now she couldn't brush her teeth without doing her face first and she never wore anything but trousers and long-sleeved tops.

"Here. It's probably a bit early for this …" He pushed a bottle of wine into her hand.

"It's well after one," Emily pouted. "Don't be such a killjoy. Besides, I've already got a bottle of sparkling wine chilling. I'm celebrating."

"So, what are we drinking to?" Paul raised his glass nervously as Emily put the plates on the table.

"I've got a new job!"

"The one with the charity? That's terrific, Emms!" He jumped up, ran round and hugged her before she could sit down.

"OK, OK. It's not that exciting!" she laughed. She was expecting him to be pleased for her, but this reaction delighted her. His eyes were lit up with joy. "Sit down, you madman, and eat your steak before it bleeds to death." She still couldn't get used to how rare he liked his meat.

"A toast!" he announced formally, still on his feet. "To Emily Riordan who's going to save the world!" He touched his glass to hers, then leaned across and kissed her cheek, which was pink with embarrassment.

Throughout the meal Emily babbled with excitement, and enjoyed Paul hanging on her every word. He was the only one who seemed to understand just how much this job meant to her. Anne-Marie and Charlotte were happy for her, but no more than if she'd got any new job. Paul understood that this was a whole new way of life she was embracing.

"I'm really proud of you, Emms. You remind me of when we were both in First Year," he said as they drank coffee, slouching on the couch. They were both sleepy from the wine. "Do you remember how when we were supposed to be looking up some boring old property or commercial cases in the library, you'd find the juicy human rights cases or the poor tenant fighting the wicked landlord. You were looking forward to the day you'd be there in court, fighting for the oppressed."

"Bit of a show off, wasn't I?" Emily grinned in embarrassment, but she was touched that he remembered her dream.

"Is Richard pleased about the job?" Paul asked reluctantly, thinking he should at least acknowledge the important part the other man played in her life.

"Hmph!" Emily snorted, frowning.

"Oh?"

"He thinks I'm wasting my talents. He reckons it's a backward step on the career ladder. No bleeding-heart liberal is going to make it as financial controller of some big multinational corporation, he says."

"That's not what it's about though, this move." Paul sat up, indignant. "It's not just a career step – it's what you want to do. There's no need to apologise for that. You look happier, more enthusiastic about life today than I've seen you in years. And I don't just mean since the accident."

"I'm not apologising. I just hoped he could be a little bit more enthusiastic, that's all." Emily looked miserable. "We nearly had a row about it on the phone this morning."

"Oh well, some people just can't talk on the phone properly." Paul wondered why the hell he was defending Richard. "When are you going to see him next? Maybe he'll have come around."

"He was supposed to be up this weekend, but this morning he said he'd forgotten some dinner party Marilyn organised. I get the feeling he's sulking because I accepted the job without discussing it with him first. He's worried that if I have to travel a lot, we'll hardly see each other. It's hard enough for him to get away as it is. He thinks Marilyn suspects something."

Paul said nothing.

"I'm beginning to be fed up of it, to be honest. Why am I still doing this? This isn't me. Not any more. Carrying on with a married man, I mean."

"So why are you?" Paul asked slowly. "Why are you still with him?"

Emily thought about it.

"He treats me like the old Emily," she said at last. "It's like the accident never happened."

"But it did. And you're not the same person."

"Don't you think I know that?" Emily's eyes narrowed. "Don't you think I see it in the mirror every day? In everybody's pitying faces everywhere I look? Poor scarred Emily. Poor Emily with the limp. Poor Emily who nearly died. Richard isn't like that. He lets me believe things are just like they were three years ago."

"Maybe because it suits him better like that."

"What do you mean?" Emily looked at him warily. It hadn't escaped her that Paul never said a bad word about Richard, although she knew he hated the other man's guts. Sometimes she was glad he respected her right to choose who she wanted to be with; sometimes she wanted to shake him and tell him to be honest for five minutes.

Paul stood up and walked to the window. Although it was early, low cloud cover was making the afternoon dark.

"Richard's marriage is over, Emms," he said without turning round.

"No, Paul. You're wrong! They worked all that through years ago. Richard told me…" Emily shook her head in violent denial.

"Two weeks ago, the property settlement was finalised," Paul went on as if he hadn't heard her. "We heard about it at work because he's a partner. I don't know why he won't commit to you, Emily, but it's not because of Marilyn."

"And the kids?" Emily scrabbled round desperately for something to redeem Richard.

"His kids are old enough to cope. They're living with Marilyn and her new boyfriend."

"Oh shit!" Emily stood up and began to clear the table. A plate cracked as she hurled it into the sink. She dropped her mug onto it from a height, but felt no satisfaction when she saw it break along the line of the crack. "How could he have hoped I wouldn't find out?" Emily leaned her head against the door of the cupboard above the sink.

"Maybe he thinks you know, and are playing along. He knows I know." Paul was still looking out the window. Emily had her back to him and was watching the level of soapy water rise.

"So why *didn't* you tell me?" she asked angrily.

Paul stayed silent.

"You thought I knew too, didn't you? That I was involved in some sort of ridiculous charade. That I got some kind of a kick out of playing the role of mistress." He didn't answer. "Is that what you thought, Paul?" she shouted at him.

"No, I … I never thought that. I could just never really understand what kind of relationship you had with him. If you loved him or not. And I love you too much. I was afraid to be the one to tell you. I didn't want to lose you, force you to choose between us … you might have hated me …"

"What did you just say?" Emily turned around and saw that Paul was still at the window. "Turn around and look at me, Paul. What did you just say?"

"I was afraid you'd hate me," he turned towards her. "If I was the one who told you … I didn't want to lose you …"

"Before that." Emily's face was blank. "Repeat what you said, just before that."

Paul realised what she wanted him to say. His heart was hammering. He spoke slowly.

"I love you too much to –"

"As a friend, Paul? You love me as a friend, as the sister you never had?" Emily's voice was stony.

"Oh for Christ's sake, Emily! Stop pissing about!" Paul's despair made him furious. He looked around wildly, as if he wanted to pick some thing up and throw it, break it. He walked over to her and seized her arms roughly. She was so thin he could have picked her up and flung her across the room. She was totally defenceless; he felt as though he could do anything to her. Well, anything except the one thing he really wanted to do; which was to pick her up, love and protect her, make her love him in return. "You know how I love you Emily," he said wearily. "I'm *in love* with you, and I always have been. Don't act like you don't know, Emily – please, allow me that much dignity."

He stared into her face and saw tears well up in her eyes.

"You didn't know!" Paul let go of her arms. "How could

you not have known?"

"I thought I'd left it too late … "

"You thought…? You mean…?" He couldn't put it into words.

Emily nodded slowly. "It took me a long time to admit it, but yes, I feel the same."

Paul collapsed onto the couch. "Oh God, Emily! How could we have wasted so much time? How could we have been so stupid?"

"That time we kissed in Castlemichael, when Sheila was sick." Emily sat in the armchair. "It felt right. It felt so right, but you stormed off … you were gone the next morning."

"I didn't want to take advantage of you like that – you were in bits emotionally. I was going to drive down at the weekend, but then you phoned me and told me you wanted to forget it ever happened…"

"I thought you were embarrassed at getting carried away, and you'd disappeared because you regretted it. I had to give you a way out."

Emily chewed her lower lip. She looked so helpless, childlike, he wanted to take her in his arms, but he could see that she had more to say.

"And then, when I woke up after the accident, I was lost and confused, and there were all these people around me. But I expected you to be there. I felt it was really important to see you, that you had some message for me."

"All the time you were unconscious I was telling you how much I loved you."

"I know. Charlotte told me, eventually. But when you

finally came in, you stopped dead at the door of the ward. You looked horrified. I hadn't seen a mirror yet, but suddenly I knew how bad it was, if even you couldn't bear the sight of me."

"Oh Emms, I'm so sorry if I made you think that. I don't know why I couldn't tell you then that I love you. I think it was because you had so far to go in your recovery. I felt that you needed to concentrate on getting better and not have to worry about some declaration of love from a man who you'd already rejected twice. And I didn't want you to think I pitied you. You'd have hated that. But it was nothing to do with your injuries or how you looked. Come here." He patted the sofa beside him.

She came and sat down on the edge of it.

He touched her face and she flinched away from him. He reached out again, and this time she didn't move, but her teeth were clamped together and her fists were clenched. Even her toes were curled up with tension. He touched her left eyebrow and rubbed gently along the outside edge of it. Some of the make-up came off on his finger. He wet his thumb in his mouth and rubbed the eyebrow harder. Emily closed her eyes and imagined what he must be able to see now. The scar tissue, still pink, still completely hairless. She would always have to draw in an eyebrow for herself. It was one of the first things she did each morning.

"When I see this scar, Emms, do you know what I think?" Paul's voice shook with emotion. "It makes me so happy that your brow-bone did the job it was supposed to do, and protected your eye." He leaned forward, and she thought he was going to kiss her eye, but it was the scar he kissed. She drew in her breath in a surprised hiss.

"And here, Emily …" He ran his finger along her jaw, pushed back her hair and followed a ridge of puckered, hard skin down her neck to where it stopped just above her collarbone. "This was nothing short of a miracle. A quarter inch to the left or right, or any deeper and you might not be here today." He let his fingers absorb the life-giving pulse below her skin.

Then his fingers dropped to the neckline of her top and slid inside it. He searched the surface of her skin gently with his finger-tips until, on one side of her chest, about two inches below her collar bone, he found a small, tear-shaped mark.

"This scar now – I don't like the memories associated with this one. This is where that tube went into you. The tube that fed you, that they pushed your drugs through. I was so jealous of that tube. I wanted to do all that for you, to help you heal. And it was attached to that pump, do you remember it? With the knob in the middle and the light displays at the top and the bottom so it looked like a face. That annoying noise it made – *whir-click, whir-click* – I was convinced it was gloating. It got to stay with you twenty-four hours a day and I was only allowed to visit for a few hours. Actually, I hated that pump. I even had a name for it. Do you know what I called it?" He let go of the neck of her top and it slid back into place hiding the small scar. "I called it Richard. That's how jealous I was of it."

Emily smiled, then her face began to soften, then

twitch and she began to laugh. Within seconds they were both in fits of giggles.

Suddenly she stopped laughing.

"Richard," she said slowly.

"It doesn't matter about him any more, does it, Emily?" Paul pleaded.

"Richard was ashamed of me, wasn't he? When we were having our affair three years ago, he offered to leave his wife for me. When I told him not to, he at least wanted us to tell more people about us. He was proud to be seen with me. I think he got a kick out of showing off his young lover. But now, even though he's free, we hardly ever go anywhere. We stay in. I cook for him. If we go out it's to small discreet places. Because of Marilyn, he said. He was ashamed to be seen with me, Paul. What do you think was the biggest turn-off? The scars? The limp?"

Emily's face looked dead as she spoke and Paul knew she saw herself as she imagined Richard did.

"Come here." He pulled her to her feet and pushed her towards the bedroom. "Where's that antique cheval mirror I helped you transport halfway across Dublin?"

"I put it in the spare room – I don't really…"

"Don't move," he ordered.

Paul came back into the main bedroom dragging the huge mirror with him. He positioned it by the window and came and stood by Emily. Gently he eased the yellow top over her head. He hardly touched her, which was difficult because she seemed to have lost all power in her limbs. As he loosened her trousers and helped her step out of them, it reminded him of undressing a child. She stood in her bra and knickers.

"Now look."

Emily opened her eyes but didn't look at her own reflection. She looked instead at Paul's. She knew that he was trying to make her see herself through his eyes. The only man she had ever loved thought she was beautiful. For the first time since the accident, she looked at her whole reflection. She could still see the scars, but she also saw the rest of her body and, to her surprise, the scars covered only a tiny percentage of it. For the first time she saw that the plastic surgeon was right: there was some improvement. For the first time she cared enough to try to remember what he had said about continuing to work on the scars to make even more progress. Emily looked in confusion at the body she thought she knew. It looked better than she remembered. A small smile escaped her clenched jaws. She felt she needed to celebrate the sudden discovery that she wasn't hideously deformed. How could she ever have thought she was?

"Paul, make love to me."

He lifted her up and carried her to the bed, then lay down beside her.

"Is this for keeps, Emily? Are you sure you won't change your mind tomorrow and tell me it was all a mistake?"

"It's for keeps. I've never been more sure of anything in my whole life." She smiled and touched his face. Still he didn't move. "What are you waiting for? A marriage proposal?"

"To have and to hold till death do us part?"

"I think I prefer 'as long as we both shall live'," Emily said, smiling. "I came a little too close for comfort to … well, to the other." She shivered and instinctively Paul wrapped his arms around her.

"I love you, Emily Riordan."

She snuggled closer to him.

"I was serious, you know," she said into his chest.

"About what?"

"The marriage proposal."

He pulled back and looked into her face.

"Yes," he said slowly, "I think I'd like that."

"It's just so romantic!" Gemma gushed. "Marrying the man who was your best friend for years!"

I did that once, Charlotte thought to herself. I married my best friend.

She was truly happy for Emily, but she had never felt her separation from Donal as keenly as she did this afternoon. He should be here with her, in the house they had made into their home, celebrating with his sister-in-law and her fiancé. She shouldn't have had to tell his answering machine.

"Have you any idea about dates yet?" Charlotte was shocked that she had to force herself to smile.

"Hey, hold your horses, she only popped the question …" Paul looked at his watch, laughing, "twenty-one hours and thirty-three minutes ago."

"You proposed?" Gemma's eyes opened wide in admiration of her aunt. "How did you do it? Did you go down on one knee?"

"Well, we …" They hadn't rehearsed this. There were children present; they could hardly tell them Emily had proposed in bed in a state of undress.

"She asked me at lunch," Paul interrupted, winking at his wife-to-be, "between the main course and the starter."

"Twenty-one hours ago?" Gemma looked at her own watch and tapped suspiciously on the table with the finger-nails she had only recently stopped biting. "You eat at funny times." She glared at them with an expression that said she knew she wasn't going to get the real story, but please don't think she fell for the sanitised version. Emily was saved from laughing by the doorbell.

"You don't have to ring the bloody doorbell – you have a key!" Charlotte hissed at Donal in embarrassment, then turned away so he couldn't see the tears beginning to form in her eyes. It was the small, thoughtless things like that, that hurt the most.

"Sorry," he whispered, genuinely contrite. Then he added out loud. "I got your message. Where's that sister of yours?" He tried to put an arm across her shoulder to atone for his faux-pas, but Charlotte shrugged it off. Then immediately wished she hadn't.

"We're in the conservatory." She led the way without looking back. "Mum's on her way up. We're waiting for her before we crack open the champagne."

"Hi, everyone! Can I get anyone a drink while we're waiting for Sheila?" Donal asked.

"I'll have a white wine please, Donal." Emily looked at him gratefully. At least he was behaving as though he had some stake in the house. She had seen Charlotte's face earlier when she explained that she wasn't sure where to reach him.

"Make that two," Paul agreed.

"Charlotte?"

"Please."

They sipped their drinks and chatted until Sheila arrived, then they celebrated all over again. They talked about their plans for the future, Emily's new job, where they would look for a house.

Charlotte had never felt so lonely in her life.

Chapter 20

Winter 1998

Charlotte licked the ice cream she hadn't really wanted. There was a ball of anxiety in her stomach as she tried over and over to tell Marcus what she had rehearsed. They sat on a bench on the seafront in Bray. It was a Wednesday afternoon, ten days after Emily's engagement. They had just climbed Bray Head and Charlotte had agreed to the ice cream, despite the bitterly cold November day, only because everyone else who had braved the elements this afternoon seemed to be eating one.

"Marcus. It's time," Charlotte said suddenly. It wasn't how she had planned to say it, but the words flew out of their own volition.

"Time for what?" He turned his head slowly from his perusal of the grey sea and looked at her with a guarded expression.

"Time to stop waiting. You told me you'd wait until I

was sure … until I told you to …"

"I know what I said." He got up, threw the remains of his cone in the bin and sat down again.

Charlotte was aware of the gooey ice cream melting between her own frozen fingers.

"So, are you going back to him?" he asked.

"I don't know what I'm doing but I know that it wouldn't work between you and me now. We could never have more than what we have at this moment."

"I suppose I always knew that." Marcus seemed resigned rather than upset. "Can we go on being friends?"

"I'd like to."

A man with two children stopped at the blue railing ahead of them. He had red hair, cut in an Elton-John style and the two girls were obviously his daughters. They shared his nose, his chin, his colouring and even, it appeared, his barber. He crouched down to their level and pointed out seagulls swooping and soaring over the waves.

"Do you think you'll ever have any more children?" Marcus asked after the family had left.

"What?" Charlotte felt her heart pounding. Had he guessed? "With the three I've already got? You must be joking. I'm just beginning to get my life back. And now that I've started college …"

"Denise and I are talking again," Marcus said as if he hadn't been listening to her. The question about children was obviously just a way of bringing the conversation to where he wanted to go with it. "Properly talking. We've suspended the separation proceedings for the moment."

"Will you get back together?"

"Maybe, I don't know. I think she wants to but ..." He sighed. "Probably not. We said too many things that couldn't be taken back. There were too many lies, accusations ..."

"What happened?" Charlotte asked, not because she wanted to know but because she knew he wanted to talk about it. And because it put off what she still had to tell him. About Gemma.

"A bill arrived at my office in New York. A medical bill, something that wasn't covered by our insurance. I opened it. It was for a gynae clinic. A fertility clinic to be accurate. Denise had had all sorts of tests. I asked her about it when she got home. She said she'd been off the pill for a year and was worried that she wasn't pregnant yet. We hadn't discussed it. Or rather we had, but years before when I said I didn't want children. Any time she raised it after that, I changed the subject. She wanted children so badly, she said." Marcus's face was filled with anguish.

"She told me."

Marcus looked at her in surprise. He knew they'd met, but not what they'd talked about.

"The tests all came back negative," he went on. "There was no reason she couldn't have children. She tried to be happy. She wanted me to be happy. She suggested that I have tests. I screamed at her. I accused her of betraying me, of taking a decision without discussing it with me. I said she couldn't possibly love me if she could do something like that behind my back. I wanted to drive her away. I even said, during one of our worse arguments that I'd only married her for her money. And all because I was scared to tell her the truth. Attacking her was the only way of defending myself. Because what I'd done to her was unforgivable. I'd let her go through all that worry and pain alone. And now I know I have to tell her. She'll probably hate me even more than she already does. Any progress we've made in the past few weeks …" He sighed and looked out to sea.

"I don't think she hates you, Marcus," Charlotte said gently. "At least she didn't when she was talking to me. But what do you have to tell her?"

Marcus walked to the railing and leaned against it. Because he was so tall and he leaned forwards so far, it looked as if he was trying to throw himself over it.

"Tell her what, Marcus?" Charlotte stood up too, and walked towards him. But then she stopped. She was afraid to move. Afraid to scare him out of speaking.

"That I can't have children. That I knew that when I married her. That I let her take the pill for five years, knowing she was polluting her body for no reason. That she went through all those tests for nothing, because I already knew why she didn't get pregnant."

"You can't have children?" All Charlotte's energy was diverted into keeping her legs holding her up. Her voice came out as a squeak.

"Well, not without making a trip to a clinic in London, where they have some of my boys in the deep freeze. I don't even know if they still have them, or if they're still viable. Have you any idea how long frozen sperm survive, Charlotte?"

She shook her head helplessly. She didn't give a shit, to be honest. There was no chance that a sperm bank in London could be Gemma's father.

"I never thought I'd need them. I … Dad insisted I go. I was only …"

"What happened to you, Marcus?" Charlotte held back her scream of frustration. How could he be meandering through his story like this? Did he not understand how important it was to her? Suddenly she realised he really had no idea, and she forced herself to look calm.

"I got cancer. When I was seventeen. Well, I was sixteen when I noticed it, but seventeen before I had the guts to do anything about it. I'd never been to the doctor's, I was healthy. Dad was my doctor, for Christ's sake. How many sixteen-year-olds could go to their fathers and say: 'Well, here's the thing, Dad, I was feeling myself up, as you do, when I found this here lump on one of my balls'." Marcus's attempt at a wry grin froze into a twisted grimace as the fear reached through the years to touch him with a chill finger.

"When I finally told him, he whipped me off to Dublin and my testicle was snipped out before I knew where I was. It was malignant so I had to have radiotherapy and chemo. I refused to go back to school in sixth year. I was afraid that somehow everyone would know. So I stayed in Dublin with my aunt, did my Leaving in a school where no one knew me.

"But do you know what the rumour was? I suspect my brother helped it spread – he knew I was paranoid that the lads would think I was less of a man or something. Somehow the story got out that I'd been sent to Dublin to boarding school because I'd got some girl pregnant!" Marcus laughed wryly. "Ironic really. I heard that rumour two days before being informed that I was one of the unfortunate few whose fertility in the other testicle had been knocked out by the treatment. It only happens to a selected minority apparently," he said bitterly.

They stared at each other for a while. Finally Charlotte got her voice back.

"And are you OK now?"

"I'm healthy, if that's what you mean. Every few years I go back for a check-up, and the first few times I insisted on a sperm count as well. Some doctor had told me there was a chance the tissue might recover. It didn't."

"So you're completely sterile?" Charlotte had to be sure. "And you've been sterile since you were seventeen?" She tried to keep any emotion from her face. It was terrifying to think that she had been about to tell Marcus that she and Donal's marriage was in trouble because they believed Gemma could be Marcus's daughter.

"Completely, totally, and irredeemably sterile!" Marcus answered. "Guaranteed to shoot nothing but blanks. Don't know why I hide it – should be a selling point really!"

But he could see that his attempt at bravado didn't fool Charlotte, so he continued in a more serious tone.

"When I was in my first year in college, there was this nurse who lived in the same building as me. She was older than me – experienced, if you know what I mean. We were messing around one day, one thing led to another, and the next thing, she was holding my balls, sorry, ball in her hand. Of course, she knew straight away what had happened – she was a nurse. I couldn't handle the look in her face. Pity. I got out of there as fast as I could.

"As far as my friends were concerned, I dropped off the face of the earth for a few weeks. I was depressed. The whole thing hit me really hard for the first time. I ended up in hospital, the funny farm, for a week, and my dad arranged for me to get an implant." He stopped when he saw Charlotte's eyebrows shoot up. "Like a breast implant only smaller. After the op, I went back to college, told the lads that I'd spent a wild few weeks bonking a married woman and failed the year. I had a reputation now and it suited me. I might only have one real ball, and a defective one at that, but everyone thought I was the greatest womaniser in the western world. I got a book on how to be good at foreplay, because I thought that was as far as I'd let anyone get. And as long as I kept to girls who had no intention of sleeping with me, I got away with it. I'd play the experienced, sensitive guy, who'd had loads of women, but wasn't going to pressurise her into anything."

Charlotte winced at the memory.

"Sorry, I guess I fed you that line too. But you were different. Usually I only lasted a few weeks, or maybe a couple of months with a girl. I got out before she could begin to wonder why I wasn't pressuring her to sleep with me. But I wanted it so badly with you. I tried to break free a few times. I'm not proud of it. I saw other girls while you were still living in Castlemichael. I'd stay away longer and longer, waiting till I suddenly went off you, but I never did. It scared the hell out of me. At last I knew I had to see if I could do it. Make love properly, I mean. And I could. And you had no idea there was anything weird about me."

Charlotte remembered how he had never undressed in front of her. She blushed to remember that he hated to be touched there.

"The next year was amazing, Char. I loved everything about you. You needed me so much, and yet you were the strong one. You knew exactly what you wanted from life. But I fought it. I told myself I was just in it for the sex. When I realised I was falling in love with you, I broke it off. I wasn't prepared to be honest with you."

"We could have worked it out ..." Charlotte felt a sense of waste rather than loss.

"You could have. I couldn't. Not yet. I didn't want to. Besides, Denise was suddenly free and I'd always fancied her. It was a new challenge. And I knew she was determined to put her career first, so she was no danger to my manhood."

"What about the months when you were seeing both of us, after we got back together? You were sleeping with me, but going out with Denise?" She needed to understand about that time. It was something they'd never discussed.

"Oh shit, Charlotte. That's the period of my life I'm least proud of." Marcus began to walk along the seafront.

Charlotte suspected it was because he didn't have to look her in the eye.

"Inside, I really didn't know which one of you I wanted. I loved you, believe me I loved you, but I was scared that I couldn't live up to what you wanted. So I made a big joke of it. The lads thought I was great keeping two women on the go like that, but I felt miserable. I wanted you, but I wanted the safety that Denise represented to me. I could marry her and never have to worry about being judged again. She was a good friend, and I did love her, but not the same way as I loved you at the time. It was doing my head in. I knew I had to tell you, let you decide for yourself, at least leave myself in with a chance. It was just how to tell you was the difficult bit.

"In the end I came up with this mad plan. Do you remember that last time we were together? The time I pretended to be someone else? I was going to tell you then. I was going to tell you the story as if it was John Smith's story, one stranger to another, and see how you reacted. I figured you'd know I was talking about me but, if you couldn't handle it, you could pretend you thought it was all part of the game. At least that was the idea, sick puppy that I was. But all evening I kept chickening out. In the end I decided to leave it till the morning, but in the morning you were gone."

Charlotte couldn't believe that one night, the John Smith night, could have had such an impact on both of their lives. If she hadn't slept with him that night, there would never have been any doubt about Gemma. But then if Marcus had managed to tell her, maybe they would never have split up and she would never have ended up with Donal. Gemma, or for that matter, Tim or Aisling might never have been born. She shivered at the thought. And Marcus, he must have wondered what would have happened if he had the courage to go through with his plan.

Maybe Denise was right and a shadow had hung over their marriage – the shadow of that night. The shadow of 'if only'.

Charlotte realised Marcus was still talking.

"You stopped taking my calls at work," he said. "I couldn't ring you at home because Suzy usually answered the phone. You refused to see me. After about four weeks I called out to where you were living and I begged Suzy's flatmate to let me in to wait for you. She told me that you'd heard about Denise, and that I should leave you alone. You were with Donal now and he was making you happy.

"So I did. I left you alone and I like to think it was the one decent thing I did in the whole sorry mess. I knew he'd be better for you than me. And I knew he was crazy about you. A couple of months later I heard you were engaged, and some part of me still wouldn't believe it. I still kept thinking you'd look me up and offer me one last chance. Then you were married and although I was as jealous as hell, at least I could get on with my life. Once I let go of you, I was able to love Denise better, in the way she deserved to be loved."

They had reached the end of the promenade, but instead of turning inland to the carpark behind the amusements, Marcus resumed his staring out to sea.

"Why didn't you tell me all this before?" Charlotte asked.

"Would it have made a difference?" He turned to her.

Would it? She wasn't sure. And when might it have made the difference? Fourteen years ago? A year ago?

"To us? I don't know. But to me, yes, probably. I had always believed in what we had, Marcus. That it was more than it had seemed to be on the surface. More than a lovesick teenager falling for the older bastard." She ignored the look of pain that crossed his face. He deserved to know the truth. How he had hurt her. "Although everyone thought you were using me, I believed in you." She was no longer looking at him as she spoke, but staring out to sea.

"But?" he prompted gently.

"But nothing." She turned on him. "I loved you, and I believed you loved me, even though you never told me. I believed I could see something in you that no one else could see … and then when I realised you'd been lying to me, that you'd been seeing Denise all that time … I felt like a complete fool, Marcus. Most of my adult life, I wondered how I could have been so wrong and I've never fully trusted my judgement of people since then." Although it had never occurred to her before, Charlotte wondered if that was why she had made so few new friends in recent years.

"Did I ever come between you and Donal?"

"No. There was never any mystery between me and Donal. He loved me; I loved him. And we weren't afraid of showing it. There was no second guessing each other."

"You said 'loved'. In the past tense."

"You asked had you come between us in the past tense. You hadn't."

"But I have now?"

Charlotte couldn't answer.

"And what about the future, Charlotte? You want Donal back. Have I screwed that up for you?"

He wanted to grab her by the shoulders, turn her round so that he could at least try to read some of the answers to his questions in her face.

"I'm sorry. I should never have come back into your life," he said at last. "It was selfish of me."

"Probably, yes. But to be honest, you never really left it. I don't know what's going to happen between me and Donal, but I don't regret having you as a friend again."

"Really?"

"Really," she sighed, but she still didn't turn around, still didn't face him. "I'd better be getting home."

"I'll drive you."

"No. I'll get the DART." She needed to be alone.

"Thanks, Charlotte." He didn't try to stop her as she turned to walk away.

"For what?"

"For listening. And sorry."

"Sorry for what?"

"I don't know. For the past. For Donal. And I'm sorry that it never worked out between us."

I'm not, she realised as she kissed him on the cheek and walked quickly towards the train station.

How was she going to tell Donal, she asked herself again and again. The train pulled into Killiney station and the almost empty carriage filled up with girls in green uniforms. Two of them sat opposite to her. They were about Gemma's age.

She was afraid that if she told Donal what she had found out and then tried to talk him into coming home, he'd think the only reason she wanted him back was to make them all back into a family again. And he was the one who moved out, she kept reminding herself. If he wanted to come back, he'd have talked about it before now.

Order turkey – Free range? – Organic?
Make cake – Puddings – Mincemeat
Charlotte paused between writing each word and then she underlined some of them. She wrote *Christmas List* at the top of the page and underlined it three times. It was supposed to give her the courage to talk to Donal when he came back downstairs from helping Tim with some homework.

Christmas had crept up on her; it was only three weeks away now. She still hadn't talked to Donal about how they were going to work it.

She still hadn't talked to Donal about Marcus's revelations.

"What are you doing?" Donal appeared at her shoulder, making her jump; she hadn't heard him come into the kitchen.

"Oh," he said when he saw what she had written.

"We'd better talk about Christmas, Donal." Charlotte screwed the lid back onto her pen.

"Yeah, you're right. Have you any idea what the kids want?" Donal sat down opposite her.

"It's the first week in December, Donal," Charlotte snapped in reply. "I already have most of the presents bought. I was talking about Christmas Day."

"What do you want to do?"

Charlotte looked at him in exasperation. Why did he have to make this so hard?

"I want to do what I always do. Cook a big huge Christmas dinner, have everyone over. Maybe Paul too if he wants to come. What do you want to do?"

"I don't know. What do you want me to do?" Donal stared at his hands. He looked at a knot in the wooden table. He fiddled with a napkin left there since dinner. He looked everywhere but at Charlotte.

"What the hell do you think I want you to do?" Charlotte tried not to cry. "I want you to be here. But more to the point I guess your kids want you to be here. Can you make it?"

"Of course, I can." Donal looked at her, his face contrite, but now it was Charlotte's turn to look away.

She stood up and fussed about at the sink.

"I'm sorry – I should have brought it up before now," Donal said.

"So should I." Charlotte had so much she wanted to bring up. So much she wanted to talk to him about. "Will you stay for Christmas?"

"In the house?" he asked carefully.

"I was thinking of Tim's tree house actually!" she snapped. "Of course, in the bloody house!"

If it was true what they said about Christmas bringing out the worst in even the most perfect of families, it was really going to have a field day with them, she thought.

"Sorry." Donal tried to grin his way out of it. "How about maybe Christmas Eve? So that I could be there in the morning when the kids wake up? It'll probably be Aisling's last year believing in Santa. I can sleep in the spare room."

"What about Christmas night?" Charlotte busied herself with cleaning an immaculate saucepan in the sink, then dabbed at her eyes with a piece of kitchen paper. What about forever, she wanted to scream at him.

"I don't think so. We still don't know where we're going. It wouldn't be fair on the kids."

"I suppose you're right." She dried the saucepan and put it away. "Look, I'm going to have a glass of wine – will you join me? Please?" she added when he looked uncomfortable.

She poured two glasses without waiting for an answer.

"Look, Charlotte, I know Christmas is going to be a lot harder on you than it is on me." Donal picked up his glass. He took a large mouthful without indulging in his usual swirl, sniff, sip ritual. "If there's anything I can do to make it easier, anything at all, will you let me know?"

Come home, she longed to say. Come home now.

"I can't think of anything at the moment. But if I do…" She smiled at him. It was hard on him too; he really was doing his best.

And then she managed to say it.

"Donal, there's something I have to tell you."

He looked surprised.

"Well, the thing is, I was talking to Marcus a few weeks ago and …" Charlotte ground to a halt when she saw the expression on her husband's face. In the space of a second, he went from hostility through wariness, to fear and then to a blank, neutral stare.

Donal unclenched his teeth for long enough to ask, "And what?"

"And there's no way he could be Gemma's father. He had cancer when he was a teenager and he's sterile. Testicular cancer, it was. One was removed and the other was zapped to hell with radiation therapy." Charlotte spoke so fast that she stumbled over the words. Her babbling was followed by a prolonged silence.

"The poor bastard!"

"Yeah."

This was not the reaction Charlotte was expecting. She didn't know what she was expecting, but not this.

"Was this when he was in Fifth Year? Was that why he didn't come back in Sixth Year?"

"Ehm, I think so? Why?" Who the hell cared?

"God, I remember what he was like then," Donal said, apparently unable to face the real consequences of what Charlotte had told him. "Up to Christmas of that year, he was a dead nice guy. Then he got all moody and aggressive. A right little misery guts. He must have been terrified, poor sod."

"Yeah, I suppose so."

"Is he OK now?"

"Yeah, he's been given the all clear."

"I'm glad, Charlotte, really." Donal stood up, reached across the table, and squeezed her hand. Then he left, without even stopping to pull his jacket off the knob at the end of the stairs.

"What the fuck …?" Charlotte shook her head in bewilderment at the closed front door.

"A few weeks ago, I was talking to Marcus …" That was what she had said, Donal remembered with disbelief. A few weeks. Why the hell had it taken so long for her to say anything to him? Had she been debating whether to tell him at all? Or had it just not seemed that important to her?

He felt rain pouring down the back of his neck. He reached for his collar to pull it up and realised he wasn't wearing his jacket.

I was wrong, he was forced to admit to himself. Somehow I thought that the only thing stopping her from coming back to me and leaving Marcus for good was the possibility that he was the father of one of her children. How could I have been so wrong? I pushed them together for the better part of a year, hoping that she would come to see, like me, that whoever Gemma's biological father was doesn't matter. We belong together, Charlotte and me.

And this whole thing about Christmas. She was so tense inviting me. Was she hoping I'd refuse? Did she want to invite *him*? Surely not? But that's how it looked.

We should have done a DNA test. Years ago. Put that baby to bed while we were still in the first flush of romance, and while she still hated his guts.

Should I let her go? Or should I fight for her? I know she'd come back if I tried; family is the most important thing in the world to her. But could I live with knowing we were together 'for the sake of the children'? Could I live with knowing someone else could make her happier? I probably could. Being with her would be enough. But could I live with it when she came to hate me? When she came to resent how I'd trapped her into staying with me?

A woman got off the bus on the seafront and sheltered for a moment at the bus stop. She looked out at the rain and seemed to be trying to assess whether it was just a shower or down for the night. Then she spotted Donal, pulled her coat tightly around herself, and crossed the road almost at a run.

Donal realised he had been talking out loud and must look a right sight. No coat, shirt stuck to his back, hair plastered to his skull and obscuring his eyes. And talking out loud. He waited until the woman was out of sight, so he wouldn't startle her when he changed direction and followed her, then began to walk back towards the restaurant.

Stop thinking about it, he ordered himself. You're getting nowhere. He clamped his teeth together to stop himself from talking out loud again, and to control his shivering. Think about something else. Think about the shortlist of applicants for Suzy's job.

They had to decide on a list of candidates to interview

at the start of the New Year. Charlotte had been upset when Suzy handed in her notice and had tried to persuade her to stay. Once again she tried to persuade Suzy to go into partnership with them in the Cork restaurant.

"I'll stay till you get someone to replace me, but no longer," Suzy insisted. "If I'm ever going to set up my own place, I have to do it now, before I get too comfortable. To say nothing of property prices – they're showing no signs of slowing down."

The whole speech had a rehearsed feel to it. Which was fair enough, Donal conceded. It can't have been an easy announcement to make. And Suzy had insisted on seeing Donal and Charlotte together, which had been hard enough to organise.

"Where are you hoping to go?" Charlotte asked when she realised that she wasn't going to be able to talk Suzy out of it.

"I'm looking at a few places in the West. Clare, Galway. I might look at one of the tourism tax-incentive areas. I'll have to see what kind of finance I can raise."

"Well, if we can help in any way?" Donal offered.

"Thanks. I'll let you know." But they all knew she wouldn't.

"End of an era," Charlotte had said sadly when Suzy left her office. She wiped a tear from the corner of her eye.

Donal, however, felt guilty at the relief he felt. They owed so much to Suzy. But although they had become close friends over the past year, he knew a weight would be lifted from his shoulders when she played a less prominent role in their lives. He was convinced she knew that there was a chance that Gemma might be …

He stopped dead as the full force of realisation hit home. He'd been concentrating so hard on Charlotte that the full impact of what she had told him had been pushed to the back of his mind. He was in the middle of the restaurant carpark, which was almost full, busy for a Tuesday night despite the foul weather. A wild grin spread across his face

Then Donal began to laugh out loud.

Gemma was his daughter! She really was his daughter. Although he was ashamed at how much of a difference it made to him, he wanted to shout it out loud. She was his daughter. He'd never have look at her again and wonder …

Donal hugged himself and looked up at the sky while the rain hammered on his face.

You poor bastard, Marcus, he thought and shook his head, grinning. You'll never know how this feels.

Suddenly Donal didn't hate him any more.

Chapter 21

Suzy drove into Cork City early in the morning on Christmas Eve. She had left Dublin just after six, so she had no trouble finding parking, even on this, the busiest shopping day of the year. She walked past Moran's restaurant, dark inside, with a notice on the door saying they were closed until December 27th. They were too far from the main shops to make it worth their while to open for lunch today. Unlike Suzy's own branch in Temple Bar, which had extra staff in to cover the expected rush.

Well, not her restaurant for much longer, Suzy remembered with a smile. There were some very promising applicants on the shortlist she had helped Donal select. She felt no regret passing the premises she had been offered partnership in. It wouldn't have been her place; she wanted to build from the ground up and the Moran's Group was Donal and Charlotte's brainchild.

Suzy ate breakfast in a café which had opened up early to catch the few people on their way to work today, and the earliest of the shoppers. She consulted her Christmas-present list with depressingly few ticks on it. But she was a good shopper, and she knew what she wanted to get. She always tried to do her Christmas shopping in Cork rather than Dublin, and her parents weren't expecting her till this evening.

Yesterday she'd rung Etienne's office to hear that he hadn't gone home to France for the holiday. After his father's death earlier in the year, he explained, his mother didn't want to spend the first Christmas without him at home. So his brother and mother had arrived the day before yesterday for an Irish Christmas. Hearing he had family with him, Suzy was reluctant to suggest they meet, but as soon as he heard she was coming to Cork and would be in town for the morning, he had insisted she come to see his new shop. He had started selling his specialist products retail now, but the restaurant trade still made up the majority of his business. The shop merely paid the rent on his new building, he explained. She had to come and see it.

So just before lunch, laden down with shopping bags, Suzy pushed open the door of the small shop. It was like walking into a small grocery in the south of France. One wall was completely taken up with wine, almost all French. A mixture of smells including cheese, herbs, and fresh bread assaulted her nostrils. The predominant smell, the easiest to identify but not so overpowering that it swamped the others, was coffee. Not brewing coffee, but the warm woodland smell of freshly ground beans.

The shop was busy, so Suzy put down her bags and examined the shelves while she waited for an assistant to be free. She didn't mind waiting. Looking at the delicacies on the shelves was making her mouth water. She imagined Etienne visiting suppliers to taste everything before he would permit it onto his shelves. Tiny bottles of truffle shavings preserved in olive oil took pride of place behind the counter. She smiled; he was fanatical about truffles. Most of the bottles and packets had labels in French or Italian on them and where it wasn't clear what delicacy awaited the buyer, Etienne had stuck on small printed labels translating the important details.

"Suzy!" He enfolded her in a bear hug when at last she reached the counter and asked for him. "You look wonderful, Suzy. How are you? Come on through to the office."

She loved the way he said her name. "Soooohzzeee" Only a Frenchman could make a word with S and Z in it sound breathy and sexy.

"So, what's your news?" he asked at last, when he had finished telling her how well his latest venture was going.

"I'm leaving Moran's. I'm going to set up my own restaurant. I've found the perfect place in Clifden." She described it to him. They both loved Clifden and she couldn't believe she'd been lucky enough to get the place. He was the first person she'd told, afraid to jinx the deal before she signed contracts. It used to be a small gift shop on the main street, she explained, but there was room to expand upstairs and in time she could build out the back if she needed to.

Then Suzy took a deep breath. "I suppose you've given up on your dream of a restaurant, have you? I mean, with this place doing so well."

Etienne stood up and moved over to the window. The laneway below was thronged with Christmas shoppers, mainly moving in one direction, arms full of last-minute purchases.

"Are you looking for a business partner, Suzy?" he asked at last, turning around to face her. His face was filled with sad regret.

She shrugged, her expression telling him she had hoped for more.

"I'm sorry, Suzy." He shook his head. "It took me a long time to get over you, to decide whether or not I could stay in Ireland without you, but I've gone on with my life now. I can't go back."

"I understand. I'm sorry too. I wish …"

"Don't wish, Suzy, and don't blame yourself. It was just the wrong time for us. You weren't ready to love me as much as I needed you to. The head can't tell the heart who to love."

He insisted on taking her out to lunch to celebrate the start of her new enterprise.

"So, has he gone back to his wife, your Donal?" Etienne asked after they had ordered.

She wasn't surprised he had guessed. He knew her so well, understood her so well. What a waste.

"No, he hasn't," Suzy smiled. "But I think he will. I hope he will."

"You have stopped loving him?"

This was her cue to say that she had never really loved Donal, that she'd just come to realise that Etienne was the only man for her, and that she'd always loved him. Beg him to give her another chance. But Suzy knew she had to be honest. Not just for Etienne, but for herself. And to her surprise, it was liberating to just say things as they were. It had taken Tara to teach her that.

"No, I didn't stop loving him," she shook her head sadly. "But I've stopped feeling responsible for him."

The Frenchman said nothing. He just raised his eyebrow in a question mark, waiting for her to continue.

"I fell in love with Donal the moment I met him," Suzy explained. "And because of that I couldn't believe that anyone could make him as happy as I could. When he and Charlotte got together, something happened. Well, I felt I had betrayed him, and from that moment on I felt I owed him something. I felt I owed him a chance to discover how happy I could make him. It took me a long time to realise that people are responsible for their own happiness, that they make their own choices. He didn't choose me. He could never be happy without her."

Etienne didn't try to tell her that she'd get over him, that she'd find someone else. He just began to talk about the restaurant in Clifden. Made her promise she'd include some of his wines on her list. Discussed recipes, which included as many of his ingredients as he could think of. Soon Suzy was laughing, as she filled pages of her little notebook with ideas and suggestion. As she thought of the months ahead, her heart began to race and she felt free. She was more excited than she could ever remember being.

Donal walked upstairs to put his bag in the spare room. Tim and Aisling followed him up, convinced that there must be presents in his bag, while Gemma waited with Charlotte in the hall. As they heard the door being opened, and his steps moving overhead into the room they had cleared out this morning, their eyes met. Charlotte longed to ask her daughter what her serious expression meant, but she was afraid of the answer. The girl looked away and went to switch on the television, and Charlotte went into the kitchen to finish making the stuffing

She wished she'd persuaded Donal to come earlier, in time for dinner, or that he'd dropped his bag over earlier in the day when they were all out. But it was nearly nine o'clock when the younger two children had called out in excitement from their vigil by the front window and Charlotte got a terrible shock when she saw her husband standing on the doorstep with an over-stuffed sports bag over his shoulder. He looked like a guest.

Charlotte checked again that she had enough glasses for tomorrow. She counted starter and dessert plates, and took a look at the table. She went into the utility room and collected the flower arrangements she had made earlier in the day. The last of the lilies had opened in the warmth, so she cut out the pollen-laden stamens and placed the vases in the dining-room. She added fresh flowers to the bunches of holly and foliage adorning the hall.

The house looked perfect.

Donal was still upstairs with Tim and Aisling. Charlotte could hear him tell a bedtime story all about Santa and the elves, and a sleigh full of presents. Tim played along wonderfully and Aisling was delighted. Most of her class scoffed at the idea of Santa Claus, and Charlotte wondered if Aisling, at nearly eight, was merely stringing them all along to maximise her presents.

Or maybe she'd had such a tough year with Donal moving out that she had to cling to some magic... Stop it! Charlotte ordered. She was determined not to let herself feel guilty.

"She'll be asleep in minutes!" Donal said as he reappeared in the kitchen. "Where's Gemma?"

"In the family room. Watching telly."

"Is she all right?"

Charlotte shrugged her shoulders and turned around to polish some glasses without answering. She heard Donal go in to his daughter. They talked, but she couldn't hear what they said over the soundtrack of the film. Then she heard them laugh and she relaxed.

"You've outdone yourself, Charlotte, as usual." Paddy said. Donal's father pushed his chair back from the table on Christmas Day and patted the belly, which, since his retirement, had grown in inverse proportion to his golf handicap. "I think I'll stretch my legs before pudding."

This was his code for saying he was going into the

kitchen to do the washing-up. He insisted on doing it every year, and he and Donal discussed politics and gossiped about people from home over the greasy turkey trays and dirty saucepans.

As she heard them clatter around the kitchen, Charlotte thought back over the day. She had managed to keep smiling and keep up a front for the kids, but she felt stretched to her limit. This was no way to live; they had to sort something out one way or another.

From the moment Charlotte had climbed out of bed on Christmas morning, she kept trying to pretend it was a normal Christmas, that they were a normal family, but small things kept getting in the way.

She had waited for Donal to go downstairs with the kids before following them, and on her way, she couldn't help seeing the tossed bed in the spare room. She had lain awake most of the night thinking of him sleeping in the next room. What would he have done if she'd gone into his room in the middle of the night and crept into bed beside him? If she'd snuggled up to his back and begun to kiss and bite that soft pad of flesh where his neck met his shoulder? Would he have given that playful growl of arousal she loved, or would he have shrunk away in horror?

Then later, in the living-room, as they opened presents, Donal produced another bag of gifts, and Charlotte watched as the kids ripped paper off presents she had never seen. She was used to her and Donal wrapping presents together.

Then they all went to Mass together and, as they

walked home, Charlotte thought that at last that they looked like a real family again. Until they reached the front door and Donal remembered he had left his key inside. So she opened the door herself and wondered when he had taken the house keys off the bunch he was holding apologetically in his hand.

All small, petty things but, added up, they made her wish the day was over. That they could stop pretending.

"It hasn't been so bad really, Mum, has it?" Gemma stood at the front door with Charlotte a few hours later as they watched Donal walk down the road.

"What hasn't?" Charlotte shut the door after he turned the corner.

"Dad not living here. I thought it would be awful, but it hasn't been. He really tries to make it OK, doesn't he?"

"I suppose so. It doesn't bother you that we're not all together any more?"

The girl sat on the bottom step of the stairs and thought about it.

"I'd prefer if you and Dad were both here, but if you can't … well, all I'm saying is that it's not as bad as I thought it would be." Gemma's face began to burn with embarrassment. "Will Dad or you want someone else, do you think?"

"I don't know, love. Were you thinking of anyone in particular?"

"Well, you know … Marcus. You see a lot of him. And Dad and Suzy seem like real good friends now."

"Do you think about this a lot?"

"No." But her face said yes.

Charlotte sat on the stairs beside her daughter.

"I can't speak for your father, but Marcus and me are just good friends. We go back a long way."

"He was your boyfriend, wasn't he? Before Dad?"

"Yes. How did you know?"

"Suzy." Gemma saw a look of annoyance on her mother's face. "No, no. She never actually said anything. It was more the things she didn't say. She wouldn't talk about the three of you. What you used to do together or anything. And she was one of your best friends back then, so I reckoned she was hiding something."

"Dad was a good friend then too. One of my best friends. Like Auntie Emmy, I married my best friend."

"He's still your best friend, Mum, isn't he?"

Charlotte nodded, choked up by the perceptiveness of her daughter.

"You're his best friend too, I'm sure of it." Gemma looked hopefully at her.

"It's not always enough, love," Charlotte admitted for the first time.

"It should be." Gemma's lower lip wobbled.

Charlotte put her arms around her and they sat on the stairs until the phone rang. It was Hannah, asking if she'd left a ring on the windowsill in the kitchen when she was washing some glasses. When Charlotte came back from checking, holding the ring in her hand, Gemma was gone. By the time she had managed to get Hannah off the phone, the light was switched off in her daughter's bedroom.

Chapter 22

Marcus arrived back in Dun Laoghaire the day after Christmas. He had spent the previous two nights with his parents, brother and sister in Kildare and was glad to be back. It was strange walking through the reception area of the offices downstairs. Daylight, and not a single person at work. He couldn't remember a day since he had set up the business that there hadn't been at least one dedicated soul pounding away at a keyboard or staring at a screen.

Upstairs he made a mug of strong coffee and stood drinking it looking out his favourite window at the sea. The pier was crowded; families were taking their traditional St. Stephen's Day walk. No doubt if he went down there now he would see a multitude of new bikes and dolls in pristine outfits being given the air in tiny prams. But he couldn't bear to join them. The feeling of exclusion would be too great. In town on Christmas Eve, he had wandered into a toyshop. Most of the shelves were empty, but he had picked up dolls and action figures, trains and jigsaws and imagined himself playing with them. He wished he had nieces or nephews to buy for. If only Charlotte hadn't made it so clear to him that there was no future for them, then maybe he could have bought something for her children.

When he had arrived at his parents' house on Christmas Eve, he had phoned Denise to wish her a Merry Christmas. They had talked pleasantly for about half an hour, then she surprised him by asking him if he wanted to meet for a drink on New Year's Eve.

"Who else is going to be there?" he asked cautiously.

Marcus hated the false jollity of New Year's Eve. It reminded him of his student days when everyone had to get drunk and try to get off with someone.

"No one," Denise answered. "I hadn't made any plans – it's just when you rang … Well, I know you hate it as much as I do, so we could do worse than be miserable together."

Marcus had laughed and they arranged to meet.

Now, as he sipped coffee and stared out to sea, he wondered how he could have so royally screwed up his life. How many men found two women that they could love as deeply as he had loved Denise and Charlotte, and how many of those could manage to throw not only one, but both away? He was in a class of his own.

He had been hopeful when Denise had asked to meet him. On New Year's Eve of all nights, the traditional time for casting off the past, and making plans for the future.

But then he remembered he still had to tell her the truth, and when he did … In her place he knew he could never forgive what he had done to her, so he could hardly expect any reaction other than disgust.

But he owed it to her. Maybe then she could get on with her life. Get the "closure" her therapist said she needed.

He picked up the phone to call Charlotte. They hadn't spoken since the afternoon in Bray. In the six months since they kissed, it was the longest they had gone without one or other of them picking up the phone.

"Hello?" Charlotte answered at the third ring, but her voice was confused, sleepy.

"Don't tell me I woke you. You've got kids, I thought they were supposed to get you up at the crack of dawn!"

"Marcus!" She brightened. "It's great to hear from you. I was afraid…"

"That I was lying when I said I wanted to remain good friends – and that if I couldn't have you all to myself I wasn't interested any more?"

"I never …" She imagined him laughing silently at her confusion. "Happy Christmas!"

"And to you. So how come you were asleep at half eleven in the morning?"

"I wasn't asleep, well, not really. Donal's taken the kids out for the day, so I was doing some study, some reading. I guess I nodded off."

"And that's not really asleep, is it?" Marcus laughed, amazed at how easy it was to talk to her.

"So how was your Christmas?" Charlotte asked, then

wished she hadn't. He would ask her the same question and she didn't want to talk about it.

"All right, as Christmases go. No major family rows. I managed to remain civil to my sister. Mum was in great form because I spent half an hour on the phone to Denise on Christmas Eve."

"Oh?" Charlotte was pleased for him. "And how did that go?"

"Fine. We're meeting for a drink on New Year's Eve."

"That can't be bad. Ringing in the New Year together, I mean."

"Well … I don't know. I have to tell her the truth. About what I told you, I mean. I might not get past the first drink, let alone as far as midnight."

Charlotte tried to imagine how she'd react if she were in Denise's shoes. Lying about something as basic as the ability to have children – and then throwing all sorts of accusations at the other person … She shivered. She knew how she'd feel.

"You'd never know. She might surprise you," was the most reassuring thing she could say. He was probably right – Denise would throw a drink over him and tell him to get the hell out.

"Hmmph! Anyway, I have to do it," Marcus snorted. "So how was your Christmas?"

Charlotte hesitated.

"A nightmare. I just couldn't wait for the day to be over," she admitted at last. "I kept imagining things were normal, that we were all together like a normal family, then something would remind me that Donal lives half a mile away, and he was only here for the day."

"Have you talked to him?"

"I talk to him every day. We talk more now than when we were sharing a house. There's so much to sort out –"

"Really talked to him," Marcus interrupted gently.

"About what?" Charlotte sighed. "He's the one who moved out. If he wants to talk, it's up to him. Anyway, I'm kind of getting used to the way things are. He probably is too. And if we can do that, is there much left worth fighting for?"

"Only you can answer that."

"And it's not fair on the kids," Charlotte continued as if she hadn't heard the interruption. "If we're not going to get back together, then we need to make the next move, so they know where we stand."

"Is that what you want?"

"I don't know what I want. Besides, it's not just up to me, is it?"

"What are you trying to talk yourself into, Charlotte?"

"I'm not trying to talk myself into anything! I'm just being realistic. We can't go on like this. That's the one thing I do know."

"Well, don't do anything too hasty. You've got three kids and –"

"It's them I'm thinking –"

" … twelve years of marriage…"

"Thirteen," Charlotte corrected automatically.

"What?"

"Thirteen. We're married thirteen years." The number scared her, not that she was superstitious. Then a horrible

411

thought hit her. "We never celebrated. Our anniversary, I mean. We never celebrated out thirteenth wedding anniversary." It was the scariest thing she'd ever said about her marriage.

"Talk to him, Charlotte. You owe each other that."

"Yeah, Marcus. Thanks for listening." She wanted to get off the phone. She had too much to do to keep nattering away like this on the phone.

For the next couple of days, Charlotte did her best to keep busy. It wasn't hard. The school holidays stretched miles into the future and Tim and Aisling were bored. At least last year Donal had been here to help keep them occupied. Now, although he wasn't at work much and he took the kids out for a few hours a day, he wasn't in the house when they got really ratty. Gemma, as usual, kept herself occupied in her self-contained way. And she avoided her mother as if the shared confidences of Christmas Night had embarrassed her.

Charlotte went down to Castlemichael to welcome Anne-Marie and Dave's new daughter into the world. After keeping everyone waiting, the little scrap had arrived at two in the morning on Christmas Eve. Seeing little Amanda in her father's arms, Charlotte couldn't help but remember the day Gemma was born.

Maybe that was where everything had started to go wrong. If only they'd known then what they knew now. If they'd known then that there was no way she could be Marcus's child, Donal would never have looked at his daughter and his wife and wondered … And Charlotte wouldn't have kept remembering that last night with Marcus and wondering what if …?

As she drove back into Dublin on the day before New Year's Eve, Charlotte concentrated on Suzy's last New Year's Eve dinner. It had become a tradition in Moran's to have a set meal on New Year's Eve, which was usually fully booked out by August. The staff finished serving before midnight and joined the diners, almost all regulars, for a drink to ring in the New Year. This year Suzy was returning to the first restaurant and they were combining the celebrations of the New Year with sending her off in style.

At half eight on New Year's Eve, Charlotte knew she couldn't delay any longer. The first diners would begin to arrive soon. She took a last look in the mirror and pulled a few stray hairs off her face. She had had the ends trimmed just before Christmas, so with the help of a straightener she had managed to give herself a profes-sional-looking hairstyle. It was the first year she hadn't bothered buying a new outfit for New Year's Eve, but this turquoise linen suit looked great on her and she'd only worn it once. She didn't like the way it creased at the front, but she wouldn't be sitting down until after mid-night, and by then most people would be past noticing.

She wondered if guests would notice a difference as she and Donal greeted them and moved amongst them as business partners and not as the golden couple they had been feted as since the restaurants had started doing so well. She asked herself idly, if they were to formalise their

413

break-up, would they stay partners in the whole enterprise, or would they break it up into parts? The lawyers would have a field day with that!

Charlotte went downstairs to Hannah who was looking after the kids for the night. She was staying over to save her the drive back after midnight.

"I'll probably be in bed when you get back," Hannah said, "so I'll wish you a Happy New Year now." She hugged her daughter-in-law.

Charlotte said goodnight to Gemma and Aisling, and repeated to Tim that he was to go to bed on the last stroke of midnight, as soon as his grandmother told him to. Hannah followed her into the hall.

"Good luck tonight," she said quietly as she helped Charlotte pull on a warm coat over her light jacket. "Good luck."

She spoke with such sadness that Charlotte wondered if her mother-in-law had read her mood and guessed that she had decided that she could go on like this no longer. Tonight, before the New Year dawned, she would have to put her life back onto some kind of formal footing.

Or perhaps, she thought with an unpleasant shock as she walked into the restaurant carpark, perhaps Donal had told his mother that *he* intended to finish things for once and for all.

If he had, he gave no sign as he helped her out of her coat, gave her a kiss on the cheek and filled her in on last-minute details. She listened impassively as he told her about the crisis with one of the starters as the suppliers had let them down that afternoon. She admired the replacement menu card he had improvised, still warm from the printer. Then she went into the kitchen to see how Suzy was getting on.

Although the first orders were only just beginning to come through, a welcome air of organised chaos greeted Charlotte. A few people looked, up but the level of noise and swearing continued unabated, unaffected by the boss walking into the kitchen.

I love this, Charlotte thought. I love what we've achieved here. It's so much more than we dreamed possible. She smiled at Suzy, who paused briefly in her preparations to give a mad grin, then she went back to the dining-room.

She moved through the rest of the night as though in a dream. She walked from table to table, greeting regular customers, topping up wine, chatting. She could remember nothing she said. Her mind was miles away, rehearsing what she would say to Donal.

At midnight, champagne was opened but she barely touched it. She felt sick and she was afraid that alcohol would make her cry.

Then the last of the guests were being shown out into the night and the kitchen staff began to assemble to make a presentation to Suzy.

Emily and Paul sat at a table in the corner and asked Charlotte to join them but she stood beside Donal as he made a speech thanking Suzy for her help and inspiration through the years. He wished her best of luck in her venture in Clifden and made her promise to send them an invitation to the opening night. Charlotte at last felt free to shed a few tears as her friend wept unashamedly as she hugged Donal and said goodbye. Suzy made a short speech, which Charlotte hardly listened to, then everyone began to filter out.

Suzy was giving Paul and Emily a lift home, so she joined them at their table. Donal brought over some drinks and Charlotte sat down as the five of them drank to the New Year again, and to Suzy's success in the future. She felt churlish at her inability to share Suzy's enthusiasm.

Could no one else see that this was an ending?

"You've been very quiet all night, Charlotte."

Donal and Charlotte stood at the front door, waving off Suzy, Emily and Paul.

"We need to talk, Donal."

There, she'd said it.

"I know."

They stared at each other.

Donal guided Charlotte gently towards the table they had just left and went into the kitchen. He came back with a plate of cheese, a basket of Suzy's breads and a bottle of wine. She shook her head.

"You've had nothing to eat or drink all night. You'll make yourself sick." He put a plate in front of her. The worried look on his face broke her heart so she cut some cheese and chose a large slice of the soft bread.

She fiddled with the fragrant olive bread, pulling it to pieces while he pulled the cork from the bottle with a few expert twists. She picked out the bits of juicy black olive from the pile of crumbs on the plate in front of her, nibbled them slowly then took a sip of wine.

"Talk," he ordered gently.

"I can't go on like this, Donal." She closed her eyes for a couple of seconds, to hold back tears, then looked up at him.

"Like what?" His face was guarded.

"In limbo like this. Not knowing if you're gone for good, or ever coming back. I need to get on with my life. I thought the past year would be a lot worse than it was, but … I suppose I've started doing things for myself. My exams, for example. And I'm doing well in college, although I've only done one term. I realise I can make it on my own now … I'm stronger than I realised. I don't need someone there to reassure me that I'm doing the right thing all the time."

"And the kids?"

"They're coping better than I could have believed possible. We should be proud of ourselves, Donal. They're great kids, and we've managed to sort out our differences doing them a minimum of harm in the process. This year's been useful like that. We've made a blue-print, if you like, a blue-print of how we should do things in the future. In the future if we …"

"Is that what you want, Charlotte? Do you want to separate formally?"

Charlotte felt the tears well up inside her. He wanted out. It was over. It had been over for a year, but he hadn't the courage to tell her. She felt a crushing sense of disappointment. What had she expected?

"Do you want to separate?" Donal repeated. He gripped his wineglass so hard his knuckles whitened.

Charlotte took the glass from him, afraid he was going to snap the glass stem. He didn't seem to notice it was gone.

They sat in silence. A car sped past on the main road and they both turned towards the window and saw the flash of headlights.

"You don't need me any more, do you, Charlotte? All your life you've looked after people. First Emily, then me and the kids. It's how you identified yourself. And now you see that I can live away from you without keeling over and dying, and the kids are managing fine."

He picked up his glass again and swirled the rich purple liquid around in it. The candle on the table, alight since the evening began, spluttered as it ran out of wax.

"And you've started this college thing which you love. You're right when you say that we've managed well this past year, but it's not entirely true. It's you who managed, and I've just sat back and watched you grow away from me. If you want your freedom, I promise I won't stand in your way. We'll work it out whatever way you think is best."

I've nothing to lose now, Charlotte realised. She took a deep breath.

"Maybe we *should* get a formal separation, Donal. We've lived apart for so long now that maybe it's the right thing to do. Cut our losses, get on with our lives, let the kids know where they stand. But I don't want that. I want you back, Donal. I want to try again. Maybe it's the wrong thing to do, but I'm willing to take that risk. As long as I have the kids, I can survive anything, so don't feel you have to come back just because I need you, or that I can't live without you. But I want you back. I never wanted you to leave in the first place, and I want you back."

"And Marcus?"

"What about him?"

"Has it ended between you?"

"It never began. It could have. We kissed and…" She stopped.

"And?" Donal asked at last, though he wasn't sure he wanted to hear any more.

"And nothing. I couldn't go on. I wanted to pretend he was you."

Donal couldn't look at her. He picked up the cheese knife, cut a piece of Gruyère, sawing savagely through the hard crust, then left it uneaten on the side of the plate.

"I love you too much to come back," he said, "unless I can be absolutely sure that you want me back just for me." He looked up at last. "Not for the sake of the kids, for the sake of our marriage or anything. For me. Do you love me like that, Charlotte?"

"I love you enough to take you back on any terms. I want you back as my lover, my husband, my best friend. But if I have to, I'll settle for the father of my children and work like hell at getting the rest of you back as well. You were wrong when you said I didn't need you any more. I do. Not in the way I used to. Not because I need to feel loved and needed myself, but because you're part of me, Donal. I need you as much as I need my legs, my right hand."

And as she said it, Charlotte knew it was true. She could survive without Donal, in the same way as she would survive if she lost a limb, but she wouldn't be complete without him.

"I know you think we got married for the wrong reason," she continued. "And maybe you're right. But whatever the initial reason, marrying you was the rightest thing I ever did in my life. And I know I couldn't be a fraction as happy with anyone else."

Donal reached across and took one of her hands in both of his.

"I'm sorry, Charlotte." He kissed her hand. "I'm sorry if I ever made you think our getting married was the wrong thing to do. When I realised you were pregnant I was happy because it made everything much easier for me."

Charlotte looked confused, so he explained.

"Remember, I wanted to go to England to work? Well, I didn't want to go without you but it was too soon in our relationship to expect you to come with me. The baby, Gemma, just made it all so simple. In a way, it was me who did the wrong thing. Remember when I said I knew you were pregnant before you even told me? That I'd seen all the signs and had a chance to think about it? Well, perhaps I took advantage of you. I knew that given your own past, your childhood and the way you felt about Robert, if I asked you to marry me, you'd accept. Whether or not you loved me enough. I suppose you could say I took advantage of Gemma too in that way. I used the fact of her existence to get you to marry me."

"Even though you thought there might be a chance she was Marcus's?"

"Yes, Charlotte. I loved you. That was all that mattered. You believe me when I say I'd have asked you to marry me pretty soon anyway, don't you?"

"Yes."

Donal gripped her hand tighter as they stared at each other in silence.

"So what now?" Charlotte asked at last.

"We belong together Charlotte. We can sort this out." He looked at her, pleading.

Suddenly there was an awkwardness between them. Charlotte realised that when she had asked 'what now?' she had expected him to provide all the answers.

"A year is a long time apart, Donal. We probably need some help to get over this. Do you think we should see a counsellor or something?"

"Probably, in time." Donal stood up and walked around to her side of the table. He pulled her to her feet and put his arms around her.

"But I can't wait that long." He kissed her and they stood like that, together, for what seemed like ages.

"Come through to the flat," he said at last, his voice shaking with desire, his eyes filled with tears. "Mum's staying the night to look after the kids, isn't she?"

Charlotte followed without a sound as he held her hand and, with the lightest of touches, led the way. They walked through the deserted kitchen towards the door connecting the restaurant with the flat.

"No, wait." Charlotte stopped, although her body tried to propel her forwards, towards the bedroom they had once shared. She pulled him in the other direction, towards the front door. "I want to bring you home, Donal. Home for good. Will you come with me now?"

He nodded and smiled. Then he swiped at the tears that wouldn't stop flowing down his cheeks.

THE END